GW00577990

MINDSAIL

MINDSAIL

Anne Gay

ORBIT

An Orbit Book

Copyright © 1990 Anne Gay

First published in Great Britain in 1990 by
Macdonald & Co (Publishers) Ltd
London & Sydney

British Library Cataloguing in Publication Data

Gay, Anne
    Mindsail.
    I. Title
    823'.914 [F]

    ISBN 0–356–18806–X

Photoset in North Wales by
Derek Doyle & Associates, Mold, Clwyd.
Printed and bound in Great Britain by
Redwood Press Limited, Melksham, Wiltshire

Macdonald & Co (Publishers) Ltd
Orbit House
1 New Fetter Lane
London EC4A 1AR

A member of Maxwell Macmillan Pergamon Publishing Corporation

To my mother and father
without whom I would never have seen a rainbow
or smelt a hyacinth

with love

The blizzard had drifted a bridge of snow over the gully and hushed the lairs of the four-footed hunters. Now and then a break in the white whirling storm ripped open a view of the night sky and it seemed as though the moonlight sang on the brilliance of the forest; crystal fragments like frozen blood cracked in the cold to fall tinkling through the branches. It was a time when all intelligent life huddled under shelter to dream of spring.

All?

Down the ragged wind rang the sounds of pursuit: the clashing of weapons; weird drawn-out yells: 'Mutinas!' Whoever it was, they must want their enemies dead with an intensity of desire that challenged the storm.

Three figures crashed out of the undergrowth and the scent of their fear went before them. In their lairs the four-footed predators stirred as the human hunters intended. Last son of First Captain was their target and his father lay dead along the trail.

'Down here!' called the old man, plunging into the gully. Snow spurted up beneath his limping footsteps. The boy slid after him but not Pyotr; he broke away and sprinted for the snow-bridge. His panicked stride shattered it, dropping him onto the ice-slick rocks below just as the first wolves belled. White bone tore out through Pyotr's thigh and his scream was masked by the animals' howls.

The old man's good eye was bright with cunning. He buried his precious burden where no-one else would ever find it. First Captain's age-old secret was for the boy alone; the enemy would destroy it. After centuries the descendants of the Crew still hated what First Captain had done to them, imprisoning them on this planet with lies and deceit.

The wolves were closer now, driven forward by the beaters and lured on by the smell of blood. It was all Pyotr could do to stand with his spear as a crutch, even after the old man took his pain away. Pyotr's fear was for himself alone, but the boy and the old man who was not his father were more frightened that First Captain's guilt would never be expunged. How could a boy and a cripple pay off the blood-debt if they didn't live?

In a thicket where the enemy could come only one at a time, they waited ...

PART ONE

Dreamlight

CHAPTER ONE

The Winter of the Wolf

Fierce and white, the bony fingers of the blizzard flung snow against the windows and the red gems spun, fragmenting. They scored the poor, worn panes that shivered at each blast. On all this world, there was none to fight the Red, save this House. But what did the storm matter on Longnight?

Tohalla told the children, 'It's the nails of the Red Woman clawing to get in,' just as Housemother had told her so long ago. And just as she had, they thrilled in pleasant terror, those little ones too tired to dance so late, because the House was old and strong around them and they couldn't imagine any other safety. Even now Tohalla could scarcely understand that safety had a price; she glanced at him.

Of all the adults crowded into the lamplit body of the Househall, he was the only one not dancing. Half-chewed joyberries dribbled from Worut's loose lips into the stubble that grew ragged on his chin. He was slumped against the steps leading up to Housefather's platform, and from her chair above him she could see his shapeless body tilted like a grain-sack that had spilt half its load. The flame of the hour-candle behind Housefather's head had almost drowned in its pool of molten tallow; when it went out there would be the darkness of the dying year and new light to celebrate the new life Slack Worut would plant in her.

She looked away and swallowed. Asdra, who was five, wriggled on her lap, trying like the others to get her back to the story.

It would have been so different if one of them were hers. But in eleven years of marriage she had failed to give one live birth. Now Pierse was dead and nine months had proved she still hadn't made him a child for the Green, not even one like poor Caramon, Red-tainted.

11

'It'll be all right,' Housemother said in her ear. 'Worut's not much, but he was normal-born.'

But he had fallen out of a tree, and he wore food on his lips like a two-year old. And all Housefather would say was, 'He's the only one left of a right bloodline. It's your duty to the Green.'

There was Granamyr, of course. He was always merry whether working or not, and their bloodlines weren't too close. But even in her own eyes it would have been a sin against the Green to give him a failure like Tohalla. It was only fair that her youngest sister Larnis should have him, but did Larnis have to sneer so triumphantly?

'Come on, Toh!' said Asdra. 'One hasn't told us the rest.' And Caelwyn her niece tugged at her hair, but Caramon just sat.

Tohalla sighed, and breathed too deeply of the amethyst dreamsmoke. She knew that in the morning she'd feel ill, but for now it made everything seem wonderfully remote.

'And that's why we celebrate Longnight,' she said in a voice keyed against the music so that her high notes wove a plaid of sound into the rhythm of the dance, 'because we've fought the Red Woman off again. Now the days will get longer and –'

The Housedoor flung open. It crashed against the wall, letting in the darkness and the terror. Snow swirled in so thick Tohalla saw only dark shapes, threatening in the Red-sparked cloud.

Inwatchers leaped down from the catwalks as the music died. Before the snow had sunk to the boards they ringed the three white-limned figures. Men and women ran to the weapon-racks, clattering knives and scythes and spears. Whoever it was in all those icy robes, they were very close to death.

Tohalla grew a smile in the middle of the Chaunt. Everyone's attention had left her and the hour-candle had blown out. In the silence where the music had died her voice sank, deeper and lower, grinding like the Book. Once she realized she was doing it, she made it stronger on purpose, her own little sound that nobody directed. Glad of any reprieve she held the children tightly, out of harm's way up here on the platform.

Somebody slammed the door and everyone was talking at once. Almost everyone. At the foot of the dais Worut crooned and rubbed at his groin.

Amid the light-shot circle of blades, a figure sank to its knees above another that seemed a corpse. Who was it in the dark doorway under the landing? Tohalla strained her eyes but the shadows were too thick out of the brightness of the Longnight lamps, and the scarves of dreamsmoke dazzled her.

Housefather ran past Tohalla, leaped down the steps into the body of the Househall. He shoved through the press of bodies, calling, 'Bring a lamp, you,' and someone did.

In its flare Tohalla could just make out a third being, half-propped against the door. She could see no weapon but size alone made for fear. It seemed a monster, inhuman, yet it had eyes and beard like a man. Somehow that made it worse. Grey tusks angled up as the lamp flamed in its face. The inwatchers hesitated and drew back, jabbing with their points when Housefather cursed them for cowards.

There was no sound but the harsh breathing of the incomers, and the nervous shiftings of the People.

'Get on with it!' Housefather roared.

The kneeling figure gasped, 'Didn't you ... see our lights?'

It was a woman's voice – her friend Trinamine's, Tohalla realized with pleasure. She knew, too, that Trinamine expected the answer she got: none. Hadn't Trinamine said year after year that they needed some other signal for storms?

From the dark fur around her hood snow plopped wetly over Trinamine's face and she wiped it off in impatience. One of the men stabbed a knife at her, feeling threatened by any motion.

She pushed aside the point of his dagger but the looming figure behind her couldn't work the same trick. Spears and a long-axe made a moving necklace of light in the skeins of lamp-lit smoke. If he moved, it would choke him.

Trinamine, still kneeling, unlaced her hood and said, 'These ... these men here are none of ours, but look!'

She hauled off the furs wrapping the thing she'd let crumple to the floor. Crystals of Red rattled onto the floorboards amid the showers of snowflakes.

Housemother snapped her fingers and two women rushed forward, emptying buckets of salt onto the glimmering Red. The crystals grew brighter, shifting down a sad spectrum to yellow, then brown, bubbling and spitting before they flattened and died. For good measure the women flung handfuls of salt over the incomer's robing, so that soon there was nothing to see of the thing on the floor but a long mound of salt except at one end, where Trinamine pushed the women away. Around it the snow was melting to a dark stain on the sanded boards.

'See? It's a man, a young one at that.'

They didn't believe her. Some even laughed, but that was probably the dreamsmoke, or joyberry juice. Maybe the arms and legs looked

13

like a human's, but the strange, knobbly head was not like a man's, and since when did a man have iron-grey tusks below where his ears should have been?

Trinamine lifted one corner of her lip and tugged the body's hood back. Her hand suddenly darted across its folds, an unnecessary movement that she masked with an empty gesture of her other arm. From where she stood Tohalla couldn't see the captive's face, but all the same she wondered. That was one of the things about Trinamine. She never moved unless she had to. She wasn't lazy, but she had a quality of stillness about her as though she were a complete person, like a tree was a complete tree. Trin didn't fit neatly in the Green either.

Only faintly curious, Tohalla drifted to the corner of Housefather's platform. Holding Asdra tightly on the waist-high balustrade – she didn't want him to fall down into the body of the Househall – she craned a little to watch as Trinamine did something to the supine form.

Tohalla thought the thing's head had come off, though wrapped as she was in dreamsmoke it didn't surprise her. Larnis shrieked, but then she shrieked at anything.

The mask, its curving tusks and green-furred muzzle, rolled free. And underneath it was a man's face.

When everyone had gasped sufficiently at the outlander's face, at the cloak with its clasp of wolf's claws whose green scales mirrored back the purple smoke, Housefather sucked in his breath angrily, about to speak, but Trinamine went on, 'Good-looking, ain't he? A body could believe he was a normal man, 'stead of a monster.'

'But it's not, is it?' shouted Housefather. 'It's a piece of the Red walking round on two legs! A murderous flesh-eater! And that's another part of the pack, is it? What are you going to do next? Bring a Wolf in here and have done with it?'

'He's a man, all right,' Trinamine said over the tide of voices. 'Nothing wrong with him at all that Mevagrin couldn't mend. A young one, at that. Makes a body wonder if he couldn't be real useful if he got to be tame. There's another one a corpsicle by now, like as not. He staggered as far as the spineders' barn and then he dropped. Couldn't carry him any further. Got some good weapons off him, though.'

Housefather gathered himself for another cloudburst of wrath but Trinamine was determined to have out her say.

'Then there's this other one behind me.' She jerked her chin at the huge, wolf-helmed man leaning wearily by the door. 'He carried this'un almost all the way, just like a human being might with a friend.'

She gathered phlegm to spit, then changed her mind as Housemother

14

glared. But she winked at Tohalla up in the firelight, still standing guard above the sleepy children all around her.

Trinamine rubbed her wind-reddened cheeks. Tohalla could tell she was weary to the bone, so that the head rocked on her shoulders, but she kept kneeling by the unconscious man, making her report. Tohalla had never heard her say so much in all her life.

Trinamine nodded over her shoulder at the other wolf-cloaked prisoner, his helmet now in the crook of his arm, his body the focus of all their blades.

'Good an' strong, by the looks of him, but he'll go short on toes this year. A body's feeling that way myself.'

The outwatcher stopped, exhausted. The crystals of ice on her collar were melted now to iridescent droplets, and her cracked lips started to bleed when she licked them. Behind her the giant Wolfman stood unmoving, staring out the People who stood staring at him. But each time he breathed, a little groan escaped his snow-grey lips.

Suddenly Tohalla understood how much it pained him to show his weakness out plain to them all. It seemed a cruel thing to have brought him there for gawping at. She couldn't understand why Trinamine had brought this enemy into their House that had never known one of his kind.

In the silent waiting for Housefather to give judgement of death, she didn't dare speak any more than the others did. But she swung Caelwyn onto her hip, and tickled the little mite until she laughed out loud into their noiseless anger.

Housefather turned angrily, but it was only a child clinging happily to Tohalla and he could not blame her for that. The little girl was still giggling, one arm reaching out to the Wolfman. Housefather couldn't see Tohalla's fingers holding up that arm.

'Tie them up!' yelled Housefather in a temper. He turned to his wife. 'See to it. The rest of you, get back to what you're supposed to be doing. And you, Trinamine, come in by the fire. I want words with you.'

Housefather didn't bother to see that he was obeyed. All round the hall the inwatchers scaled the ladders back up to their windows above the catwalks, at the turn of the two staircases in the long wall opposite the Housedoor, or at each end of the gallery between them.

He stalked to his end of the Househall. People stepped out of his way and shaped back into clusters behind him, their talk crashing into the stillness like a breaker on the shore.

He stamped up the steps to his platform, stepping over Worut's outstretched legs since the idiot obviously wasn't going to move them. When he had planted himself before the dreamsmoke fire, feet as far apart as a striding-post, Housefather put his hands behind him to the blaze and grimaced up at Trinamine. It had always annoyed him that she was so much taller than he, a feeling he didn't trouble to hide. Of Tohalla and the children at the corner of the dais he took no notice. The musicians by the other fire at the far end of the hall struck up a ravelled chorus when Chulain twanged on his fiddle.

Taking his wooden mug of mulled ale from the mantelshelf, Housefather said, 'Well? What d'you mean by leaving the striding-post? That's what it's there for, isn't it? To keep the Red out! And there's you inviting in servants of the Red as if they were human beings! It's a fine harvest I'm reaping for trusting you, isn't it? How many more of 'em are out there waiting to attack? And what about their litter-mates? Hm? Well?'

Trinamine shivered and rubbed finger and thumb over her red-veined eyes. Tohalla felt sorry for her but knew better than to offer her House-comforts now. If she did, Housefather would keep Trinamine waiting all the longer.

Besides, Tohalla had enough else to do with seeing to the children, who were all excitedly watching the men string ropes around the Wolfman. Even Caramon's dull eyes were round with fear.

'Does he bite?' shrilled little Caelwyn loudly, pulling Tohalla's sleeve, and, 'You won't let him eat me, will you, Toh?'

The Wolfman turned his head, tusks and all. Tohalla's insides crawled with embarrassment – and just a touch of wonder whether he might eat them after all. His eyes, one dark, and one marble-white gotch, seemed to touch something inside her head. It was as though a dust-mite were heaping grains of dust against the wrinkles of her brain. She was afraid to look his way in case, like the mite, he built a heap of Red within her.

He limped past, reined like a spineder going out to the plough. She tried not to notice as he went by the platform – and failed. The lines were tight around his neck and wrists, but he looked at Tohalla as he stumbled against the nooses on his feet. And winked.

'Here, Asdra!' she said when she had recovered herself. 'Run and get us some joyberries, hey? Tell them a body sent from Housefather's platform if they ask.' Tohalla had to bend low to make the little boy hear her above all the disjointed noise of the roundel they were dancing in the Househall below her. Asdra jumped down the seven steps, twisting through the dancers.

16

She was on fire to know what Housefather and Trinamine were saying, but she had to wait until the children were settled again around the bowl of dried golden fruit. Even then it was hard to hear, because for once Housefather was remembering to keep his voice down, yet every now and then she would know he was watching her, discussing her, settling her life as if she were a field to be planted or a tree to be stripped clean.

'... but she is promised to the Tine strand,' she heard Trinamine say. 'You know a body ....'

But Tohalla didn't know what she ... Nor did she find out, because her sister Larnis glided up to the platform and smiled winsomely through the balustrade, calling, 'Housefather dear, isn't it time the hour-candle was lit again?'

Tohalla felt a pain inside at this reminder. Why must Larnis be so eager that she didn't care about her sister's direction? But Housefather beamed back and stepped closer to hear his favourite child, and you could have heard Larnis's whisper from the Edge.

'A body knows you must have seen it go out, Housefather, and there must be an awful lot to think about with all this incoming.'

How Larnis went on, looking like the Corn Dolly through the carved bars of the railing. For just a second she cast a malicious glance at Tohalla, then she was smiling sweetly at Housefather and saying, 'I'm sure you must be doing something about it.' *'I' and 'you' as though Larnis counted for something in the Green!* Tohalla listened in amazement as Larnis went on, 'Everyone's looking forward to your fertility plans. Especially Tohalla and me. It must be nearly time for your speech.'

Almost, Housefather looked back at the dead hour-candle in its niche in the chimney-breast, but he stopped himself.

'You're right as usual, Larnis, but I haven't forgotten you. I've already sent for Housemother to do it. Not long now. You go off and enjoy your last night as a child.'

When Larnis had gone, he beckoned Tohalla over. She disentangled herself from the three children, pouring a heap of the joyberries in Caramon's lap so that Asdra couldn't take her share, and hoping Caelwyn would stay quiet. For a wonder Tohalla had to bend to hear Housefather whisper so that Trinamine would not be able to hear, 'Go and get your mother.'

Turning his back on his daughter, sure that she would obey, he rounded on the shivering outwatcher again. The last words Tohalla heard him say as she went down the steps were, 'Just you remember, Trinamine, it'll be your fault if there's any trouble at the Edge.'

17

CHAPTER TWO

The Red Invades

In a little while everyone stood back to let Housemother through. The musicians left their instruments and came to join the crowd around Housefather's platform, anxious to know how he'd direct them this year. Larnis elbowed her way to the front, pulling an embarrassed Granamyr in her wake. The youngest women ran to put out the lamps in the hall as Housemother mounted the steps.

Flickering firelight lit her silhouette, with the year's Corn Dolly held high. The wheatstraw had darkened in its place above the kitchen range, but the long plaits on its head were still good for their purpose. From the blue-flamed embers of the dreamwood, Housemother set the Corn Dolly alight.

Its wizened blueberry eyes glowed through the smoke; its painted mouth burst out on fire. In all the Household there was not a sound but the crackle and hiss of burning. If the wind from the door hadn't blown out the hour-candle, they'd have watched it die, listening to Housefather's plans for the new season as it guttered in the winter's dark.

But this time there was no emblematic dying of the old season. Housemother prised out the pool of tallow and embedded the new hour-candle in the sand. She touched the blazing Corn Dolly to its linen wick. Even Mevagrin had come in from the kitchen to watch, and everyone cheered the baby light of the New Year.

No-one said anything about Longnight being in the wrong order, but they would remember it later. For now, though, they fell to standing quietly, last year dying with the Corn Dolly's embers in the grate.

Longnight, with all its freight of dreams. Not that there was much to

18

celebrate, nor much to celebrate with, this year. But the children didn't know that. They snuggled into Tohalla's lap for comfort and all was secure and familiar for them. Around them on the platform were Housefather and Housemother, and here was Auntie Larnis coming up the steps, but Tohalla wouldn't let her shout at them.

The silver-mauve coif of dreamsmoke shone above their heads, plaiting itself as Housefather talked and waved his arms expansively, but it was brightest here on Housefather's dais by the fire. It breathed serenity even as the snowfall sizzled onto the flames. Tohalla was sure that was why Housemother had set it this year: not just to fill the air – so thin of spiced punch and joyberry scent – but to make her oldest daughter, Tohalla, accept what was about to be made of her. Tohalla's eyes had changed from innocence.

In the middle of Housefather's rambling speech, Housemother leant across from her seat by the dreamsmoke fire and Tohalla jumped as the implacable old woman tapped her arm.

'You be ready,' she whispered. 'When he finishes, it'll be Larnis's turn and yours. You won't let me down, will you?'

For a moment Tohalla panicked, but she gulped smoke into her lungs, and almost at once became calmer. Looking at her mother, Tohalla thought, *She seems so far away!* But she shook her head vaguely, not trusting her voice now above the cheers and stamps of the Household, and settled the children on cushions by her feet while Housefather began on plans for an Intake, stopping every few sentences for the Household to express their amazement.

From its strange, smooth case of real plastic, Tohalla took out the zither. Automatically she caressed it, just as she had when she was ten and Housefather's favourite girl. Before she'd failed the Green. He'd handed it down to her from the shelf that she couldn't reach and said, 'Here! Have this. It's yours as long as you want it – but take care with it. It's hundreds of years old.'

She'd struck two notes just right for all that its shining strings were untuned. He had smiled and patted her shoulder too hard, and said, 'There! That's my girl! You make music with it for the House, just like someone's done in every generation, right since they boarded the Ship on the ruins of Erth. All the time Good Captain kept our people locked in the dark hold of the Ship away from the offsers' treachery, someone made music to cheer them. It came safe through the crash, though the first Housefather said many things were smashed. That and the glass windows and the Book, they're about all that came through in one piece. But we don't need anything else from the world of death and destruction. And Erth's long gone. We've been here, building our world and doing Good Captain's will for more than three hundred years, and the zither helps bind us all together. It's yours for all your lifetime, and your children's too if they want it.'

But there'd been no children, and memory was no tangible escape. Tohalla's eyes drifted unfocused round the Hall. Just as she must make their music she must live their lives in hers. Shuddering, she resolved not to fail with Worut. Housemother had said, 'You can stand anything for a few minutes, can't you?'

It was a thought Tohalla clung to, to stop her from thinking how soon it would happen. Housefather was still talking, still raking in the applause. *If only he'd never stop!* Then she wouldn't have to play for Larnis's Ripeness Chaunt, or gather song in her dry throat for her own.

Housemother gave her a sharp look that Tohalla didn't even notice. Then she gave a sign – just a slight raising of her hand that you had to be watching to see – and Tohalla's youngest sister smiled and left the lad beside her while everyone else down there was talking around him.

Larnis seemed so young and eager to Tohalla, climbing onto the steps in her new green dress with her hair shimmering from the moondust. On those long, perfumed waves of white-gold hair, the wrack Tohalla had gathered for her first wedding really did look like moondust, so long had it matured in Tohalla's kist. There'd been none this year with the sad, grey weight of Autumn fog and the half-ripe crops black-rotten all around.

And down below the dais, Slack Worut slumped against the steps, a drool of saliva hanging lower and lower from the corner of his mouth. It shone in the candle-light and Tohalla wondered remotely why somebody didn't wipe it off. He probably didn't even understand why all of a sudden he was seated so near the fire. His fat fingers were still between his legs.

Eventually, Housefather's speech came to an end with a well-worn joke that brought, with relief, laughter thicker than honey. Tohalla, pale as an icicle, saw it all: the reciprocal blaze of fire at the other end of the hall; festoons of greenery, sharp-scented; meagre sheaves of wheat hoarded from the wretched harvest; and worst, 127 faces watching her disposal.

Into the gathering silence, Housefather coughed his impatience. Tohalla heard her fingers, so obedient to others' will, skittering on the strings of the ancient zither. Larnis started to sing her Ripeness promise.

It really was happening, then. Even the dreamsmoke couldn't make it go away. On Longday, Larnis and Granamyr would join. *They'll probably have fifteen children as easy as finding the Red*, thought Tohalla bitterly, and strummed the zither harder.

And there was Tohalla, twenty-seven and childless with her husband composted and out on the fields under the snow, and nine dead of lung-fever and eight of Red sickness this year alone; and Tohalla had to think of others now. That's what Housemother was always saying. 'You have to think of others now. You have good children and maybe you'll be Housemother some day, like me and your grandmother, and her mother before that.'

And all the time Tohalla's hands and arms flickered over the zither while Larnis sang her bloodline.

'What's it about anyway?' hissed Housemother. 'A few minutes of pleasure or pain, and then he's asleep. You can stand anything for a few minutes, can't you? And let's face it, we know Worut can function if nothing else.'

Tohalla snorted and Housefather glared at her, but the music still rose from her fingertips as she spoke. 'Hard to stop him, wherever he is, but who knows if he can play a duet?'

Housemother laughed softly at her daughter's joke; Tohalla didn't think it was funny. She ducked her head, trying to hide behind the blond curtain of her shoulder-length hair.

So a woman alone was a horrible thing to the Green. So Worut must count for more than she did? Or was it Housefather's web of ambition?

Grief and humiliation twanged in hard chords, and Larnis glared at her eldest sister, but fear lent Tohalla its distance and the dreamwood burnt out her feelings, disconnected sight and hearing from emotion. And her cold fingers slid from one chord-shape to another while Larnis, ten years younger, slid her eyes slyly at Tohalla and Granamyr stood proudly to answer her parentage with his own.

Tohalla, in her own stiff green dress, the green for birth and marriage and death, for Longnight and Longday and forever, plain green because Tohalla could not celebrate this – this – Tohalla almost forgot to breathe, though far away her hands kept on plucking out the notes. Granamyr was almost finished. *If only somebody would stop this!*

Wintry lights exploded in her darkness. Tohalla hated herself for not *wanting* the good of the Green. It was her duty to make sons for the House even if Slack Worut with his loathsome, bloated body were the father. *I should want this!* But she didn't, and this new self-loathing etched into the old like lye. Then, when she realized she did not want to live if living meant this, Housefather growled into the silence left by Larnis, and her lungs hauled in air. Before Housefather could say a word, Tohalla sang as though surprised.

'Through black night we came, lit by beacon stars and guided by Good Captain who gave us this life in giving up his own, blessed be his name. I, Tohalla, daughter of Mirame and ....'

Trinamine woke up with a start and nearly fell off the top stair. She'd sat unnoticed by the balustrade, as close to the fire as she dared to get with Housefather around, and had nodded off from exhaustion and the effects of Housefather's speech. At a high note in the middle of Tohalla's song, Trinamine gaped round in surprise and scrambled inelegantly to Housemother, whispering so fiercely that Tohalla almost raised her voice to be heard.

Housemother listened, questioned once, nodded.

'Change it, Tohalla. Do the Outwatcher's song!'

Tohalla struggled into her wool-skins in the long back porch where they kept the Winter clothes. Lines of thick coats hung on their pegs like waiting animals. She had been afraid to go in there when she was a child, thinking they would get her, but they dangled motionless unless she bumped into them. Even now, she tried not to.

As she came back into the kitchen in her thick wrappings, one of the inwatchers bent suddenly over the woodbox. She could see part of a tankard sticking out when he straightened. He tried to look casual but missed.

'Just putting another log in the stove,' he said unnecessarily.

'Mind the handle doesn't burn!' she answered with a laugh.

Housemother hadn't explained why she'd postponed Tohalla's Ripeness to Slack Worut, still less why she'd blocked Housefather's will – and the argument while Tohalla struggled through the Outwatcher's song had been fierce for all it was in whispers – but she *had* said, 'Get out on Outwatch now, Tohalla – quick, before your father sticks his hand to the plough, else you'll be Worut's come Summer. Go on! Move!'

Tohalla didn't understand, but she'd got out with almost indecent haste. She'd jumped over Worut's feet, still clutching the zither, trying not to run past the lines of watching faces.

With the Hall door banged shut behind her Tohalla had laughed wildly, shaking her head, not explaining to the People in the kitchen what she couldn't explain to herself. She'd not even glanced at the Wolfmen tethered in a corner, where Mevagrin swilled brine over their shivering bodies, and couldn't have cared less if a dozen of the Outwatchers had been derelict of duty.

Crossing to the back door, she took the peg out of the latch and heaved. The wind screamed back wildly, but one of the inwatchers came to help her. Together they forced the heavy wood open. It banged loud against the side of the house, a sharp reverberation. Tohalla shuddered, more afraid they'd make her go back to the platform than of the shrieking cold. The kitchen lamp flickered sideways as snow gusted in, rattling on the ceiling and the floor.

Mevagrin cursed them, barely glancing up from the young Wolfman's bleeding torso, but it wasn't worth answering because Mevagrin wouldn't have heard.

The inwatcher held on to Tohalla while the wind pulled her this way and that. He didn't let go until she had fixed a loop to the guide-rope. Together they swung the door shut, straining this time to keep the wind from smashing it against the jamb.

Outside it was white. White air, white ground, the sky invisible, or more like tangible all around her. It was cold, so that the hairs stood up on her body even inside her layers of tideswool. The wind sucked at her breath like some monster. Like the Red Woman who tried to kill them all.

And it was deafening. Head down to keep the stringing snow out of her face, she pushed through the malevolent air along the deepway to the barn.

She couldn't see it. She could hardly see her sleeve when she lifted up her glove to guard her breath, much less make out the barn. But on either side she could feel the banks of snow they had cleared from the path. They were over her head, though the fresh fall reached almost to her knees. Even without the guide-rope she could hardly have got lost.

Past the barn, though, it was different. At the corner where she had to reach round for the next guide-rope, there was no deepway. From where she was held, she clutched at empty space. Tohalla stumbled sideways.

She panicked. Groping around, she could feel nothing with her bulked-up hands. Nothing!

She would have to go back, then. And Housefather would have her back under control, might marry her regardless to Slack Worut and his fat, clammy hands. Tohalla knew she could not count on another reprieve.

Until Longnight was over, she'd couldn't risk going back in. And if she stayed out in the blizzard, she'd die. And still she couldn't feel the

23

hook and its life-keeping cord however far she stretched.

The thoughts circled each other in her head like geyrlizards at a kill. The dreamsmoke haze was their hunting-sky and her future was their prey.

She shook her head, angry with herself. There *must* be a way out.

Yes! She'd have to spend the night in the barn with the spineders and their awful smell that nothing could wash off. But that would be better than Worut and his rancid sweaty fumblings, and she'd have an eight-month reprieve 'til Longday.

She took two steps back into the lee of the barn before she knew she couldn't leave the other Outwatchers all alone. They'd – but who? Tohalla couldn't even remember who was on watch that season – they'd be all alone on the striding-post at the Edge, up high with the post swaying in the icy wind, the whole thing built with one leg either side of the Edge so that part of the striding-post was actually *outside* the safety of the Green, and who-knew-what coming in from the Red to prowl below or swoop down the white wind. All their lives might depend on her and she stood like an idiot, fumbling while the snow smothered her ... Of course! The guide-rope would be *under* the snow on the other side!

Delving into the snow's wind-packed solidity, she got her hand onto the line. It didn't seem to be anything else; nothing living, anyway.

From here she couldn't wade through to hook her belt on. For a moment she had to clamber up, not anchored at all. Tohalla felt very unsafe, knowing that even one or two steps away from safety she might not be aware of it. She had read in the Book about people who'd been lost in blizzards and not seen again until the Spring thaw left their bodies out in the open. Very pale, those bodies were, with the blood all sunk down to the lowest part; not rotten at all, but their eyes all bloody where the Red grew on them, and toothprints on their faces.

From the barn to the orchard; from the pear-trees to the joyberry vines on the high stone wall at the end. It had been Trinamine's idea to string the snow-lines so that no-one else would be lost when the Red Woman smothered the world with the killing white. Tohalla's lungs hurt as the prickly air shrieked in past her muffler.

More often than not she could see nothing as she waded through the snow. Sometimes, though, the wind dropped and for a time she could see darker patches of sky with now and then a star adrift between the tides of cloud. It was strange, the magic of the Red Woman: the snowflakes were black when she looked up at them, and white when they fell to earth. And here and there, like a drop of blood, shone crystals of winking Red.

24

Then the world closed in on her again, and the ice clawed at her eyes until her lashes were caked and her eyelids stung. But always there was the knowledge that Worut was waiting behind her, and the wonder of why she'd been spared freewheeled in her mind, far off behind the dreamsmoke. Without the drag of the snow-line on her belt she would have died.

When her legs were shaking so much with the effort of floundering hip-high that she thought she would rather sleep on the soft snow pillows, the white grew suddenly brighter and the skirts of the blizzard swept past. Dumbfounded, she could only stare about her. The wind still screamed and buffeted, so that her bulky clothes billowed against her like a sheet on the washing-line, but she could see starlight. It was an unearthly radiance, glimmering back from the streamers of snow blowing off every slightest rise, but it was enough for her to make out a massive blackness. She was so close to it that she began to be afraid. She had reached the Edge.

The striding-post was nowhere in sight.

Slowly she checked the guide-line running through her belt-loop. She knew it was there, even without seeing it, because the weight of snow upon it still pulled her sideways and down, but Tohalla couldn't see the Outwatchers' refuge. Conscious reason told her that the line had broken. The striding-post must be somewhere, and she tried to feel comfort that she was within the limits of the Green, but there was no landmark she knew in this strange rolling landscape.

Yes, there was.

A pack of wolves belled from beyond the Edge and she flinched even though they couldn't get through. The sound quivered through her body, disturbing her slow thoughts.

Oh, yes. A landmark. She stood nodding for a while, working it out one step at a time.

'All a body has to do,' Tohalla told herself, 'is follow the Edge down to the stream.'

It was false dawn when she reached her destination. Tohalla had long passed the stage of shivering. Continual shudders ran through her, and she fell down so often that she couldn't always remember which way was up. Her head was burning.

The stream itself was invisible in its valley, but the great pronged legs of the striding-post towered upwards. They straddled the glittering spikes of the Edge which the day had paled to bronze. Where the legs joined, lights shone out of a lattice in the ironwood bole. She couldn't see anyone limned in the slits of the tracery. There were no

Outwatchers watching out for her.

She tried to shout out, but her throat tasted of blood and no sound came to disturb the still, white dawn.

Unbelievably weary, she hauled herself up the notch-steps to the watch-room, too tired even to look for danger as she climbed the exposed part above the top of the Edge, much less to wonder why no-one had seen her. All she knew was that the scent of woodsmoke and soup promised rest and safety.

A discus of stone smashed into the bole only a nailspan from her fingers.

CHAPTER THREE

The Red Woman's Teeth

Tohalla jerked back. Fragments of ironwood scored her cheek where the metal rim of the discus zinged off the bole. The whole striding-post sang, its lacy bark thrumming under her fingers.

By a miracle, Tohalla did not fall. Reflex kept her gloved hands clinging to the snow-covered lips of the notches. She scrambled higher, frightened, her icy boots slipping on the steps. At any moment another missile might come ...

Reckless in her panic, she pulled herself up. A notch higher ... another notch ...

Behind her, Whitesun leapt over the horizon, its light bursting on the Edge. Dazzling, it glanced off each bronzy tine, hurling lances of molten amber to glitter in her vision.

Blinded, dizzied, she began to slither helplessly down to the living spikes of the Edge. She cried aloud; but the cry of fear choked on the Red-scored rawness of her throat. She was falling ...

The door-flap above her slammed up. From the shadowy entrance, hands reached down to grab her.

They hauled her up over the sill. The Outwatchers' post seemed like the inside of some Red creature's mouth, cavernous and secret after the cold glare of the snowfields. Tohalla felt suddenly trapped. The weight of the domed roof oppressed her. As they slammed the door shut, a great shout of laughter rang out from the Red beyond.

Tohalla wallowed onto her back, hampered by her bulky wraps, head down towards the curving hollow of the floor. Her breath grated her throat. Sparks of colour wheeled behind her eyelids. That at least was normal: a reaction to the dazzle – and the fear.

When it had passed she opened her eyes again, to see the

Outwatchers finish sealing the door. While they worked Tohalla did nothing but breathe until her bruised chest moved in a more natural rhythm than that of sheer terror. She could feel the side of her neck pulsing where panic pumped its pressure into her blood.

Backs towards her, the two could be – Tohalla floundered to a half-crouch, groping for her knife. Her stiffened fingers found it hanging from her belt, held it shakily, ready to defend herself against Sons of the Red.

They put the resin-pot down in a niche and turned to face her.

With relief, she recognized them: Adiokcle, her aunt of the Chrysobal strand, and her uncle Sibulkrin. She should have known by the clothes they wore that they were Greens. Adiockle looked the same as always: unperturbed by anything, even an attack by the Red. Of medium height, spare-boned, everything about her was an angle, even her greying eyebrows, whereas Sibulkrin looked older than she remembered him from before the Winter began. He seemed to have shrunk, to have grown paler, but he was just as wiry and brisk in his movements.

Neither of them recognized Tohalla, muffled in snow-caked, Red-spattered wraps. Sibulkrin, eyeing her as an unknown stranger, balanced a knife point-down on his horny hand and said nothing. Adiockle made up for it. 'Who've we got here, then?'

'Tohalla.' It was a hoarse croak, unrecognizable. Tohalla laid her knife carefully aside and sent it slithering down to the middle of the room.

She pulled off her gloves with chattering teeth, struggled to unlace the frost-encrusted drawstring of her hood. Red crystals tinkled unheeded to the floor. All the time Sibulkrin shifted his hand, keeping the dagger upright, but his eyes never left her. Adiockle moved to one side, stepping easily on the hollow floor. From there the intruder couldn't hope to cover both of them. Tohalla could just see her on the corner of vision. Adiockle was standing casually by a rack of spears.

At last Tohalla tugged at the tideswool muffler covering her mouth and nose. As it came loose, Tohalla gasped.

Sibulkrin tossed his knife into the air and caught it on its third glittering arc. Adiockle said only, 'Oh, it's you, is it? Sit still a minute, Toh, and let me look at that.'

Firmly, she turned Tohalla's chin to catch the cold light of Whitesun coming in through the lattice. 'Nothing to worry about.'

Adiockle scratched out the shards of ironwood with her nail, hardly glancing at them. Tohalla didn't feel that half as much as the stinging below her lip.

'It's just where your breath froze your muffler to your skin, Toh. Come in by the fire and let's warm you up. You could do with some raspberry tea by the seeming of it.'

Adiockle asked no questions. She stripped off the snow-caked layers of clothes since Tohalla's fingers were too numb, and wrapped her in some sleeping-wools that she'd warmed at the fire.

Tohalls was shuddering from a cold that seemed to be an empty cellar, dark and sucking in her heart. While Adiockle helped her drink the hot brew laced with willow-bark, Sibulkrin toured the round room, peering through the lattice that circled it from one side of the chimney to the other.

Tohalla scarcely noticed when she slipped over the edge of sleep.

It was a friendly silence Tohalla woke to. Sibulkrin was stirring a kettle full of something savoury on the ironwood grid over the embers while Adiockle twisted fibres into a rope. Neither of them spoke as Tohalla wriggled her bedding closer to the fire, but Adiockle smiled at her and nodded.

Whitesun and Redsun were both high, casting a coloured tracery of light and dark into the neat room. From outside came an endless pattern of silvery chimes, faint and elusive. Tohalla had never heard it before; it puzzled her. Other things were meant to puzzle her too, she remembered that, but she was feverish and couldn't recall what.

The gentle clangour reclaimed her attention. What was it? Why was it so strange? Why hadn't she heard its melody in all her twenty-seven years?

Then the thought came to her that she'd never really been on Outwatch before, never wanted to, and the logic of it fitted neatly in her mind. So she lay still but for the ghosts of shivers, following the tune in and out of sleep.

Redsun was shining flat across the room when Sibulkrin brought down the lamps. It was the soft gurgle they made as he filled them that woke Tohalla again. Her chest still ached at every breath, and her throat was thick and swollen. Though the fever had lessened, she still felt light-headed and unreal.

Adiockle looked up from some needle-weaving as Tohalla stretched languorously in the soft sleeping-wools. Never before had Tohalla felt them all over her naked skin.

Her aunt's sharp features suddenly swam closer and a calloused hand felt Tohalla's forehead. Adiockle nodded positively.

'You'll do, Toh, and I should think so too after four days. Here, put those on. It's cold down the compost steps.'

29

'Those' were petticoats and a dress of soft tideswool hanging on the chimney-breast. In the ruddy sunset, they glowed like the path of Redsun over the darkening sea. It seemed an unwholesome colour to one born to the Green, but Adiockle shook them gently under Tohalla's nose, saying, 'Get on with it, Toh. I want my supper.'

Tohalla took them reluctantly, noticing how odd it seemed that Adiockle had said 'I', as though one person's wishes were more important than the group's. But Adiockle was clicking with her tongue, and Tohalla obeyed.

She wriggled into the things under the bedclothes, as she had done when she was little and dreaded the cold air in the girls' room. Even so, Sibulkrin turned the other way.

Smooth-knit socks, leggings and quilted slippers completed Tohalla's outfit, but over everything else Adiockle made her wear a hooded shawl whose point touched the backs of Tohalla's knees. After all that Tohalla giggled to herself, wondering why her aunt didn't remind her to wash behind her ears.

Tohalla stood up experimentally. The room had a distressing tendency to spin, but if she stared hard it behaved more like the familiar rooms of the House. Tohalla hadn't seen the striding post more than three or four times in her life. At the moment she wasn't quite sure what things on the Edge did or didn't do.

Sibulkrin pulled back a padded rug and flipped up the trap-door leading to other rooms below. All of them had been hollowed out of the single ironwood tree that formed the striding post. The trap-door revealed a flight of steps that had been rounded out by the same acid the first Housefather had used. It was the only thing that would cut through ironwood.

Tohalla walked over to the trap-door on wobbly legs.

Adiockle said, 'Can you manage?' and when Tohalla nodded, passed her a hand-lamp.

Tohalla was glad of its wavering light for the stairs were little better than gentle, uneven ridges that flowed downwards in a loose spiral. As soon as her head was below the curve of the floor, Sibulkrin shut the trapdoor to keep out the cold.

Tohalla put her hand on the outside wall to steady her as she went down a full turn. She felt a faint warmth seeping through the ironwood under her fingertips, but the draught from the stream far below was still cold enough to bring goose-pimples to her skin.

She passed the first opening and went down another half-spiral, uneasily wondering if she were in the leg of the striding-post that stood out in the Red. A faint, nameless dread urged her to hurry but her body wasn't strong enough. It was letting her down again, as it had when it couldn't keep her poor dead babies alive.

Here, the compost chamber swelled out from the edge of the bole into its centre. There were two wide tubes in the floor, since urine was kept for setting dye and making a wash to kill Red-mites before they could tunnel into people's brains, or bore into the trees of the orchard.

In the clean-room above it, Tohalla used the bowl of tepid water for a quick, shivery splash with the soap, then emptied the water back into another tube. She could hear it gurgling as it found its way down to the stream. She conscientiously piped more water up from under the ice, so that it could warm up for the next user. The tubes were nothing more than dead arteries of the ironwood.

Wandering weakly back up by the dim light of the hand-lamp, Tohalla remembered the puzzles that had beset her before she slept. Why had the Wolfmen thrown the discus? Had it been the start of an attack that she'd slept through? Maybe. But someone had laughed out there, and she reddened, all alone in the dark stairway, that she'd made a fool of herself over a practical joke.

But she could have died! Would that have made them laugh all the more?

Not only that, Adiockle hadn't seemed to do anything much about the crystals of Red Tohalla had brought in on her clothes. Was life on the Edge eating into her aunt's thinking? She'd done nothing back to that discus-thrower ...

And what about Worut? Why had Housemother made her sing a different song? What was Housefather doing, to let Housemother direct Tohalla's life? What would she be going back to?

Tohalla's feet slowed on the steps, as much from confusion as weariness. The dim twists of the passage made her feel she was trapped, breaking open the nightmares she'd forgotten.

Unaccountably, she felt better when she climbed back into the warm, lamp-lit watch-room and slammed the trapdoor down.

Still not asking anything beyond, 'More salt, Toh?' Adiockle helped them all to the meal Sibulkrin had made. It tasted strange – a vegetable stew with rich gravy. Maybe they did things differently out here at the Edge? Still, the buttered oatcakes tasted of home, though Tohalla couldn't swallow much,

As an umarried woman, it was scarcely Tohalla's place to start up a conversation with her elders. Consequently the silence went on as Adiockle checked through the lattice and Sibulkrin washed up. It was plain they didn't share her feeling of awkwardness.

Just as Tohalla's problems were growing to fill the sunset quiet, Adiockle settled down on her chair.

'How'd Housefather like the presents we sent him?' she asked.

'W–what presents?'

Sibulkrin chuckled over his washing-up. 'Your Wolfmen, of course!' His voice was rusty, out of practice.

'Oh!' Tohalla flushed. 'Sorry.'

'Not to worry, Toh,' said Adiockle kindly. She'd unrolled her needle-weaving this time. 'It's being Redified that's snarled your brain up. Go on if your throat's up to it.'

'Well, one of them died by the barns.' Tohalla wondered if she'd stumbled over his corpse. It was an uncomfortable thought. 'The other two made it, just, the big one with the white eye and the skinny blond one. Housefather was all set to kill them but ...'

It seemed silly to say Housefather hadn't because Tohalla had tickled a little girl.

Adiockle nodded anyway. 'But he didn't. We didn't think he would, or we'd have kept 'em here. Easier though at the House – more to watch 'em, like. Still, I wonder he let you go, Toh. I didn't reckon he would, but Trinamine said it was worth a try.'

There it was – Adiockle had said 'I' again!

'He didn't,' Tohalla answered. 'Housefather, that is. A body was on my strand-naming when Housemother stopped me. Made me change to the Outwatchers' song. She said to get out here before Housefather ... He was furious! They were quarrelling right there on the platform in front of Larnis and Worut and everybody! I couldn't work out what was going on ...'

Aghast, Tohalla stopped. *She*'d done it now. Worse, a suspicion came to her that she *did* know what was going on. Hadn't Sibulkrin said, 'Your Wolfmen'?

Adiockle chuckled, watching horrified comprehension tiptoe across Tohalla's face.

'They're not human, Adi! Even Worut's better than –'

A sharp, bell-like sound made her break off. It was the clash of something heavy crashing into the ironwood. Some dark shape bounced off the Red-side lattice, sending a shadow across Tohalla's eyes and making her duck. The whole room was singing as the bole vibrated: a bass note and five harmonics. Lower tones, unheard, tingled through Tohalla's body.

'Not to worry, Toh,' Adiockle said, and crossed to where the lattice

32

stopped at the chimney-breast. 'They often do that if they're passing, like they did this morning, just to let us know they're ...'

'Attention, colonists!' The stentorian shout from outside interrupted her for a moment, but Adiockle continued placidly, '... there. They say *they* planted the Edge to keep *us* out of the Red.'

'Attention!'

At the second shout, Tohalla made her way as stealthily as she could to the lattice. She cursed under her breath when she stubbed her toes. This curved floor was uncomfortable.

Kneeling on the windowshelf with her aunt out of sight behind the chimney, Tohalla peered through the lattice, quite forgetting she would be silhouetted by the lamplight. The intricate whorls and knots of the bark were all that the acid had left there. It was like looking through lace.

Outside, beyond the blue-shadowed clearing, shapes were moving in the Red scrub. They were just visible in the afterglow. The whole scene was weird, unnerving. Everything seemed just off true, trees that weren't trees, as if there were a disturbing new dimension to perspective that Tohalla's Green-trained eyes couldn't quite perceive. Even the figures were not quite human in outline.

One came forward now, her feet – his feet? – crunching on the glittering snow. Breath smoked out between her tusks. (Adiockle whispered, 'It's a woman – look at the shape of her.') The wolf-cloak glistened red and mauve and green and blue as the wind flapped it back from her shoulders. The woman threw back her muzzle-helm.

As the Wolfwoman stooped to retrieve her discus her shaggy hair streamed back towards her friends. Tohalla forgot to be scared. She stared at the long russet strands, amazed that any childless woman should be so confident. The woman was grinning, unafraid. On the still air rang faint chimes, gently discordant. The woman straightened, and for a long moment there was no other sound.

'Colonists, perception is. Signal if you me receive.'

Slowly Tohalla raised her hand to hit the lattice. As her fist met the ironwood, the bole gonged again and again. It was as if, for the first time since her first Ripeness, she felt she could be seen. Each blow said, 'I exist! I exist!' She beat and beat at the lattice until her aunt elbowed her impatiently.

The Wolfwoman laughed derisively. 'Signal received. Message follows: locate the Axe.'

Tohalla longed to answer, but she didn't understand. Adiockle and Sibulkrin looked at each other, as baffled as she was.

'What axe?' shouted Sibulkrin.

'Young male Caucasian, wounded. Two followers. Messengers me inform the squadron this way passed in pursued by squadron of wolves. Locate!'

Adiockle called, 'Why do you want him?' before Sibulkrin could speak. He shrugged. Even if it was not Adiockle's place to speak, it was a fair question.

'The Axe with mutiny is charged. When located, for him execution is. Give exact location?'

Tohalla longed to answer but Sibulkrin shouted her down. 'We don't know just where he is. We ain't got him.'

And the Wolfwoman walked away. Tohalla wanted to call after her, to make her turn around, but there was nothing left to say.

That night before the moons rose, Sibulkrin lit a driftwood flare when the fifth star showed in the dark sky. It burnt a crackling blue and he waved it three times from the doorflap, which faced the House in the combe, to signal all was well. In the code Trinamine had made, there was no signal for wolf-questions about strangers.

Next day, Sibulkrin repaired the guide-lines under a gentle snowfall, and there was nothing left of the whole episode, except Tohalla's Red sickness. Neither he nor his wife talked of the Wolfmen at all. It was as if the whole thing were her fever-dream.

It was Spring before they let Tohalla go outside.

CHAPTER FOUR

Red in the Orchard

A warm wind was blowing from the shore, carrying with it the boom of the ice cracking in the bay. Tohalla felt the warmth of both suns and heard the steady drip of the thaw despite the racing cloud-shadows. She begged to be allowed back to the House, but Adiockle said no. Below, in the combe, a faint mist of green wove through the branches of the orchard, and the wattle domes on the House shone wetly. On bare patches of ground the Red grew overnight, and every morning the children raced round the fires that burnt it off. Tohalla felt cut off here and useless.

Adiockle set up a hand-loom for her and tutted if she sang out loud.

At last the mud dried out and on that day the new Outwatchers struggled up the hill with salt to trade when the Iron Men came. Their faces were black with the ash of the Spring burning.

One of them was Trinamine. They'd been so close as children that it was like living inside one another, Trin-and-Tohalla, but something had happened after Trinamine's Ripeness, something she wouldn't talk about. After that, Trinamine had spent as much time as she could up here on the Edge, away from her husband Grensham who preferred to stay below at the planting. Still, at least Trin talked to Tohalla as an equal, which most of their age-mates would not. Maybe it was because Trin's one son had died at the age of eleven, crushed beneath a wagon-wheel.

While the other Outwatchers stopped by Adiockle, Trinamine strode over the cracked ground to her friend.

'Hello, Toh. How d'you like the Edge?'

Tohalla grinned despite the personal question. 'Good in small doses. But doesn't the Red look fierce in the Spring?'

'Surely, the way it grows. Colours are nice and bright, though. Makes a change from the Green.'

Tohalla gasped and looked around to make sure no-one could hear.

Trinamine laughed. 'Still pretty stiff, ain't you? Even after a Winter on the Edge. Don't you even like its song?'

But Tohalla wouldn't admit that she loved its dancing harmonies. The sight of their ancient enemy, the Red, still disturbed her even after months on the Edge.

Trinamine smiled at her confusion and changed the subject. 'Your Wolfmen have survived – don't know how. Housefather wouldn't give them enough to feed a hen. But times were tough – look how skinny I've got. Grensham says he hardly knows me. Still, he never did. I'm glad to be back.'

I ...

They had no time for more. Adiockle called loud good-byes that Tohalla wasn't allowed to ignore. And Trinamine hurried through the secret good-bye she and Tohalla had made when they were children. Her fingertips scarcely brushed the inside of her friend's wrist: eye in eye, they savoured the coming-together that would follow the parting. But Trinamine kept looking through the gaudy tangle of the Edge to the burgeoning Red.

Feeling somehow jealous without being able to put a name to the feeling, Tohalla followed Adiockle and Sibulkrin. They walked down beside the chattering stream in its vale of rocks. Grass – real grass from seed brought all the way from Erth – pushed up, pale and green in little crevices. But the hard shine of invading Red hurt Tohalla's eyes wherever she looked.

Adiockle had made her wear most of her Winter gear, and Tohalla sweated under its weight. They made frequent stops for her shaky legs, and took time out to throw stones at the geyrlizards hovering in the thermals over the waterfalls. Even so, Tohalla was exhausted by the time they got down to the fields.

Tohalla, waving to the children busy with their chores, smiled; but she didn't know how she felt about coming Home. After that one moment of existence when the Wolfwoman spoke to her, she had become again a nothing. Still, it had been easier at the striding-post without having to duck Housefather all the time. And life on the Edge had been straightforward, though spiced with alien smells and an informality that was more than just Adiockle's way. Tohalla's pockets held a weaving she had done just for the pleasure of creating. Housemother certainly wouldn't have allowed that, but Adiockle had

36

said, 'Well, it keeps you out of mischief.'

The Wolfman she wouldn't think of at all. But what, Tohalla wondered, would happen about Worut?

The first Tohalla saw of the Wolfmen, she was sowing seeds in the herb garden. She had strict instructions from Housemother to stop when she was tired, but that was more for form's sake than because Tohalla was valued. Still, Tohalla liked to feel the warm earth crumbling under her hands and to smell its fragrance mingled with the soft sea breeze. Every now and then a snatch of song drifted up from the salt-pans on the beach. The salt would kill off the Red and keep them safe, or bring them metal in trade, and the cheerful singing seemed all part of the garden's peace.

Tohalla heard a shriek from the orchard. It was a cry freighted with fear.

She dropped her trowel and ran. From all over the infields people dashed to the orchard. The yell went up again from among the blossoming trees, and chickens squawked away into the pink and white branches. She didn't even notice that she had stopped beside the older of the Wolfmen. She was too wrapped up in the horror of the attack.

A seastalker was bouncing over the line of bee-skeps, slashing its long jaws sideways. At each pass it filtered a mass of bees from the air. How it found them, blind as it was, Tohalla couldn't understand, but its hard-shelled head was sucking thousands of them in. Without the bees for pollination, there'd be no crops. Next to nothing left of the brave Green. The seastalker meant death.

Galvan shot another arrow at its iridescent hide. The beast was as high as Housefather's platform, its sinuous neck even longer. And jaws the length of Tohalla's arms carried a web of fibrous teeth.

The arrow-point glanced off, missing Asdra by a span. Asdra screamed, then pretended he hadn't been afraid after all.

Beside Tohalla, the old Wolfman swallowed a grin.

Someone had sent for Housefather who strode through the crowd. He'd gathered inwatchers with spears and swords. Caramon came, drifting after the other young ones, but her thin face was shut to all emotion. The mindless girl stayed half-hidden on the edge of the crowd, watching blankly.

Housefather ordered the children back, and the swords and spears flashed in the noon light. The seastalker hardly noticed them. One of the inwatchers slashed his wife's arm by accident and the Wolfman chuckled softly.

37

Housefather said loudly, 'You. Get her back to Mevagrin. A fine pair of inwatchers you turned out to be!'

As they left, Housefather pointed accusingly. 'And you, Wolfman! You've taken the bread from our mouths all Winter long and all you can do is laugh! How would *you* kill the thing?'

The Wolfman, with all the dignity of his age and height, stood to attention, not that the Greens knew it, and turned his one good eye insolently on Housefather. 'I my work for short rations traded, sir.' It was amazing how much contempt he could put into that one outlandish word, 'sir'. 'No need for the destruction is. The alien on short-range radar operates. Let it those stingers as fuel take in and it will leave. Seldom is that one homes in of the same location twice.'

Housefather took a minute to sort out some meaning from the words. Then he shouted, 'D'you mean to tell me that we should let our bees be eaten?' His ruddy face darkened and he flexed his muscles, as if only respect for his position kept him from striking the Wolfman down.

'You ignorant savage! You don't understand what's good for you!' Housefather snorted his disdain. 'You're no use to man nor beast! I've half a mind to put you out of your misery right now!'

The Wolfman moved not so much as a muscle in his face, but somehow words came into Tohalla's mind in the Wolfman's gravelly voice: *In you not that much possession is.* She was surprised that behind his grey face the Wolfman was laughing infectiously.

All the time the seastalker was jumping blindly on its six plate-ended legs and the hopes of the Green were dying by the swarm. Around it, some of the children were leaping about with excitement but many of the older ones were crying, caught in the web of the adults' blighted emotions.

Housefather swung his head round as if that would help him find what to do. Behind him the hard round belly of the seastalker seemed to swell. Bees buzzed frantically, their stings failing to fight off the intruder that dwarfed even the old Wolfman.

Housefather caught a glimpse of a slim, blond figure sandwiched between two bulky farmers. A crafty expression crossed Housefather's face.

'Grab him!' he shouted, jerking a finger that way.

Hands seized the young Wolfman, who struggled until he realized it would do him no good among so many enemies. At the same moment, his gotch-eyed elder started forward and was promptly tripped up by an out-thrust rake. Booted feet pinned his shoulders to the ground. Tohalla hadn't moved.

Housefather made no threat but it hung on the air anyway with the salt tang and the peaceful scent of blossom.

'Tell us how to slay this killer!' and Housefather rolled his head towards the shiny giant over the hives.

The young Wolfman shrugged. 'No point is.'

The boots thrust more cruelly on the old Wolfman's shoulders. The slim boy – *that must be the Axe!* realized Tohalla – said hastily, 'Where killing is, his kind will come for defence.'

'Answer me, boy!' roared Housefather, red-faced with fury.

The boy said, 'With killing this, suffering for the Green is – but I'll inform. Hang tidenets in the trees on the flight-path from the sea.'

'We'll be cut to ribbons!'

The boy shrugged. 'Then half a watch wait and the beast's mission will be done. A sufficient of those stingers for you and him is.'

At the headland, where grey rocks draggled strings above the swell, six frightened farmers waded out with broomstales. Here, where the arms of the combe almost touched, the tidenets hung just above the sea. Already they were stroking glands below their red eyes, pulling out a dull fibre that hardened in minutes to glassy sharpness. With it they were plastering over the holes in their nets that the seastalker had torn in its passage. Other tidenets, further out, were harder to see. With every passing cloud or drifting wrack, they changed colour so that they were all but invisible with their translucent bodies.

The farmers, Jeremas and Kerstaf at the fore, raised the wooden handles and lifted off the strands that were still sticky where the tidenets walked. On the sandy beach, practically everyone had come to watch. The elder Wolfman laid his arm casually about the thin-fleshed shoulders of the Axe, not seeming to mind the heavy log to which his leg-chain was shackled. Apparently Housefather wasn't afraid of the boy: Tohalla noticed that the Axe was free to come and go. He still looked skinny, fine-drawn by the sickness from his wounds of last Winter. His long bright hair blew wildly like the Wolfwoman's, and Tohalla's heart lifted at the reminder.

They're playing with the tidenets! thought Tohalla. *It's like some puzzle for children – every time the tidenets walk up near the handles, our lot lift that end and the tidenets slide back down.* On a level lower than thought was the impression that the Wolfman were clever to have worked out such a plan.

Housefather was galled he hadn't thought of it. And for the first time, he really began to believe the Wolfmen were smart enough to escape – if they wanted to do so. It seemed they didn't. So what did they want? Striding along the path from the beach, supervising noisily, Housefather stopped so abruptly he was almost cut by the tidenets.

It was obvious! The Wolfmen wanted to stay warm and comfortable and well fed. Why should they go back to their old barren life in the Red? Perhaps Housemother was right, after all. They did have a certain animal cunning. But whether they were human – well, that was another matter. Tohalla could practically see the thoughts reflected on Housefather's beefy face.

Coming in through the gates of the orchard, Housefather met the watchers he had set to guard the monster. Privately Tohalla wondered why, since there was nothing anybody could do to the seastalker in its stone-hard casing.

'He's slowin' down,' said one of them.

'It! It!' shouted Housefather. He was always shouting, as if that made him right. 'String these tidenets up and let's see if those outlanders have the right of it. Where d'you suggest we put it, Gotch?'

The old man, still a giant compared to the farmers, looked down his long nose at Housefather. It was a gesture of superiority calculated to annoy. 'Diagonal above the stingers' camp.'

Housefather looked furious. 'On your head be it, Gotch. Do it, men!'

Tohalla could see no reaction in the Wolfman's face to this cruel nickname. But then, she was careful to show no reaction when she was taunted either.

Gingerly, Kerstaf and Jemeras scraped off the sharp strands onto overhanging boughs, then the other farmers followed. The tidenets piped shrilly, their thin bodies changing wildly from the pastel of blossom to the blue of the sky. Below them, the seastalker bounced on its bendy legs – and screeched. A clear fluid oozed from a cut in its skin.

The sound resonated horror in Tohalla, setting her teeth on edge. The Wolfmen walked away, the Axe carrying his friend's log easily in his wiry arms, but Tohalla's gaze was pinned on the awful spectacle. The seastalker, blind, was bouncing this way and that, not even his bony jaws able to break the strands that glittered with his blood. Out at sea the beast could snap the tidenets with its massively-protected feet. But here, caught beneath the web of branches, the seastalker couldn't jump high enough to bring its feet into play. At each leap another gaping wound appeared in its body. The strands cut with a sound like the shriek of iron on iron, and the seastalker's cries made more than Tohalla turn away. But she was one of the first who stumbled off through the pink and white glory of the orchard, heedless of the cackling hens she scattered.

Tohalla walked faster and faster, breaking into a trot as if she could get away from the sound. Yet down the dusty road it pursued her, growing fainter only when she reached the sheltered herb-garden on the far side of the House. She turned in through the gate and stopped, panting. The Wolfmen were sitting on the doorstep in the wide shade of the House eaves.

'Oh!' she said, and was embarrassed.

'Regrets, mate.' It was the older one who spoke.

'I – I'm sorry. I was startled.' Tohalla heard herself say 'I'. The seastalker's screams hung on the air so close about her she could have touched them.

Not knowing what to do, she walked to the pump and drew water into a leathern bucket. She offered them the dipper first.

'Gratude,' they said one after the other, and pretended not to watch her while they drank. In her position, she scarcely dared look at them. But they had long hair too. She didn't know that in their world, it was no sign of disgrace.

The younger one, elbowed by his companion, got up and dipped water for her. Tohalla was surprised by the courtesy.

When she hesitated, the older one said, 'Take it in, mate. By your respiry you it need. I you from Tree Valley could have heard.'

She took the dipper from the boy's hands and drank, working out what he meant. Swallowing the lot, she gasped her thanks.

'You could reline your pipes with marshstar.' The old man seemed to hear her thoughts and went on, 'My name's Edrach, rank ex-leftant of the Captain's True Crew. This here one Ain Tsui Battle-Axe is, but since we were docked here no axe to him is. His mother Marchidas of the Seven Battles was, and the last at finding the Ship.'

He looked up at her quizzically when she made no answer. 'Is there a name to you?'

'Yes. A body didn't know you wanted it, though. It's Tohalla.'

'Tohalla.' They said it with a rounding of the first a, making it more like an o. It made her feel strange and mystic, like a new identity. But she still didn't know what to say to people she'd never met before. She'd never had any practice.

'Sit down, mate, before you fall. We no teeth for biting have.'

She leant back against the Housedoor in the shade. All three sat on the sill, their legs stretched in front of them, six brown woven pipes going baggy at the knees. She could see no difference between them

41

and her, but they had nothing in common.

'D'you know what marshstar is?' the Axe asked. It was the first time he'd spoken and in his rich, tenor voice was the same shade of contempt she'd been used to for the last ten years since her baby died at birth.

Tohalla shook her head and wished she hadn't. Just like Housemother had told her not to, she'd strained herself running and the fever was nibbling at her brain. Though the seastalker's cries had subsided, she could hear children crying through the open window of the creche, and the sound pierced her head. She couldn't even go and comfort them, not Redified as she was.

'Marshstar a plant is. Small, ankle-high, pale mauve it is and on the meadows floats when the meltwater high in Spring runs. Six points it has, jointed up even all the way on the main stem. Top joint like a cup is shaped. Know it?' the old man asked.

Head down, no cap because she wasn't married, Tohalla muttered, 'No, I've never seen it.'

'Burnt it up, most like,' the Axe said suddenly, fiercely.

'Oho, tongue to you, is?' laughed Edrach. 'Give this one time to open.

'What does the old mo you for this sickness give, mate?'

Tohalla said, 'Willow bark for the fever, and raspberry leaf tea for the throat, and ... and ... I don't know.'

Edrach asked, 'Fast remedy is?'

Tohalla said, 'It depends. Some people never get better, not really. I got it on Longnight and it only bothers me now if I do too much.'

The Axe said, 'Then no good remedy for it in the Green is!' He was still angry and Tohalla didn't understand why.

Edrach glared at him and said, 'Fifth column, lad. And you, Tohalla, attention.'

It was that word again that raised excitement in her.

But she never got to hear why she must pay attention, because Housemother opened the door at their backs and all three nearly fell flat.

'I thought I'd find you here, Tohalla, but I never thought I'd find you loafing when there's work to be done.' Housemother's chins wobbled fiercely. 'I'm surprised at you – in your position, too! The sooner you're properly directed, Toh, the better.'

'And as for you!' Housemother clicked her fingers at the Wolfmen. 'I can't believe such ingratitude when we've fed and clothed you ...'

Tohalla scrambled to her feet, swaying more than was necessary.

42

'Don't blame them, please, Housemother. A body felt ill and they fetched me water and looked after me ...'

'Don't interrupt. They'd have done far better to bring you in to Mevagrin and get on with their own work. Now you come with me, girl, and you two get back about your business.'

Tohalla was not so ill this time that she had to stay lonely in bed in her age-mates' room. Not that they were her age. Again she was back with the giggling youngsters of fourteen and fifteen who were coming up to Ripeness, and with her youngest sister Larnis. Not content with winning Granamyr on Longnight, Larnis dug at her with petty meannesses.

All the same it was boring in the kitchen with only old Mevagrin to talk to – and she was deaf. Since her head ached, Tohalla could not sew for long, or spin, but for the moment she was content to sit in her quilt and doze by the stove when no-one was cooking. The tisanes she had to drink relieved her bone-deep aches, but the disease lurked nearby, ready to pounce back into her lungs. She wasn't even allowed to sit by the window.

Only the children came to talk to her, and Mevagrin's voice, that harsh, off-key mumble of the deaf, frightened them away. 'Don't let Housemother catch you!' she said to Caramon, pushing her away because the girl obviously didn't understand why she had to keep her distance from Tohalla, and 'You'll feel the back of my hand if you go and get Redified from this 'un.' Caramon might not follow the words but the meaning of Mevagrin's upraised fist was plain enough. Still, puzzlement drew an expression of pain on the little girl's features as she trailed reluctantly outside.

Mevagrin mumbled off to the compost one morning when only Whitesun had risen over the blue waters of the bay. It was after breakfast, and Coril and Beran chattered more than usual over the washing-up. They both had children to talk about.

Tohalla wished they wouldn't clatter so; the willow-bark left a dry bitterness in her mouth and hadn't eased her yet.

'Hear that?' asked Coril, cocking her neatly-capped head towards the open window. Faint shriekings came in on the morning breeze.

'Another seastalker.' Beran nodded and tipped the dishwater into the run-off. 'A body gets fed up of 'em. Everlasting racket.'

'Dozens of 'em there are now. A body can't hear yourself think outside. There's too many to burn – they're tipping 'em into the sea the other side of the point now. Housefather's got Jemeras on it today.' Coril put away the last plate and wiped her hands on her apron.

Beran re-tied her cap strings, saying not a word to Tohalla. Her swift footsteps clacked on the boards by the hall door. 'Nothing good ever came out of the Red. The sooner it's wiped out, the better.'

Coril shut the cupboard and followed her. At this time of day there was no-one in the hall, except maybe Worut. Tohalla could hear their voices echoing.

'Coming to help with the Intake?'

'Soon as a body gets my britches on. Meet you at the house-stead gate, all right? Won't be an eye-blink.'

'First time, then.'

Tohalla heard someone moving softly around the kitchen. Thinking it was only Mevagrin, she didn't open her aching eyes until a gentle voice beside her said. 'Marshstar is. The boy it for you got.'

Edrach was holding out a wooden cup to her. 'Go on. Take it in. Good smells, is?'

The dark liquid that came up to the rim had a fragrance like bean-flowers. Tohalla murmured her thanks and swallowed it. Its warmth stroked away the pain in her throat. The scent of it stayed in her airways so that for once she could breathe easily.

Surprised, she thanked him, eye in eye, the way the other farmers wouldn't look at him. Even the children didn't look at him aright: they stared at his sightless, bulging eyeball and called him Gotch until a fierce grin split his lips apart over his teeth. Then they were frightened.

'When tomorrow is,' Edrach said, smiling down at her, 'you out again will go,' but she didn't believe him.

He nodded, friendly-fashion, and walked into the pool of sunlight at the open door, but Tohalla called after him.

'Is it true that the seastalkers keep coming?'

He said simply, 'They distress-calls receive. They'll keep coming while a single one strung-cut in the orchard is. The tidenets dead are, but the strands not yet are broken. Could you a distress-call hear and not come to help a crew-mate?' He stared at her out of his one brown eye. 'Or loyalty not in the Green is?'

And while her surprise searched the shafts of sunshine for an answer, he limped away carrying the heavy log in the crook of his arm.

That night, lying in bed with Larnis's lungs pumping the slow, ironic rhythm of sleep across her own wakefulness, Tohalla felt strange. She had dozed most of the day. Now a wide-awake feeling tingled through her limbs, carrying the message to her brain; her fingers twanged with it, and worked patterns of guilt into the crinkles of her bedspread.

Restless, Tohalla moved to find a coolness in her sheets. There was none. Her throat, her chest, glowed, it seemed. She wished she'd never taken that marshstar from the son of the Red. If it wasn't wrong, why had she hidden it? It kept tracking across her mind that she might really be Red-tainted now. She might die. (Hadn't one of the offsers tried to kill the Captain once? By poison, with a smile?)

She forced herself to lie still, to think of something that wasn't the galloping of her heart. Opening her eyes to blind them to such inner thoughts, she sat up.

Faint, mauve shadows reversed the path of the Amethyst Moon. From seawards, its light shortened until it hovered on the run under the seaward window. The tide was turning, the tide of full moons and melting snow. It kissed the beach and sucked at the reefs. Out where the Edge curved down to the shore came the dying whistle that meant wolves had killed. So Trinamine said.

And nearer, suddenly, sounded the howl of a seastalker. Another one. And the Greens who never killed had cut that shriek out of its body with glassy tidenet strands.

She wriggled lower under the suffocating warmth of the quilt. She could do nothing about the seastalker's mutilation. She knew she couldn't. But it went on and on screaming while it cut itself to kindling, calling its distress. So its crew-mates — wasn't that what Edrach had said? — would come. To die.

Wasn't anyone going to do something about it? Not even help it die so the Greens could sleep in peace?

From the pegs on the wall she took down her trousers, her tunic, slid silently into her leggings. Larnis didn't stir, nor Hella, nor Cervel. Tohalla half-wished they would.

If only someone else would do it instead! But she didn't let the 'it' gel in her mind as she stealthily dressed.

As the light of Amethyst Moon spilled outwards over the sill, so did Tohalla. Her body remembered the hollows in the Housewall, her fingers curved to the same knobs of flint. But then she'd been creeping to meet Pierse, when to touch his face was to share her soul.

But it hadn't ever been like that, not really. It had been only a reassurance that she wasn't alone. As her foot skipped the rocking stone by the downstairs window, she couldn't remember his face, not even from the day they'd poured him into the slurry-pit so he'd go on feeding the Green as a farmer should. What had she been feeling when his body sank through the crust of scum and they cropped her hair? She still didn't know, but was secretly afraid part of it had been relief.

45

She could only remember the feel of him in the dark of their room, his whisper in the blackness when he'd done his part of their duty: 'Now keep your hips on the pillow. I'm sure that's where you went wrong last time.'

Since then her dark blond hair had grown a palm-span …

Tohalla's feet, careful not to trample the cabbages, hit the ground with a faint thud. But the inwatchers were laughing, attention focused on their jokes in the Hall. How could there be a threat from beyond the Edge, here in the heartland? Even the beasts of the field were bedded in the barns where geyrlizards and flying ticks could not get at them. And what threat could they suspect against Housefather's authority from within?

Ducking low, she kept in the moonshadow until she had scaled the wall of the vegetable plot, but no-one had seen her. No-one called after her. No-one came to share the blame.

Lonely, sliding along the base of the seaward wall, Tohalla turned the corner to southward and ran through the long grass of the ley. At the next corner she was safe in shadow again. But the safety was unconvincing to her constricted arteries.

The House seemed both far away and frighteningly near, but only the watch-lights were burning from the Hall and the landings. Not a single silhouette stood watching her as the seastalker's hoots shivered her flesh.

Her bootheels clicked faintly when they found the stone road, but nobody could have heard the sound above the immense anguish piercing the air.

Abruptly, Amethyst Moon leaped over the domes on top of the House and she was pinned in its light. Fear took her over the wall of the orchard; fear of the smooth-shelled monster hid her in the safety of the apple-trees.

How could she, *she*, go against Housefather's will?

Pain bellowed out ahead, rang so heavily against her that it was a shock of light in her squeezed-shut eyes. And from the sea came its answer.

Tohalla slid forward with reluctance. The seastalker kept bobbing about, trapped, growing feebler and more desperate. It was smaller than the one Housefather had forced the Wolfmen to tell them how to trap, but still Tohalla's head was on a level with the joints of its shoulders. She danced forward and back, retreating from its shrieks and blunderings. Its body – twice as long as hers – gleamed dark and smoky, limned silver-mauve when it jumped up into the light – and pain hooted from it as it darkened amid sobbing whistles when its ballooning foot-plates sank again into the grass. Milky gems of fluid slid down its sides, glowing briefly until they splashed onto the trampled earth. The smell of it was thick, acidic, but sweetened with cherry-blossom, and bees still hummed, disturbed.

Appalled, she saw that dozens of tidenet strands now angled between the boughs. They were glowing in the light of Amethyst Moon.

Tohalla dared not touch them. With a knife she might have cut them, given time. But she hadn't thought to bring one.

A sidewards glance boiled panic up inside her. The other seastalker was bounding out of the waves now and onto the beach where Tohalla once gathered wrack for her Ripeness. She couldn't bear to watch this invasion of the Green.

Helpless, she tried to find something she could do. Anything. And saw that one of the glassy strands had almost cut through a branch. Gingerly, keeping as far away as she could from the seastalker's blind-slashing jaws, she broke off the branch. And another and another, until her palms were bleeding from the roughness of the bark.

The strands slithered over the seastalker's shell, not cutting now there was no tension to their sharpness. Deadly ropes, they lay shining in the grass, and wherever the moon touched them they shimmered with milky blood.

The seastalker jumped again, one footplate tangled in a coiling strand. It wailed its distress and rocked from side to side, its knees angling all ways, its head turned towards the sea. Tohalla crept forward, terrified, but she could not back out now. As the second monster jumped high over the wall, she twitched the fallen strand aside. Then she scrambled back into the currant-bushes.

Just in time. From the seaward wall, the great, shiny beast came jumping. The three footplates on one side landed not a hand's breadth from her. She lay prone, hugging the ground, trying to pretend she wasn't there. The hideous shrieking stopped.

Scared, she lifted her head out of the grass just enough to see. Her fear flew away on the breeze as she watched. The two seastalkers, each both taller than even Edrach, whistled and hooted, but gently. *As if they were talking to each other*. Tohalla was entranced.

The new one rubbed the first, and she could hear the soft scales under its jaw scraping its wounded companion. She could not understand what they could be doing, but gradually a new smell came and the translucent blood stopped flowing, and Tohalla understood.

47

Then, side by side, the seastalkers bumped slowly away over the wall. Tohalla peeped over the coping. She watched them until they reached the sea. Their bodies were dark against the path of Gold Moon, and they seemed to rise higher on the sparkling waves.

CHAPTER FIVE

Deaf Green

The clack of the loom was jaunty in the bright afternoon. Cropfields were greening, silver-sprayed where the warm breeze combed them. Most of the adults were out making hay, and beyond the distant hills, gold-crested with the glittering spikes of the Edge, blue smoke spiralled where the others were preparing the Intake. Mevagrin had stayed behind, but she was snoring in the rocker by the banked-up stove. Even Worut was far away under Housemother's eye. Only Tohalla was left to look after the youngest children.

Enjoying her freedom, Tohalla had wheeled her loom out onto the grass north of the House. Her hands had healed completely in the last heart-squeezing days while she feared discovery, but it was the Wolfmen whom Housefather accused. Now the Axe too dragged a heavy log from leg shackles, and his name seemed far from right.

Tohalla breathed in the sweet, warm air, glad that the lurking ache in her lungs and throat had gone, miraculously. Even Housemother had to agree, reluctantly, that she was well again.

Under the awning, Tohalla moved hands and feet rhythmically, glad to be alive on such a day. Around her, fascinated by her weaving, little children circled happily.

She smiled and started to hum the tune of a clapping dance. It fitted neatly with the slap of the heddle and the shuttle's rush.

Asdra bullied the little ones into line. 'You do what I say!' he yelled shrilly. 'I'm going to be Housefather one day.'

Tohalla had to keep looking up from the loom to watch him. He was six now, with a cheeky grin and one front tooth missing. Housemother thought he had pulled it out to make way for the new one to grow in, but Tohalla knew different. That tooth had been knocked loose in a fight, and Tohalla had pulled it off the string of flesh it dangled from. He'd winked conspiratorially, and Tohalla had promised not to tell. But he hadn't listened to her warnings and his age-mates grew bruises and wouldn't tell why.

Keeping up the weaving-rhythm, she still glanced at the little ones. Asdra soon had the other children where he wanted them. He was taller than any of them except for Caramon, and he hit out if he couldn't get what he wanted. When no-one was watching, of course.

Caramon was seven, and should have been out gleaning with her age-mates in the fields, but she was simple. Asdra was exasperated when she didn't understand what he wanted. Looking to make sure Tohalla's eyes were on her work, he pushed Caramon roughly, unafraid even though she was half-a-head taller than him.

Caramon cried out wordlessly and Tohalla spun round on her stool. The girl was rubbing a red mark on her dark, skinny arm but Asdra had carefully jumped away and was blithely scratching under his blond curls. Caramon didn't even look up from under her downswept lashes when Tohalla said loudly, 'You leave her alone, Asdra!'

All he did, of course, was look hurt. 'I didn't do anything!' he shouted. Housefather would have believed him. Asdra was the boy he'd wanted Tohalla to be. But what could she do?

Tohalla started the song again, swinging her voice with the motions of her hands and feet:

Firemoon to burn the Red,
Sparks to make her die,
Ploughing moon to make Green's bed,
Then watch the Green grow high.

Asdra jumped forward from one end of the line and, still singing with the rest, stopped clapping long enough to scratch the earth all the way to the other end of the line. Loud above the other voices, he yelled off-key:

Asdra ploughs his furrow straight,
Asdra sets the harrow,
Asdra sows his barley straight,
Asdra reaps full barrow.

One after the other, all the children followed his movements – except Caramon. She slipped away to hide behind the cloth-bolt and Tohalla winked at her and smiled. But as soon as Asdra checked that the line had formed straight behind him, he noticed she was missing.

The second child started her verse, but Asdra shouted, 'Shut up!' so fiercely that the girl stopped.

Asdra whipped his head around and it was all Tohalla could do not to laugh. She bent closer to the snapping heddle, her shoulders shaking.

'Where is she?' he shouted, squatting down to look under the swinging tassles on the weights that held the warp-threads.

'Leave her!' Tohalla said sharply, but Asdra had already pulled Caramon from her hiding-place. He thrust her into line and said, 'She *wants* to join in.'

And before Tohalla could say anything else, he'd started the tune again. Caelwyn the toddler had to hurry to get her furrow ploughed before the end of her verse, and Caramon was trying to clap in time, so Tohalla left her.

At the end of the song, Tohalla stood up to wind the bolt so the cloth was held taut. Two steps took her to the bolt-handle – and she stopped dead. The Axe was there.

Tall, outlined against the bright gold of the hayfields, he seemed as aloof as ever. In one hand was the leather water-bucket, in the other he carried his shackle.

Before she could ask him what he was doing at the House when he should have been out working, he hefted the bucket and said, 'Take in drink?'

Not knowing what else to do, she dipped out a mugful and drank it. Clear and refreshing, its coolness arrowed down inside her and she gasped her thanks. She hadn't known how thirsty she was.

Ain the Axe leaned forward to take the dipper. His unbound hair covered his face and tickled Tohalla's ear. Under the scent of hay and spineder and fresh sweat, there was a strange musky odour, like the Red beyond the Edge. His hand touched hers on the dipper's handle and he whispered, 'The night the seastalker freed was, your footprints clear in the dew showed.'

Tohalla dropped the dipper as if it burned her. The Axe shook his hair back and smiled distantly at the little ones around them.

Most of the children hung back, but Asdra shoved his way through and stood facing the Wolfman, to show that he wasn't afraid. Strangely, Caramon came too, drifting silently to stand head down beside him. *No*, realized Tohalla. *Not beside Asdra, but in front of Ain.*

Asdra held out his hand imperiously, but the Axe seemed not to

51

notice. He dipped the wooden mug and held it out to the silent girl. Her eyes looked shining up into his, then down again in her ordinary shyness, but she took it and drank. Asdra moved suddenly, as if to snatch the mug, but the Axe moved fractionally too, and Asdra's gesture died in embarrassment.

None of the other children came near the son of the Red. Even dressed in plain homespun, the Axe looked wild and strange. His long hair flickered in the sunlight, and Tohalla suddenly longed to set her own hair free from its childish stubby braids. But she didn't. She wondered again if he would tell Housefather how she'd broken his tidenet trap, and why he wasn't out at work with the others.

'A spineder today lame is so I it back to the barn brought. Sing again that song?'

His voice hovered on the borders between question and statement. Under the pale eyebrows, his eyes looked pale too: a clear grey that was surprising in the sun-brown of his face. He was so young that his blond beard scarcely hid his jaw.

Tohalla remembered she was staring, and said abruptly, 'All right.'

Tohalla sat down and threw the shuttle between the two ranks of warp-threads, slapped down the comb and treadled so that the weft was caught and the way open to throw the shuttle back. In moments the rhythm was there again, hanging in the air, waiting like Ain Battle-Axe and the children for her song to start up again. Tohalla swallowed and sang.

With only seconds to spare from her weaving at any time, Tohalla was slow to realize that Caramon was clapping almost in time. She was doing everything almost in time – and in the right order.

Then Mevagrin hobbled out and yelled. Tohalla lost her rhythm; when she looked up again the Axe was carrying more water to fill the trough in the spineders' barn. And, strangely, Caramon the simpleton was closer than she'd ever been to following the dance.

Late that evening, Amethyst Moon and Gold Moon were thin crescents lying lazily over the Red hills. In the sultry air, their glitter on the growing spikes of the Edge was misted, and the sweet, clean smell of the hay rose up around the House.

Tohalla sat with her back to the garden wall and watched the first stars glimmering over the glassy sea. It didn't seem to be getting any cooler. From the front of the House she could hear giggling chatter where groups of young people sat out in the yard, and from the orchard there were shrieks of laughter as couples pelted each other with the little hard apples of the first-summer drop. Larnis should have been with them, but she and Granamyr had had a row. Now Larnis was stamping about in the House, and Tohalla was keeping out of her way.

Footsteps swished in the long grass, and she looked up to see the Axe and Edrach close to her. Tohalla was surprised. Hardly anyone ever sought her out, only Housemother to tell her off, or Trinamine. But Trinamine had chosen to go on Outwatch again, and here were the two Wolfmen wanting to talk with her.

Smiling, she said, 'Isn't it beautiful?'

They put down their logs and sat on them. Edrach nodded comfortably. 'Rosaria a beautiful world is. From up there it shines, like one of your raspberries ripening in the dawn.'

Surprise pulled in Tohalla's breath. 'Have you been up there? Out where Good Captain came?'

Edrach puffed down his nose for a sound of laughter, and Ain said, 'No. It so in the Book says.'

Tohalla said nothing. There was a hollow feeling inside her that told her of wrongness. These outlanders were not supposed to know anything about the Book. It was something special for the Greens, not for murdering sons of the Red who lay with the wolves. She felt guilty just knowing they'd found out about it.

The Axe twitched, as if to get up, but Edrach made a gentle sound deep in his throat, and the young man sat still again. There was another silence then, as if there was something they weren't saying either. Tohalla wondered if she ought to go in, but didn't want to be rude. Yet the difficulties that lay in talking to people she hardly knew haltered her tongue. She knew everyone in her world – except the Axe and Edrach.

She sat very still, gazing at the darkening sea where silvery tidenet strands made pictures if you looked hard enough. It was still silent, except for the shrill whistling of summer flyers along the shore, but the silence had somehow become comfortable again.

The Axe said, 'That girl in the dance. She clever is.'

Tohalla knew better. She smiled sympathetically and said, 'She's not. I've known her all her life and ...'

The Axe said, 'No!' It annoyed Tohalla that he thought he was right and she was wrong just because he was male, like Housefather, like Asdra. If he said it, then it must be true, was that it?

There was that tickle in her mind again, like the sifting of Red-mites in their dust. Edrach said gently in his rough voice, 'Not that. The little girl deaf is. You all in words think. She in pictures. So she can't think your thoughts until she how knows. Do you her well want?'

'I don't know what you mean. Look, she's ...'

53

The Axe interrupted her. 'Confirm or not confirm. Her well, or her not well is to be?'

Tohalla sighed through her nose. 'Of course I want her well. It's just that she can't be, not ever. She's Red– ....' She stopped.

'Red-tainted.' The Axe sounded hateful. Full of hate. She had forgotten that he was a son of the Red. Like the Household forgot she was a woman.

Quickly she apologised but Edrach made a sign with his hand, then added, 'Not important is. Rosaria patient teaching is. Now to –'

'What's Rosaria?'

The Axe passed his hand quickly in front of her eyes, as if to check that she could see. Then he pointed to the looming shapes of the Redwood beyond the curving arms of the bay. He grabbed her hand and shook soil into it. 'Rosaria. Understood?'

'Oh, you mean this world! We call it Saria.' She pronounced it Sarya.

Ain said again, 'Ro-zar-i-a. Name in the star-charts is. On Erth – if Erth still is – they it Ro-zar-i-a call.'

Again Edrach made the sign that said, It doesn't matter. 'We her one night to a place will take where she can hear. Then she to be better is. No hurt to her will be. Before morning, she back in the Green is. You too will come.'

The Axe said fiercely, 'No trust for us in her is. She will come – or we the girl without her might take.'

Edrach shook his head, and his long, grey hair bounced around his shoulders. It smelt of hay. 'No. Tohalla will come; cause? She will want to see.'

But it was all of six days before the Axe whispered, 'Tonight.'

Caramon lay wide-awake beside her sleeping age-mates when Tohalla came for her. Tohalla laid her fingers to her lips and beckoned; Caramon crept out of bed. Tohalla remembered which were the squeaky floorboards they had to avoid from when she was a child full of promise with her age-mates, and signed to the uncomprehending figure in the skimpy summer nightdress. When Tohalla pointed to her own bare feet, Caramon picked up her boots and hung them from their strings around her neck. She didn't ask any questions: how could she? But after two loud steps Tohalla swung the deaf girl onto her hip and carried her.

Tohalla's nervousness didn't seem to affect the child outside the House. Instead, once they'd climbed out of the window, and slipped their boots on, Caramon seemed to be pulling Tohalla along as soon as she'd seen that they were sneaking down to the shore. Her skinny fingers were warm in Tohalla's. And she didn't flinch, though Tohalla did, when there floated on the wind the long, hooting shriek of a wolf that had killed.

Tohalla didn't really expect the Wolfmen to be there. It was probably some sort of joke that they played in the Red, like the discus on the Edge, and she'd let herself be caught in it. They were probably somewhere she couldn't see, watching her, laughing. But that wasn't the worst. She kept following Caramon's trot, looking behind her. All she was really worried about was Housefather finding her out. The only good thing was that Caramon wouldn't be able to tell tales on her.

Off the sand-blown path between the straggling grasses, Tohalla walked more and more slowly towards the one low cliff with its jumble of rocks in the sea. The waves were clashing shingle on the boulders, pulled fiercely by the rising wind. Tohalla wondered if they were in for a storm, and hoped they wouldn't get wet on this drake's egg hunt. She didn't understand why the Wolfmen had chosen this of all places to meet. Skinners whistled overhead, racing on the wings of the wind, and Tohalla knew that they trailed thunderclouds far behind them, still below the horizon but coming surely to attack the lonely outpost of Green.

A strange thought came to Tohalla: *Is Beran right? Will Housefather really burn up all the Red so we can have it for the Green?*

The fallen stones became thicker, higher. She shivered and pulled Caramon up to hold her for comfort. Whose comfort Tohalla didn't know. Peering over the nearest boulder, Tohalla saw nothing to show the Wolfmen had ever been here. She held Caramon's hand more tightly, and the girl's boot-toes stuck into her ribs as Tohalla stretched up on tip-toe to see more clearly. The dim shadows cast by the crescent of Amethyst Moon tricked her eyes, and she squinted.

Caramon's other hand touched her shoulder and Tohalla put up her free hand to cover it reassuringly. Her breath struggled on a gasp: the hand was large and calloused. Housefather!

She jerked her hand away and stumbled backwards. But the Axe's hair danced over his smile, and Tohalla said crossly, 'So you can scare people by creeping up on them. Big surprise! Now what?'

'Now we the little girl here to the Dancing Forest take.'

Tohalla smiled her disbelief. Not understanding, Caramon smiled too, sitting astride Tohalla's rounded hip. Edrach said, 'For her, understanding in the Red is. No harm to her, or to you.' Even against the pounding of the waves, Tohalla heard how he freighted his words with sincerity – and she mistrusted him. He used sincerity like a tool to get what he wanted. The Red-mites crawled inside her head again, and Saria seemed a large, hostile world that threatened her security.

She said loudly, 'There's no such place. A body knows every span of this place, and the only trees here don't dance.'

The Axe bridled. 'Say it loud, then it's so? From Housefather well you learn.'

'That's not true!' But Tohalla stopped, because it was.

Edrach reached gently towards her. Tohalla stepped back, not trusting him, but he looked into her green eyes with his one grey eye, and while she fought against the embarrassment of the whole for the flawed, he laid his hand on her arm where Caramon sat looking from one to the other. 'We can be there and back before dawn comes. We will have helped her, or not helped her. But we will have tried.'

No argument stood against that, but still Tohalla said, 'You won't get past the Outwatchers.'

Edrach smiled, but the Axe laughed out loud. Tense, Tohalla shushed him, feeling the worry tighten in her stomach.

The Axe said, 'Shout! The old man you can't hear. Listen to the wind!'

It was true. The Red Woman was coming closer, weeping angrily somewhere over the sea. As yet only small clouds ran across the sky, flaring at the edges where the moons' light touched them. In the deep bowl of night, distant stars burned fiercely. Something of Edrach's haste caught Tohalla in its knots, and she followed them quickly, hoping they'd get there and back before the rain soaked their clothes. Wet clothes might give them away.

Edrach went first. Tohalla stepped close behind him, wondering if he could see where he was going in the blue midnight gloom. She stumbled, and from behind the Axe took her arm gently to steady her. His hand felt warm even though the spray washed over them. Then the surf began to drag at her feet.

She stopped suddenly, but the Axe said, 'All right is. Edrach knows. Soon the dry part comes. Let me the little girl take. Is?'

Caramon *was* heavy. Tohalla hesitated, but Caramon slipped easily into the Axe's arms when he stood close.

Heavier clouds covered half the sky now, and it grew darker, but Tohalla's eyes grew more accustomed to the dim slither of starlight on wet rocks, and without Caramon squirming round her neck, her footing was easier too. Up, down, across, like a dance with the rocks, she found it hard enough even so to climb where Edrach climbed. She admired how the old Wolfman managed with his limp among the boulders, even with –

'You're not carrying your shackles!' In her own ears Tohalla sounded small and scared.

Edrach turned back. 'Tomorrow we'll wear them.' In his face she thought she could read amazement that she wanted chains on someone who'd helped her. Quickly she looked down. But in her mind she found something like the thought that she'd be wearing hers again then too. Some part of her that wasn't her seemed to think it was funny.

It was when footsteps started to follow their footsteps that she realized she was in some kind of a hollow place. It gathered the crash of the combers until her head was so full of the sound that she couldn't hear herself speak when she asked where they were. But the way twisted again and again until the sea was only a hiss and the darkness so stifling that she had to say something just to prove to herself she was still alive.

'Not perfect the Green is,' the Axe answered. 'Rosaria cracked is. All around this Green.' She felt his breath on her cheek as if he were still talking. Saying, 'Around all this Green.' *Did that mean there were others?*

But then his voice came louder, 'See above now – stars. One day you will look up, and one of the stars me will be.'

And tilting back her head while his words seemed to sing in the darkness of herself that was part of the darkness around her, Tohalla saw a twinkling. 'How – ?'

Edrach, a little way ahead, called low, 'Here stay.'

When his footsteps were gone, Tohalla felt the Axe squat down beside her, then Caramon's little fingers shivered over her leg. Tohalla knelt down and cuddled the girl whose fast breathing showed her fear. Caramon slid her arms around Tohalla's neck, and gradually her heartbeat stopped its syncopation and patterned itself on Tohalla's slightly calmer one.

Tohalla tried to rub some heat into the skinny body. Her fingers met the Axe's on Caramon's shoulder. Some of his warmth crept into her.

Gold Moon was high enough now that some faint hint of its light covered the vine-strung walls of the crack. Realizing suddenly that the vines were not any kind she knew, Tohalla drew back, shrinking into herself so that the Red wouldn't touch her. Sheltered from the wind, the Axe laughed gently.

The cold yellow gleam lit Edrach's familiar homespun, but Tohalla saw that the man inside them wasn't doing anything a man of the

57

Green would do. He was leaning spreadeagled on one of the curving stones that she thought must once have been part of the roof of the crack. His hands were stiff, forcing contact with the rock but not holding it. Then, slowly, slowly, he was shuffling backwards with tiny steps. And he wasn't dragging the massive stone. It was following him.

She cried out and Caramon caught her fear, making ragged sounds unconscious of what she was doing. Edrach's whole body jerked, and Tohalla saw his fingers straighten even further. The Axe hushed her, and Edrach twisted one foot sideways to keep it from being crushed as the vast stone teetered. She held her breath, pressing Caramon's head more tightly into the crook of her shoulder, and the Axe sighed his relief as Edrach began his shuffling again.

Against her will, Tohalla whispered, 'Ain?' She would have felt silly calling him the Axe to his face even though Edrach did. 'What's he doing?'

The young man shrugged. 'For you, seeing is. Then you must know.'

Tohalla stiffened with anger. But when she stopped seething, she knew the Axe was right. All the same, she wished he would talk gently to her, not coldly or with such contempt.

Her arms round Caramon, Tohalla watched the old Wolfman moving the stone without pulling it.

When it was where he wanted it, Edrach sagged against the weight of the boulder, and it seemed orange where his shadow didn't fall. When he stood back, one after the other they edged round it and into a tunnel, or rather, a series of arches where gigantic stones leant precariously against one another. Sometimes even Caramon had to crawl as the shadows deepened beyond the moonlight's touch.

The wind was stronger when at last Edrach summoned them out into the open. All around them the night was full of noises: tinklings, keenings, faint rumblings that were just below the threshhold of sound. Tohalla felt them grating in the tiny bones of her inner ear. And behind them, spiked with light, rose the Edge.

She was in the Red.

No wonder the Axe had laughed when she said, 'You won't get past the Outwatchers.' The striding-post wasn't even in sight. She and Caramon were beyond all help, alone with the Sons of the Red.

CHAPTER SIX

The Dancing Forest

The night was alive. It was hostile. On every side was the Red, shrill-voiced and alien in the rising wind, and Tohalla was afraid. She should never have come with the Sons of the Red. For all she knew, they were planning to feed Caramon to the wolves – and as to what they meant to do with her ...

Edrach and the Axe ran easily, changing pace but never slackening to a walk. At first the footing was over ground-cover plants that crunched underfoot, but soon the Wolfmen were loping among strange, glistening growths which loomed taller the further they went from the Edge. They cut off what little light there was. Tohalla blundered along, wondering how the Wolfmen managed to see where they were going.

Louder and louder keened the gale as the sharp-edged crystals cut it. The sound unnerved her, yet Edrach and the Axe were happy, grinning and passing Caramon from one to the other on the run. Above, the clouds raced too and the darkness was all but complete.

Tohalla's breath came short, and not just from exertion. She was too scared to stop, and when a wolf hooted far off, she jerked into a faster run so that she wouldn't be left behind. Ahead of her, Edrach and the Axe were dodging now between towering clusters of crystals that whistled and glimmered in the roaring wind.

The very wind seemed unreal, charged with odours that never existed in the safe familiarity of the Green. Tohalla felt she had been running forever and had lost all sense of direction. Panting, she forced her trembling limbs to greater efforts. Whatever happened, she must not let Caramon out of her sight.

Besides, she didn't want to admit the Wolfmen could do something she, a Green, could not.

At last she had to gasp, 'Stop! Oh, wait! I can't keep up!' but the harsh wind stole her words. The stitch in her side burned, and she was furious, yet just when she was on the point of collapse, Edrach dropped back and shouted to her above the howling blasts of air, 'Not long now is. See how good marshstar you has run made?'

And, with one arm around her, he guided her through the huge clumps of glistening crystal. Abruptly they rounded the end of a low escarpment, and Edrach stopped.

The Axe was at the bottom of a natural hollow, some fifty yards below them. He was holding Caramon's hand, and she was yawning, looking not at all afraid, only tired. She saw Tohalla standing between sparse pillars of rock, and waved.

Tohalla struggled downhill against fierce gusts of cold air. The wind was louder here, as if the scarp bounced it back, and the storm was not far off. Amethyst Moon had set, and Gold Moon was only a fitful gleam as the last stars were curtained by the clouds. The fickle light showed nothing like a tree, let alone a forest; only irregular spires of dully-gleaming rock in a barren, windswept bowl.

Breathless, Tohalla rested her hands on her knees. When Edrach's uneven lope brought him level with her, she straightened and glared at him.

'What are we doing here? I don't see your precious dancing forest. There's just a lot of rocks –'

'This the dancing forest is. When the storm comes, you will see. Now we rest.'

'With this racket? I can hardly hear myself think, let alone rest.'

Calmly he sat down, his face just a pale blur under the lee of a rock pinnacle. Seething with rage, she squatted before him, saying, 'Let's go back. You've had your fun. Or at least show me the way back so I can get Caramon under cover before the storm starts.'

'You mean the rainstorm, or the Housefather storm?' The Axe. Disdainful as ever as he made his way towards them. Tohalla's fury rose higher. She stood up to stare him in the eyes. He was only a little taller than she.

'How can I make you understand? Housefather has to be stern, to keep so many people safe and working for the good of the Green. What do you know about him anyway? About anything? You're an Outsider.'

'Then run!' he shouted. 'The girl take so she never knows. In Housefather's chains stay!'

Edrach stroked a hand along each of their arms, stilling their voices but not their rage. Caramon looked distressed. She might not understand their words but she understood anger.

Then the rain struck. It lashed them with a force that stung, that beat at them from every direction as the wind caromed off the slick rocks all around the basin.

And the hairs at the back of Tohalla's neck rose because where the rain touched, the rocks moved.

Ribs of crystal creaked outward from the rocky spires. They swept upwards like outreaching arms, slow and majestic, and the rain pooled where they joined the trunk. The crystal, washed clean, shone with some strange inner light, and finger-like projections sieved a series of whistles from the wind as it backed.

Lightning crashed on the crest of the scarp so loud that it frightened Tohalla. And then she saw why this place was called the Dancing Forest.

Tohalla reached to shelter Caramon from her fear but the girl ran out of her grasp. For the lightning had struck an echo in the crystal trees. Light like fire ran up and down the tinkling branches, and everything vibrated to the thunder. Wild music belled from the glassy boughs. Leaves of turquoise and sapphire jangled at the edge of sound, flashing notes as pure as Tohalla's zither. And, under everything, the blue-sparkling trunks rang octaves below the threshold of hearing so that the music was in her body.

She didn't know when she was jerked to her feet by the savage harmony; only that she was impelled to move, as Caramon was, and Edrach and – the Axe. And that Caramon's face was transfigured.

Leaping, whirling, Caramon became the nature of grace, thrilling to the living song of the trees, a song so deep that even she could hear. Edrach forgot his limp and moved stately yet with a profound joy that Tohalla felt when his touch led her into the dance.

Now the trees were singing to their own motion, so that each movement's harmonies shattered a melody and transformed it to another, with the deep chant of the tree-trunks guiding all.

Edrach spun Tohalla towards Ain. He looked now what the Wolfwoman had called him at the Edge: an Axe, sharp and young, his dance fluid yet savage, his body glistening in the rain. He belonged here. And as he wove his steps into hers beneath the glowing trees, he lent her his belonging.

Too soon the Red Woman called home her summer storm and her lightning-lances speared at other prey. And the trees darkened and the music stilled until there was only a knot of tired people in a grove of starlit trees. The sky wheeled slowly to show a rim of grey that put out

61

the last sparks of treelight. And the trees closed over the precious moisture caught in their joints, hoarding it against the summer's heat. They shrank, dulled; the music died.

But hearing had reached Caramon from the swelling throb of music. She had been taken out of her silent isolation into a joining with the majesty of the singing sapphire trees – and with humankind.

Her hand in Tohalla's, Caramon walked proudly homewards through the rain-swept Red, and joy was in her face.

CHAPTER SEVEN

The Wolftrap in the Book

In the lamplit evening of that special day for the Green, Housefather pushed back his chair after the meal and said heartily, 'Go on then, Tohalla. Go and get it. You still remember where it is, don't you?'

Tohalla froze.

Around the long trestle tables, conversation stilled. Heads turned to watch her – and Housefather. In the sudden silence everyone heard Coril shout an explanation to Mevagrin and break off in embarrassment.

Mevagrin wasn't embarrassed. Loudly, she said, 'Let Tohalla get her hands on The Book again? Whatever for? A body thought Housefather didn't like her any more. Nasty, sly, barren thing she is, thick as thieves with them two wastrel sons of the Red. She don't belong here!'

Her wrinkled, apple-yellow face puckered belligerently as Coril nudged her. 'All right, all right, a body's going. A body knows when she's not wanted. And from the sound of it, a body knows more than some as is called my betters.'

Mevagrin's boot-heels slurred across the floorboards as she stumped out with a pile of supper dishes balanced in her arms. Just before the kitchen door slammed they heard her yell, 'And don't be all night gossiping, Coril! A body's not washing this lot up on my own.'

The day had started well enough.

When Redsun leaped out of the sea to chase Whitesun through the morning, heat had already lain heavy on the land, drying up the freshness of the morning along with the opal dew. And after the cheerful chatter of the long breakfast table, the people swarmed eagerly outside to disturb the stillness and the song of birds.

Tohalla was deafened by the racket in the yard. With everybody trying to get ready at once and talking at the tops of their voices, it was an assault on her senses that she didn't want. Her head ached with tiredness and her legs were trembling with the strain of the long run last night. She needed quiet to assimilate the wonders of what she had experienced scant hours before. Echoes of the Dancing Forest still swam in her blood and her bones vibrated to the ghosts of colour and the song.

But the suns were climbing into the vaulting blue sky; everyone had their part to play today and she was no exception. Besides, this was a great event in the life of the Green and she didn't want to be left out, even if Housemother kept nagging on about her not being well enough yet to risk her lungs beyond the Edge.

While everyone rushed to complete their ordinary chores Tohalla yawned over her loom; she wanted to finish off the loose ends. More than that, she wanted to hide the bolt of cloth altogether before Housemother saw it, because she had raised some threads and underlooped others, so that a diamond pattern showed faintly on the green twill. She didn't know why she had done it and now she wished she hadn't, but it was too late for that. She had stolen time to make the only pattern in all the Green and guilt was strong in her, though that was the least of her sins against the Green.

Despite the confusion, Edrach and the Axe managed to back the spineders smoothly between the wagon-shafts. Tohalla shocked herself by feeling relief that the Wolfmen's shackles bound them once more to great chunks of cedarwood, but the Axe and Edrach affected not to notice them. Working as a team, the two men soon had the massive beasts inspanned to each of the two wagons. Edrach winked at Tohalla as he swung himself nimbly onto the driver's seat of the lead wagon.

At a word from Housefather two dusty bottles easily waist-height were loaded onto deep straw in the wagon-bed behind Edrach, and covered with more straw and a platform of wood. Then people clattered hoes and ploughs and spades on top of boxes of seed behind that, and Tohalla climbed stiffly aboard the other wagon with the children.

Full of himself, Housefather called, 'Walk on!'

And the people surged forward to put his dream into action. Out of the yard swung the long wagons, and once through the gate of the lea the men and women spread out to walk swiftly beside them. Chulain raised his voice in a happy planting song, and when everyone joined in to swell the chorus, tears rose to Tohalla's eyes.

She couldn't have said why she felt like crying. The universal gaiety was only a part of it. There was the joy beaming from Caramon's face, where before there had been only passivity. There was the sense of being one with all the people of the Green, and that was a two-edged knife. So long had Tohalla been cut off from them by her failure to do something as ordinary as having children – the sneers, the taunts, the threat of betrothal to Worut after Pierse went to the Green – and Housemother's disappointment in her that was nowhere near as strong as Tohalla's own. But she had helped give Caramon the gift she most wanted …

Yet they were going to kill the Red, and the Wolfmen had shown her it deserved to live.

Tohalla dashed a hand over her eyes as if it had been a speck of dust that irritated them. Glancing at her exuberant charges, she saw they were all happy to sing and so she felt free to scramble over the picnic boxes onto the seat beside the Axe. She had so many questions she wanted to ask him …

He looked once at her tight-braided hair that had danced free in the Forest last night, and said, 'I a pattern in your last piece of weaving saw.'

Nervously she said, 'A body saw a pattern …'

He puffed a snort of laughter down his nose. 'Irrelevant is. Call yourself a body but you still Tohalla are. Communication the most important is, not the form. Why are you a pattern making when no other pattern in the Green is?'

Tohalla looked round guiltily, but in all this bright song-filled morning there was no-one listening to them. The others were all stepping out, swinging along joyfully to the lilt of their purposeful tune between the broad acres of the summer fields. They couldn't even hear the whistles of the flying lizards that were black shooting stars high above.

She sighed. 'They say pattern is a waste of time, that natural things are so beautiful they need no adornment, that the Green needs all a body's work to survive.' ·

'But what do you think?'

She looked at him, his brown hands strong on the reins. Of course he knew no better than to ask personal questions. Defiantly she said, 'It takes only a second to raise a few threads here or there, and the material's no weaker for it. And if I do have to marry Worut on

65

Longday, I'll have one small thing of beauty that I made all by myself to cheer me in the night.'

The Axe slapped the reins between the animals' ruffles of grey spines, not at all put out by her statement of individuality. His hair – Housemother had cut it short this morning, like every other farmer's in the Summer – flew in blond streaks as he shook his head angrily. On the wagon up ahead, Tohalla noticed that Edrach's was short too, and their beards were gone. Perhaps they had put off the cutting until that thing with the Dancing Forest? She wondered how long they'd been planning it. And she wondered if their calves, too, were stiff with all the running last night.

'For you of the Green, marrying a long thing is?' asked the Axe, and his voice had the edge of anger in it. Tohalla didn't know why.

Casting her gaze round guiltily, she whispered, 'Not the marrying, but the being married. It's forever.'

'And you this Worut like?' The Axe jerked his head back over his shoulder, to where Worut sagged against the tail-gate between the children. Tohalla noticed that not one of them touched Slack Worut's lolling, bloated body, though they were so crowded that many of the older ones had brothers or sisters on their knees.

'You don't understand!' Tohalla said just loud enough to be heard. She scarcely moved her lips, as if to pretend it wasn't her talking at all. She wouldn't look at the tall man beside her with his smooth, young face. He had to bend closer to hear above the singing of the Greens.

'It's not a question of liking,' she said. 'It's his Bloodline. He's of the Tine strand and I'm of the Chrysobal. He's the last unmarried one and now Pierse is dead and I have no children to give to the Green, I have to marry him because we're the only Bloodlines compatible. It's – it's a body's duty.'

'Wrong is. You a choice have –'

'I don't!' Tohalla practically yelled, 'I –' and stopped, appalled. She'd been on the point of speaking as if her wishes should count for something against the good of the Green.

The nearest singers turned to look at her, but there was no time for the argument to develop because for the last miles the crowd had been climbing steadily and from the wagon in front Housefather signalled a halt. They had reached the Edge.

Along the crest of the ridge it stretched for miles in a glittering arc that reached from one headland to the other. Cruel amber, its dagger-like thorns made it impenetrable to anything bigger than an

66

insect. Within its shelter nestled the smiling fields of the Green, safe from the Red and the sons of the Red. Only the geyrlizards that could swoop down to carry off a spineder or a child could make light of its barrier. And the first Housefather who had planted it had shown his People how to deal with them.

Yet it had one weakness. Where the stream came tumbling down from the foothills of the mountains, the Edge would not grow. From the high water line on its banks, the wicked branches leaned across until they joined as solid as ever, yet the first Housefather had warned of a danger: that the evil sons of the Red might swim beneath the net of branches, hidden in the fast current, and so steal and murder and carry off the children of the Green.

And that was why he had caused two huge trees that he called oak to be planted alongside the thorns of the Edge on the north bank of the stream. And through something that he called 'genetic engineering' he made the oaks grow from their two separate seeds, one on the Red side of the Edge and one safe in the Green, so that, on the day they out-topped the tallest spines of the Edge, they twisted together as swift as a flying needle until they became one tree, and the tree grew wider and its bark grew thicker and the first Housefather said that something in the soil had made it grow strange and dangerously fast.

But it was too hard to cut with saws and axes and fire wouldn't burn it, so he made the acid and poured it in high up, making a bigger hole each day, and in time and in time the acid-pool had eaten away all the wood in a big circular shape, with a twisting passage going lower down inside. And that was the striding-post.

Around the two wagons the line of people bunched up, as if they had been a strand of tideswool that had been stretched and then let go. From all their throats the song rose in a crescendo and the song was a glorious thing.

Then the people fell reverently silent and Housefather filled that silence with a speech that stopped them getting on. At least he had the good sense to cut it short when they began shuffling about and mumbling to one another.

'All right, now, stand back there!' boomed Housefather. 'Two of you get those jars out, will you? *Two*, I said!' as half a dozen men and women sprang forward.

'It says in the –' Housefather glanced at the two Wolfmen who were outspanning the spineders, and cleared his throat. 'We must keep well clear of the fumes, especially the children and those with weak lungs.'

With long-handled ladles Hanumarn and Threlleck sent the liquid from the huge bottles spinning in dazzling rainbows over the clear gold thicket of the Edge. Which hissed and smoked.

Tohalla and the Wolfmen gasped with the rest, but Housefather's harsh features relaxed from concern to satisfaction. The acid still worked.

Gradually the farmers grew bored with watching the Edge writhe and blacken. Whitesun was high now and Redsun had almost reached its zenith so they sat well away under the shade of a rowan spinney, drinking cold leaf-tea and eating the food Mevagrin had packed.

The double shadows had merged and barely separated when Housefather stood up and shouted for silence. His deep voice reached even the furthest of them, his words hard to catch in their bass rumble.

'First fruits'll need cutting tomorrow. So we've today to plough and harrow and sow the Red to grass. This is the first Intake in three generations. So don't stop to chew the oats!'

With a cheer they surged forward. Yet they wavered where the wicked beauty of the Edge was breached.

'Don't fret!' shouted Housefather. 'D'ye not think I've been smart enough to make it safe? I had Kerstaf put the neutralizer on while you were all stuffing your faces. Come on!'

Tohalla stepped with the others over the black, greasy slick, the Axe and Edrach leading the spineders at her side. Edrach had thought to put down a bed of straw for the animals to walk over but it took all the Wolfmen's strength to urge them across. In the end it was the Axe who laid one hand on each of the heavy necks, just in front of the clashing, dangling spines. Then, as he crooned wordless encouragement to them, the spineders stepped onto the Red.

But it was Red no longer. For weeks Housefather had had farmers firing the crystalline growth inside the new Edge he'd had laid. Their virgin land rose in a great curving sweep almost to the edge of the forest where Tohalla had first seen the Wolfwoman's pack. And every step of it was a ruined, charred devastation.

Housefather wouldn't trust the Wolfmen to plough a straight furrow. In fact he wouldn't trust them at all so close to the wild with the soft breeze stroking music from the lips of the Redwood.

'Got those chains, Kerstaf? Well, don't just stand there, man! Put 'em on! We haven't got all day.'

Kerstaf fastened a heavier shackle to the Wolfmen's free leg, and the end of it was a stake driven deep into the ground. Tohalla's heart thudded dully with each blow of Kerstaf's mallet. One glance at the Axe's face was enough; naked pride kept his features stiff in a neutral expression, but his grey eyes roved to the wilderness beyond the new-born Edge and he was pale under his tan. She could only guess at the depths of humiliation experienced by the young man whose wild dance last night had invited her to join his free spirit.

Edrach winked at her. Face working, she had to turn away.

Housemother bustled over to her, skirts kilted up around her plump waist. Housemother never did like wearing trousers. She said from the back they made her look like two marrows hung up for the winter.

'I knew we should never have let you get this close to the Red, Tohalla, not Red-bitten like you were at Longnight. Don't you do any digging now, nor running after the little ones. Here – ' she laid her hand briskly on Tohalla's forehead which was burning with shame.

Tohalla pulled away, saying, 'A body's all right! Leave me alone. Please.'

Housemother ignored her. 'Hmm, not too bad, but you're as red as beyond already and you haven't done a lick of work! You sit in the shade under the striding-post and take the water round later when everyone's ready for a drink. Look at me when I'm talking to you!'

'Yes, Housemother.'

When Tohalla sank miserably down in the shade of the ironwood tree that nothing had killed, not even the ancient acid, the Axe was staring at her.

Above her, Adiockle and Sibulkrin stood guard behind the lattice in the striding-post. Trinamine prowled along where the new Edge angled away from the old, stepping lightly over the fallen crystal tines. All three of them spoke to her, but Tohalla didn't answer. She didn't even hear them above the thoughts spinning in her head.

Only when Caramon crept over to kiss her did Tohalla notice how swiftly the afternoon was passing. The little girl's face was no longer blank; the thin features were alive with interest and affection. Tohalla hugged her for a long moment then shook herself free of her lethargy.

Scooping a bucket of water from the tumbling stream, Tohalla went first to the Wolfmen. Caramon walked with her, even copying the rapid rhythm of her steps. At every stride, soot puffed up from the scorched earth that last night's rain had scarcely softened. Soon they were almost as filthy as the diggers and ploughmen that they passed.

Tohalla stopped in front of Edrach. She scarcely dared face the Axe. Both were digging in the circle their tethers permitted. She swallowed.

'I – I'm sorry,' she said. 'It hurts me to see them do this to you, and know how bad you must feel. I – I know just saying it's not enough, but I can't do anything. I can't believe the strength it must take you just to

69

keep digging as though nothing was wrong ...'

Impatient at all this talk, Caramon grabbed the dipper and held out a drink to the Axe. He grinned at her and emptied it in two swallows. A drip ran down his chin, drawing a clean, tanned line through the layers of sweat and soot. Then he widened his smile to include Tohalla.

'All right is. All systems go. A crewman anything can take, if not too long is. And you more a prisoner are than us with your Worut. Not long now before we Marchidas's trail take.'

He smiled again and leant over to dip water for Edrach. Tohalla stared at the Axe in disbelief. *How can they go? And where? What for?* Edrach just drank.

The Axe smiled at her again. 'Close your mouth! Wide enough is to catch a geyrlizard!' As Edrach splashed the dipper back into the pail, the Axe ran one forefinger up the inside of Tohalla's arm. In the hot afternoon, she shivered.

Then Caramon, dancing with impatience, dragged her away, and there was only a faint streak among the sooty marks on her arm to show that the Axe had touched Tohalla in friendship and in trust.

Indigo shades of evening reached out in long shadows as the suns sank behind the tops of the Redwood. Housefather called his people together with a voice grown hoarse from an afternoon of shouting.

'We've done it! Dug and ploughed, harrowed and sown, even dunged it! Every one of us, working together. We'll pasture the beasts here in Autumn, and plough grass under for green manure come the spring. And we've done it together for the food we'll have next winter, for the good of the Green in years to come! I'm proud of you! Now let's see what Mevagrin's cooked up for us at the House!'

Then, tired but content, everyone walked down through the evening-misted fields, past the striding-post that was no longer on the Edge. A gentle song hummed from them all, united in the knowledge of work well done. Below them, in the gentle valley by the sea, lights twinkled through the windows of the House, and the arms of the bay cupped a golden reflection of sunset.

When Housemother lit lanterns and hung them on the wagons, not because they were needed but just to complete the picture in the lilac gloaming, Tohalla smiled. At least the Wolfmen would have a memory of beauty to take back with them into the Red. Caramon was snuggled in her arms – even Housemother had commented on how lively the girl seemed today – and Tohalla could feel the warmth of the Axe's body beside her on the wagon seat.

70

Then Housefather called to her from the wagon in front. The Axe crooked his arm invitingly and Tohalla shifted Caramon across, smiling to herself when she touched him, and glad the darkness hid her smile. Her smile vanished as her foot rattled on his chain. But the Axe said, 'No problem is. Go now. All right is.' And he twitched his shackle aside so that she could climb down.

The wagons turned into the lea. When Tohalla ran up beside the wagon Edrach was driving, Housefather jumped down to walk beside her.

Housefather said, 'I've settled it. Today just proved I was right and they were all wrong. Your Wolfmen there have been touched by the Green or they wouldn't have worked so hard for us today. I'll marry you to that young one come Longnight and we'll get ourselves a new bloodline into the bargain.'

Tohalla stopped, shocked. *Are they human now, then?* And she thought of the shackles. In a strangled voice she said, 'So you don't trust the Axe without a chain, but you'll marry me to him?'

Housefather scarcely slackened his swagger. His walking-stick swung ahead, casting a long shadow by the light of the dancing lantern. Certainly he took no heed of her objection. She had to run a few steps to hear Housefather's next words.

'Worut'll never know the difference, Tohalla. I'm not calling him the Axe, though. I think I'll call him Hearnor after my father. That's a nice, suitable name for a farmer.'

And Housefather had lain his heavy arm over her shoulders like he used to when she was little and he still liked her, pulling her against the roughness of his stubbly chin. Unwilling, but caught up in fulfilling other people's expectations, living her life in the light of their dreams, she put her arm around Housefather's thick waist. When they turned into the yard he led her straight into the House and told her to put on her betrothal gown and the moondust. She couldn't even get away to warn the Axe of the noose settling about his neck.

Now the festive dinner was over and Housemother had set dreamwood blazing in the earth on the platform. The candle-light was thick, like jars of luminescent honey, and from the long tables the scents of new bread and joyberries mingled sharp and heavy on the hot night air. Tohalla heard Housefather's words echoing in her head, 'Get the Book.'

Dazed, she moved to obey. There was no escape for them, then. No last-minute reprieve. Unless ... unless Edrach knew of a way. But she must keep her hope hidden from Housefather. *He was always so sure he was right ... And anyway*, Tohalla thought, *maybe it won't be so bad. They can still get out into the Red when they want to, visit the Dancing Forest. It'll be our secret. It'll be fun, having a secret like that. And I suppose I'm lucky to get even a son of the Red, even if I am nearly old enough to be his mother. It could have been Worut ...*

Tohalla concentrated fiercely on each step she took down from the dais, past Worut drivelling at the end of the trestle-tables, up the stairs to the landing. She couldn't look down to the foot of the tables where the Axe sat cheerfully over his mug of honey-squash, yet she was aware of the light gleaming on his tanned face and sun-streaked hair, and of the way his grey eyes smiled when they rested on her.

What did he want out there, anyway? Scratching his living from the death of animals it might kill him to hunt. A prey to all the sicknesses the Red could inflict ... Tohalla shifted the arguments angrily around in her mind, afraid he might not see his life the way she did. And not altogether convinced that he was fully human ...

She crossed the creaking floor to the Housefather's private room, where she'd been born, where she used to play with baby Larnis. And where Housefather had always kept the Book safe in the locked windowseat the first Housefather had built.

The summer night lay heavy on the ripening fields beyond the House. From the yard Chulain's bass dominated the children's faltering song: he was teaching them the Longday Chaunt because the few who were still awake were far too excited to sit and listen to speeches, let alone sleep.

'No, no, no, no!' Chulain said loudly, though he kept his voice just short of shouting. 'Look, we've got three weeks to get it right. Let's try again, shall we?' And, past the ragged line of barefoot children, Tohalla could see Caramon, kneeling in the pool of light by the open door, busy at the little hand-loom the Axe had made her and that Tohalla had threaded, back when she still thought Caramon was stupid. Since then there'd been the Dancing Forest ... Not stupid after all ... even though Housemother still said she was ... Just having a good day ...

'Get the Book, I said!' rumbled Housefather. 'Don't spoil this now, Tohalla.'

And from the way Housefather called, she knew he was thinking of how it had been when she was small, before Pierse, before her poor little dead babies, before she couldn't conceive any other whole ones ... He'd hugged her then, had Housefather, tossed her up to the ceiling, and said, 'There's my clever little girl. D'you want to put this day's entries in for me? I'll tell you what to put.' And just like now, she'd fetched the Book for him.

Running downstairs with the Book, she dropped it on the table in front of Housefather. There were ooh's and aah's from around the hall, and many furtive glances at the Wolfmen, but Housefather made his announcement in front of all of them though it wasn't Longnight. And Tohalla didn't hear a word of it.

Head down, she watched the Axe covertly. And saw him jerk upright, though not at first when Housefather said, 'Since this is not Longnight we'll dispense with the strand-naming. Anyway, we're founding a new strand here, so what do we need all that for? These two young people are handfasted, that's the main thing.

'Come on, young man. Yes, you, the Axe.'

The boy – that was how Tohalla saw him now, nothing but a slim, blond boy in borrowed clothes – stood up warily and stepped hesitantly behind the lines of people on their benches who turned to stare at him.

'That's the way, lad,' Housefather boomed. 'Can't keep on calling you Axe, it's silly. That's right, step up here on the platform.'

Ruddy-faced, balding, tubby, Housefather descended a couple of stairs from the dais and leaned down across Worut's sprawling legs to grasp the young Wolfman's wrist and pull him up beside him. Housefather beamed jovially. 'From now on, lad, we're going to call you Hearnor. That's a proper farmer's name, that is. You and Tohalla, you're betrothed now.'

Housefather looked sideways at the youth whose arm he held, trying to make out whether or not he understood. It was difficult to tell. The Axe kept his face still, in some unreachable expression.

'You're going to be married.' Housefather spoke louder, more slowly, like he did to Worut. 'You and Tohalla. On Longday. To make babies. Understand?'

But that wasn't what made the Axe react.

It was when Housefather prodded his daughter's shoulder and said, 'Go on then, Tohalla! Get on with it!' And she took the thick cylinder out of the scroll, and laid her hands on its metallic tube, and it began, faintly, to glow.

No dancing, no Chaunt to name the strands. It wasn't a real Ripeness at all. Tohalla knew they would say in after years that she was never properly betrothed at all. But the people in the House were too tired to do more than raise a half-hearted toast to their future as she put down

73

the words on the Book.

Not the proper Book, of course. That was so old and worn-out it could only glow feebly, and scarcely slurred a dissonant growl when you asked it a question, but it was still the same Book Good Captain had given the first Housefather hundreds of years before when they blasted off from the war-torn shell of Erth.

No, what she wrote on was the parchment scroll that Housefather's father had started when he finally realized the Book was wearing out. And Housefather directed the words Tohalla should write in her shaking hand, looking over her shoulder and tutting when she didn't make the letters fast enough. But her writing was still better than his.

Then Housemother stood to make a toast in her turn. The swirling dreamsmoke seemed alive with her hopes. 'Let's drink to my girl starting the first new strand since Good Captain brought us to set the Green on –'

'Come on, a body told you!' bellowed Mevagrin, slamming open the kitchendoor. 'A body wants her bed.'

On Longnight of course, at a proper Ripeness, the betrothed could whisper in corners under cover of the dance. But there was no dance for Tohalla on this Intake day, so Housefather said, 'You can take a walk outside, if you like. Tell him how lucky he is we're keeping him. Make him understand. Get along with you now!'

'With the Axe in chains?' Tohalla asked sharply.

'What? Oh – no, of course not. Here, you, Granamyr, fetch a peg to knock the pin out.'

Granamyr moved so slowly that Grensham elbowed him out of the way rather than risk putting Housefather in a temper they'd all suffer from.

Tohalla said, 'It's all right now, is it, for Edrach to be freed as well?'

Housefather swigged at his honey-squash. 'Eh? Edrach? Why not? Him and Hearnor'll be sons of the Green before you know it. Won't want to run off then, will they?'

And Tohalla wondered why Edrach was only Edrach but the Axe had never told anyone else in the Green his given name.

'Satisfied now?' Housefather said when Grensham had hammered out the shackle-pins. 'Right, Hearnor, she's all yours. Off you go.'

It took the Axe some moments to recognize himself as Hearnor but then he held his hand out towards Tohalla. Numbly she climbed down from the platform, took his hand stiffly, and allowed herself to be led out of the Househall.

Away from the staring faces and Larnis's flush of anger, the Axe took Tohalla down to the bay. When he sat on the dunes, she did. From their seat on the salt-grass they could hear the wild melody the tidenets harped from the wind. But Tohalla's thoughts chased each other in ugly circles. *This skinny Wolfboy is better than Worut, but he's still a badge of shame ... Does he even understand that his life's been taken from him?*

He moved closer to her, draping one hand gently around her neck and onto the soft skin below her collar-bone. It was the very softness of his touch that got through to her in her confusion. With his other hand the Axe stroked her fingers lightly.

'Oh, Ain!' she burst out. 'They've used me to trap you here forever! They've even taken away your name! They never even asked what you wanted.' It didn't occur to Tohalla that no-one had asked her either. 'A body's sorry ... I'm sorry.'

He chuckled. 'What all this talk of sorrow is? We of the Crew often our lives change to be with the partner we have chosen. You kind are. You others help, and don't betray. You beautiful are, beautiful inside; you wisdom have to know that when you open, for you learning is.'

Me? Beautiful? thought Tohalla wildly.

He shook her gently. 'No problem is. You your new strand will have, a thing of honour that you with pride will wear. A daughter is what you want? To love and guide and show how to be free inside? And if it me is that you want, not Worut, then I you will have. Will you my crewmate be?'

Dumbly she nodded and he felt the movement of it in the velvet starlight. In answer he hugged her. 'Listen, Toh! For us the tidenets sing. All the wild things of Rosaria for us sing. Will you not their song in your heart hear?'

She returned the caress of his fingers, thinking that she knew what he meant. She felt his hands, their dryness, their strength, reluctant to take more than he was willing to give. Laying her cheek in the hollow of his neck so that his heart drummed steadily against her face, Tohalla whispered, 'Will you – will you stay with me?'

The Axe slid a knowing finger down the curve of her jaw. Careful to make his words after the pattern of her language, he said in her ear, 'I will stay with you until my flight is a star in your sky.'

She clung to him in response, and one strong arm held her until she ceased to shake. Tenderly he lifted her long hair where the shimmering moondust was caught in its silken skeins, and inhaled the perfume of her. His bare toes tickled her instep until she laughed and tickled him too.

75

'Tell me, Tohalla of the Loom, what was it that your Pierse did to give you pleasure?'

Embarrassed, she answered, 'I – I'm not sure what you mean.'

He kissed the top of her head and she could feel his face move in a gentle smile. 'I mean, my Tohalla, how did he help you making love to enjoy?'

'I don't know.'

'He just did?' the Axe teased.

'No. He just didn't.'

Unbelieving, the Wolfman waited for her to go on. Tohalla took a deep breath and said, 'The sons of the Green take pleasure in it, I suppose. Not the daughters. For us it's only a means to an end. The way to give children to the Green. It's not a thing to enjoy or – or disenjoy. It just happens, like the weather.'

He shifted slightly so that his elbows were resting on the turf and she was nestled half against him. 'My poor Tohalla! Then we slowly will go, and you will tell me what you like and don't like. And if you want to stop, we with no cross word will. For if you no pleasure in me find, how can I find pleasure in you?'

As the Amethyst Moon drew their shadows together, she knew she ought to tell him that in the Green you had to wait 'til you were properly married. But he had given up his life for her. How could she deny him? Besides, though he was skinny and years younger than her, it was very good.

CHAPTER EIGHT

The Cage Door Opens

'You're what?'

Tohalla's anguished shriek rang through the hot dry afternoon.

Even up here on the headland you could hear the clatter of the cutter-bar and the distant shouts of the women urging on the spineders at the reaping. Whitesun was low in the sky; at this time of year it rose and set early. Soon it would be time for dinner, and the dawdling evening of song and good cheer.

Faint squeals of laughter came up from the beach where Chulain and the children were gathering ripe tideswool. From beyond the harsh dazzle of the Edge, strange whistles and popping sounds drifted lazily down the land-wind with its freight of musky scents.

But amid all the warm-dreamed activity only Tohalla and the sons of the Red were up in the scrubby trees on the headland, gathering joyberries from the brambles.

For tomorrow was Longday and her wedding to the Axe.

Far below her perch, among the jumbled rocks, Chulain looked up at her sudden cry, and waved at her. Obviously he thought it was just a shout of merriment because he bent back to his game-of-work with the children in the surf. But for Tohalla it was no merriment. It was almost-death.

Because the Axe had just told her, 'We leaving are. Tonight.'

She wriggled further out along the branch, ignoring the prickles and Edrach's yell to 'be careful'. Now she could see the Axe's face between the dull green leaves of high summer; the sea made a dazzling crown behind his head.

'But you can't!' she shouted. 'You said you were staying with me! You said you were staying with me until your flight ...'

77

The Axe climbed higher up the cliff, his brown body glistening in the light of the double suns. He reached up one hand to cover hers. '... until my flight is a star in your sky. And it will be, Tohalla. Before the autumn rains begin. Because we true data have: where the Ship is.'

He fell silent a moment, remembering how he knew. Then, wiping a forearm across the dust on his face, he went on: 'But it a long way south of here is. We time to travel need.'

Tears started to her eyes and her face puckered. She felt childish and ridiculous. These last weeks she had burst into tears at nothing. She recognized the feeling. She recognized many of the feelings that assailed her, because she had been pregnant before: the ache in her womb; the tingling in her breasts; the smell of her urine in the morning.

And ten days ago Edrach had come upon her in the drying-shelter on the roof. He had taken her hand, smiling at the secret joy he could sense in her. In the slatted light that filtered between the hanging bundles of fruit, he had shared her happiness. His affirmation thrilled her. She didn't ask him how he knew. She hadn't even told the Axe at that time; she'd been saving it for when they slipped out of the sleeping House under the moons' light to their languourous secret pleasure.

'To you gratulation is, Tohalla!' Edrach had said, and she had breathed in the rich odours of the fruit as if it were her private feast. 'A girl is, to fuse the Red and the Green. Take care, Tohalla, because you precious are, and not just in the child.'

But now it was the day before Longday when she was to have been married and up on the cliff the joyberries in her mouth grated on her teeth like sand. She stared down at the Axe, suddenly as cut off from him as all the Green was from the Red beyond.

'You said you wouldn't leave me!' she repeated childishly.

The Axe smiled gently at her. His hair was the colour of new rope and he smelt of homely things, not like the wild creature he had suddenly become.

'You mean you with us won't come, Toh?' He sounded strange, but her hurt was more important to her than the riddle of his mood. 'How can I?' she retorted.

I'm too old for him, that's what it is. The years from seventeen to twenty-seven are more than that in experience. I wish I didn't want to cry! It makes me ugly, and I so want him to stay ...

She shook her head like a spineder who'd tangled his horns in the Edge. 'I can't! I'm going to have a baby!' As if he didn't know. He'd been so happy when she told him.

78

The Axe stroked one finger down her forearm in a gesture that was laden with memories of their time together in the warmth of summer nights. He pulled her gently down to the ledge beside him, his hold steadying her lest she fall to the tidenet strands above the heat-pressed surf. When she was safe-balanced on the broad shelf of rock, he sat so that she had to do the same, and he turned her chin to kiss her but she wasn't reconciled and the kiss landed on the angle of her jaw.

He gave her a gentle shake while Edrach eased himself up to the branch where she'd sat a moment ago. The old man looked at her with his one whole eye, and swung his legs idly above her. Tohalla felt surrounded, but for once there was no stirring of Red-mites in her brain to comfort her. Did that mean Edrach wasn't going to help her any more? She'd forgotten until now just how much he had done for her.

The Axe stroked a pattern on the back of her wrist. 'I in the Red was born. Edrach in the Red was born. Hundreds of Crew there all their lives spend. Beauty in my heartland is. Don't leave me.'

'Don't leave me, then!' she snapped tartly. 'You know how important it is that we have this child here. Think of it! You want to take the new future I'm carrying away from the Green! You must know the dangers of inbreeding!

'No.' She corrected herself bitterly. 'I forgot. I allowed myself to forget that you're sons of the Wolf. You don't know anything!'

His gray eyes poured their disappointment out onto the ruby sea. Whitesun had sunk now; only Redsun was spinning over their shoulders, and the ledge was cold in its growing shadow.

After a time the Axe broke through the net of silence her words had cast. 'We of the Red many things know that the Green to you denies. Fair?'

'Fair,' she admitted in shame. 'But you know I can't leave! I can't take this baby away from my people. There's been so many lost these last years, Red –'

'Red-bitten. Yes.' The Axe was letting his anger out now too. Edrach sat picking a thorn-tip from his stubby fingers, but Tohalla knew he was hearing every word she said – and for all she knew, every word she chose not to say.

The Axe said fiercely, 'Many of us new lives choose their partners to follow –'

'But not you! You're too selfish!' Tohalla pulled away from him, jumping to her feet only a fingerspan from a leap to death. Death would be a relief ... But her life was not even her own to take. She had to carry this child, who was to be a greater gift to the Green than even the Intake. Her body had trapped her.

The Axe climbed to his feet too, and the ruddy light made a Red beacon of his hair. His movements were short, full of violence suppressed, but not by much.

'I you of the Ship tell, and you call me selfish?' he shouted after her, but she was swinging recklessly downwards towards the normality of Chulain and the children on the beach. In her savage haste to reach them before they had finished packing up, she dragged her shoulder-basket free of an outcropping rock and the joyberries for her wedding spilled in a dull gold river.

Then Edrach spoke in her mind. Now it wasn't a comforting presence, but an alien thing and she hated him: his ugly, distorted, inhuman ruin of a face. And his invasion of her being.

'Leave me alone!' she shrieked over her shoulder, but she couldn't run away from that sound that left filthy Red prints in her mind. She should never have allowed herself to be tainted with those sons of the Wolf, whatever Housefather had said ...

But Edrach's voice was closer than Chulain and she was tired through her bones ...

Travel with us or stay, Tohalla who to us was good. But I dying am. And the Red one lesson more to teach you has.

Then, because he knew her weight of guilt, Edrach added, *This you must learn, your daughter for the good of the Green to tell. And tonight we all your celebration will eat before Redsun's setting from the sky has faded. But tomorrow? Who that can tell?*

So – and she later said it was by her own choice and not through compulsion – she abandoned her duty to the Green for the second time. But she always intended to come back ...

ENTR'ACTE

The Heart of the Messenger

CHAPTER ONE

The Messenger

In the embers of Redsun's light Edrach led them down to where the Edge fought – and lost to – the battalions of the sea. Sullenly, Tohalla followed his limping descent, down between the ribs of the headland. Behind her, fierce and sullen in his own way, the Axe clambered easily.

From time to time Tohalla glanced back up at him, disguising the movement as a look at a handhold, or a motion to throw back her tangled hair. In the same way he pretended not to notice her, only the task in hand.

That was enough. The rocks were razor-edged, and lower down where they winnowed the sea, they were sharpened by sting-shells and slick with growing things. Too, the dusk was thick and red. Blue had gone from the sky now, and green from the dunes back in the safe curve of the bay. Only infinite reds remained, and Tohalla's vision was uncertain. She was more than a little scared; she would have turned back, but she was even more afraid that Edrach would storm her mind by force.

What could she lose? What was left for her to lose? Only the baby, and she was terrified of what might happen to the little one growing inside her.

A ghostly booming erupted from a hollow in the crumbling rocks. Tohalla screamed: there was no need. A pillar of pale water leaped upwards, drenching her; it was only the force of the tide.

'Take off your leggings, Toh,' said Edrach. He didn't watch her. Like Housefather he assumed she would obey.

She was glad she did. They were wet enough already, and now Edrach was leaving his hanging above the wrack of the high-water line and wading out into the surf.

The old Wolfman led them some hundred steps through the waves. Around the point, he turned inwards to a small shingle beach and crunched up its steepness, slipping back half a pace at every footfall. Reaching an overhanging rock at the top of the slope was a real triumph, and Tohalla was already exhausted. The pain in her belly was dragging her down. Even the Axe was breathing heavily. Evening had brought no relief from the fierce heat of the day.

'You now rest must, Toh,' said Edrach. 'I you will protect. Ain Battle-Axe, cast around. You the right messenger must meet.'

Meet a messenger? Tohalla whirled her head from side to side, terrified anew. *Were there other Wolfmen around? Hostile ones? How? Had Edrach summoned them in some arcane fashion?*

She was ready to believe anything of him now; her hand fumbled over the shingle, sifting for a stone that was round and heavy and would fit in her hand ...

The Axe trotted off through the rocks behind the beach, leaving her alone with Edrach and more frightened than she had ever been in her life.

But Edrach lowered himself stiffly to sit facing her, not close enough to threaten. Half in shadow, still he held one hand up to protect his eyes from the slanting rays of Redsun until the Axe was out of sight.

Edrach relaxed, wriggled until he had hollowed a seat for himself in the shingle. Then he looked at Tohalla and chuckled.

'No harm to you is, Tohalla of the Loom. But many questions, yes? And not enough answers to keep you from fear's prowling.'

Tohalla's tongue tripped over half a dozen questions which fought to control her tongue. Edrach smiled serenely. 'Then it better is if I start?'

'No!' She gathered her wits, fed up of always being directed by someone else. She was no Red fragment, sent at the whim of the wind to be strewn on good ground or bad.

'Who is the messenger? And what is this ship that you have to go chasing off now of all times to see it? And why now? Why didn't you both go before – before the Axe ...' She abandoned that one in confusion, but her voice raced on, 'How did you know the messenger would come here? Who's she from? Or he? And that rock –'

'Enough is!' Tohalla could hear the laughter in Edrach's throat, but it was companionable, not mocking. 'Maybe tonight all we have is. That for you to decide is: what you with your life will weave.

'Here!' He fumbled in the pockets of his sleeveless jerkin and threw something towards her. She ducked and hurled her rock at the same time. It didn't make for accuracy and the stone danced off down the beach, nowhere near his head. Edrach laughed heartily, pointing to what he'd thrown.

'An apple is! Old and wrinkled, last year's end of harvest!'

Tohalla looked, and blushed. But she was ravenous. She picked it up, examined it and bit out the bruise. Then, chewing his own apple in harmony with her, Edrach began.

'Last winter, when the snow hard in our flesh stung, another Crew us tried to kill, because we the true Crew's descendants are, and the Axe's father the only true Book held.'

Edrach took breath for another sentence but Tohalla interrupted, 'That's not …'

He held up his hand, brown and gnarled, and in the coral light she saw scars along the inside of his wrist. '… not the Colonists' book is. This the *Mosckva*'s log is. It all the redows of the *Mosckva* has, the Ship that us all from Erth brought, so we will know how it to fly when the time comes.

'Anyway, the mutinas us through the Longnight blizzard hunted, and the wolves from their sleep in the warm places by our fear were woken. Den-Xiao died but the mutinas the wolves drove, and us in a dead-end pinned, between spike-trees and stone, and the Axe and Pyotr and I a wall of wolf-carcases built up at each stab and swing and thrust.'

Tohalla couldn't make the picture complete: the whirling snow, slate rocks and a tangle of cruel thorns, but of the wolves she had no picture. 'These wolves – what are they like?' she asked, the apple forgotten in her hand.

'A man's head to their jaw comes – a tall man like your Chulain. Four feet they have that in claws end, and the legs in scales like steel are clad.' Tohalla didn't know what steel was. She decided to ask later.

'Then the body strong is, like your spineders, but no crest of spikes and lower at the back, to a tail like an extra leg. And the scales give way to fur that blue and purple and green with different light is.' Edrach smiled and nodded to himself. 'And they teeth have!'

Tohalla said, 'But you got away?'

'Pyotr a wolf-head cut off that not quite dead was, and it on his spear stuck. That when his stomach ripped was. But he the spear used to hurl the wolf-head into the ring of mutinas. So the wolves them attacked instead.'

Tohalla felt the round familiarity of the apple on her palm and seemed surprised to see it there. Around another mouthful she said, 'So you got away?'

'No. First we the Book hid and then we away tunnelled, through the snowdrifts under the thicket. The wolves us would kill, and the mutinas, and the cold, if we first to death did not bleed. So we to your Edge came, and just before the last mutinas of that Crew up with us caught, Adiockle and Trinamine us in took.'

Tohalla nibbled the last of the flesh from around the apple-core and pressed finger and thumb to fire the pips across the beach. It was only an idle gesture, but Edrach said, 'And so the Green grows, with flame and seed, until the Red is killed, or to a herb-garden is trimmed, with a wall of grass around it.'

Breathing in sharply through a mouth open in indignation. Tohalla exclaimed, 'Yes, but we wouldn't –'

'Not a battle is, Tohalla.' For a moment he thought how to rephrase, to put his meaning in words that would fit her thoughts. 'For us, Tohalla and Edrach, not a competition of arguments is. More urgent questions you have, na?'

'Ummm. Why do you back to the Red want to go?' She laughed faintly down her nose. 'See, Edrach, you've got me doing it now! Why do you want to go back, if it's so dangerous?'

'That the messenger will tell you better than I.'

She sorted her thoughts a moment. 'Then who is this messenger? And where is she from? Or he?'

'Not a person is. Not *from* a person is. That also you will see and know, and best before Redsun gone from the sky is. If the Axe quick enough is ...' Edrach finished quietly, more to himself than her, but Tohalla was as hungry for knowledge as she was for food.

'Well then, can you tell me why you have to go *now*, just when the Axe and I were supposed to get married?'

Again that sudden shift to tears. Tohalla hated that; it made her feel weak and vulnerable. Inside she began to rage again, at herself, at all of them, Housefather included. *Why did I have to get pregnant now? Wouldn't even Worut have been better than all this fear and uncertainty? What foul influence is the Red going to have on my baby? What have I got myself into?*

Edrach did just what she needed from a man she didn't love; he ignored the writhings of her face and the silent tears that flooded from her eyes, and he talked of something else.

'The Axe now coming is. Can you him hear?'

He helped her to her feet and together they crunched over the shingle. Where the rim of the headland dipped to a notch, the Axe stood limned against the sleepy eye of Redsun, beckoning.

'Not far is,' he said triumphantly to Edrach. He made it clear that he

86

wasn't even going to look at Tohalla yet. He turned and began to trot; Tohalla could not have kept up, but suddenly the Axe dropped to a swift walk, ducking under arches of ruby or ochre crystals that grew above a carpet of hookweed. It was lighter up here out of the hills' shadow, and the chiming song of the Red was soft around them. Still she felt the threat of its alienness.

Edrach, following her, said, 'Your feet low keep. The hooks in your shoes stick.'

Tohalla took a second to glance down. Just as the old man had said, there were dull brown, feathery hooks clustered on her shoes. If she lifted her feet there was the danger that she could brush them off on her legs. 'In flesh they fester,' Edrach told her. The barbs were as long as the joint of her thumb. She could believe him. It did nothing to make her feel better about this latest in her string of disobediences to Housefather and the teachings of the Green.

Soon they came to a clearing in the last light of the afternoon. The hookweed didn't grow among the thick shale. Instead crystals of vermilion scattered the sun's rays so that pink light flecked her clothing. Mostly the crystals rolled loose underfoot but some were clumped together almost to waist height. They grew in fans of ruby needles that were as thick as her body at their base. Along each shaft were joints where other fans branched out, thinner and clearer, but the fans had lost their symmetry now.

'This one the right message lives?' asked Edrach, nodding to a plant where the Axe stood expressionless. Broken points lay all around it on the stony ground. To Tohalla, born to fear Red crystals, it was a terrifying sight. She wished she were anywhere else, and tried to hide her trembling.

The Axe nodded brusquely. Edrach said, 'Then wolf-guard keep, na?'

Edrach took Tohalla's hand and she was glad of the contact. 'Are there wolves near here then?' she whispered.

'Always near messengers wolves are. They hunt from the messages the crystals live, but Ain Battle-Axe will wolf-guard keep.'

'I don't understand. What is all this? Why –'

'Hush now.' Edrach squinted at the westering sun. 'Not much time left is. See where the heart of the plant blood-red is? There live the oldest messages. Kneel and your two hands around the stem cup. Your eyes close, and wait.'

Apprehensive, she obeyed him. Nothing happened. Around her the evening breeze plucked a harmony from the crystal growths, then she heard something slither behind her. Whirling so fast she almost fell over, she still wasn't quick enough to see what it was.

Edrach clicked his tongue impatiently. 'The wind a crystal rolled. Now hurry! The Axe and I you safe keep. Hands back on the heart of the messenger!'

CHAPTER TWO

Marchidas of the Seven Battles

Behind her closed eyelids, Tohalla seemed to be in a world of warmth and comforting redness, the colour of Whitesun seen through outspread fingers. Between her palms there was nothing, then a tingling came that spread gently through her like a fire that did not burn. Lifetides washed over her, the tiny feelings of myriad small creatures; the sharper emotions of more sentient species plucked at her own. Gradually she ceased cataloguing these sensations. Now she was only a vessel waiting to be filled.

At first the kaleidoscope of images in motion was dim, red-hazed, too swift and too alien to comprehend. Then, as her mind came closer to the burning heart of the messenger, the swirling slowed and little by little a figure appeared, and the figure was her, but it was a young girl too, dwarfed by –

The Wolf lowered its tusks to rip up into her flesh, but Marchidas was ready for that. She used the broad haft of her spear to pole-vault back and to one side. Lumbering, off-balance, the beast turned to face her. In a copse in the heart of the violet forest it glowered down at its puny foe.

She could smell the strong muskiness of its body, see the broad sunlight rippling from mauve to blue to green as the huge muscles worked under its hide. And she could feel its impersonal desire to eat her change slowly to anger and puzzlement. *This meal was too quick! And – more puzzling still – it wanted to kill the Wolf!*

Marchidas feinted to the left. In her was the joy of youth and strength now come to their full morning; the blood sang through her and she chanted as if the deed were already done, 'I my Wolf killed!

89

See how his skin becomes me! I my Wolf killed!'

The Wolf could not hear, of course, since he had no ears, but he could sense the intent behind the words. Woken from his torpor under the branching spearwood, he had lolloped out of his lair for an easy kill. Now the feeling of puzzlement grew, and with it, against the wind, Marchidas's Wolf scented human and animal spiced with fear. He whistled softly, lips curling back from his fangs.

As he became more awake, the Wolf pounced forward and slashed with both front paws. Marchidas was not quite quick enough: her knife-arm burned with pain where five runnels in her flesh dripped blood.

Again Marchidas vaulted back but the tip of her spear tangled in the sparkling trees. She fell, rolling, to spring to her feet. Now the prickly undergrowth was at her back, hampering her. The spear lay beyond her grasp.

She began to breathe faster, frightened that the watchers behind her would step in and finish her kill, and she would be dishonoured. She began to wish that she had allowed her Wolf to leave his lair; there would have been more room to manoeuvre on the open plain.

Marchidas was wary now, with the wariness of the Wolf sharp in her mind. He pivoted on his front paws, flicking his dagger-point tail at her. She ducked and his tail-claw spun the spear further out of her reach. Hastily she lunged after her weapon, crawling on all fours under the lilac gleam of the spearwood, but the Wolf was there before her. Marchidas backed away. It was as far as she could go.

Behind her she could hear the watchers rustling nearer through the purple forest. She had to do it *now*, before they took over! She had to be promoted *now*, before it was too late to save her father!

The Harifon's mind-voice plucked at the fringes of her awareness. Marchidas shut him out. Again she feinted with the knife, a long extended movement. As she intended, her Wolf snapped viciously; she cut at his exposed neck, but he was becoming attuned now and sensed what she was about to do. Once more he whirled on his front paws and his tail speared her shoulder.

'This child not for promotion is,' sneered the Harifon. 'Now her out get so that her superiors the chore can finish.'

Edrach shook his head at his senior offser, motioning 'Quiet!' Marchidas, bleeding, was grateful to him.

Don't I have enough to do? Her Wolf's temper soured her thoughts, clouded her eyes with ghosts of his vision: a girl, long dark hair snared back in a loop of shells, lithe body crouched under the cramping

90

spearwood, and the suns' dazzle limning her long knife in black. And Marchidas could smell her own blood as her Wolf could. Appetizing …

Through his eyes she saw the Harifon and the other offsers, kneeling, parting the low branches to watch her failure. This one he could handle, with her nostrils breathing fear.

But three more? Large ones?

Marchidas sidestepped low to the ground and skimmed a broken branch at her Wolf. He jibbed, blinking. She rolled forward in a flattened handspring and snatched up her spear.

Daring a glance behind her, she saw Khowdris had drawn back. In a flash from the corner of her eye Marchidas watched Edrach press a hand on the Harifon's arrow. A tall youth not yet come to full growth, still Edrach was a head taller than the older man. The Harifon bared his big teeth in a mockery of a smile. 'I herself let kill. Why not? I none of that get have lost!'

And Khowdris watched, impassive.

Marchidas shifted her gaze from the tableau framed by the spearwood. Deliberately she firmed contact with the Wolf: eyes into eyes, thoughts into thoughts. She paced his breathing; it slowed with her own. Then, when she could taste her scent on his tongue, she made herself small in his mind. Small and lonely and afraid.

It wasn't hard to do. Marchidas was terrified. She had never before thought of death as something that could come to her. And now it was close, with her life dripping crimson from the fiery wounds in her arm. Her pride of life shrank. Will fled. She felt the Wolf's longing to eat her. And she was the Wolf …

But somehow she had to leave a thread of self-awareness that her Wolf could not reach, a shining thread of strength he could not touch.

She sank lower, her thigh-muscles stretching as she bent her knees wide apart. Now she could feel his claws flexing in the weed-strewn earth, knew the sensation of crystal stems sliding over the hard scales on his paws.

Marchidas's Wolf pressed harder with his mind, and the prey cowered, thoughtless, unaware even of the blood dripping from its spindly arm. He probed: no response.

The Wolf surged forward, jaws gaping, fast as an arrow from a bow. Unnoticed, Edrach sucked in a shocked gasp and the Harifon's smile widened. *The girl had gone too far! She couldn't pull out of it! The Wolf was …*

Faster than an arrow from a bow the Wolf sprang onto his

empty-headed prey. But from that distant glimmer of light that was the essence of Marchidas flooded a shining river of battle-joy and she pulled up the tip of her spear. The butt of it was firm in the blood-red growth, the shaft of it braced by her legs into the stable point of a triangle, and the blade of it ripped through the throat of the Wolf.

The girl screamed in his mortal agony. Barely she leaped aside from the crash of his fall. Marchidas's Wolf lay dead at her feet.

The skein of Marchidas's life was bright with pride when she came back to the Crew's camp in the bloody hide of the Wolf she had made her own. In a circle of stones the fire leaped, and its amethyst smoke blended with the lilac of the sunsets. Around them spread the darkling plain, but the camp was nestled in a motherly fold of earth.

First Marchidas sent food to the outwatchers, but there was meat for all, that Marchidas cooked, and her Wolf's head went for honour to Captain her father. Old Khowdris nodded and smiled at that. But the believing heart went to Edrach. That night she chose him for her brother and though he limped, he limped proudly at her side.

Once the meat was gone and the dreamsmoke shared its spell with the thirty-odd Crew, Marchidas scattered fire-crystals on the embers. Sparks flew to challenge the stars behind her and their light encircled the Crew-folk.

Her battle-poem was fierce and strong. Even Arno Wordweaver was open-mouthed with admiration, though her son slept peacefully in the crook of her arm.

Cross-legged between Captain her father and Edrach Chosen Brother, Marchidas wove the strands of her tale so that everything was laid out for the Crew's inspection; if they did not share knowledge the Crew could not survive. And she made the point of small heart while showing all its dangers:

Almost I died. Small heart the enemy draws on,
But the tide of life in strength is.
Hold the tide. Ride it! Bright as a lake it shines.
Your self all is you can believe.

She looked across the flames to the Harifon, named for the hot killing winds of the South. His deep eyes glittered in the dark skin of his face. To either side of his hooked nose pride drew shadowy furrows. Marchidas, unseeing, reached back unerringly to lay her hand in her father's. She had only her feelings to tell her that the Harifon wanted

92

Captaincy – of course an offser as wily as he would do nothing in her sight that might threaten her father. But now she had been promoted, and her father had another defender to stand beside Edrach.

The awareness came to her that her battle-poem had gonged through the Harifon's dark soul as it had reached many others of this fragmented Crew. Now Marchidas sharpened the song to its edge.

And in your friends trust is
With loyalty to The True Crew.

But the Harifon smiled maddeningly, and turned sooner than politeness allowed to chat to the man at his side.

For Marchidas, promotion to adulthood meant all she had hoped it would.

Now came free hunting as the suns raced across summer skies. She gloried in the running over the tinkling plains, to track game by its imprint on the coral fans of messengers and to roam wide, matching her pace to Edrach's experience while the column of privates trekked slowly across the hollows. *Maybe, too*, thought Marchidas, *I the one shall be who the Ship finds.*

Her Wolf's-hide she carried in a roll, skin-side innermost, wrapped around a paste of crystal plants and earth to cure it. It wasn't heavy, but its bulk flapped awkwardly on her back when she ran. Yet the iridescent fur stroked her bare skin pleasantly, and the size of her Wolf-pelt drew admiring comments of how much so brave a promoted could contribute to the Crew. She was too young yet to be an offser. But she could shape her dreams to the rhythm of her stride …

And at night Marchidas drilled quietly into the claws of her Wolf's hind feet, ignoring how it made her shoulders ache. The pain of her wounds had been nobly earned but sometimes Marchidas allowed Edrach to draw the pain outside her with his mutant gift. He was glad to do it; his mutation had robbed him of so much else, even the chance of fathering a child. But he was Chosen Brother and Marchidas loved him … Slowly the stripes of her Promotion hardened into honourable scars and the necklace of Wolfclaws grew.

Almost as good as the hunting was the time when she had tanned the hide to clean suppleness. Its softness made a comfortable pillow in the dark; it re-affirmed her dignity and proved she was no longer a child. It gave her the right to sit near the offsers and listen to their talk. She knew she had much to learn. Besides, there was always laughter by their fire even when Captain her father led them into land where game was scarce. Sometimes Arno or another would sing of glory or their star-home. Sometimes even the Harifon and his woman joined in, though more often not.

And, watching those two, though she mentioned it only to Edrach, Marchidas knew the time would come when her father needed all his friends at his side.

When Redsun rose at the centre of Whitesun's disc, that was when it happened.

Under the clear pale sky of Autumn dawn, the Crew stirred sluggishly to life. Marchidas, wrapped in her warm Wolf-hide, leant up on one arm to snuff the cold air.

Around them the broad sweep of the plains was no longer richly red. White frost sparkled on each crystal so that the vast, rolling land was shaded from alabaster to coral, and there was a cobweb of ice fringing the stream that rolled out of the Northern Hills. Marchidas shivered.

After a scant breakfast of yesterday's meat, the Harifon detailed the outwatch. That was the job which Captain had given him last night when the arrowfalls had begun to fly south in search of warmer lands. The Harifon himself was to be point, since Captain's leg had been torn by a hungry groundtrap some three days before. But it was all right – Marchidas hoped. Captain had told him the route he was to follow.

Marchidas walked at her father's side, supporting him. She was as discouraged as he was to be going back to the winterground after another fruitless trek. They all were.

She had pored over the Book as long as he had in her last years. Bearing the weight of his shoulder on hers, she said brightly, 'Not to worry, Captain my father. Next spring if Rosaria kind weather brings, you the Ship will find.'

'I it *feel*!' he said. 'So close we were. I wonder that no-one yet the Book like us this time has interpreted. It so obvious is when you know.'

It was strange for Marchidas to be back in the familiar column of privates, instead of roaming free with the promoted. Yet there was pleasure in the sociability. In front of her a toddler held up a trophy: the empty shell of a pinger. The child chortled as she began to fire small crystals at her friends. Soon Marchidas and Captain were surrounded by a minor battle. It was not so long ago that Marchidas had played pinger-wars. Laughing at an accidental hit on her Wolf-cloak, she joined in. In between times, she carried on her conversation with her father.

94

'Do you think that someone it has found?' she asked him.

It was an old argument between them. Still, Captain considered the problem, shuffling forward and stopping to let her fire a pinger. 'No. No-one else the True Book has. Loi-tsu mother of Captain's son, who it from the *Moskva* saved, it carried to her death, and her line it beyond carried. And my grandmother's grandmother' – it was a phrase meaning an ancestor long ago – 'the words on skin copied when rustworms the metal of its pages clouded. All other copies such as the mutinas have are nothing but twistings of the truth, to make this one or that one important seem. No-one yet the Ship has found. It my destiny is. Inside me I it feel.'

Captain her father hobbled a step further, turning to look into Marchidas's eyes. His hair was the colour of basalt streaked with snow and the tanned skin of his face was mottled with liver-spots. Smile-lines decorated his cheeks, and his eyes that gazed into distances were saved by the wrinkles of long laughter from being those of a wanderer.

Marchidas recognized the force of her father's intellect, but knew too of his ambition to be Shipfinder. He'd spent half a lifetime leading his people on searches, convinced each time he'd find the Ship that Ain Tsui, First Captain, had wrecked and whose location had been disguised by his followers. But for generations the Crew had spent their lives searching, longing for the way to join the star-kin and end their isolation, though the march was cruel on young and old.

And each year of his Captaincy, Nawaz her father had searched the Book for clues to free his people of the summer treks of error. Marchidas smiled at him, her gaze as open as his, for she trusted him. After all, didn't they share the same ambition?

'When the arrowfalls north fly to chase the snow away, we the Ship will find, you and I,' she said.

Marchidas looked around. All the parents and the privates were some way ahead, laughing still at their running battle. 'But unless we catch up, we'll still here be!'

At noon the outwatchers scarcely allowed them time to boil water for wintertea. Captain kept looking around, shading his eyes against the brightness. Old Khowdris looked worried too. And Edrach didn't come in for his meal.

All afternoon, on the trek once more, Captain seemed more and more uneasy. Marchidas shifted her rolled-up Wolf's-hide to let the sweat on her back evaporate, because the suns had soon boiled the frost from the ground. Once again the carpet of glittering red swelled and dropped away to meet the blue horizon.

95

Captain called, 'Tearlach!' and a short, handsome man swung out of his place in the column and trotted forward to join them.

'Captain?'

'I your help would welcome as my second leg. I words for the Harifon have, and Marchidas them must carry.'

Tearlach looked up at the pain-lines on Captain's face that were deepening with the length of the march. He smiled willingly, taking Captain's Wolf-hide cloak and knotting it next to his own. 'No problem is.' One of Tearlach's teeth was missing. It made his lop-sided smile engaging. Marchidas would have trusted him with her life.

Captain took her to one side. 'Find the Harifon, but warily. This not the way to the winterground is. He us too far west is leading. Also the trek too long for one day is. Already our shadows are growing, and the children need rest. And let Edrach with you go, but out of sight.'

Marchidas gulped, nodded. It was a lot of responsibility for a girl of fourteen winters, even if she had been promoted, but Captain could hardly send any of the parents in the column. They might be needed for defence. They would want to be with their children if an attack came. The night before they had all seen the smoke of fires to the west.

She trotted away, smiling as if her father had freed her for the pleasure of running over the undulating plain. She circled wide along the left flank, where she knew Edrach had been posted.

Once out of sight of the line of privates, Marchidas waved violently, made the sign for 'brother' and pantomimed a search. She was not foolish enough to skyline herself but there was a good chance he might see her from beneath the crest of some slight ridge.

Soon she saw movement. Her keen grey eyes scanned all sides for danger, but it was only Edrach, she saw, when he was near enough. Loping swiftly over the uneven ground, she caught up with him. He had never minded that others could run faster than he could with his twisted foot. Edrach knew he could run further by the strength of his will.

Edrach accepted her explanation readily. 'The Harifon some other plan in mind has. But Captain right is. We the children and old ones to the breath of northern winter must not expose.' Neither of them mentioned those fires, knowing the other knew. Mutinas and Wild Men were everywhere.

Together they ran, he keeping watch to left and front, she to right and rear. It was automatic. Other crews than theirs roamed the red plains. Yet there was no smell of danger sweeping down the long winds.

Marchidas stopped when she saw a messenger. It was only a stub of ruby hidden among the more orange-red of the ground cover. Around it, shattered by the heat of the past midsummer, the broken tines of its fans were scattered. Some had already rooted and from the horizontal crystals' ends shorter points were thrusting upwards, making use of the last warmth of the dying year.

She cupped her hands on the heart of the messenger, reading the little lives of grazers and lizards and the stronger imprint of a wolf-pack. And, stronger still because more recent, the passage of a proud and angry man.

He had stopped there too, seeking knowledge of what dangers might lie ahead. He had not guarded his thoughts: Marchidas was shocked to realize he intended to lead them along another trail to the Ship, which he thought lay in the marshes at the foot of the Purple Mountains. *He wrong is! He us all for his ambition is risking!*

The Harifon had broken faith with Captain.

Abruptly she disengaged from the messenger. Running faster now, Marchidas told Edrach as they leaped over holes and scattered rocks. A curving wall of shale blocked their path. They slithered upwards, not knowing or caring that it was the grave-mound of some ancient glacier.

Dropping flat to peer over its rim, they saw the Harifon's dark barrel of a figure jouncing only two arrow-flights ahead. He was running easily, a man a little past his prime. Grey salted his hair, and there were folds of skin at the back of his neck. *The only reason he never before has taken over*, Marchidas thought suddenly, *is that up to now the Crew in Captain my father has believed. And now they him as a weak old man see, who once again them has let down, for he the Ship after another Summer's trek still hasn't found ... Or maybe they not yet have realized where the Harifon us is leading.*

Marchidas summoned all her awareness but she could detect no-one else. Nor, even with his twist-born powers, could Edrach. That was strange. Surely the Harifon must know by now he'd be found out? Or was the man so arrogant he couldn't believe anyone would seriously contest him? Anyway, who could he get to follow him?

Marchidas nudged Edrach and mimed two curving paths. He nodded and winked encouragement at her. She smiled then into his steady brown eyes, and pressed his hand briefly to seek and give reassurance.

The Harifon was angling down into a dip now. His pursuers separated, each intent on making ground as quietly as possible while their quarry was still unaware.

They caught him in a pincer movement as he crested a gentle swell. Marchidas rose up before him out of the shadow of the land.

The Harifon's spear-arm swung backwards in instinctive response. Before he could complete the throw Edrach tore the javelin out of his grasp.

Marchidas's voice was high with tension. 'You too far west have led. When the snow-winds come, our Crew safe shelter must have.'

The Harifon arched his brows disdainfully, as if at a child's presumption. 'Our Crew in the Ship can shelter. And not all old women are, like your father. If he so sure is, why the Ship long before has he not found?'

The Harifon turned slightly as if the suns were bothering his eyes. Marchidas edged round to face him directly. His long knife was still in its scabbard at his back. She tried to stop her legs trembling.

The Harifon yawned in her face, stretching his arms high and wide. She was above him on the slope but he could still look levelly into her eyes, and she was afraid. But she had fought and slain her Wolf, though she'd been afraid then too. Fear didn't matter. It helped. It made your senses sharper. So long as you didn't give way to it.

The strong muscles in the Harifon's arms knotted as he stretched still wider. Marchidas balanced her long-knife, a warning not to try and reach up for his in its scabbard at the back of his neck.

But he laughed. 'Children all are that Captain has to send? He not fit to be Captain is!'

To either side of him now his henchmen appeared, arrows nocked to their bows. Captain's messengers had been too intent on their quarry to notice the stealthy approach.

It wasn't even a battle. Neither Marchidas nor Edrach struck a single blow.

Marchidas sheathed her knife, sick within herself at her failure. The Harifon pivoted, casually taking the spear from Edrach. Two men seized Edrach's arms. Marchidas swallowed, tensed …

The Harifon whirled the spear so that it sang under the blue vault of the sky. Then struck Edrach with its butt, again and again.

Marchidas sprang forward at the Harifon's first hint of movement but from behind her Harifon's Woman leapt onto her back, jabbing a blade into her neck. Marchidas bucked and writhed even so, but Harifon's Woman twisted the girl's head until she could not breathe, forcing her to watch, though internal lightning splashed over her darkening sight.

They held Edrach upright long after he had lost consciousness. Frenzied, the Harifon still beat Edrach's head and chest. The Harifon was *laughing*. Only when he struck a blow that landed on the side of

Edrach's face did the Harifon stop. Now there'd be no more opposition to his leadership. Marchidas was crying. For Edrach's eyeball had burst and its juices were tears on his once handsome face.

Harifon's Woman jerked Marchidas's head up by the hair. 'Shall I her throat slit?'

Quickly, before they could stop her, Marchidas dragged breath into her bruised lungs and yelled, 'You no honourable challenge made, but trickery and evil!' She was crying with rage and self-loathing.

They laughed.

Harifon answered his woman. 'No need is her to kill. Who her will follow? Or her father now? She dead is to the Crew.'

In a far hollow just outside the copper-gleamed spikes of the Edge, Tohalla moaned. She felt clear to her bones that same self-loathing as Marchidas had lived. Just so had Tohalla been when she couldn't make her babies live. Helpless, dead to her People ...

Yet the Axe could stretch out his hand and save her. Except, he didn't want to. He wanted to leave, to go back to his cruel heartland where the brutal wrought this violation of flesh and spirit on Marchidas.

All but unconscious, Tohalla crouched still by the messenger, while Marchidas's life slipped through her fingers and into Tohalla's brain. She didn't understand why the Wolfmen had brought her here; she knew only that Marchidas was closer to her than even Trinamine who loved her, and Tohalla had to know the rest of her story.

Then the shock faded and Tohalla's mind was cleared to the life that flowed through her, and Redsun inched down to the hills ...

Marchidas, Edrach, and her father once Captain were dead to the Crew and the Harifon had stolen the Book and their ranks. That was why the Crew huddled shivering in a gully in the foothills of the Purple Mountains when they should have been in the warm cove to the south of the Big River. Rain and sleet leaked from the low sky where the hill-tops bruised its belly. Only the Harifon and his friends could get into what shelter there was from a slight overhang – the Harifon, of course, now having more friends than he used to. The rain had hissed the night-fire to extinction. Now there was only smoke-reeked darkness.

Marchidas shifted her numb body on the muddy slope. She could have crawled into the bivouac she and Nawaz her father shared with Edrach: their three Wolf-hides fastened together. But she was more than ordinarily uneasy. Besides, the coughing and fevered moans of the sick kept her guilty and awake. Edrach muttered and tossed in the half-dreams of delirium. She didn't want to disturb him when only sleep eased the feverish pain of his ruined eye. *I should have stopped the Harifon ... Edrach would have been well and my father would still be Captain and caring for his Crew.*

The rim above crumbled and a new rivulet bubbled under the sleepers. Marchidas strained to hear one cheerful sound, but everything alive was still. There was only the drone of the wind that made the spindly black trees cry.

Marchidas hunched lower. An arrow chirred through the air her body had worn a moment ago. It chunked into a Wolf-cloaked sleeper.

'Attack! Attack!' she yelled, rolling onto her stomach to seek the arrow's source. Since that day on the plains, her spear was always close to hand, but it was useless now. She couldn't throw it with her own people struggling to their feet, falling to arrows.

The fierce, incomprehensible cries of the Wild Men terrified her. A score of figures burst through the trees and slithered down the gully on a tide of mud. Marchidas darted aside, swinging her spear at knee-height to bring two men down. Then it was knife-work in the dark. She couldn't even use her Wolf-hide to shield her, laced as it was to the others.

Edrach and her father were back to back, ringed by clashing weapons. Without compunction Marchidas stabbed Wild Men in the back, the side, the neck. All around, screams punctured the moaning wind.

Then it was over, her second battle. The last Wild Man left alive crashed babbling through the sodden undergrowth: no food, no captured children, no-one to tend his wounds.

And Nawaz her father was dead.

In the dawn, the Harifon said, 'A platform for the fallen build.'

Wordless, Marchidas climbed up to the bare hill-top. After a moment, Edrach and other promoted followed her. They had no heart for the task.

The sky was still harsh with rain; nothing was dry enough for a pyre. When the dead ones' Wolf-hides were lashed on a tower of black boles, Edrach laid a comforting hand on Marchidas's shoulder. She shook it off. Nevertheless he said, 'Not the honour of a pyre is, I know. But this platform on the hill still the dead as far as possible raises to the stars they came from. They a way will find. And I wolf-fire have.'

He shaking with fever and weariness is! she thought, wondering at the inner strength of someone wounded but still trying to ease others.

With an effort she said, 'Gratude. That something for honour is.'

'More. That something for annoying the Harifon is.'

And, against her will, Marchidas laughed rustily.

When the bodies had been laid at salute on the skins of their Wolves, the death-poems began, lacing each life's pattern with bravery and humour. The Harifon listened to them with growing impatience. Some were from privates only seven winters old. Other offsers stiffened their faces against tears, but not him. He stood hip-shot, tapping his foot, scratching his nose. The Crew noticed there was no discipline in him for himself.

It was a bad sign. They had enough of those already.

At last Marchidas began her father's epitaph, chanting in the weeping rain.

The Harifon turned away, issuing orders against that counter-point of glory to his rival. But many of the score of survivors saluted when she touched the wolf-fire into flame, and joined in the last line of hope:

Now Nawaz once Captain his ship has found
To take him to the stars.

The Harifon led them upwards. At the night-fire he said, 'A pass up there is. An Iron Man I traded with to me it described.'

Normally he brooked no questions but Marchidas, reckless in her grief, said, 'How an Iron Man would know?'

The Harifon's eyes reflected back the fire-light. His face was thinner after this march, and his eyes were fierce in their caves of flesh. 'When you your winter breeks were soiling, dead Captain's father us to the Mouths of the Big River led. There where the Iron Men live is.'

It was insulting of him to state something so obvious when talking to the promoted but Marchidas had trained her thoughts not to come to her face. When she made no sign, the Harifon went on, 'The Big River many sources has on the far side of the mountains. And in the summer the Iron Men the mountains walk to find ore. They boats up the River ride, and when they the boats leave, they search. Now do you understand?'

Marchidas nodded. 'You a very clear explanation made have. To you gratulation is.' And her voice stopped just short of a mother's warmth to her infant.

Upward steps made the backs of her legs ache; downwards her toes

101

were crushed in the ends of her boots. But there was more up than down. The Harifon hadn't found the pass. And winter was closer than the winterground …

One day, when the sky was only an aching blue bridge high between the walls of a chasm, the Crew slowed to a panting halt. The Harifon, Resik and Tearlach were way above, striding onward.

Tearlach didn't care any more; since his wife and daughter had died of lung-fever he offered no resistance to new Captain. The Harifon used him as a pack-carrier, a shameful thing. Only children and the sick couldn't carry their own loads. What did that make the Harifon?

'We should go back!' gasped Arno Wordweaver when she could speak. Her legs shook with weariness; her son Brachan trembled against her knee. Frost weighted her hair, sheathing its auburn curls in polished loops. The rock-fault they stood on was slick with ice: the waterfall deafening them cast a chill spray that hung in translucent icicles beside the trail. Behind them was the grim-shadowed valley. Sunlight was a blessing out of reach above.

'Back to the winterground,' murmured Lorwen, her old bones shivering.

'Or at least back below the tree-line,' Edrach said. His voice shook with the weakness that still wracked his body.

'The Ship us will shelter and feed,' said Harifon's Woman harshly. 'Then it the strong back to Erth will take.' No-one had heard her creeping up from the rear-guard. She wasn't there to protect the Crew but to keep them under her eye. Once she'd been Tarlas Ebony, but since her alliance with the Harifon, her character had been eaten up by his. Captain only called her 'Woman'. To her face the rest called her nothing at all.

'Oh!' Arno said. 'You me startled, up like that sneaking.'

But Marchidas had seen her, and Edrach. They would not be taken twice from behind.

Harifon's Woman smiled grimly. 'You just a private are, ha? Where the strength of the True Crew now is? Long ago we the sacred nineties ore found. Less you are than your grandmother's grandmother? Or in you faith in the Ship not is?'

Arno thought how easy it would be to strike Harifon's Woman, have her sneers silenced. Her sword was sharp.

As her friend tensed, Marchidas jerked her arm sideways. It distracted Harifon's Woman, as Marchidas meant it to. The girl was well aware that Harifon's Woman had nasty ways of making reprisals against children. Marchidas shuffled casually sideways, half in front of

Arno, covering Brachan's body with her Wolf-cloak, staring into the deep brown eyes of the one woman who could tolerate Captain's strange sexual tastes.

Before she could speak, Harifon's Woman said, 'And you! Dead Captain you did not tell it wrong is your betters to interrupt?'

Marchidas spoke without turning her head. 'Regrets, Arno.' Her gaze was fierce; Harifon's Woman found it funny.

'Oho! A bite from the crawl-frog!'

'Nowhere it in the Book says that the Crew of a mountain Winter should die. If the Ship really beyond the mountains is, it still there will be when the Summer comes.'

Harifon's Woman glared at Marchidas, an ugly look on her face. Marchidas could feel the waves of hatred radiating from the Woman. The vibrations were strong in the icy air between them. *I better careful had be!* Marchidas thought. *It a long way down to die is.* And from deep in the chasm a wolf's belling echoed.

'Your father never in the stars believed,' Harifon's Woman said conversationally. 'He us all on this mudball wanted to keep, where he power over us had. Why else he us all over its face would have dragged? He us from the star-family kept. Yender knew it! Hannis knew it! And where they now are?

'Gone, that's where!' Harifon's Woman was cruel in her triumph. 'And your father never them to challenge dared. He a true son of Ain Tsui was!'

Edrach said, 'The Harifon.' And Marchidas was glad of the warning, for Captain was pushing his way down through the knot of Crew on the ledge.

Marchidas stepped further away from the lip of the chasm. The statement of distrust was obvious. Arno slipped Brachan behind her out of harm's way.

Marchidas lifted her chin. 'Yes, my father a son of Ain Tsui's flesh was. And because of that he the debt wanted to repay! But it not our family was who the Book's path muddied.'

She knew she shouldn't have said that the moment the words were out of her mouth. Still, everyone knew Loi-Tsu was a grandmother's grandmother of the Woman and that she'd abandoned her son, the son of Captain Tsui, and had kept the Book from him after she'd taken it from the *Mosckva*. She'd given it instead to her new lover's children and they and their heirs had mauled it 'til the words could hardly be heard. Yet Tsui's descendants had finally stolen it back and on the hide copy that they made, Loi-Tsu's line had deliberately – so the rest

103

of the Crew said – smudged and scored out whole passages so that the way back to the Ship had been lost for centuries.

But Marchidas should never have said it to the Woman's face. Swallowing her fear, Marchidas still couldn't prevent the thought flashing through her head, *I now can't die! I all the flesh of my line left am, the debt to repay.*

Caught between two spears – the Harifon and his Woman – Marchidas eased back her cloak from her knife-arm. Even in the shadow of the canyon her Wolf-hide's colours rippled. Unobtrusively Edrach shifted to stand at Captain's back. Marchidas knew she could rely on Chosen Brother. But the ice was slippery under her feet and his.

'You again!' Captain snarled.

'She a mutinas is,' his Woman said quickly. 'She says my line the one was that the Ship-path hid.'

Captain stopped using his spear as a staff and levelled it at Marchidas's throat.

Harifon's Woman said, 'She mine is. With my bare hands. She my personal Crew will be when I with her have finished.' She threw her cloak back from her shoulders so that her hands were free, but the Woman was so contemptuous she didn't even bother to unbuckle its claw-clasp and roll the hide round her arm for defence.

And the Harifon, seeing the difference in height and weight between his Woman and the hunger-gaunted girl, slowly dropped his spear-point.

With a savage yell like a wolf's killing-note, the Woman leaped for her adversary. Her hands were clawed to tear at Marchidas's eyes.

Small heart! Marchidas dropped, and the Woman flew over her body in a tangle of arms and legs. And slid on the slick green ice.

Marchidas's scream was covered by the Woman's. For Harifon's Woman was skidding not up the trail but sideways, right off its edge.

Marchidas flailed for and found something to hold, anything to stop the Woman plummeting into that awful void. Her enemy's Wolf-hide. She spreadeagled herself, waiting eternities for the sudden strain that would tell her the Woman wouldn't die.

She groaned with the pain of it when it came. Edrach was already lying on her feet, pinning her so that she wouldn't follow Harifon's Woman into the abyss.

Everyone was shouting at once.

And, with other willing hands, they hauled up the Wolf-hide.

Harifon's Woman gave them no help. She couldn't. Her whole

104

weight had fallen against the claw-clasp around her neck, and her head was at a sickening angle. The claws were red, not steely grey; above them the bulging brown eyes would mock no-one, ever again. Gone was the cruel spirit of self-interest that had distanced the Woman from the Crew, the more since she had allied herself to the Harifon. In death she became again an individual with a name, Tarlas Ebony, to take beyond Rosaria to her sky-home.

The Harifon, breathing fast in the threatening atmosphere, thought about death and violence. Then, looking at his ex-possession whose blood was already freezing on the ice, he up-ended his spear instead.

'Her over the side tip,' he said.

'But – '

'No kindling is. Nothing for a platform is. You her to the top want to carry?'

He strode off, his face impassive, though he deliberately hid his eyes. Marchidas could only guess at the trouble building there for her. One by one the rest of the Crew fell in behind him, even Lorwen, too old for trouble and Wordweaver with her vulnerable son, until only Marchidas stood beside the corpse with Edrach Chosen Brother.

And Marchidas wrapped Harifon's Woman in her Wolf-hide and laid her at salute on the trail.

'This half-way to the stars already is,' she said, with a twisted smile. 'Now Tarlas Ebony not so far to go has.'

CHAPTER THREE

Transparently Dying

Tarlas Ebony was laid to rest, but it took time to get over the killing. Already the others were high on the chasm wall when Marchidas and Edrach began the long slog up to sunlight.

As so often, Marchidas let her spirit fly above her while her body was chained to the painful demands of this earth. She needed this mental escape from the bitter disloyalty of killing another member of the one True Crew, even if it had been a cruel accident. While her spirit soared in airy realms of imagination, singing epics whose jewelled words enshrined her future deeds of greatness, she and Edrach were struggling upwards to reach the rest of the Crew. Neither of them had any doubt that the Harifon would abandon them if he could, but they knew they stood little chance of surviving the mountains on their own. A sick man of nineteen winters now, worn thin by fever and the lightning pains in his head, and a girl in her fifteenth winter, a season Promoted and all but skin and bone. She would not have put it past the Harifon to murder them with an avalanche ...

At last they burst out of the gloomy canyon beside the crest of the thundering cascade. It was as if the world had changed from one moment to the next.

They stopped, leaning against fissured boulders to catch their breath. Mouth-speech was impossible. Even their minds were numbed by the din of the falling waters, and the glory of the suns-bright snow.

It stretched before them, sparkling, its broad smoothness broken into ugliness only by the marks of the Crew's hard passage. Even the melt-river was bridged by its sheer white crust. Upwards it swept, almost to the horizon, but far above the winds had swept clear the black bones of the col.

To their right the peak reared, jagged, harshly naked. While the shoulder of the mountain to their left was smoother, it leaped up from a vertical wall sheathed in shadows. The Crew were tiny dots of colour a third of the way up the bald snow of the saddle, and the snow they had trampled down followed them like a broken tail.

'On come, Edrach!' Marchidas encouraged. 'At least we suns' light now have.' Already she was striding forward, tossing the words over her shoulder, but there was no answer. She turned back.

Edrach was slumped against the banked snow of the Crew's passing. His face, even by Redsun's light, was grey. He was breathing stertorously through his mouth.

'Regrets,' he panted, and she could have beaten herself for driving him to such straits. The Harifon's forced marches had not given Edrach time to recover from the ruinous fever in his burst eye.

'Mine the regrets should be,' Marchidas said, kneeling beside him to rub warmth into his limbs. 'Will you some snow drink, if I it first in my hands warm?'

He nodded, too weary even to speak. Then, when she had eased his parched throat, Marchidas opened his cloak and hers. In silence they shared body-warmth under a double layer of Wolf-hide. Her hand stole up into his over-long sleeve – none of the Crew wore gloves – and as Redsun passed zenith they rested, fingers entwined in friendship.

At last Edrach felt strong enough to move. Chewing on strips of dried meat to keep their mouths moist, they made their way slowly in the wake of the Crew. And swift shadows swept over the white snow towards them.

Above each double shadow was a triangular dot, circling upwards. 'Look, Edrach,' called Marchidas, trying to interest him in anything. 'Geyrlizards!'

Still clasping her hand, Edrach stopped toiling upwards long enough to say, 'Not this high. Mountain lizards are – see? Their flesh transparent is, not the bones or the guts. Good eating, though. More meat than geyrlizards. Maybe the Crew one of them for supper will kill.'

The Crew had to share knowledge to live, but his duty had worn his sick body out. Doggedly he began to put one foot in front of another. He kept his gaze on the rough pathway, seeming too appalled to face the endless trek upwards.

Marchidas, though, was entranced by the gliders. She wondered how it would be if she could ride one across the skies, looking down *through* the blood-tracery of its wings. The thrill of it sang in her blood,

107

making her forget how cold she was. *I Edrach to the warmth of the winterground could take! And in Spring, when bright new crystals fresh beauty to the Red bring, we straight to the Ship would fly ...*

The Ballad of Edrach and Marchidas! We for ever sung will be, wherever campfires the darkness of the plains throw back!

'Down!' Edrach jerked her off her feet. A glider's obscene talons raked over her, retracted at the last moment so as not to foul in the snow-bank.

Marchidas rolled to a crouch, spear-head thrust upwards. Each lizard circled, hungry; three of them. *Where were the rest?*

The first lizard wheeled overhead again. In the gap between wing-arch and dorsal-ridge, Marchidas saw two more slip-streaming past the face of the black peak. She jabbed and saw the mass of the lizard above her shrink from her spear-tip. At the edges of her mind she could feel the huge beast's puzzlement.

Unbeknown to her, far above, Arno had begun to hurl herself downwards, sledging desperately back towards them on her cloak. The Harifon yelled orders to her, unheeded.

The three lizards banked into a climbing turn. Marchidas watched them, trying to learn something to give her an edge. Each vast wing projected more than a spear's length either side of the ridge which held it up from the lizard's body; the membrane stretched over the rigid frame of cartilage was clear but an ugly pink where veins showed through. True gliders, they could not flap their single wing, only unfurl it so that when the dorsal-ridge rose, the wing funnelled air under its delta of membrane to lift the racing body that hung underneath.

Marchidas turned slightly, tracking the nearest lizard with her spear. It seemed pitifully inadequate, a tooth-pick pitted against a winged beast that dwarfed even Edrach. But it was all she could do, except lie down and be eaten. Her spear-tip quivered, but she held to it nonetheless. Behind her she felt Edrach do the same.

Oh, the comfort of Chosen Brother! But there was no time to feel it: talons clawed down at her. Marchidas linked her mind to her enemy's, searching for a way to undo its plans.

She held her aim, breath stilled by fear and the lizard's concentration. When the beast was almost upon her, she fought the lizard's presence in her mind and straightened and the spear buried itself in the scales of the lizard's breast. She cried its death-scream's echo.

The thing fell on her, its weight knocking the air out of her lungs. From its absurdly small beak, blood trickled down into her mouth.

Marchidas retched, choking. Her limbs were pinned, helpless, under the hot writhing pink glass of its scales. She could see nothing but the dying canopy of lizard-flesh, yet beyond the roaring of its blood in her ears she heard Edrach grunt with effort, and the creak of other glider-muscles.

As the wind leaked out of the dying glider's sail, the corpse pressed down harder on Marchidas, pushing her deeper into the snow. She was stifling in whiteness, her eyes blanked out, her ears stopped ... But the lizard wasn't quite a corpse. Its heart-beat drilled through Marchidas's chest, its labouring breaths compelled her lungs. The thread of its life-blood forced into her gasping mouth. And its mind screamed in hers.

Frantic, she struggled. Strained every nerve. Cramped her muscles to fight off the lizard's weight ...

But it was struggling too, its resistance varying as it spasmed towards retreating life. She could get no hold on the slithering, pulsing scales of its thorax, and death battled it, a dark numbness that crushed it even as she was battling in terror against her own crushing death.

The more she fought, the closer her mind was linked to the dying lizard's. Individuality was gone. Only the blackness remained to them, and it was coming closer.

Then their awareness was in a tunnel that was flawed with life, and life's brightness faded ...

CHAPTER FOUR

Edrach Unnamed

A flicker of awareness returned to Tohalla. Self came back. She was kneeling in the irrelevant glory of the sunset before her un-wedding, in a glade outside the Green, and through her hands had passed another woman's dying.

Tohalla shuddered with the shock of life beating in her veins. She had forgotten to breathe; or, with Marchidas, her lungs had ceased to function. Now a sharp, ragged breath tore through her fossilized lungs and she swayed, on the point of collapse.

A strong hand reached to steady her.

Edrach!

She flinched from him, the old man with the shambles of a face. Tohalla saw him at her side, knew he watched her recoil, knew he understood and that the understanding hurt.

Good! How could he have left Marchidas to die? She had chosen him for her brother. He could have saved them both, but he had thought only of himself. His body's disfigurement was nothing to that of his spirit.

Tohalla pulled away from him, supporting herself by her hands, her forgotten hands which still clasped the heart of the messenger.

Edrach cried out, 'No! Tohalla! Tohalla?' but she had abandoned him as he had abandoned Marchidas ...

It happened faster this time. Already linked to Marchidas's experience, she was pulled out of herself and through the life-tides of smaller things that overlay the expected emptiness in the life-space of –

Marchidas! A faint, glimmering strand of awareness: life! And the sheer surprise of it was strong enough to fan the feeble gleam. The wonder that life could be at all. The vision of death's black tunnel was overwhelming ...

110

Something lurched on her and she felt the weight of it pinning her down. The noises she hadn't noticed became clearer, more defined: whistles, hoots, a bellowing of defiance. The mountain lizards!

Adrenalin pumped into her, panic ripped at her eyes because she couldn't see. She couldn't open them! She was stifling!

Again whatever-it-was jerked on her chest, suddenly heavier. Marchidas (*that* was her identity!) groaned involuntarily as her ribs were squashed, but then the thing shifted and her diaphragm succeeded in dragging air into her lungs once again. Her own lungs, not the lizard's, for she was on her own once more. Poignant regret for the creature's dying lanced through her, but at least she, Marchidas, had not died with it. Her purpose might yet be accomplished. If she lived, she could steal back the Book. Last Daughter of First Captain's line, she could pay back the debt of blood to the Crew ...

Moreover, she could now move one arm.

The terrifying shrieks impinged again and there came into her dull sensibility a realization: her life was at the mercy of the mountain-lizards' hunger! By sheer will-power Marchidas moved the numbed arm. Fiery sensation tingled in her fingers as her blood scorched sluggishly down through them. *I hurt, so I alive am* ... For how much longer?

After eons her hand found her face. There was something sticky, crusty, bad-smelling on her eyes.

I blind am! Like Edrach I blind am! But to have lost *both* eyes ...

By touch she felt her eye-sockets, dreading to find the caved-in, ruptured orbs leaking slime.

But her eye-lids were rounded. Complete. And the same scabby stuff trailed down her face and choked into her mouth ...

The lizard's blood! Marchidas could have laughed at her own stupidity – if she hadn't been so stunned by relief. But the corpse above her heaved again – lizard-scales resolved out of abstract *touch* – and the harsh sounds of the gliders frightened her more in her darkness. Hastily she worked up spit in her dry mouth, but it took too long.

Another sensation settled itself into a feeling of great cold. The snow! She smeared it on her fingers, scrubbed at her eyes.

Light was a pain that cleansed her when she prised one eyelid open. And then Marchidas understood why the corpse wouldn't rest quietly. The gliders were fighting over the corpse of the one she had killed. She flinched as, a scant hand-span above her hard-won eyes, bloody talons tore gobbets of meat from the steaming rib-cage. More daylight stabbed down at her as the lizard, with constant glances around, snatched its booty up to its tiny mouth. And she'd be next on the menu if someone didn't do something about it.

Edrach! Where was he, Chosen Brother? Marchidas reached out for his comforting presence in her mind. And there, where it had always been, was nothing. A void.

Edrach had gone.

Frightened now as she hadn't been before, Marchidas thought, *Edrach too weak to fight was. Too weak to stand.* Self-loathing swelled in her. *I him let die! For my father he blinded was, and beaten, and I him let die.*

Marchidas lay motionless, forcing herself not to move as the lizard rent its prey. Between the arching ribs of the corpse she saw its cold eyes, one at a time as it turned its head. She saw the wicked claws stuff meat into the obscenity of its mouth, and the mouth spill it clumsily, and when the lizard swallowed she saw the meat jerk down bloodily through its almost transparent neck. And, in the reeking space between dorsal-ridge and sail-wing, she saw the other lizards coming back.

They swooped down on the raptor. Almost she could have warned it, so unaware did it seem, so intent on stuffing itself with the dead glider's stomachs.

At the last moment it shrilled a whistle of defiance, fouling the nearest lizard's wing-tip with its own forcing the beast to crumple into the banked-up snow.

The lizard feeding on her dead lizard – the complexity of the idea burned her brain in dazzling confusion – ran a few paces, lofting its canopy, and the wind caught and held it, let it fall to run again. The flying lizards chased it off. Then they turned on their fallen comrades, one struggling, one empty.

Even though she was tunnelling through the snow, Marchidas gagged at the stench of ripped intestine.

She burrowed downslope, heading for the undersnow river. Though she tried to keep her hands inside the long sleeves, still they stung with the cold. Whenever her tunnel grew stuffy Marchidas fought off the dizziness, the darkness in her vision, the loneliness, until she could bear it no longer and she must pierce a hole to the sky that the lizards might see. *That wrong is! Edrach! Why you not in my head are, to put my thoughts all neat?*

Alone, with the white radiance roofing over her and the melt-river for cold company, Marchidas stayed until almost dark. The cruel waters thundered black beside her and she knew if she slipped on the icy curves of the tunnel they would dash her down the waterfall to her death.

At dusk she hoped the lizards would have gone. In any case she couldn't stay here, so she began to cut her way free. Mistrusting the tunnel-mouth's strength, she dug away from the roaring, echoing death of Whitesun at the lip of the abyss, and forced a way with her longknife through the packed snow above her.

Clouds were dulling Rosaria's stars, mopping them up one by one as Marchidas dragged her trembling legs back to the site of her fourth battle. Her long hours chewing dried meat in the melt-river's hidden way she had spent composing an epic. A fitting death-poem for her Chosen Brother, shorter than it should have been for such a man, cutting off suddenly as his life had been cut off, before the honour of finding the Ship. And unless Wordweaver dared speak of him wherever the Harifon camped tonight, Edrach would have no other death-song. Because Marchidas very much doubted she would get out of this alive.

She searched. She lifted up the almost colourless lizard-flesh with its dead weight of bones. In the faltering light reflected from the snow she tried to find Chosen Brother's body to honour it. Tiny scales of snow feathered downwards and still she sought him with her cold-stung hands.

But Marchidas did not find him, because he wasn't there to be found. Not even half-eaten. And footsteps tracked upslope to the Harifon's crew.

Chosen Brother had deserted her.

Edrach had lost his name.

Live will I and the Ship find, sang the pattern of her footfalls. *I about Edrach no longer care. I never did care* – but she cut that bit from the litany that kept her going. Marchidas couldn't make herself believe it. When she dug for rootbalm in the frozen earth, she did it because Edrach had shown her where to look. When she burned wolf-fire, it was Edrach who had shown her how to ignite it without searing her mind.

I the Ship will find and Edrach from the glory keep. I him will show! I for the line of Ain Tsui the debt will repay.

But the shadows in Marchidas's thoughts kept her from going over the pass to find safety with the True Crew. Weren't they the True

Crew? Didn't they have the Book now? *And* – pain comes in many shades of night – *that me a mutinas makes. If I children have, I to them as children of Ain Tsui another shame bring. But if my Chosen Brother, who his name in joy sought … if Edrach now the Harifon follows, I with the Crew not long enough for children would live.*

Edrach …

The dissonance of thoughts vibrated like a knife ringing on stone – and fracturing.

A winter alone was more than she could bear, together with the knowledge that even Edrach didn't want her. Only death looked for her, though sometimes she didn't hide from him. Yet deep within her Marchidas knew that even the Iron Men would be better than dying with no-one to know but herself. Sometimes she thought of the messenger – she'd record her death. That would shake him. Them. But the messengers were sleeping under warmer ground. *Besides, I the last of my line am. I yet can't die, not until the treachery's undone. I the Ship have to find …*

And each lonely step down below the tree-line was a step further from the True Crew, from rightness. But when she saw smoke spiralling or the flicker of a fire in the chilly dusk, Marchidas could not make herself go closer. By knives or distancing, people hurt.

In a wooded valley on the southern slopes, where the suns had banished snow to the hollows and to a skim of ice on a suns' bright lake, she found a dead razorback. Cousins to the spineders, traitors to the Green, the Edge had not kept them out of the Red. Now the colonists wouldn't have them on the land their alien Green scarred.

Marchidas, feral in her hunger, dropped to the ground, watching. Whitesun cast long shadows, sinking below her over the plains. And cunning, shifty Redsun was her friend, arcing so fast that movement would have shown a running shadow, arrowing towards anything that might rob her of her meat. Out here, beyond the lilac spearwood trees, she waited.

Ears – mind – tremors in the coiling mountain-red under her palms – there was nothing but a distant belling of geyrlizards on the breeze. Here, with odd lumps of rock sitting on the low, rippling growth, Marchidas had weapons enough to scare them off. She could find no animal scent to disturb the sharp breeze of the winter's dying.

Marchidas lay long enough to be sure that no beast, not so much as a ripperclaw, was working towards the razorback. Nothing lurking outside the shelter of the distant blue-trees.

114

And the juices of her mouth made her stomach echo through her body.

Abruptly Marchidas rolled to her feet and ran, her toes automatically avoiding the painful stones.

Anyway, no beast of prey had killed the female razorback. She had obviously caught her forefoot in a crack between two up-thrust rocks. The foreleg was still there, upthrust at an angle that had splintered the bones through the kneepad.

Circling, Marchidas saw the poor beast had taken a long time to die; white sweat crusted the slatey hide and the mountain-red was torn and scattered where the razorback had tried to plunge free. Her glorious collar of spines had been no use to her at all. And at this time of year, with grazing sparse, the rest of the herd might be days away from the breeding-lake. She had had no comfort in her dying.

Which also meant Marchidas wouldn't have to fight the herd-mother.

Still she could scarcely trust her luck, but the razorback was barely cooling. The meat was fresh.

And as she laboured happily over the butchering, a voice said, 'Enough for two is?'

CHAPTER FIVE

The Ironman and the Razorback

Marchidas almost fainted with the shock. Another voice. Another human after the winter of cold and dark thoughts milling down the sharpness of her mind. And she had lost the habit-groove of people which might have helped her react.

Mutinas! Iron Man or Wild Man or Crew, whatever he was, he was not of the True Book. Murderer. Outcast. *Mutinas!*

Her pupils widened in fear – reflex so that she could flick a glance wider to scan for attack.

But he didn't attack.

He didn't even look at the butcher-knife dripping red in her hand.

'I with no-one else stand,' he said. 'If not enough for two is, I go will,' and his voice shook with a tremor that he could not suppress.

Marchidas tossed a haunch at his feet. She meant him to go away, to leave her in safe loneliness, but the winter-thin man said, 'I a fire will make. I salt have. Sodium salt.' Which she needed.

Better him to have where I an eye on him can keep, thought Marchidas, and said, 'For tonight, then.'

'Until Rednoon I your blood will share.'

Wary one of the other, they dipped thumb and finger in the razorback's blood and touched it to each other's hand. Because, if a mutinas could keep his blood-sealed word, until then Marchidas would be safe from him.

And by what he did, she saw in his eyes that he hoped he would be safe from her.

He had no Wolf-hide. He cooked in a vertical tunnel in one of the walls of his camp and Marchidas could hardly see the embers of his fire caged behind – metal?

116

The camp itself was dark, with straight walls softening to curve low overhead. She had had to crawl through a hole in the earth-bank to follow him in. On her skin there was no feel of the living wind, only warmth. Marchidas felt as if she were dead.

Redsun hurled itself below the rim of the world. When Whitesun set, she made herself be still as he cut off the last light from the sky with a weaving of blue-wood over the crawl-space. Now Marchidas could feel the flesh of the hill pressing down overhead. It was worse than in the cave the river had made under the snow. At least there she hadn't had to pretend she wasn't afraid.

But the meat smelled good.

In the dim ruddy glow from the tame fire she saw him reach forward at last to lift the strange oval – pan? box? – off the coals. Marchidas was very glad. Game had hidden from her as the winter-beasts went to sleep, and the summer ones had not yet set foot on ground still moist from snowfall; she felt half-starved. Also she had made up her mind that once she had eaten, she would leave this trap under the earth.

What he handed her was an oval of blue-wood. Marchidas didn't know what to do with it.

Studiously looking at the task in hand, he – *what his name is?* – unhinged the two halves of the shallow oval dish and handed her one full of meat. Marchidas could feel the herb-scented steam of it on her face. He balanced the dish on the blue-wood on his knees and ate. It was strange – the Crew always shared a common bowl; that way there was less to carry on the trek. Wary, Marchidas copied the mutinas.

Afterwards, when both of them were too full to want to move, it seemed less important that she couldn't put the distance of an ordinary camp-fire between them.

'Will you dream-smoke share?' he asked.

'Mmm.' Marchidas was drowsy from the heat and her full stomach. She heard the rustle of his clothing as he moved, saw its piebald patches more clearly when the dream-wood clinked and poked sparks from the embers. Soon its strange, entrancing light let her see him as an individual for the first time, now that her hostility had guttered and he wasn't just *enemy*. But she was too sleepy to care much. Besides, she had either too much to tell, or too little to say. What was the point of beginning?

When the wreaths of dream-smoke bound them together, he said, 'Benhannon my given name is.'

His voice was firmer now, and it recalled her mind from a great distance – a tenor call that seemed only another part of the

117

pleasantness that wrapped her.

'What response from me do you want?' Marchidas didn't mean to say that, but her rational filter seemed to have got stuck in the dryness under her tongue.

He moved abruptly. She jerked awake, ready to defend herself, but he was merely shifting to lounge more comfortably on the earthen floor. 'Dreams to share, each the other's indentity at least a little must know, or the dreams in common no sense will make.'

Marchidas nodded. It felt good in the dream-smoke so she did it again. 'That sense makes.' *But outside the Crew, who I am?*

'A name me give,' he prompted.

And that was easy. 'Only Marchidas. I not long enough promoted was an earned name to have.'

'A secret, no?'

Marchidas smiled sadly, liking the romance of it now it was all so far away. 'Not in the True Crew. It no secret was to them.'

'But you not with them now are, Marchidas.'

'No. They left me. *And I why don't know!*' Her thought was outside her now, resonating on the cosy air like the drops of a waterspout.

He let it settle, and she seemed to see its rainbow fall to peace. At last he said, 'I in the Iron Caves was born. I it hated. I left.'

'You your people *left?*' Marchidas said, incredulous, and in her brain it rang: *Mutinas!*

Benhannon ignored her recoil. 'They not my people were. By birth, perhaps, but not by choice. My spirit did not know how metal to guide. They only metal love, and fighting. They said, "You of the Red have eaten." Even my mother it said when I in the pits a captive would not kill. I her face now can see; contempt in the folds around her eyes, and the men and the women in the torch-light me with their hate battered when I the brand-rod threw down.'

Benhannon's face changed; half a smile grew. 'I said, "I in this place no longer will stay," but they me didn't hear, so loud did they roar. That a sound you know is? One voice and one voice and one voice, they together as another sound out come. They me out kicked, but I it first said, "I in this place will not stay." '

He shrugged one skinny shoulder, dappled in the purple light. 'So that my secret is, that even my once-people never will know. And they think that they it all know.'

And Marchidas, through half-closed lids, watched him fall silent. She did not know what to say, and so she said nothing, and the longer she said nothing, the worse the silence became. Then she feigned

118

sleep to break the embarrassment, and the dream-smoke interlaced their paths, not together, but side by side, with a barrier through which neither could reach the other's hand.

In the cheerful morning Marchidas slipped out of her furs. She had meant to be quiet, to let Benhannon sleep on, but the only light in his camp was a dusty ray breaking in through the cook-tunnel. She was clumsy in the dark and cursed under her breath when the wicker clattered aside. He merely groaned, and stretched, and seemed to fall asleep again.

Marchidas was glad. She wanted time to herself, a time to get ready and go away from the discomfort she had caused Benhannon. She would be long gone by the time he woke up ... There was the rest of the butchery to do too, if the ripper-claws and geyrlizards had left her anything on the carcase. But she stopped, on hands and knees, at the mouth of the crawl-space.

Overnight Winter had birthed Spring. Marchidas brushed the dirt off her knees and stood, just breathing. Air rushed pure and clear into her, seeming to pour along every blood-way until she was as clean and light as the morning.

Crystalline tinklings sounded elusively on the breeze off the lake. A million tiny rainbows sparkled to confirm the sounds of new growth bursting out into the warmth. Everywhere was the scent of fresh growing, and the mountain-red coiled and danced at her feet. The suns behind the blue-wood were curtained by a tracery more complicated than yesterday's, pale, mauve-tipped, translucent. Her spirits rose on the flashing wings of the arrowfalls high in the morning, and when she heard their chiming calls she felt she could have flown beside them.

'The arrowfalls Winter back north have chased,' Benhannon said.

Marchidas hadn't heard him come out. His words dropped like stones in a pool to muddy her experience, but the morning was so bright that the ripples refracted her joy and her annoyance disappeared.

'Look! The ice nearly all in the sunshine has gone.'

'Yes.' He moved to stand beside her. 'There only a little is where the trees their shadow on the lake cast.'

His elbow almost touched hers. She could feel the warmth of it, companionable now rather than an invasion of the mind-space she needed. She glanced at him shyly, a little sideways flick of her eyes, and saw him smiling too with the same joy she felt. They shared a grin and his face felt like the winterground: a safe place to come to. It didn't matter that it was unfamiliar, that his nose was broken and one cheekbone far from smooth. His skin was young between the wrinkles.

'The razorbacks soon to the lake will come to hatch,' he said, glorying in new life.

'Then we the butchering over and done with must get, or we the herdmother will have to fight.' They both sighed at Marchidas's practicality, but it was true.

'I back in ten heart-beats will be,' Benhannon said, and climbed over the roof of his camp with such comical angularity that she laughed as he had intended.

Redsun on the edge of Whitesun's disc was a scant finger's breadth above the spearwood when they set off after their morning duties. At first they jogged but that soon became a race. Marchidas won easily. 'Anyway,' Benhannon said, trying for a dignified drawl between his laboured gasps, 'Iron Men don't run.'

'So it appears.' She mimicked the mockery of his tone. Both of them laughed, but Marchidas was concerned for his weakness. *Perhaps he ill has been?* Now that she noticed he certainly didn't seem very strong.

'Look!' he said a moment later, 'A crawlfrog!' And they laughed when the azure lizard hopped in surprise. Sunning itself placidly, it hadn't heard their thoughts approaching.

They enjoyed the walk. It didn't seem half so long without the suspicions and weariness of the day before. The spring sunshine had melted the frost, evaporated its moisture. Rosaria sparkled, rejoicing. When they panted up the hill, it was more from laughter than breathlessness. Then, as a flight of geyrlizards raced away from the chewed remains of the female razorback, they sobered.

Once again Marchidas quartered the area, but there was no trail of anything larger than a ripperclaw. Bent low to examine the ground, she scarcely noticed that Benhannon took no precautions at all, just walked up behind the shell of bones and hide and spines.

When he was almost on top of the carcase, he yelled, jumped backwards and fell in a startled tangle of limbs.

Alerted to danger, Marchidas ran to him, drawing her long-knife. 'What it is?' she called, sheltering behind the creature's back.

'She not dead is!' Benhannon said.

Marchidas touched the slate-coloured corpse; it was stiff as a board where it wasn't hollow. 'Yes, she is.'

'But she moved! I her saw!'

Marchidas looked. There was no arrow plucking at the flesh and away in the sky over the lake, the lizards were only feathers against the blue. Scanning the wood's edge, she could see nothing hiding in the sprawling shadows of the undergrowth.

Benhannon called, 'There it again is!'

And Marchidas laughed. Because what had jolted Benhannon was a ripperclaw tunnelling into the meat to hide from him. At first he was hurt by her mirth, retreating into huffy formality, but soon he grinned too as he saw the funny side of it. 'What can you expect?' He shrugged, quirked an eyebrow so rapidly that she smiled. 'This land strange to a dweller in the Iron Caves is.'

'Now you here wait, and for bigger enemies out watch,' she told him. 'I some wolf-fire must find. Ripperclaws from smoke always run.'

'What wolf-fire is?' asked Benhannon.

Marchidas looked at him, amazed. To her fifteen winters' perception Benhannon seemed quite old. The wrinkles around his eyes and mouth must have been the same age as she was; the flesh that wore them twice that in the broad light.

'How you so long have lived without wolf-fire making?'

He countered her youthful scorn. 'We Iron Men no wolf-fire need, whatever it is. We not primitive are. You no fire-box have?' Benhannon sounded amazed. 'Here, a fire lay and I it will light.'

An Iron Man thinking a Crew-woman primitive? How dare he? I'll him kill! Yet Marchidas laid her anger by until there was time for it. Food came first.

Marchidas kept a weather-eye out for enemies as she ran, but nothing human or animal was in sight. In the fringes of the blue-wood she found old, dull vegetation that was cracked and dry. Breaking off a double armful from under the new season's growth, she trotted back with it, squatting beside him.

Benhannon struck sparks from an earth-crystal. The sparks jumped out from between his striking-stones onto some soft, grey stuff that he quickly covered with her purple spearwood. Then, as the flames popped and crackled into light, he and Marchidas flapped the smoke towards the razorback.

As the blue smoke curled into its body-cavity, they both heard the ripperclaw scrabbling at the stiffened hide. When they looked moments later they saw not one but two ripperclaw tails disappearing downwards. In a matter of heartbeats, even the tunnelling sounds were gone.

'Benhannon? Regrets that I so rude was.' Marchidas studied the ground between her feet. 'Your fire-box well works wherever you are.'

Knee to knee with her, he gave the same spurious attention to the red crystals budding at his feet, but he said just as softly, 'Will you one day me show what your wolf-fire is?'

Marchidas nodded, forgetting that he wasn't looking at her. The tension of anger eased in her stomach. For the first time he didn't feel like a stranger. All the same, she said briskly, 'Better on with it get. I the herd-mother on us don't want, thinking that we her sister killed.'

Already her knife was slicing into the meat, cutting out the chunks the scavengers hadn't had time for. She squeezed out the intestines and coiled them over her shoulder.

'The hide spoiled is,' Benhannon pointed out. 'Enough there is new boots for me to make?'

Marchidas didn't understand how he could be ignorant of something so obvious. She glanced up at him, squinting against the strong morning light. And, by the slight movement the gesture gave to her body, her hand touched something that palpitated in the entrails.

It was her turn to be startled. She fell over backwards, automatically rolling to land on her feet again, one boot-heel in the ashes of the fire.

'What it is?' Benhannon asked her, struggling to contain his mirth.

'Another ripperclaw ... I think. But they all with the smoke should have gone.'

Squatting again, sharing his grin, she probed among the creature's stomachs. Her grin faded.

'See, Benhannon.' Her fingers tapped something hard, oval, pale grey. 'The sac almost ready to break is.'

He came to kneel beside her. 'Truth is. Look! They moving are. And can you them hear?'

She nodded. Dark shapes moved erratically inside the hard birth-sac. 'So close they came ... she came.' Marchidas stroked the lifeless fur behind the razorback's knee. 'She brave was. And for nothing.'

'They die will?'

Again she nodded slowly. 'Yes, without water to hatch them. And the herd them from predators to keep safe.'

'At least we them to the lake carry can, na? Then they a chance will have. Agree? Or shall I it do?'

'No.' Marchidas felt quite protective to the tiny razorbacks all of a sudden. She had the feeling that she, as a woman, should finish off the dead female's mission. 'Your fingers mind,' she told him abruptly.

Quickly she cut out the birth-sac. It was easy – the internal connections were already withdrawn; she knew the razorback would

122

already have deposited the sac safely in the shallows if she had lived. The ripperclaws had gnawed away most of the stiffened muscles, but they hadn't been able to breach the hard, crystalline shell.

'A race is,' Benhannon warned her. 'See down there? Where the blue-trees down to the lake reach? The herd coming is.'

Marchidas looked; it was true. Some thirty blobs of grey were moving fast, throwing up white spray as they galloped over the edge of the dazzling waters. From this distance she could not hear the clashing of their collars of spines, but she knew the razorbacks would be upon her soon, wanting to tear and rend and spike her as a predator on their kind. On their four webbed feet, a bundle of spines sticking up from a single vertebra between their shoulders, the razorbacks raced over the lake towards her.

She worked urgently. The sac came free at last and, running, Benhannon beside her, she carried it in her bloody hands down to the wind-rippled shallows. Almost at once the shell began to dissolve, except where she had left sticky red hand-prints on it.

'On come!' Benhannon yelled above splashing and clattering. He was already wading out of the ice-cold water, head turned back in fear as the herd came to defend its kind.

Marchidas risked a glance. Huge, dark, the razorbacks loomed half-seen in the pale clouds of spray, and the suns' light slid along their neck-lances. They weren't called razorbacks for nothing.

Already three little razorbacks were swimming in the clear waters around Marchidas, examining the pebbles, nuzzling her hands, waiting to be fed. Their webbed claws tickled, still soft, and the tiny spines on the backs of their necks fanned without co-ordination. But the last two would die unless she could scrub the thick blood off the crystal rim of their birth-cells. Frantic, Marchidas scooped gravel from the bottom and ooze muddied the water so that she couldn't see what she was doing. She lifted the unwieldy sac above the surface, trying to ignore the herd's thunderous approach. Already the herd-mother was gonging a challenge.

'Run, Benhannon!' she shouted. 'I you in a heart-beat join. Run!'

He hesitated, ran. Marchidas was clumsy with fear and the hard shell was slick between her fingers, but she couldn't leave the dead mother's job unfinished. Heart galloping like those webbed claws on the surface of lake, she scrubbed furiously one last time.

Then she threw the sac from her and swam. Beneath the dazzling surface she was hardly more than a scented shadow. The herd stopped, milled and plunged, allowed themselves to sink in a semi-circle around their leader. They could see that there was only one small enemy; their champion needed no support. Enjoying their conversation and the coolness of the lake on their heavy winter coats, the razorbacks watched their own sacs dispersing.

Marchidas, lungs straining and lights exploding in her eyes, surfaced at the point of fainting. Eyes level with the surface, she looked back to see the joyful union of the hatchlings with their kind.

And was appalled. Though the rest of the razorbacks were spreading peacefully, dropping their own birth-sacs or flirting with the smaller, weaker males in their midst, the herd-mother took one of the new-hatched in her teeth and shook it. Water spun from it. And blood. And a thin desperate belling which stopped abruptly. Then the herd-mother threw the tainted thing aside.

'*No!*' Marchidas cut off her own yell. Anguish fuelled her; she swam underwater, so fast that a current surged out in front of her, carrying her scent to the muzzle of the herd-mother. The razorback's head was submerged, sniffing out the other two hatchlings who bore the alien scent. She would deal with them the same way she dealt with any deformity.

The odour on the new current distracted the herdmother. She lifted her muzzle above the surface, shaking the water from it in a flashing arc. Her eyes, unlike the scent-fronds grouped around her mouth, were much more acute in air.

Marchidas's foot broke the surface. At once the herd-mother spread her claws and began to paddle faster and faster. Her body rose higher in the water until she was galloping on its waves, and iridescent arches of water winged in her wake.

Dimly Marchidas saw the dark claws in their clouds of bubbles. No time to fight the razorback's mind. Instead Marchidas gulped air and spun back sideways, under. The razorback's speed worked against her and she overshot.

The herdmother churned at the surface, sinking as she lost momentum. Over her shoulder Marchidas could see the beast fighting the water's drag. The dagger-sharp spines clashed from forward attack to point rearwards, lying flat along the razorback's flanks to lessen resistance.

Marchidas flailed towards the remains of the birth-sac she had carried. Desperately she tried to find the hatchlings but the water was silted with the razorback's passing. In the one unbroken birth-cell the tiny razorback was dead. And wavelets slapped Marchidas's skin where the herd-mother was charging her again.

124

'*Where are you?*' yelled Marchidas at the unseen hatchlings. Rage and frustration thickened her ragged voice. Fright ran trembling along her limbs impelled by her racing heart.

'Give it up, Marchidas!'

Marchidas heard Benhannon's voice. Instinctively her head had snapped round at hearing his call. *Does he nothing know?* She turned back, angry at being distracted (Edrach would never have done that), needing to know where the herd-mother was – and something nibbled her toes.

The herdmother clawed viciously out at her and missed. She was so close that spray was flung into Marchidas's face. Marchidas slapped the shower from her eyes and dived sideways under the muddy water.

Again the razorback sped past, pulling up in a welter of webbed claws. The huge spines swivelled forwards, swinging out level with the massive head. Marchidas could see the herd-mother as a giant darkness on the water. Speared on the razorback's fury, Marchidas was terrified.

The hatchlings were back, scrabbling at her legs. Absently, almost, Marchidas grabbed them and stuffed them into the depths of her pocket. She backed gently towards the shore, her long-knife in one hand. It was a fraction of the neck-lances' size.

Step by step the herd-mother advanced. There was less and less depth for Marchidas to manoeuvre in. First her arms and then her feet struck bottom. She pulled her legs under her in a crouch –

And leaped up, yelling.

The herd-mother shied. Recovered. Reared so that falling she could impale the intruder on her cruel spines.

Marchidas rolled aside and floundered to her feet again. The razorback plunged after her, a powerful jump that put her only a skin's width from Marchidas.

Marchidas swept her arm round and let go a fistful of mud. The razorback caracoled, gonging in fear. By the time she landed Marchidas was out of the shallows and running as fast as she could in her soaked clothing.

Behind her she heard the rumble of the champion's claws, felt her fury flowing out to tangle Marchidas's feet. Marchidas stood no chance of outrunning any razorback, let alone the strongest in the herd. The razorback would be on her in a heartbeat …

Marchidas, helpless, went on fighting the cling of her clothes, the herd-mother's hate. *In give*, howled the blood in her ears, *rest …*

Then, as the razorback's spines punched through her flapping tunic and her heart threatened to stop from fear, Marchidas spied a thread of smoke curling in the breeze. If it was smoke. If it wasn't a spore-dance behind those chameleon clusters ...

Dodging, leaping, she cleared the orange brush. And landed in a volcano of ecstasy. She was safe.

Benhannon had lit a circle of fire.

Hands still cupped unknowing on the heart of the messenger, Tohalla felt the tears flowing down her face, tears of relief that the girl who lived inside her mind had been strong enough to save the little ones. And tears, too, that Tohalla had not saved her own dead, and fear that this murderous Red might taint her unborn child. Yet Marchidas's joy shone in a smile beneath Tohalla's tears; this woman from when Edrach was young gave strength to the daughter of the Green and the purpose was becoming clearer ...

CHAPTER SIX

The Sixth Battle

By the time dusk reached down to encircle them with its gentle caress, the tiny razorbacks were nestled in Marchidas's mind as well as in her arms. And on a level below his awareness, Benhannon was jealous.

They sat outside the crawl-way to his camp; or rather Marchidas did and he did too because he didn't want to be alone. Both of them were chewing the bitter-sweet buds of new marwit so that the hatchlings could eat the pulpy mess when the humans spat it out into their hands. Marchidas was enraptured by the creatures' simple dependence; it made her feel wanted.

Rialon-star lifted above the shoulder of the hills, bringing down the cool winds of evening. Benhannon shivered ostentatiously. Marchidas didn't even notice.

'Cold is,' Benhannon said. The tickling of the razorback's paws on his palm was beginning to get on his nerves.

Marchidas took a time to answer, 'Yes. The spring-star too young is much warmth to bring. I suppose we soon in should go.' But she didn't move until he got up himself.

She set her hatchling down beside his in a bowl of water near his strange, captive fire. The baby razorbacks swelled almost visibly as they splashed about. Kneeling, Marchidas flicked a finger for them to chase. 'Look, Benhannon! Already they the size of my hand are. At Whitenoon they only the length of my little finger were.'

He grunted but she didn't know it meant *stop playing*. Finally he said, 'Let them sleep, na?'

She sighed with content, lying prone with her chin cupped in her hands to watch them curl up on the sand she had heaped in the middle of the water. 'I a baby want.'

127

Benhannon said, 'Because you a couple of little animals as playthings have, you a human child want? What for? So you with that too can play until you tired of it are?'

Marchidas rolled sideways to touch him. He shifted away a fraction, but she laid her fingers gently over his and said, 'Please?'

He snorted. 'Please, Benhannon, me a baby make because I one want?' Even he was repelled by the bitter mockery in his tone.

'No,' she said as evenly as she could. 'Please your mind with me share. Or if that too much is, at least your feelings.'

The same words but two languages. They thought they understood each other.

Instead, he replied in words. Marchidas felt the rejection that wasn't there. How was she to know that the Iron Men didn't have Red-speech? She listened to the sounds his tongue formed, really tried to listen for his meaning, but she heard it resonate through her reality that he didn't comprehend, and her pain was a distant feeling that sat somewhere in her body.

'On Rosaria,' he said, 'death is. Everything fights – wolves hunt, and then each other for the prize kill; razorbacks outsiders kill. Men the whole planet for their living fight. For land or a brooch or a drink they knives into each others' hearts plunge. Or for leadership, or a new truth they to glory can ride.'

Already Marchidas was longing to interrupt. *You so wrong are! No – how I say what I mean can, in words that inside him will reach?*

And fighting through his thoughts, against the current of hers and back again, some of his meaning came through: 'Everywhere, even on the homestars that the *Mosckva* us from brought, where life is, death is. Anger and pain, and for what? There no point is.'

'No!' she yelled. (Did he think, as she did, *You wrong are?*) She lowered her voice half an octave after her stupid shouting, trying now to be soothing and reasonable. (In the firelight he reached behind him to check that the blue-wood shield was hiding them from enemies.) 'Life is!' (*Please believe me.*) 'This morning you it felt, like I did. Everything growing, rejoicing, filling the gaps of the Winter-death with sparkling forms and bright song.' *Why you with me your mind won't share? I this to you could show, but you me won't let …*

He drew breath, his answer wanting air on which to imprint itself, but she would listen to him in a minute, she knew what he was going to say. Marchidas hurried on, cross-legged now and leaning forward in her urgency, 'This time round, maybe one hatchling dies, but another lives, and maybe it a better kind will be, or a child who up will grow and something better to us all show. We not the end are. We not alone are. Somewhere' – her arms waved – 'others like us are, or not like us, and one of us or one of them the next step will be. Here no warring crowds are. Rosaria all this space with us shares. We can grow. We hope bring. But not if we dead are.'

Benhannon cursed. She didn't know the word, didn't hear its syllables because they were unknown, but she recognized the emotion it spelled: anger and frustration. 'How can you so stupid be, Marchidas? Do you think you a saviour are, better than us, better than anyone? How arrogant can you get?'

(The offsers' rule in the True Crew: talk more quietly so that anger doesn't soar.) Marchidas said, 'Benhannon! It not arrogance is. I not perfect am. Nobody perfect is. (*There something terribly wrong in me is, or Edrach me wouldn't have left ...*). But because I here am, I something must do. If I nothing do, what point there is in me at all living? Yes, it sweet is, something small and helpless to care for. It me makes feel good. But on my own I not truly important am, or only to myself and my friends. I only a link in a chain am, right back to the first ancestors who the first world trod. And it my duty is, not a weak link to be. I to the future on must pass what they all in the past to me gave.' *And Ain Tsui's debt repay, but how can I tell him that? He only an Iron Man is ...*

'Oh.' Benhannon groaned in frustration. 'You don't understand.'

He turned over, so that he faced the shadows in his life, and said, 'It not to you worth talking is.' She thought, *I that was going to say.*

And the firelight glowed in its cave of metal and Marchidas turned to the razorbacks for comfort, but they were asleep.

'It easy is,' Marchidas told the two half-grown razorbacks trotting beside her, 'a decision not to make.'

They didn't understand her words, but they enjoyed her fingers sliding up to scratch under the knot of clinking spines on their withers. Around them the hills rolled in a tapestry of reds and ambers, fading into lilac distances and dazzling snow-crested mountains. The heat of late Spring soaked pleasantly into the bones of all three, a contrast with the breeze of their walking.

Arno and Mumtaz – Marchidas always thought of the razorbacks in that order because Arno was much bolder than the gentle Mumtaz – Arno and Mumtaz played 'starting at shadows' when a puff of cloud danced two racing patches over them, and shied not very seriously when Marchidas tried to echo their bell-like calls. She knew which sound-shape each made to call the other; which one meant her, and the one for danger. She knew what 'I'm hungry' was, and 'I'm lonely'. Marchidas practised that one often.

Benhannon was mostly good company when he was talking, but the silences between them were unhappy. They traded songs, they knew this fact and that fact about each other – though he didn't want to talk about why he'd been so weak when they'd met – but they were no closer than they had been on their first walk to the meat that had saved their lives.

That was why, this sleepy Whitenoon, she had left Benhannon scratching around in the forest for the plants he liked to eat. He liked the shady blue dimness under the canopy of lacing crystals, the stillness of the air. He liked not being with her.

And Marchidas wanted someone to listen to the language of her heart.

She had the lake to herself; Arno and Mumtaz raced over the mountain-red on the slopes, not having learned yet to run on the water. Their scent-fronds were still only buds that they hadn't learnt to control, so every now and then, in mid-gallop, they would put down their heads to sniff something, almost tipping on end.

The rest of their old herd were far away by now. Neither Arno nor Mumtaz was afraid, and yet Marchidas was nervous.

Am I the right thing doing? Will Arno and Mumtaz all right be, if I them Red-speech give?

And, like the bigger decision of when (or whether?) to leave to find the Ship, she kept putting it off. Stripping, Marchidas dived in and swam furiously, the water stroking her naked body firmly, but wherever she went, her problems went inside. *If I Arno and Mumtaz leave, will they die? Or themselves wear out, trying me to follow? Will Benhannon hurt be if I go?* And: *He so little of survival knows ...*

Marchidas smashed her palm on the water, sending a silver arc of spray into her eyes. She shook her head savagely, a punishment or an exorcism, and her long hair spun out in ribbons of black and suns'gold. *At least I Arno and Mumtaz can ask ... if I them Red-speech give.*

Careful not to touch anything, she baked herself in the streaming light until she was clean and dry. Overhead a geyrlizard clanged; moving suddenly, Marchidas showed it she was still alive and it winged away in the clear blue sky. Then she approached the chameleon cluster where Benhannon had saved her with his fire-box. She recalled, sensation by sensation, her ecstatic leap to safety and a friend:

And plucked, full of that joy, a great, round, coppery crystal. At its perfect moment it was with her, it was in her and she in it,

130

complementary parts of Rosaria's essence. Only faintly yet, though ... Gleaming in her double palms, with Redsun centred on Whitesun's leisurely disc, was the heart of the Red.

When the cluster dimmed to a dusky pink beneath a passing cloud, she left it to its own company, carrying the crystal next to her solar plexus.

And that night, even in in the earthy darkness of the dugout, the cluster and Marchidas knew when the Amethyst Moon rose to its highest. Marchidas slipped from her warm bedding. She had propped the wicker loosely against the entrance to the dug-out camp. Now it was easy to sneak out between the familiar things. Arno and Mumtaz were splashing in the shining waters of the stream nearby; they came when she belled with her tongue.

Marchidas touched the chameleon (night-blue now, with a core of purple fire) to their lips, then bit into it. At once the low stars grew brighter, closer. She took out that bite and gave it to Arno, stole a bit back and shared it with Mumtaz, shared her own bite with Mumtaz and took some back for Arno. Friends of the wind, of the night, they were sisters to the moon, part of all Rosaria ... *If only he was too*, they thought.

They heard the unbrother's feet squeaking through the coiling mountain-red. They heard him say, 'What you doing are?' and they longed for him to understand. The two-legged one tried to make him see:

'Benhannon! Please – share with us. With me.'

Marchidas pressed herself to him, reaching into him with a kiss that tasted of the tang of chameleon. He took a bite then of its deliquescent sapphire ...

He does! He himself with Rosaria shares!

Kissed by the starlight, at last he understood.

At last the hours melted the edges of the spell. Under the Amethyst Moon the razorback colts drifted down to the murmurous stream, still sisters. On the slope outside the dugout camp, in the clean song of morning in the Red, Marchidas stretched up to kiss him because he wanted her to. Or she wanted to kiss him. Her spirit and his had forgotten the differences that lay like a crevasse between them. This was a time out of time, like a snow-bridge spun white and tempting from safety to danger, waiting to wreak its fragility on those who dared to cross.

Lying atop her Wolf-hide on the soft red by the chuckling stream,

131

Marchidas didn't know which was warmer: the iridescent fur sparkling against her skin, or Benhannon's body touching hers. Full length beside her, every part of him seemed to be an endearment. She moved her head in the crook of his shoulder and his hand moved too, gliding the dark strands of her hair in rivers over his chest.

Caressed by the summer-scented air, her hand feathered circles on his thigh and pleasure echoed from him into her. They melted into each other, so that there was no end or beginning to Marchidas and Benhannon, and no guilt or self-doubt.

Quickly now, quickly life races by. Grab it, remember it, it'll soon be gone. The new-born strength of Spring, Summer's long golden heat ...

But under the temptation of a loving haven, the suns were ripening the glacier ...

And guilt won in the end. Benhannon suggested, asked, argued that she couldn't possibly set off in her condition.

Marchidas told him as soon as she was sure she was pregnant. She had to go. Fear impelled her; she knew the risks of childbirth. For the sake of Ain Tsui's descendants, she had to find the Ship. 'How can I the whole meaning of the Crew give up? I want to stay, Ben. I want to.'

Marchidas tried to bring his hand up to feel the life swelling inside her but Benhannon pulled away. 'It my child too is, Marchidas. You it away can't take.' And she knew he was thinking, as she was, that she might die.

'That just it is, Ben. I the only one now am who knows where the Ship is. I now have to go, before it too late is.' ·

But Benhannon said again, 'For the sake of the baby, you here have to stay.'

Their closeness grew thinner, like old tidenet strands.

'All right,' Marchidas said one melodic dusk with the crystals singing in the change of light and warmth. 'You here stay. I'm going.' *How can I him tell of my fear of too-soon death, when he so little hold on the joy of life has?*

'Can't you wait?' he shouted. 'At least until next year? Why do you want me on an alchemist's quest to drag?'

He had to explain that one. And while Benhannon was trying to make her understand, and to find out why he'd wanted to hurt her with his unbelief – his doubts were scouring the wounds of her own uncertain faith.

Marchidas was too frightened to stay. She had to find the Ship

132

before she died or her life, and her father's, of all of her line, would have been in vain. Yet she dared not say it aloud in case it came true: her death in childbirth before she'd lived her purpose. And she couldn't explain her fear of failure and death; it was too personal. She wouldn't let him come that close to her any more. Her body wasn't her own any more. All she could hang on to was her mind.

'Then I too am coming,' Benhannon said. And wouldn't let her touch him lest she feel his confused feelings, so little did he understand of the power of Red-speech. Still she knew what he was thinking: *I a man am! I the one to decide should be!*

And the year turned with frightening speed as they began the search for the Ship. Marchidas's urgency grew with her belly.

Swiftly now life carries you. Here comes fertile Autumn with the seeds of peace and decay. Soon the arrowheads' silver call will melt with the land in the rain.

Gentle Mumtaz carries Marchidas-with-the-new-life-in-her, because it makes her human body weary. Even the smoothest jog Mumtaz can manage is sometimes uncomfortable for Marchidas, because it drags her belly jouncing up and down, but Mumtaz carefully bears her burden. Arno helps when Marchidas lets her, but Arno's spirit is too fiery to walk for long.

On his two long legs that have grown accustomed to the pace of a nomad on the trail, Benhannon trots alongside the rider in case she is hurt. Arno scouts ahead, the way Marchidas tells her, always southwest by the Book.

Benhannon's strength has grown, his sickness of heart has shrunk. There is a new pride mapped in the lines of his face: he needed acceptance and now he has it, now he can accept himself – a little. Marchidas has taught the Iron Man to smell things softer than the acrid reek of soot and molten metal. Benhannon's twisted nose guides him to the streams and pools of standing water in the scorched land, towards the marshes where the skate-lizards cry, and Arno Razorback sniffs out a trail ahead, her scent-fronds blessed by rain after the drought.

Follow the winding river from its birth high in the mountains to a new burst of life in the arid south downs. Who would have suspected a flourish of crystals between the baked hills?

But Marchidas is torn by anxiety: Benhannon isn't sure the Ship exists any more. *Won't it rusted be? He an Iron Man is. He should know.* Still Marchidas makes herself go on. She is ridden by doubt, but honour – and faith? – drive her.

To the marshes the Book says are there (*Do I it right remember? Captain my father, am I your honour renewing? These marshes are – but the right ones? When the Crew not a day from here our trail to the winterground made? Benhannon not really believes. Oh, Edrach, if I only your belief had, to lean on ...*).

A sound within the sounds of the rain on the water.

'Stop!' hissed Marchidas.

Benhannon did, surprised. Marchidas, fierce?

She flash-read his face: *Is she the baby now having?*

'People!'

Her people. Or at least Crew. Who would anyway think she was mutinas. And an Iron Man with her? Death would be quick – or very slow.

Ungainly, Marchidas slid off the razorback, Red-speeched: *Hide!* and slid into their minds the image of the heaps of living-stones across the trail by the undercut bank.

Crouching, Benhannon and Mumtaz Razorback ran to cover. Marchidas ducked low, walking as fast as she could with her belly not a month from bursting. Under the edge of the bank they huddled. *Small heart ...*

Time stretched. They shivered. The dripping rain steamed on Mumtaz's flanks. Marchidas breathed open-mouthed lest the air hiss in her nostrils and betray her baby's life. *Where Arno is?*

Marchidas fingered the rain-slick hilt of her long-knife, wiped her palms on the inside of her cloak. Its fur was dull grey, reflecting the weeping skies and the mournful ochre of the marsh. The stones' life was faint and grey ...

Benhannon was trembling, his mind a turmoil that dimmed Marchidas's senses. He was wondering whether to break his principles that had exiled him from the Iron Men, or fight for the life she carried ...

As if they had a choice.

A scrape of claws on the crumbling rim of the river-bank.

Arno Razorback decided it. In a spatter of mud she leaped down into the gully. Just ahead of an arrow.

Arno scuttered back, pressing into their inadequate shelter. A warrior jumped down, whirled and shot.

Arno screamed: a shrill echo of the herd-mother's savage gonging. She half-reared, staggered sideways, fell. Her second scream wavered, its pure tones muddied by the froth of blood.

Marchidas, horrified, risked a glance over the razorback's red flank

134

as another warrior braved the jump. The warrior met her eyes. He slammed his friend's arrow downwards before the woman could shoot again.

'Don't!' he yelled. 'Don't shoot, Wordweaver. It Marchidas is.'

Mud streaked his face, but not his eye. Not the gotch eye of Edrach, Chosen Brother.

'You dead were. I in your mind was, and me you didn't know.' Edrach said it for the fourth or fifth time. 'Wordweaver and I, we for you looked, and you carrion were, blood-caked.'

Benhannon was beyond the camp-fire, outside the bivouac of Wolf-hides, in the streaming darkness with his arms around Mumtaz. Marchidas could understand it; Benhannon knew he was an intruder here and it hurt him. Just the same, she wished he were here.

There were nine of the Crew, counting Marchidas – but no-one was sure whether to count her or not. They were toasting the dead razorback on its own spines – and Marchidas wouldn't. She sat, arms cradled round her knees, shivering in the firelight and the smoke. Her nausea was not all physical.

'Your mind in a black place was, a tunnel of death.' Edrach's voice was cracked with his urgency to make her believe. 'I couldn't stay, Marchidas, it closing in was. You dying were. I couldn't make you hear ... Wordweaver will tell. But no-one our regrets can tell.'

Arno Wordweaver, cradling her emaciated son, said, 'You white were. Death-white and streaked with blood.'

After whatever had happened to the Harifon – Marchidas could hear the way they skirted round the subject whenever they came close to it – it was Arno who had taken over. She was the one who had said they would go back to their old place. They were on their way to the winterground – all that was left of them after the seasons with the Harifon. And they had vowed never to risk their lives on a summer's quest again.

Wordweaver looked older, tireder. They all did. She stabbed Marchidas with her gaze, willing her to believe. 'I never Red-speech like Chosen Brother could. He said you didn't hear when he you called. I him heard your name call. It like the grief of all Rosaria was. And you weren't breathing, Marchidas. I swear you weren't.'

'Then – ' the pregnant girl's voice came high and broken. Marchidas cleared her throat, tried again, 'Then why you me with honour didn't leave?' There was nowhere she could go to talk of all this without baring her pain to the rest of the group. Everything she wanted to say was just words, a thin pastiche of her grief. She needed to share how it had hurt when even her Chosen Brother had abandoned her but pride wouldn't let them in to her vulnerability.

'Marchidas –'

'I –'

Wordweaver and Edrach began at the same time, hesitated. All this could have been resolved with Red-speech but Marchidas wouldn't trust any of them any more. They had left her to die. Wordweaver glanced at the younger girl with her swollen belly then back at Edrach. 'You it say,' she ordered.

Edrach reached a hand towards Marchidas, who moved her knees so that he couldn't touch her. He left his hand there, a mute plea she ignored. So in words he said, 'I too weak was. And we afraid were of what the Harifon might do. Arno's son there with the Harifon was. She her life and his for us risked, Marchidas. In my heart I your death-chant made.'

Marchidas swallowed her tears and the taste was salt and slime in her throat. She shrugged; too much to say, and no way anyone would win the battle without time. And the pain of raking it over was gravel on her grazed emotions. She relaxed slightly, but not enough for Edrach to touch her. Swallowing again, Marchidas said, 'Unimportant is. I the Ship have found.'

The tired chatter stopped abruptly, cut off by a knife: the Crew's old life was severed by those words. It would never be the same again.

Wordweaver said, 'No you haven't!'

Marchidas said angrily, 'In all our days together I never you a lie told, Wordweaver. I not one now am telling.'

Slowly, as if the words weighed more than she could bear, Wordweaver said, 'I sure am that you believe what you say, Marchidas. But Rosaria full is of people who knew where the Ship lies, and most of them are dead. Like all the Captains back to Loi-Tsu's betrayal, each one sure that they knew where the Ship lay.

'I your father followed from when I born was. Even when I in my mother's womb was, I him followed. Each season he us all from the winterground dragged, sure he knew this time where it was. And every Autumn when the arrowflights down the storm-winds belled, he sure was that next season we the Ship would find.'

People were nodding, their tired heads bobbing on their spindly necks. Marchidas hated the way they were looking at her, their eyes shining hot in the light from the flames.

136

'But Wordweaver! You faith can't break! You Captain of the True Crew are!'

'But nothing. Your father dead is, because the Harifon sure was that *he* knew where the Ship lay. It stupid is, Marchidas. We won't –'

Marchidas stared across the fire that was fed on the grease from Arno Razorback whom she had saved – for this. Stared straight into the weary face of Arno Wordweaver whom she used to call friend. Arno's ruddy hair was lank and streaked with grey. And no-one else spoke.

'Wordweaver,' Marchidas spoke through clenched teeth, 'Wordweaver, I you to battle challenge.'

Strain stretched tangible between the two women: the one who'd grown old early in her year as Captain, and the girl of almost sixteen Winters. Even trying not to be netted in their thoughts, Marchidas felt them: *She all the long march of the Harifon didn't suffer. She dead was. Now she back to life has come, pregnant to a hated Iron Man. How dare she our Wordweaver Captain challenge?* People edged back from the line a long-knife might take.

'You can't, Marchidas,' said Arno. The tension that had been building collapsed. Pent breaths sighed under the flapping canopy of wolf-hides. 'I your challenge won't accept because you pregnant are.'

'Arno Wordweaver,' Marchidas said with a lift of her chin, 'my challenge you must accept. You weak are. I strong am, with the strength I need, my son from a lifetime in your useless settlement to save. That no fit life for the True Crew is. And I my challenge won't cancel.'

Edrach shifted violently, stifled the protest he was about to make. Marchidas thought suddenly, *He still believes!* And from that too resolution grew inside her until she felt big enough to contain every one of them that sat in the leaking shelter.

Fat sputtered and smoke flared yellow above the fire. It shone on Marchidas, limning the architecture of her determination.

The set of Marchidas's face did not deter Wordweaver. Marchidas was softer, round with the padding of youthful reserves, aglow with the juices of pregnancy. Kneeling, Wordweaver sneered down at her rival's stubbornness. 'You like a petulant child look, Marchidas. You not even a name yet have earned.'

'Then I one now will have, Wordweaver. Marchidas Shipfinder.'

She fumbled in the pocket of her tunic, drew out the stiff folds of cord she had made from her Wolf's sinews. And Edrach, who would have been her body-lover if he could, tried not to think of the unborn

137

child that should have been his, but tied nine strands of sinew to her wrist.

Slowly Wordweaver stood, holding out her hand above the stuttering fire. Marchidas stood too, and over the wavering heat Edrach tied their wrists by one long strand. The two women pushed back the sleeves of their soft hide jackets. Then, either side of the flames that rose and fell, they glared at each other while Edrach knotted more cords on Wordweaver's wrist, so that both women trailed eight dangling ends.

The fire was hot beneath their outstretched arms. Neither Marchidas nor Wordweaver showed their discomfort, but it was there. A battle was a serious thing, not to be undertaken on a whim. It could maim – or kill.

Instinctively, as Edrach tightened his last knot, both women pulled back. The cord twanged taut, cutting into their wrists as each woman strove to put distance between her arm and the flames.

Wordweaver said, 'I Arno am, of the strand of Leftant Vassily, third in command of the Ship. But I not on her ranks rest but on my own deeds of glory.

'And I the name Wordweaver won by the battle I fought with Chulitskaya Mutinas, who my first son tried to take, and who now a stump of bone has where his battle-arm was, because I him by fire and logic beat.

'And I Captain am because I also the Harifon battled though he fierce was as the burning wind that him his name gave, and he fell so the flames roared through his hair on the red sands of the Unnamed Desert. I challenged because he my friends to their death on this search for a ghost-ship led. And when he died we laughed.'

The crowd roared – six of them – though in the cramped space of the shelter they seemed like more. Marchidas could feel their minds beating on hers, sure of her failure and wanting it that way. Only Edrach stood silent, but he tied a loop to shorten Marchidas's end of the firestrand, because no-one could deny that Arno had earned her Captaincy by valour.

'I Marchidas am,' the girl declaimed with the firelight shining on her tight-swollen stomach. 'I my Wolf have killed, and more. I the one am that you abandoned. You the old ways left: you no death-chant for me made, so one of the True Crew – your Crew, Wordweaver Captain! – alone and injured had to survive. What do you think the regulations for are? To stop you against survival going!'

The people shifted uncomfortably. By the same regulations

138

Marchidas could have compelled a knot against the Wordweaver. Yet Marchidas let her off this hook so that she could gaff her rival, 'But there the Harifon was. He his offsers beat, and on mad ramblings many deaths made. Sickness, and hunger, and suns' fire in the desert. But he the Book did not have, did he? And still you him followed! Who the greater fool is, the fool who leads, or the fool who him follows?'

And no-one stopped Edrach tying the first loop to shorten the distance between Wordweaver's arm and the searing fire.

Wordweaver said quickly, 'He said the Book was destroyed. And I say the Ship was destroyed like the Drone-Ship, or into the marsh sucked! Didn't the Book say, "By the second day the *Mosckva* disappeared"?'

Again Wordweaver's supporters yelled. Edrach swallowed and reached towards Marchidas. She jerked her arm away.

'No, Wordweaver! It said, "Heavy rain. *Mosckva* submerged by nightfall of second day." Not "disappeared", not "destroyed", or why did the First Offser us send all those years ago to search for the mountains where the nineties ore is? Why do we still ore in our Wolf-skulls keep? Because we it to repair the drive need!'

And in the hissing of breath all about them – because what was the Crew if there were no Ship for it to man? – Edrach tied the second cord round the fire-strand and back round Arno's arm. But along with his belief he gave a Red-speech gift to Marchidas.

Tears of pain stung Wordweaver's eyes. She shook her head fiercely and spoke the hub of her Captaincy: 'Wherever the Ship may be, we it do not need! There nearly thirty of us were, na? And now how many?

'Survival most now matters. Getting to the winterground, getting more children, not some stupid chase with an un-corpse and an Iron Man that us won't help!'

Wordweaver had won. The roar of approval lifted her head and shoulders above the younger woman. The boy in Marchidas's belly kicked; Edrach tried not to feel the pain that seared Marchidas as he fastened the second cord to bind her more tightly to the fire-strand. The hairs on Marchidas's arm curled and sizzled; the stench of their burning pricked her eyes.

But Marchidas said, 'Get more children, yes. But why? Where from? We them from another crew steal like Chulitskaya Mutinas your Brachan tried to steal, because this life against all survival is! We attacked are every time we another crew meet because they think we murdering mutinas are, the same way you think that of them! There not enough of us are to survive!'

Wordweaver opened her mouth to protest, but Marchidas glared at her in the flickering yellow light and yelled, 'Look at you! All of you! In a leaky shelter in the rain, the wind blowing smoke in your eyes and shivering your backs, half-starved, diseased, your friends murdered or crippled or born awry ... We no better than Wild Men are!'

Marchidas was panting, staving off the agony of her burnt arm. She had to win quickly or face life maimed:

'What more proof do you want? There not enough of us are to go on this way! We that ship *need!* We here orphaned are, abandoned on one rock. We cut off from the stars are. From the glorious suns that in the dark void beckon. From the family of the star-folk. From our home.

'What else are we Crew of, if not the Ship? And we filthy mutinas must be, if we our star-home do not seek.'

Wordweaver recoiled instinctively, pulling on the firecord, and Marchidas gasped as it cut into her charred skin. But Edrach ignored the fire's scorching on his own hands to realign the blackening thongs: no-one stopped him putting it to the position Marchidas had won. And he knotted the loop to shorten Wordweaver's side and pull her arm closer over the flames.

The Captain's thin face worked; Brachan looked at his mother and whimpered. Wordweaver spoke hastily: 'By what right do you us order? Why should we your blind fumbling for a trail follow?'

And Marchidas accepted this gift from the man who had been her chosen Brother: 'Because I the True Book have. The Log of the *Moskva*, and Leftant Vassily's person-log. And I can prove what I say.'

In the flaring flame-light, the Crew stilled utterly. The smoke of singed flesh stung their disbelieving eyes. Edrach moved to shorten Wordweaver's firecord yet again, but Wordweaver shrieked triumphantly, 'You it can't have! The Harifon it destroyed!'

Marchidas said only, 'Edrach.'

From inside his tunic he took the battered cylinder. With his fingers he compelled it to a feeble greenish glow. In a tortured copy of the first Ain Tsui's voice it groaned, '*Moskva*'s log, Captain Tsui ... Drone-ship off course ...'

From all sides hatred and disbelief tied Marchidas's emotions, but the Book was there. It cut Marchidas free just as Edrach bound Wordweaver's flesh above the flames.

'The Book proves what I'm saying, Wordweaver! When you young were, didn't you the Book like everyone else learn?'

Marchidas quoted from the old hide copy. Reluctantly, silently, Wordweaver's lips mirrored Marchidas's: 'I can only believe that the

140

same action which wrecked the *Moskva* perverted all our instruments as well.'

The Crew knew it. Wasn't that why mutinas happened? Because nobody *knew* any more? The faint sussuration of whispers died in the smoky shelter.

Marchidas hurried on, 'That's what your own Leftant Vassily said. And she described from memory where the Ship lies. "In the southern marshes where the river spreads." Don't you, remember, Wordweaver? Wouldn't this be the south if they'd explored the Iron Mountains for their nineties ore?

'This Autumn only, Wordweaver,' Marchidas gasped. The words jetted out of her, impelled by the urgency of pain. 'If we the Ship don't find before it too late is to go to the winterground, then we our lives another way must live. Your way.

'But when the north wind the snow down to the plain chases, we under cover will be. I, Marchidas of the Six Battles, promise. Do you accept?'

Wordweaver knew she had lost. Her face contorted, she shouted quickly, 'I accept!' and wrenched her arm sideways, away from the fire. Blisters swelled whitely from her raw, red flesh. Her son Brachan was sobbing, 'Ma! Your arm!', his stick-like limbs flailing against the hands that held him back.

Marchidas staggered, jerked along in Wordweaver's wake. Wordweaver had plenty of supporters to cluster round her, pointedly ignoring Marchidas though she had won fairly.

Benhannon, the outsider, watched from the doorway. It was Edrach who slashed Marchidas free and held her to his chest.

Hot winds from the south dulled the red with Autumn's dust. Whitenoon, but the year was so far gone that the double shadows forked long over the undulating plain. Yet the land was baked hard under the feet of the Crew; the Autumn rains had all but failed. Late arrowfalls belled overhead in a piercing blue sky. Here, where the river snaked into the edge of the marshes, the sluggish waters threw back its colour.

Taking a deep breath to steady herself, Marchidas strove to throw off her aching exhaustion. 'We a nooning here will make. There water is, and shade and food.'

She signalled to the outwatchers. Already the pathetic column was sinking wearily on a gentle rise where the ground was firm. Around them, nodules of crystal crimsoned erratic boulders, climbing over one another to form weird peaks.

Not until all her people were settled and the food shared out did Marchidas allow herself to rest her throbbing feet. When she saw that Benhannon was riding to take the morning's gather to Edrach and the other two outwatchers, Marchidas finally closed her eyes against the glare of the suns on the shimmering marsh. She was too worn down to combat the dragging ache in her back or the sting of her arm-burn.

Benhannon, astride Mumtaz Razorback, rode a semi-circle back across the plains towards the weary privates. He skirted round the others – little Brachan pointedly turned to avoid seeing him – who kept a small but perceptible distance from Marchidas. Benhannon stopped beside her.

'I no-one could see,' he said, sliding from behind the trailing crown of the razorback's spines. 'Mumtaz restless is, though. See how her scent-fronds are writhing?'

Marchidas felt too ill to pay much attention to anyone else, least of all an animal. Maybe it just is that she the water can smell.'

'Are you all right?' Benhannon asked her. Her face was thin and drawn; even under her tan he could see the purple shadows beneath her eyes. They made an ugly contrast with her skin.

He came to squat beside her, concerned. Marchidas was sitting with her legs sprawled out in front of her. It was too hot for trousers, so her swollen, veined legs stuck out beneath her long tunic. Crushed bluestone had soaked through the bandage on her burned wrist.

A ripple of motion distorted the supple hide where it strained over her belly.

'Are you all right?' he said again.

'No.' The admission was torn from her.

He unwound a length of razorback gut from his shoulders and pulled off the metal ring that sealed it. 'Here,' he said helplessly, 'maybe this will make you better feel.'

She didn't even open her eyes to take the water, but he sloshed some from the gut into his hand and wiped her face with it. As always, she smiled at his gentle touch, her eyelids flickering so that her grey-blue gaze drifted across him. His damp fingers brushed delicately at the dust and sweat on her neck; she had always liked the touch of his hand along her collar-bone.

She smiled, though her lips thinned against a wave of pain. Mumtaz came and snuffled at a spreading patch of moisture that came from beneath Marchidas. Benhannon pushed the razorback away but Marchidas sketched a caress on the grey hide.

'She her winter coat is getting,' said Marchidas, in an attempt at normality. Then she stifled a groan. 'My waters have broken. Fetch Wordweaver!'

Arno Wordweaver was good. Swiftly she organized old Lorwen to brew the women's drink, then held it to Marchidas's lips, saying, 'Come on, my Captain. This only another journey is. A journey through pain. Your boy on the other side is waiting. Come on now. Drink this.'

And, quietly, Arno sent Tearlach to deputize for Edrach on outwatch. She didn't call; she walked over to the others as if to fetch padding, but all the same Benhannon saw Tearlach's gap-teeth smile. The man nodded curtly, then he was trotting out towards Edrach, and Benhannon knew. Because he knew Marchidas would rather have had Edrach's child than his. Only Edrach was born twisted; Edrach could not father children, and he, Benhannon, was only an accidental meeting. Hadn't he seen in the dreamsmoke that his path and Marchidas's lay side by side but didn't quite touch?

For Marchidas the journey seemed to last a long time. Around her she saw the towering spires of crystals on the rocks, and the crimson was her blood. Her womb was a black tunnel – she remembered the mountain lizard – and the tunnel-floor swelled to engulf her. The tunnel was fear and death and her eyes burst open in terror.

Edrach's mind reached out to Marchidas, a bright gleam of love and faith and hope. Her panic faded; her eyes ranged over the landscape and fastened on a coruscating clump of red spires half-rising from the marsh. Benhannon, beside her, squeezed her hand encouragingly but she was so far from him that she didn't seem to notice. He thought she said, 'The Ship! I the Ship can see!'

Arno looked at him and shook her head: *she's delirious.*

'I his head can see,' crooned Arno. 'You, Benhannon, sit her up now. He's coming.'

Marchidas muffled her screams on a strap of hide. *I mutinas must not bring! I will not out cry I willnotcry –*

Two, three tearing pains that she thought would rip her apart – then she knew they hadn't. She strained. With a slither her son squelched out into Arno's waiting hands.

Marchidas was crying with relief, astonished by the look of pride and wonder that transfigured Benhannon's face. Edrach gazed at her, his brown eye wide in soul-pain and wonder, the white eye dead and staring. The others were just coming over towards her as Arno laid the blood-streaked baby on her belly.

Marchidas smiled. The world was the right shape again, the right

143

colour. And, rising from the sinking of the river, a twisted ruby spire poured fire into her dreams.

Her hands moved to encircle the child, to wrap him inside her tunic so that he stopped his mewing to nuzzle at her breast.

She said, 'It's the Ship! I the Ship have found, to take us home to the stars!'

'There now,' lulled Arno. 'You're not going to die, it's all right.'

Incredulous, Marchidas said, 'It's there, Arno! Can't you see –'

Rocks rained down on them. Arrows. Wide-eyed, Marchidas writhed to shelter her baby with her body. *Mutinas! I so weak am! Oh, let him not die. Please, let him not die. Not when I the Ship to him can give …*

Everyone was scattering on the slope which rang with mutinas battle-cries. Benhannon fell backwards then scrabbled to his feet. For a second, Marchidas looked straight into Edrach's eyes.

Then, so the mutinas could claim her child for themselves, a stone smashed Marchidas –

PART TWO

Lifetides

CHAPTER ONE

The Colours of Dawn

Tohalla's hands slipped unnoticed from the red crystal heart of the messenger; a breath broke into her lungs. Tears tracked down her cheeks; laved by the baleful stare of Redsun sinking, the tears were like tears of blood: Marchidas's fear for her son undercutting the knowledge that no-one believed she truly had found the *Mosckva*. Only Edrach, mutant born, mutilated, whose belief no-one followed. And Tohalla's bereavement, because Marchidas was her inside-friend and she was dead. So many griefs! *How she had hurt Chosen Brother. Who was she?*

In the closing blackness that was the womb of death, Edrach reached out to her –

To Tohalla.

The thread of life, continuing. The sound in her body of breathing, the sibilant rush of blood to every part of Tohalla. And the shining touch of Edrach that warmed her aloneness, an outcast woman of the Green pinned far in thought from her House in the Summer-ripe combe. A woman who had failed her people so many times, whose body had denied life to Pierse's child, Cren, a plain, freckle-faced woman whose dull gold hair shone rubescent in the forbidden Red.

Yet her dutiless womb had quickened to the Axe's tainted seed before ever she should have lain with him, and now the Axe was abandoning her to Housefather's justified anger.

But colder than that and darker was Marchidas's death that she had lived, and Edrach's childless bereavement. *How could I have been so cruel to my friend's Chosen Brother? Hasn't his life been hard enough already? And he looked after Benhannon and kept faith with Marchidas's son even after his Chosen Sister died.*

147

What have I done? But it's not too late! How can I reject Marchidas's son?
'Oh, Edrach! I'm sorry!'

She longed to comfort his pain.

Tohalla reached out to him. Old though he'd seemed when he came to the Green, Edrach's warmth and strength reassured her of life as he held Tohalla against his chest. She pressed in towards him, full of the sensations of death and birth and the knowledge that living swiftly goes ...

Gradually the dim red glade of the messenger grew around her.

When she was quieter, he murmured, 'Now do you see why we soon have to go? While I still can? And while the mutinas and the Crew too far north to catch us are? Brachan Arno's son in that raid died. The mutinas us never would have caught if Marchidas us there hadn't led. Wordweaver never a forgiving woman was.'

His words came to her gently, a warm breeze in her hair. He made the deaths seem commonplace and very far away.

Tohalla nodded, shivering. She felt that the pain was closer to him than to her who had just died –

'But you the Ship in her mind saw?' Edrach persisted.

Again Tohalla nodded, with Marchidas's belief implanted in her.

Edrach slid his touch down Tohalla's arm. 'On come, then. Redsun nearly set has.' Chosen Brother squeezed her hand. 'Do not grieve. Marchidas in life almost everything had. And she Ain Tsui's blood-debt repaid.'

'But you, Edrach! You've had so little!'

A strange smile moved his cheek on her forehead; Tohalla felt rather than saw it. 'I a friend had. Her life completed was. At the last, she knew I knew. And her son mine to raise was. To me she gave the way to deliverance for our people – when he old enough was the debt to repay. The rains this year light have been. The Ship above the water will be.'

Edrach raised her solicitously to her feet. He smiled. 'Can you the twilight music hear?'

Tohalla nodded again, knowing he wanted to bury his sadness. Soothed by the melodious chiming of the Red, she sniffed and wiped her eyes on her sleeve and joy in life rose shakily in her. For such a hope as the freeing of Rosaria Tohalla would follow her happiness beyond the savageness of the Edge. On a jerky breath she said, 'Yes, the Red in beauty sings.'

But the ghost of another life followed inside her.

Marchidas's son and her Chosen Brother led Tohalla back to the

148

bright shelter of her House.

Longday. The Axe's gift to her: a day for a life. But Tohalla didn't see it that way then.

When the suns had burnt off the dew from the fields, Housemother said, 'Well, go on! I suppose we can manage without you now.'

In the cool, shady Hall Larnis said dutifully, 'If you're sure you can spare us,' and giggled coyly at Granamyr over the loaded trestle tables. It was her Ripeness too, of course. On the threshold Worut's tuneless humming rasped the bright morning air. Coril bustled in from the kitchen with another platter for the feast. She winked at Larnis, standing demure in front of her mother, and touched her cap to remind Larnis that soon she'd wear one like it over cropped hair: the signs of a wife of the Green.

'Ha!' Housemother said to her favourite daughter. Though she was gruff, her affection was real; Tohalla remembered her other Ripeness, when she was given to Pierse. The affection had been for her, Tohalla, then. Even with the promise of a new strand from Tohalla's direction, Housemother wasn't sure about her any more. But Housemother was saying to Larnis, 'Off with you! You're getting precious little done anyway.'

Tohalla only touched the Axe lightly on the arm to make sure he followed. With two sets of perceptions she could see how strange it all was to him. At the back of her mind was the guilty thought: *If I don't say anything, perhaps Housemother won't find out ...* Tohalla was sure Housemother could see that other woman, the Daughter of the Red, inside her. For a moment, too, she was convinced Housemother knew about her baby, but how could she? Tohalla tried to convince herself it was only her own habit of guilt. She was glad to take her difference upstairs out of Housemother's sight.

As soon as they had turned the first corner of the dark, creaky stairs, the Axe put one arm gently around her. Ahead of them, laughing along Housefather's corridor that led back over the kitchen and storerooms, Larnis and Granamyr were all but running. It was all Tohalla could do to walk, though she was still trying to please the Axe by not wasting time, as if he were a Son of the Green.

'The pains soon go,' the Axe said in her ear, so that the Outwatcher at the end window thought it was only lovers' chat.

Tohalla looked up at him in puzzlement. Plain work-shirt, fair hair cut short so that it seemed almost brown, he looked like Hearnor the farmer. Normal. A Green man of seventeen Winters. Yet he seemed to

149

care about her as a person, not just as a vessel for the new child of the Green. Not just a womb on legs, like Pierse had done.

The Axe smiled and shook his head faintly. 'Of course I the aches of pregnancy know. Did you think I my own mother's life have not lived? How do you think her death-message here came if she her own end could not implant? Edrach for me it brought. I know.'

He's so handsome! she thought, now she believed she understood him. *Why did it take me so long to see?*

Patiently climbing the steps to the roof-store, Tohalla panted, 'Would Arno really kill you if she caught you?'

The Axe nodded blithely. 'Oh, yes. Marchidas and Edrach, they both right are. We the Ship need, to stop all the killing. To make us one people.'

Tohalla thought 'us' meant the Sons of the Red. Why do we never know what the right questions are at the time? She didn't even consider the changes the star-kin would bring to the Green.

The Axe stopped when Tohalla did. While she rested at an angle of the stairs where a small window glowed gold with the cornfields beyond, he said, 'Now me something tell. Why are we up to the dome going?'

'It part of the celebrations is. The making of the perfumed bed of Ripeness.'

He laughed at the same time Tohalla did, 'Now you my speech are learning!'

It was a conscious act for her this time, 'I from you have a lot to learn, if I'm going in your world to live.' He thought, *Yes, you still much to learn have …*

The morning light spilled glinting dust-motes liberally on the old, dim wooden walls. The deep scent of fruit played a rich counterpoint to the fresher green smells of the summer harvest. Doggedly she began to climb the last few stairs, doing what was expected of her, still drifting through a life that was dreamed by other people. But at a level below consciousness she was aware that this was almost the last act of that dream of the Green. In the dawning Tohalla would do something that wasn't the enactment of other people's expectations. Then an idea came to her: *Aren't I just doing what the Axe wants instead?*

She tried not to be afraid of the change …

Another step, still the pain above her pubic bone, another step – Beyond her soft panting, in the sunlit dome above, they heard Larnis.

'A body's ashamed to stand beside her, even if she *is* my own sister! Mooning about in that stupid way with a filthy Son of the Red! Why, he looks half her age.'

Granamyr said soothingly, 'Now then, Larnis, be reasonable. If Housefather thought there was any danger, he wouldn't be giving her to him. Anyway, aren't you proud that it's your own flesh and blood who'll be starting a new strand?'

Below, down half a flight of steps, Tohalla whispered, 'Oh, Granamyr, that's the wrong thing to say!'

Larnis snorted. 'Her! She couldn't even bring one child to birth by a decent Green like Pierse. What chance has she got with a sub-human freak like him? The thing'll be born crooked, you see if it isn't! If she comes to term at all, that is. They lie with wolves in the Red. What'll Housefather say when his proud new line starts off with a misbegotten sport?'

The Axe tightened his hold on Tohalla's waist in support and warning. 'It doesn't matter what she says,' he murmured softly.

But it did. For all Tohalla had learnt of Marchidas's life wasn't enough to break her conditioning. Larnis was putting into words exactly what Tohalla feared.

'Don't be silly, love!' Granamyr was saying. They heard his bootheel slur on the planking; Tohalla flinched. 'Honestly, Larnis, there's no real danger. Mevagrin tended him when he was ill with his wounds. She says he's built just like a real man.'

Larnis's lighter steps sounded, brisk and sudden. Evidently she had turned away because she said petulantly. 'Not you too, Granamyr! A body thought you at least would be on my side, but no, you're against me, just like them.'

'That's not true, love,' Granamyr answered. His tone was one of forced patience; Tohalla knew by the sound of it that this argument was an old one. 'But do be sensible. Don't you want a new strand for the Green?'

'A body doesn't want to be murdered in my bed!' (Larnis ignored his saying, 'I'll protect you!') 'A body doesn't want every last one of us to be Red-bitten come Winter, and why it hasn't happened yet a body doesn't know. Half the folks don't wash in brine like a body ought to, but they'll be sorry, you wait and see. The Red'll get them sooner or later – it'll get us all!'

There was the sound of material rustling and Larnis's upset breathing was muffled. Down the stairs, Tohalla and the Axe heard it all. The Axe deliberately scraped his boot on a riser and Granamyr hissed, 'Ssh!'

The Axe helped Tohalla firmly upwards, though for a second she resisted. When they arrived in the doorway with his arm around her, they looked like any other couple coming to make their perfumed bed. But neither of them was laughing.

Granamyr, flushed, said, 'Oh, there you are! We were wondering what had become of you.' His voice was unnatural but at least he was making an effort.

Tohalla rested on the threshhold of the sunny dome. Two of the slatted panels had been moved aside so that an arc of summer-blue sky dazzled her momentarily. Larnis and Granamyr were only two silhouettes pasted darker against the dark-and-gold pattern of the half-full stores. At their feet the plain green ticking was scattered with fresh hay. The warm scent of clover rose, friendly, to mingle with the smell of dried apricots and last year's apples.

The Axe tactfully left it to Tohalla to speak. 'Oh, we were just talking.'

When Tohalla's eyes adjusted to the suns' light, she walked out through the opening onto the flat roof of the House. She had always loved the feeling of being high above the meadows. Now, with the freedom of Marchidas's life burning bright within her, she could put a name to that feeling: the urge to fly on willing wings along a course she alone had chosen. Further out, past the dunes, the two arms of the headlands almost encircled a perfect sea, and the distant kiss of the waves calmed her.

In a moment the Axe joined her. In his embrace – even if he was ten years younger and a Wolfman at that – Tohalla felt safe, though she couldn't have said why.

He helped her bring in their ticking, which she had left earlier to billow in the fresh breeze from the bay. Granamyr talked too much; Larnis scarcely said a word. And, in an atmosphere that gradually lost most of its tension in a few attempted jokes, Tohalla and the Axe filled their own secretly-patterned mattress with the perfumed hay.

No hour-candle to mark the middle of Longday and the coming of harvest, but when the laughing people gathered in the clearing in the orchard, a glossy chestnut shone on a pale wooden platter beside Housefather on his make-shift dais. As the double shadows of the nut shrank and merged, everyone around the platform slowly fell silent, shushing the children.

From the leafy branches the sound of bees grew more plain, and hens scratched and squabbled in the lea beyond the orchard-wall. Into the murmur of the sea-breeze in the leaves, the plop of windfalls pattered suddenly. Tohalla wondered if anyone else but her was listening to the harping of the tidenets down by the shore. She swallowed. Her tiara of bright plaited straw itched and stuck in her head. Her long, dark blonde hair caught other colours from the suns as the wind drifted it tickling past her face.

Slack Worut sprawled in the clearing. Granamyr kicked him when he fingered his groin. A trickle of saliva drooped glistening onto a tiny withered apple in the grass. Beside her, through the suns' heat, Tohalla felt the warmth of the Axe's skin. Her soul swelled with love; he was beautiful. Their anger was forgotten.

Under the chestnut, where the two shadows fell, they darkened.

Then there was one shadow.

Housefather's voice boomed and Tohalla jumped. 'Happy the brides the suns shine on – even though the wheat could do with some rain!' He chuckled at his own humour, lacing heavy witticisms into his directions for the Ripeness of the Green.

Tohalla heard it all from very far away, deep inside her own head. *I'm still not part of it.* The knowledge hurt; she stopped her gaze wandering over the people in their new green clothes – Trinamine, beside her stolid husband Grensham, winked at her – and tried to concentrate.

'We came here,' Housefather was saying, 'to make a garden in this wilderness, and we'll do it yet. The Intake's only a step on the way, but it's lush with good grazing already. If things keep going well, we'll start a new House next year. And I'll be looking for a new Housefather.'

Tohalla looked away from the stout, balding man that was her father. All around her in the sun-shimmered orchard men and women were trying to stand straighter, seem more responsible.

Housefather nodded approval. 'One day all the Red with its filthy taint will be gone, and wherever we look there'll be Green. We've got two converts already! Fresh blood, fresh enthusiasm that's proved itself, and here's one convert now to take my Tohalla and give her sons for the Green!'

His ruddy face beamed down at the Axe beside Tohalla. *I can't do it!* she thought wildly. *I can't betray Housefather and go to the Red now.* Even the zither on the seat beside him was a reproach.

Housefather held out his hand, inviting her up on to the platform. He was waiting for her to name her strand, sing her Ripeness Chaunt –

She couldn't move.

Larnis, behind her, kicked Tohalla's ankle. Green encircled her – green trees, green clothes – everyone was waiting for her. Even the baby inside her was supposed to be theirs ...

Red tickled in the folds of her brain: *Part of you always here will belong. But you wholly your own are. This your life is, Tohalla.*

And, before the whispering grew louder yet, Tohalla took the Axe's hand and led him up onto the platform.

The Axe surprised her: in his turn he named his own strand, from Marchidas of the Seven Battles back to Ain Tsui, Captain of the *Mosckva*.

Hubbub. Housefather overturned his chair, waving his arms and roaring for quiet.

Of course the Greens obeyed, reluctantly. Only Worut's groaning croon carried on, rising and falling, rising and falling. Beside Tohalla, where she sat with the original plastic zither shining on her lap, Larnis turned white with angry red spots in her cheeks.

'Well I never,' Housefather finally said. 'So you're descended from Good Captain, are you? Well, it's turned full circle then, hasn't it? You've come back to where he wanted you to be. Welcome to the family, son.'

So Larnis, for all her youth and golden beauty, glowered through her own Ripeness, eclipsed.

In solemn ceremony Housemother stood behind her daughters and cut off their long hair, a straight line across from ear-lobe to ear-lobe. Married women had too much to do to be bothered with fripperies like plaiting or coiling their hair.

At each crisp snick of the scissors, Tohalla felt vindicated. *I am a proper woman, whatever they say! And I can have children!* Her hand moved softly over her stomach, still skinny but not for much longer. *I'll bring them all up to respect the Red as well as the Green … I'll do what no-one has ever done, what Good Captain must have intended .*

Tohalla smiled beatifically, weaving hope in nebulous dreams, and Larnis, pretty even without her fall of golden hair, sulked. In the dance Larnis moved like a wooden doll in the sun-dappled circle of trees. Tohalla plucked all the old favourites from the shining strings of the zither and hoped her youngest sister would get over her jealousy. Larnis would be favourite again soon enough.

For herself, Tohalla was happy to have the Axe beside her, and glad to play the stream of bright traditional tunes that set even Worut's toes tapping. It was the one parting gift she was glad to make to the Greens: their music. *I never fitted in here,* she thought, *only when a song bound us all together, heart-beat to heart-beat.*

On the outskirts, among the swirling children, Caramon swayed to the dance, radiant.

154

The Axe woke her in the pre-dawn shadows of their married-room. She saw his young face silhouetted against the opalescent glow from the window; somewhere the stars were trying to pierce the early mist.

Tohalla smiled at him and shared his kiss. *Isn't he young? It's like a picnic to him, he's so excited.* It made her feel old and motherly. She kissed him again, on the side of his neck this time, for Marchidas's sake. Memories of Marchidas gave her strength to get up and pull on a tunic and leggings against the chill. Things would be all right.

It only took a moment to brush her short hair and slip on a cap. Pride and memory struck her at the same time: *Pierse's face, the first morning when I tied on my cap and he saw I really was his! I was a proper daughter of the Green then –* The Axe coughed softly. Tohalla smiled at him. The past was over.

It was simple. Tohalla's bare feet glided over the smooth old boards to the bag she had packed 'for moving'. She simply hadn't laid out her things in the kist at the foot of the bed. The Axe had already rolled his few possessions in a sack.

The room was bare, used to being untenanted since the lung-fever last winter. It wasn't home. It wasn't hard to leave. And the perfumed mattress with its patterned cover had given them its blessing. Ain Tsui's destiny lay before them: to find Good Captain's Ship and draw errant Rosaria back into the bosom of the star-kin. Tohalla still didn't quite understand the urgency she had caught from Marchidas and Edrach and the Axe but it was just as potent a force in her.

The Axe lowered Tohalla two storeys to the ground. Her foot was safe in a loop of rope Marchidas's touch remembered: Wolf-gut. It was a strange descent into white stillness. The hens that might have given warning were asleep in their coop. Not even Mevagrin was awake to rattle pans on the kitchen stove. All the Greens sighed and turned over into deeper sleep as Tohalla left. *Not one of them cares –*

Edrach met them, a wraith in the mist, but she felt her loneliness less when he was there. Past the spineders' byre – Tohalla felt relief never to have to smell that again, and remembered her fears on Longnight. How circumstances had changed her life! At the wall of the lea, she was far enough away to pull her boots onto her dew-damp feet. Housemother would have had a fit …

The lane – there was a lane now, since the Intake – helped her lean into the long slope. The Axe's hand was warm around her chilly fingers in the sad, cold, greyness. Whitesun had risen somewhere behind the thick fog but its light scarcely reached the earth. Dark trees dripped tears in the world that closed about her. It was the only sound but for

155

the hollow boom of a seastalker out past the headland. Neither the Axe nor Edrach spoke.

At the top of the hill she turned to look back. The fog was thinning; in the tiny domed shape of the House, odd lights sparked the windows into wakefulness; Tohalla's heart lurched painfully large. But they wouldn't be looking for a newly-Ripe woman yet – she hoped.

The sparks flamed into fire –

Red lightning scorched inside her eyeballs. The world roared around her, terrifying, formless. Tinglings jabbed at her fingers; breath burnt, cut short.

'Tohalla. Are you all right? Tohalla?'

So far away! Too far ...

But the distant voice came closer, and the smells of damp earth and bruised grass. A strong hand was heating the ache in her womb while her skin shivered to the clammy touch of the mist. She was lying in the lane.

'What is it, Toh?'

She felt guilt for the worry so plain in the Axe's voice. That was the first symptom of recovery. When her eyes opened, they conjured his face out of the blur in the fading whiteness. 'The House – the Green. I thought –' *It sounds too silly to say it.*

'What is it?' he said again, and Edrach was kneeling by her, too.

'I thought the House was burning.'

The Axe smiled fondly at her foolishness though one look at his face told her he was thinking something like: *It's enough to annoy anyone!* 'Here,' he said, lifting her shoulders slightly so that she could look down to the valley. 'It only Redsun rising is.'

A rim of gold fire crested the mist out to sea. Friendly lights twinkled in the weathered House that was certainly safe and normal. Only she wasn't in it, where she belonged. Nearer, treetops mushroomed, floating darkly on the haze. A cock crowed to possess the morning.

Tohalla shivered again. 'I'm all right now, honestly. Let's get a move on.'

The Axe helped her up. 'No need for worry is, Toh. No-one after us will come.'

But she wasn't thinking of that. She was thinking of the seastalker's hoot and Edrach saying, 'Then loyalty not in the Green is?' and of Housefather burning the Red.

Even when the leafy canopy of the striding-post spread over her and its lattice glowed a cheerful welcome, her feeling of dread wouldn't go.

156

Of a sudden Adiockle flipped open the hatch and called, 'I thought you'd be here sooner or later. Come on, up with you. I'm cold standing here.'

I again! The sickness of the Red. I.

Tohalla's unease grew. Never mind the wolves. What sort of people was she going out among?

And – I – have chosen to live with them … Or am I just being dragged along by the Axe so Marchidas's grandchild will be born out in the Red?

In lamplight and firelight, Tohalla's aunt said, 'Here, drink this, Toh. You look like you've seen a ghost.'

'But –'

'Do as you're bid! And give your cloak here. It's soaking. Sibulkrin!'

As usual he was pacing quietly around the circle of the lattice. He turned his head and the tendons pulled at the wrinkled skin of his neck.

Adiockle handed hot drinks to the Wolfmen and said, 'Typical. Never uses a word where one would do.

'Sibulkrin? Why don't you take these two here to spy out the Edge?'

'At least let them finish their drinks.' Adiockle's husband creased his face in a grin at having had the last word. Then, as Edrach stood and dwarfed Sibulkrin, the older man banged their mugs on the windowledge and from a cupboard handed them wolf-hides and heads, knives and iron-shod spears, hidden since the blizzard on Longnight.

They all but hugged their old things. Then, with all three men grinning, Sibulkrin unsealed the door. The striding-post rang to their footsteps.

Adiockle tutted into the growing silence. 'We had it better arranged when the striding-post was on the Edge. At least we could see both ways then.'

She peered at Tohalla. Something about her niece's expression was obviously worrying Adiockle because, uncharacteristically, she put one angular arm around her. Adiockle wasn't wearing her cap. *But she'd only just out of bed.* Tohalla hoped it wasn't an excuse … She was very conscious of the strings of her own cap fluttering against her neck. A badge of dignity – and success.

'Come and see, Toh.'

Wary on the curving floor, Tohalla drifted over with her aunt to stand beside the lattice. Side by side they looked out over the Green.

For it was green now, pale as pale on the breasts of the hillsides where a new breeze was trying its strength. Lower down, cupped between the swelling fields and stitched with the darker green of hedges, the mist was gilded with fresh sunlight. And the House was nestled in the heart of the combe.

'They have to go back to their place, Toh. But this is your place. Can you leave it?'

Adiockle wondered if Tohalla had heard, so long did her silence spin its thread. Then Tohalla snapped it off. 'I have to.' *I sound like Housefather: I this and I that.* 'He's my husband and he has to go.' She fiddled with the edge of white linen by her ear.

Adiockle was Green enough to understand that. She pulled the muscles of one cheek into a facial shrug, tilting her head. 'Then you'll need this.' She reached into a cupboard Tohalla had never noticed, recessed below the rippled floor. 'We got it off the dead one last Longnight.'

It was a wolf-hide, its fur striking mauve and emerald in the light from the window. The skin of a creature someone had tricked and killed selfishly, without respect. (*In her limbs she felt the actions of Marchidas, battling mind and body with her Wolf: respect? Yes. but of a most un-Green sort ...*) Now Tohalla was going to wear it, the skin ripped off a mutilated and steaming corpse.

The growing suns made it sparkle in colours the House had never known.

'Put it on then, girl!' Behind Adiockle's brusque command a silver lizardsong chimed from up in the striding-post's branches. The Red enticed and repelled ... Meanwhile Adiockle said forcefully, 'Well, don't just stand there, Toh! You'll need to be long gone when they come looking for you.'

Tohalla, obedient, slipped it on and fastened the claw-catch around her neck. The wolf-hide was soft as tideswool and surprisingly light about her shoulders, though when she moved the head, with its tusks and empty eye-sockets, jiggled on her spine. But she was committed. Wasn't she? And, with shaking fingers, she unloosed her shorn hair from its marriage-cap.

All the same, Tohalla was slow to follow her aunt's footsteps down the ringing bole. On the threshhold she paused, her eyes drawn to the strange and beautiful room. Sunlight embroidered a pattern through the lacy bark lattice, splashing brightness on the dear, familiar things: the windowsill, the rug, and a cloth-covered bowl of rising dough. Farewell to the welcoming Green –

'Will you get a move on, Toh! I've got better things to do than wait around on your good pleasure.'

Farewell.

CHAPTER TWO

Red Ways

The Axe went first, shinning up the plank framework of the pulley used for trading salt and spineder-calves for the Iron Men's wares. But her eyes were fastened to the Axe's beauty that she had been so long in seeing, to the smooth flow of his wiry body.

The framework creaked a little as his weight shifted its angle against the spikes of the Edge but he was sure-footed and didn't fall to their amber cruelty. Balanced at the top, he reached a hand down to steady Tohalla, and Edrach came behind her to catch her if she fell. Apprehensive, Tohalla began to spider up the planks, not sure she could still climb. It had been so long since she had ... *What if I fall? Will my baby be all right?* But in a few moments she was up and over and working her way down the outside of the Edge. Her feet crunched irrevocably on the crystal carpet of the Red.

Easy, really. I wonder why the Iron Men don't invade? But Tohalla didn't voice her question. Words seemed too small to bridge the distance that was growing between her and all that was familiar. Goodbye was the hardest word of all. But Tohalla had to say it *now*, before Housefather found out that Adiockle and Sibulkrin had helped them.

She could hardly see them between the sparkling thorns. Even their voices seemed cut off. Adiockle's yell was muffled: 'You, Axe, take care of her. And Tohalla! Reap full harvest out there.'

Her answer was a pale trickle of sound in the glittering Red. 'Goodbye! And thank-you. Give my love to Trin ...'

Ain Tsui of the Battle-Axe tugged Tohalla's hand. The Redwood and safety lay just beyond the clearing.

The Axe and Edrach ran for the joy of it, their arms outstretched to their homeland. Their spirit of adventure infected Tohalla, so that she jumped little outposts of the Edge that grew like sparkling topaz, happiness singing in her. Around her the Red sang too as the suns' light struck notes from the crystals' expansion, or the freshening breeze combed chords from musky, rosy fans. Shafts of sunlight danced between overhanging trees whose colours rainbowed down upon her. In hollows, the emerald of new grass had escaped to colonize. She stopped surreptitiously to greet it with her fingers.

And the scents! Rich, deep as earth, as fresh as spring in a beanfield. Soon the Edge was hidden by the towering Redwood but her new life soared in front of her with the columns of clear honey light. How her husband's hair gleamed! Tohalla's whole being smiled with delight.

Edrach, slowed, so that she easily caught him up. And on a sudden leap the Axe stopped too. Tohalla wondered if Edrach had Red-speeched him for the sake of good manners, but it didn't matter. She and Edrach walked to him arm-in-arm. Together the three of them went on, single file where the man-thick trees crowded in against the light, or side by side where the wood was open. In one broad, sun-filled clearing Tohalla grinned in pleased surprise: the yellow flowers of oil-seed smiled familiarly at her, set here at random by off-shore winds. The Axe trampled it as he passed.

Tohalla hastened after him. To redeem herself she asked, 'What's this?', crouching by a bush whose movement had caught her eye.

The Axe scarcely glanced at its opening buds. 'Stenchweed.' His tenor voice floated casually back over his shoulder while he strode on. 'Don't close get.'

Edrach, now beside her and now at her back, kept up the lesson in a low voice, 'It the movement of ripperclaws feels, or other small creatures. The stench a venom is. It them to the ground glues, and their flesh melts, so that their goodness into the soil goes and the roots feeds.'

Plants that kill? All Tohalla's fears of the Red came back.

Tohalla was beginning to tire. She was unused to walking so far and the ache was burning in her belly again, but she still strode out to keep up with the Axe. Every time he waited for her, he started walking again as soon as she got near.

She swallowed her annoyance and asked Edrach, 'How does he know where he's going?'

From behind Edrach said quietly, 'The suns. The lie of the land. And we both this way before have been. Even though it different in Summer looks from that wolf-driven trail in the snow.'

160

Wolves. Tohalla had forgotten about them. The mauve and scarlet shadows seemed colder than before. And darker. A mutinas with nocked arrow lurked behind every alien tree.

Now she could see nothing Green here, nothing at all. The ground was red with crystal, or the feathered brown of hookweed. The trees were trees only by courtesy of their size: they were rounded, or spear-straight, or lilac fans that dwarfed her. Some were pyramids of ochre, or spires of russet like apples on a string. And though the song of the Red had charmed her when she was in the safety of the striding-post, it threatened her now from every side with its unfamiliarity. Even Marchidas's life inside her had not prepared Tohalla for its outlandish reality.

Around midday, they dropped down into a steep-sided gully that seemed to trap the heat. There was not a whisper of wind to cool the sweat sticking to her face. The Redwood thinned out here. Sudden noises, bell-like or crackling from the scrawny vegetation, kept making Tohalla jump. She wished they would make their nooning soon; this endless, nerve-wracking trek was troubling. Her womb ached, and the hot flare of light on alien vegetation was hard on her eyes.

The Axe came back to consult with Edrach. Tohalla sank down into a crouch, reluctant actually to sit on the covering of red crystals that bit into her boot-soles. *Red-bitten ...*

'On come, Tohalla of the Loom.'

The Axe's impatience broke off Tohalla's gathering fear. Irrationally, that made her resentful.

Deliberately lagging behind so that Edrach would come to her, Tohalla said behind the Axe's back, 'Doesn't he think about me? Or the baby?'

Edrach touched her; calm flowed through his fingertips, but after a moment she rejected its comfort. *Surely the Axe should be caring for me?*

'We there in a moment will be. Then you by a cool stream can rest.'

Sulkily she followed her husband's distant back.

The scramble up the far side of the gully did nothing to improve Tohalla's temper. Filthy, scratched by who-knew-what diseased Red plants, she cannoned into the Axe when he stopped. Absently he put an arm round her to steady her, but he wasn't really aware of *her*, Tohalla, a person. That grated too.

Edrach came up silently behind them. Again Tohalla noticed how tall he was. Abnormally tall. But at least he patted her shoulder and said, 'Well done, Toh.'

'Can you it find?' the Axe said over her head. Tohalla was angry at the perfection of his profile.

Edrach nodded, his brown and grey hair plastered to his forehead by perspiration. A few steps away he rummaged in the dark gap between a tumble of rocks and the fallen lances of amethyst trees.

Tohalla was too tired even to ask what 'it' was. At least there was shade here …

At last Edrach grunted and heaved aside a couple of rocks. 'I it have,' he said breathlessly, and Tohalla could feel the joy radiating from him.

He turned. In his grimy hands he held the Book.

Tohalla sucked in breath, gasping. Edrach turned the bulbous end of the cylinder and it glowed, faint and greenish, as she had known it would. She recognized the blurred, dragging speech: a different page but the same kind of Book the Green thought was unique.

The Axe snatched the cylinder before she could touch it. His hands turned it swiftly; his examination was prosaic while she was rapt in wonder. And Edrach was digging at something else in the shadowy roots of the rock.

A writing book. *They told me, but I didn't believe they could write!* Tohalla felt humbled.

Edrach unwrapped its weight, leafed through its curled and battered pages that were so thick compared with the squashed pulp the Book itself had told the Greens how to make, almost with its last whole breath.

No, thought Tohalla. *Ours is not* The *Book, it's only* A *Book. There could be dozens –*

And the Axe took the thing from Edrach and read, ' "So we her out of the marshes followed, because Captain Tsui" –'

Edrach's sudden warning stopped the Axe from telling Tohalla more. 'I a Wolf feel,' he hissed.

'There no –' began the Axe, but Edrach was chivvying them: 'Time to be gone.'

Fear, that was what Tohalla remembered afterwards of the long walk. Fear and boredom, and the harsh glare of the suns on a thousand sharp-edged crystals. No soft Green, smiling in tame fields, but the vast, hungry Red that lay waiting all around, sometimes beguiling her but more often hurting with its jagged edges and scents that buried her in the heart of its wrongness.

After the first excitement came days that were always the same. The Redwood smothered her with its cavernous arcades, and who-knew-what ready to pounce from hiding. Under the canopy of red and mauve and blue, the air hung still and breathless between the endless aisle of

162

trees. Strange stirrings were crystals fragmenting to root where they might – or small crawlers that made Tohalla shriek when they fell suddenly into her hair. Red-mites burrowed and festered in her skin. They didn't bother the Wolfmen. Edrach said, 'If you Red-meat eat, Tohalla, they you won't touch.'

Tohalla shuddered. 'I'd rather have Red-mites than eat dead animals.'

'Your privilege,' shrugged the Axe with all the disdain of youth. At least Edrach poulticed her sores with marshstar when they camped for the night, and took her pain away with his twist-born touch. Tohalla wondered for the thousandth time why she had come.

At last the trees thinned. The rolling hills tended downwards and midsummer dazzled in a broad swathe of light. Then, as they jogged down into an enormous valley – Tohalla's legs had been strengthened by days on the march by that time – the openness frightened her, because anyone might see them exposed on the flatlands that shimmered in the heat.

The Axe was seldom with her in daylight. Tohalla would not let him see how much that hurt.

Edrach, limping beside her, tried to explain: 'He the scout is. He a safe way must find, or enemies, because he more swiftly than us moves. And we quick must be the rains to beat.'

On one day whose awfulness Tohalla never forgot, the Axe cupped the ruby heart of a broken messenger. She watched his face slacken as his mind sank into it. Beneath the racing shadows of clouds on the hillside, she saw his head rise as though he snuffed the air. Behind his closed eyelids, the eyes themselves moved, seeing something she couldn't see. Apprehension seized her.

She stared round wildly. Edrach was out of sight – no, under cover, guarding them from a hiding-place beside a knobby cluster of round, gold growth. Hadn't he said where there were messengers, there were wolves? Tohalla discovered that she could be so tense she shook with the effort of not running.

Blind emotions worked the Axe's face: his jaw dropped in fear and pain forced lines between his pale eyebrows. Then a lewd, unfocused leer thinned his lips into a grin of lust that made Tohalla feel unclean.

Was I as naked as that? she wondered in horror. *Did Edrach's heart twist when he saw in my face how Marchidas made love with Benhannon? – No!* – but the thought was hard to squash back out of sight.

Tohalla hadn't seen the Axe let go of the blood-coloured fan of crystal but he looked like himself again. *What's going on inside him, though?*

163

The Axe put an end to her wonderings by saying, 'I so thought. Edrach?'

Edrach hauled himself stiffly to his feet and came closer. Tohalla noticed all of a sudden how the skin hung emptily on the big man's frame. But Edrach was saying as though he weren't on his way to death, 'Comets, is it?'

The Axe nodded, squinting south-west into the glare. 'A line of 'em, not long after second mating. They hungry are. Their pool's dried. They for the Big River are heading.'

The two men nodded, though Tohalla didn't know why. *They never tell me anything!* This time Edrach walked ahead with the Axe, and even Tohalla could tell the line of their march into the lowlands had changed.

They walked faster now, and the dried-up crystals shattered into red grit under their feet. It whirled up around them in a glittering cloud that the hot wind dragged at. The Axe looked round and she waved to him, but it wasn't her he was looking at.

The men began to draw ahead. Tohalla wanted to shout at them to wait, but the heat had pressed a silence on the burned-up land and she was loth to break it. She walked faster. The dust gritted between her teeth, chafing at her groin and armpits where her clothes rubbed. But the Axe and Edrach did not wait for her as they usually did so she ran to catch up. At least Edrach had found medicines that stilled her aches, but the forced pace worried her more than the hunger and thirst, more even than the suns that made her eyes ache and her head throb.

What are comets, anyway?

Tohalla ran downwards into the valley that was so wide she could see no rim on the horizon. Its garnet vastness unnerved her and she was glad when she skidded to a halt by the Axe.

'Don't run,' he said, putting a hand on her shoulder to turn her around. Where he pointed, swirling puffs of dust hung against the hillside, pale against the fierce glitter of the Red. Footprints written on the air.

Tohalla shook his hand off. 'I only ran because you wouldn't wait for me,' she said defensively. 'What's all the rush for?'

'Comets.'

That was all he said. Then the Axe turned and crunched away down the slight incline.

It was left to Edrach to explain. Arm in arm with Tohalla he walked, but swiftly, following the Axe's trail of broken crystals. The clouds of pink grit left by the Axe ground at their eyes and set them both coughing but it couldn't stop Tohalla asking questions.

164

Between spasms, Edrach said, 'No running? Because it those dust-devils bigger makes. Anyone them could see.'

Tohalla interrupted. 'But there isn't anyone to see them! We haven't come across anyone at all since we left the Green.'

Edrach coughed over the last part of her sentence, a fit so cruel that he had no breath to answer while the crystals of the lowlands split tinkling in the heat. At odd intervals other growths erupted, tall banks of maroon or brown that looked dull and withered.

Finally Edrach said, 'Mutinas. Haven't you their smoke in the distance seen? They us now will follow – if they hungry are. Or if they a woman need.'

Alarm beat in Tohalla's blood. She whipped her head from side to side, trying to look in every direction at once. 'Why have we left the shelter of the forest, then?'

Edrach squeezed her arm reassuringly. 'The Axe ahead looks, I behind. Our supplies of Green stuff almost gone are. Now we by the speed of hunting are chained.'

'Hunting?' Tohalla almost spat the word out, so great was her disgust. 'It's – it's –' but she couldn't think of any word strong enough. *Hunting! To kill a living creature and strip it of its dignity by eating the flesh you had mutilated. No Green would even contemplate such a thing!* She pulled away, leaving the hideous old man to choke on the dust-devils that sprang up where she strode. Yet however hard she tried, the Axe's dust still gritted in Tohalla's mouth.

When the Axe stopped at last, Redsun was a ball of pulsing fire that finally gave black definition to the horizon. The ground was sand and gravel now with climbing ruby spires puncturing the air at intervals. From higher up Tohalla had seen the wavering threads of a stream, but now, in the dried-up bed of the Big River, she could only scent damp earth in the shadows. Footsore, she limped up behind the Axe.

He was urinating.

Tohalla moved back, embarrassed by the splashing sound; such things were kept private in the Green. But the Axe said, 'You too. Just here, where the bubbles rise.'

'Why?'

'Don't ask why! Just do it. This my land is. Fair?'

He moved aside, retying the thong that laced his trousers.

Tohalla squatted obediently – *Why should I?* – but the habit of obeying was deep in her.

'Not there!' snarled the Axe. 'There!'

'Don't watch!'

165

'Well do what I you tell! Don't you want to eat?'

Disadvantaged by her squatting, Tohalla still managed to say, 'Eat?' in a strangled voice, but she was too late to stop anyway.

'Yes, eat! And quick be, if you your foot don't want to lose.'

Scared, revolted, she moved aside, stumbling over her trousers, and as the bloody sunset leached colour from the sky overhead, Tohalla heard, in the darkness that closed about her, Edrach going through the same performance. *Why just here? Why now? Why won't the Axe ever explain?*

Suddenly the ground lurched under Edrach's feet.

Tohalla shrieked and sprang back, still fumbling at her waist-string.

Edrach rode the heaving earth, spear tight-held in his hand.

Tohalla gagged. Noxious mud slurped under the ruptured surface. Beneath it bulged some obscene thing, dripping gouts of feculence. Higher it rose, until Edrach was marooned on its reeking back.

Then a three-fingered hand snaked from underground darkness into the half-light. Soft and pudgy it was, almost like a human fist reaching back towards Edrach.

Horror pegged Tohalla in place. The Axe swung his spear-tip; its iron edge severed the hand which fell to the gravel. And a wail like a burnt baby's shivered through Tohalla's soul.

She longed to comfort the creature but now Edrach was plunging his own spear over and over into its back and the thing was crying and she was screaming, 'Stop it! Stop it!' and all the Axe would do was slash at its imploring arm.

Tohalla slapped her hands to her ears but there was no getting away from the piteous cries. Even after she stumbled blindly into the black reaches of the river-bed the awful, human blubbering followed her. The last time she fell she stayed hunched, her head pressed on her knees, arms straining to block the sobbing from her ears.

I'll go back! she thought. Tohalla swayed to her feet. 'I'm going back,' she croaked and her voice came from eons beyond the thick dusk. She splashed, staggering, towards the night side of the sky. 'I'm going back to the Green!'

Her words echoed in the sudden stillness vacated by those hideous sobs. She careened sharply off an unseen spire of growth and said again, 'It's all right. I'm going back.'

She blundered into the Axe and fell into something yielding and sticky. She wouldn't let herself think what it was. 'Sorry,' she said quite normally. 'I'm going back now.'

Tohalla tried to stand up, twisting her ankle on the slobbering,

166

pitted surface and the thought swamped her mind: *I'm walking on dead flesh! It's like a nightmare!* Trying to walk when something grabs at your feet, slipping back or sideways at every slithering unseen step, trapped in a hideous night.

The Axe leaped up and grabbed her savagely – she couldn't hear what he was shouting for the roaring in her ears – but Edrach came and stroked the back of her neck. Was it in words he said, 'See that light on the plain, Tohalla? That a camp-fire is. Mutinas. We other bait than you must use before we tonight the river cross.'

Mutinas would steal her and her child. Tohalla stayed.

The Sons of the Wolf butchered the carcase by touch – but not by Tohalla's. Apart from them, she tried not to watch the way they skinned the round body of the trailing spines that gave the beast its name, but in horrified compulsion she could not take her eyes from its single arm that still twitched even after Edrach cut it from the beast's head.

Away beyond the foetid mud, the acrid alien scent of the comet's blood still stung the back of Tohalla's throat, and the tiny campfire so distant in the lee of the Redwood disappointed her cruelly with its beckoning welcome: *Mutinas! I won't let them get my child.* But Tohalla's vehemence was only to try and make herself believe ...

Gold Moon's light showed only three lumpen shapes dark against the gilded, tinkling plain. And when Tohalla had watched in revulsion as Edrach and the Axe blew up sections of the comet's hide to float them all across the last, deep, golden stream, even those shapes disappeared into the maze of channels.

At least in the dark Tohalla could try to pretend she was safe in the Green. First light, though, dragged a clangour from the Red all around her as the suns' heat began to creep over the horizon. Seeing the mauve and amber creepers on the rock walls of their hideout completed her disillusion.

'Eat, Tohalla,' urged the Axe, mumbling round his food and pointing at dead comet. 'There nothing else for you is.'

She was hidden with him in a cleft at the base of a low bluff; Edrach was prowling outside the maze of muddled stones. A chill of dawn made Tohalla huddle over the small, fierce fire but her shivers were mostly from fatigue and fear. Hunks of brownish meat sizzled blood into the flames, but the Axe was chewing something blue.

'Why can't I have some of that blue stuff?' Tohalla asked.

The Axe shattered another long crystal to get his teeth into the pulpy mess inside. 'Because it no good for the baby is. I nothing for you could find.' He gestured again at the meat speared over the fire. 'It ready by now should be.'

'I'm not eating a dead animal!' she said. 'Especially not after you made us all pee on it.'

'Only on the skin. In dry seasons comets in river-mud hide. It them cool and moist keeps. We the skin of one wet so it thought it was raining and it out came. Anyway, it in the river got washed, didn't it? Now we enough food for days have.'

'Well I haven't.' Her face wrinkled in disgust. 'I can't eat some poor creature that cries like a human child. You're nothing but a filthy animal yourself!'

He snorted and spat out a bit of blue pith. 'You a hypocrite are. Everything kills to live. But you and your precious Greens, you a whole planet are killing! Remember the seastalkers? Remember when Housefather us in chains dragged so we the black-burned earth could dig? What survived those flames?'

'At least we Rosaria respect.'

Tohalla shifted suddenly on her haunches to sneer at him through the fire's haze. 'Respect? Respect? You don't know the meaning of the word!' Pointing fiercely at the cooking flesh she yelled, 'Call that respect? At least we care for every creature of the Green!'

He smiled with withering scorn and she could have hit him. 'You dead bodies in a hole full of shit tip and that respect call? You me Pierse showed, remember? I his funeral through your mind saw, na? I that to a mutinas wouldn't do.'

'Pierse wanted it that way! He part of – He was part of the Green! His body went back to the earth, to nourish it, just like he did in life!'

The Axe laughed. That hurt so much that she could hardly keep still. But he made it worse yet: 'And you the food ate that his flesh nourished? You nothing more than a cannibal are!'

Tohalla's face was ugly in her fury. *How dare he reject me?* 'Yes, I ate what he gave! Part of him is in me still. We both Greens are. We belong to each other even in death.'

'Even though he you unhappy in life made? Tohalla, Tohalla –'

Edrach sidled back in through the gap in the stones, his good eye asquint with anxiety. 'Ssh! Do you want the mutinas to hear? They only the other side of the river are, up to their chests in the comet's blood. A pregnant woman even better prey would be.'

Edrach lowered himself to the ground, swinging his leg out stiffly before him. 'Rosaria big enough for us all is. We all here belong, even

168

with our different ways, because this one little planet all we have is.'

He stared at the Axe. 'Isn't that why you here are, Ain? And you, Tohalla, our ways to learn and teach? Now stop squabbling. You like a pack of privates sound.'

But she wouldn't eat the meat.

The mutinas passed, and the days passed, each hotter than the one before. Tohalla and the Wolfmen marched north and west up the steepening valley of a tributary, and the baby began to kick. The old man – Chosen Brother looked older by the day – often laid a hand on her belly and reassured her that the baby girl was well and whole inside her. On the trek after the Axe's retreating back, he showed her which crystals to eat, and which to use for medicine, but there wasn't much food with the drought.

When she fainted with hunger, the Axe ordered her to eat meat. But Edrach made her a meat broth that smelled delicious, and said, 'If you don't eat, the baby may die.'

And, trying to overcome her nausea, she began to worry meat down. The Red-mites stopped boring into her flesh. She grew stronger, and she needed to, because the Axe watched the skies and marched faster than ever through the dried-up crimson wastes.

For the Axe was obsessed with paying back the blood-debt of his line. He strode relentlessly ahead. Tohalla knew she was slowing him down, but though she tried to keep going through the iron-hard hills, she had to rest. She didn't like to be a burden, but she couldn't quite understand why the idea of going to see the Ship possessed him so utterly. *Would a day or two make so much difference?*

But Edrach, limping beside her when the trail allowed, took time to be her friend. He showed her things, and made jokes and allowance, and told her stories about when Marchidas was a little girl, and how he and Benhannon took care of Marchidas's son. He explained how Benhannon came to give the boy an Iron Man name when he was old enough to earn it. And when evening shadows raced down from the hills, Edrach pointed out the beauty of the Red he loved so much.

Yet when she was alone, Tohalla's thoughts spun with herself at centre, since there was no work she could do for others so far from home. She felt lonely, and frightened, and sick with herself for having made such a mistake. She knew she should never have come into the cruel Red lands. But Housefather had married her to the Axe; she was stuck with him. And guilt at such ideas anchored her more surely to herself in the hours and days when she plodded endlessly through the hot and hostile Red.

But the nights … when the cook-fire had burned from viridian flames to homely coals and the stars swung low and sparkling in the soft summer nights, Edrach would say, 'I crackwood for this leg of mine must find,' or 'A hot-pool of mud my aches would ease,' and leave her alone with the Axe and her resentments.

The Axe shared none of her awkwardness. The skill of his fingers would untangle the mesh of her nerves. Tohalla kissed him then with her whole body, as if she could pull his being into hers. Her own passion frightened her, so surprising was it to a woman of the Green, but the Axe always knew what she wanted, though she would have died of shame before talking of such a subject.

Of course he knows, Tohalla thought, relaxing gradually on the Wolf-hide as the Axe stroked her softly and then harder. *He a son of the Wolf is*, and she would listen to his breathing to test whether she was pleasing him. But then sensation would blot thought, so that she forgot even how swollen and alien her body had become with the Daughter of the Wolf inside it …

Just looking at him next day, so distant on the hot and dusty trail, made her remember the pressure of his hips, or the caress of his tongue on her skin. And an echo of orgasm would vibrate through her.

In the night, she never doubted that he loved her.

Then one night, afterwards, when the Amethyst Moon and Gold Moon threw shadows of a different black, and the living stones glowed ghostly above a marsh where strange creatures chimed unseen, Tohalla lay in the borderlands of sleep.

The Axe said dreamily, 'Tomorrow we our Ship will find to take us to the stars …'

CHAPTER THREE

Three Flights

Mist-white dawn. Chill silence even in the marsh where the secret animals were waiting for the suns.

Tohalla felt the Axe kissing her. She groaned, reluctant to wake from a warm dream of the House, but his excitement was contagious. Yawning, she returned his embrace.

He was lying on one elbow above her. Tohalla's fingers found something hard around his throat. She explored – and sat up with a jerk.

A necklace of claws gleamed dark and steely on his naked chest. She had never wondered before what might be in his pack. Around his wrists and arms were pointed teeth. She looked further: they were on his ankles too. And each point was traced with scenes of battle and of death.

She could tell the Axe sensed her mental withdrawal by her physical one; he said quickly, 'I Captain am! When I the Ship find, I need my ranks to wear.' He looked at Tohalla to see how she was taking it. Certainly she didn't feel impressed, as he had obviously hoped.

He rushed on, trying to recapture his enthusiasm. 'Look.' His fingers fondled the claws around his neck. 'This my first Wolf was. See the battle? I never Marchidas's thought-powers so strong had. But I him anyway beat.' Smiling, the Axe held it out to her. 'Go on, Toh, you can read it!'

Tohalla didn't move. She could feel his baby kicking hard inside her. *Will she be a killer too?* Tohalla couldn't think of anything to say that wouldn't wound him, so she said nothing.

Ain Battle-Axe dropped the heavy cone back on his chest. It rattled against the others and she only just heard him sigh. Then he slapped

171

her companionably on the shoulder, like he did with Edrach. 'On come, Toh. This the start of Rosaria's greatest adventure is.'

Tohalla rolled awkwardly to her feet, her belly getting in the way. In the time it took her to splash water from the length of gut onto her face, he pulled on a waistcoat and short kilt of hide.

'The start?' Tohalla asked sleepily, struggling to pull on an overtunic against the chill morning mist. The familiar tideswool she had spun and woven in her other life muffled her words. 'I should have thought it was the end. Still, I suppose if you do find it, you'll have to find someone to tell.'

Her head popped out of the neck-hole. 'What are we going to do, Ain? Go to this winterground place?'

He looked up from blowing on the fire's embers. His eyes were red and squinting from the thin smoke. 'This the Ship is, Tohalla, that we about are talking. The Ship! Don't you understand?'

Tohalla came to kneel by the other side of the fire, wondering where Edrach was. She had that old, familiar feeling of hopelessness because she could tell she and the Axe were going to argue again, and it never got anywhere. It never seemed to resolve anything, or bring them closer. They just did what the Axe said because this was his world – but sometimes Edrach could make the two of them feel better about each other. Now, though she could hear Edrach's halting steps out in the scrub of rustling marsh-growth, he did not appear. There was only her husband.

Confronted by this Wolfman in his death-soaked trophies, Tohalla didn't feel conciliatory.

'What's to understand, Ain? We're going to find Good Captain's Ship. It's exciting, it's what you were born for, but I can't believe like Marchidas did that it's going to stop your people marauding up and down this world killing each other.'

'But it's the Ship, Toh!'

'The suns will still go on rising and setting and the grass back home won't grow any greener. I can't see what difference it'll make.'

'*Everything* different will be! We on this prison won't be held! We our star-family can rejoin! You and me, Toh! And our baby. We to the stars will go.'

'Don't be ridiculous! The Ship's a wreck anyway – it only got down at all because Good Captain gave up his life to land it. We're where we wanted to be, safe on a planet with good soil and water, where nobody can wage wars on us.'

'But the star family –'

172

'Ain, listen! There is no star family. Doesn't your Book say about how Erth was when Good Captain saved us from the smoking ruins?'

The Axe tried to interrupt but Tohalla wasn't listening. 'Ain, if anybody's left out there it's only the wicked ones! The ones who have things that kill hundreds of people at a distance. They don't even have to see you to hate you. They're not human, not some loving star family. If they were family, would they have left us alone? Wouldn't they have come looking for us, to help us?'

The Axe stared at her, his handsome face not handsome any more but cruel and mocking. 'Have you finished?' he asked in a voice that scorched her like the cold of snow. 'Then ready get. And don't to me talk about things you don't understand. Didn't your version of the truth you tell that Captain Ain Tsui his ranks in war won?'

In crude Red-speech that made Tohalla's head ache, the Axe thrust a picture of dying and burning and a thing in Good Captain's hand that exploded against his people. The Axe watched her face lose colour until it was the same sickly white as the waiting sky.

Tohalla couldn't stand looking at him any more. She heard a creature shrill alarm from the mist drifting over the brown-spiked marsh; a splash and the shrilling was choked off. Something else had died in the Red.

Slowly Tohalla looped up the length of gut that held their drinking-water. It sloshed as she draped it over her shoulder. She didn't even notice the animal feel of the dead intestine.

'Now, Tohalla, we the *Mosckva* are going to find. And then we in our bodies to the stars will go. Fair?'

Why answer? He is dancing to the beat of a different song.

Frightened now but not quite sure what of *(surely even he knows the Ship was broken in the crash? Even Benhannon thought it would be rusted through.)* Tohalla scrambled after the Axe.

As usual he kept well ahead; Tohalla kept looking back to see where Edrach had got to. She kept telling herself that Edrach would be able to track them, that he'd know where the Axe had taken her. But even when both suns burned off the mist she couldn't see Edrach limping through the mud behind her. She hoped he was all right ...

Redsun raced past Whitesun and long shadows raced over the marsh. Even here at its edge the light scared thousands of clangs and whistles out of unseen creatures. As the earth warmed up, crystals of scarlet and ochre and acid yellow gonged, but Tohalla could find no harmony on the hot wind. The discord throbbed painfully in her head.

173

Memory: the shape of the land folded into a pattern Marchidas had known. With it came a hint of Marchidas's excitement. And Tohalla heard Marchidas repeating the ancient words of Leftant Vassily: 'In the southern marshes where the river spreads.'

For here the shrunken river spread and wandered, and living rocks had hunkered down the shrivelled banks to dip their feet in the water. Dried mud crazed slopes the river used to shelter. Scummy hollows sank between dead and broken crystal. Tohalla found it hard to breathe; the marsh was stiff with the stink of decay.

And spires of ruby twisted up towards the sky.

'You see?' the Axe shouted, ahead of her. 'You see, Tohalla of the Loom? I you told! Don't you it from Marchidas remember?'

The awful thing was, she did.

With Marchidas's vision doubled over her own, Tohalla stumbled on clumps of yellow-weed Marchidas hadn't known. Her foot fell through air where Marchidas had walked on a sand-bank time had washed away. The shadows of pain burned her wrist and an echo of Ain's birth gripped her belly and back and thighs. *What is this doing to my baby?*

'There!'

Tohalla looked up at that glad and glorious cry. The Axe was pointing, exultation in every line of his lean, tanned body. *He so right in his ranks looks!* Tohalla thought unintentionally, knowing it wasn't her own thought even then. *Marchidas would have been so proud ...*

Because Tohalla followed the line of his quivering arm out towards the steaming marsh. Double shadows aimed like an arrow at a crusted tower of ruby that blazed where their green and black hearts mingled. And she was sure with Marchidas's certainty that it was the *Mosckva*.

The sparkling crimson clusters could not disguise the soaring arabesque of a tail-fin. Joy surged in her, lifting her spirit so that she felt she could fly into the great blue dome of the Autumn sky –

Abruptly Tohalla was her own again. Doubt dashed her down. It was only another burst of red crystals, climbing over one another in their need to grow away from the ooze. Even the weary aches inside Tohalla were her own. It would be months and months yet before she gave birth.

The Axe was splashing through the marsh, moving exuberantly, without his usual care and control. Tohalla pitied him for the disappointment that was coming to him. The Ship must have been huge to bring machinery and people and livestock; there was nothing near big enough in this neck of the marsh.

174

The muscles of her cheek pulled her mouth into a grimace and she sighed.

Where's Edrach?

Even on tip-toe she couldn't see him. At least there was no trace of mutinas either. Her adrenalin crawled back out of her blood-stream, leaving her exhausted. Tohalla slumped to rest in the shadow of a rock, but it was no cooler there.

So high they were invisible, the first arrow-falls flew belling overhead.

A clangour shocked through her. All the marsh seemed to call back that violent sound with strident jangles of crawlers and fliers and crystals. Tohalla started to her feet, then thought better of it and ducked into cover while the hideous breaker of noise still pounded in her head.

Momentarily the thumping stopped. 'Tohalla! Tohalla, on come! We work have to do.'

She could see the Axe madly waving, though the rest of his words were drowned out. Sighing again, Tohalla dumped her pack in the shade and pulled off her boots. She had discarded her trousers miles before when the morning mist had evaporated. Edrach had been nowhere in sight even then. She still had no idea where he was.

Wading out through the tepid water, Tohalla tried not to think of what might be lurking in it. The mud writhed up between her toes like something alive. *Something with a hand? Like a comet?* She shuddered in spite of the heat that dried her sweat, and pushed herself faster …

The Axe was balanced on a rock half in and half out of the murk, chipping away feverishly at the clusters of crimson and vermilion that winked in the suns' light. It seemed that however many of the dish-like crystals he prised off, there were always more underneath. *It's hardly surprising*, Tohalla thought. Glittering red dust puffed out in choking showers that clung to her skin too when she got close enough.

'On come, Tohalla!' he panted. 'Didn't you the arrow-falls hear?'

She pulled herself up onto the knobbly rock, annoyed by his haste. The crystal-mound was hot under her unprotected thighs; she curled her legs up clear of the water and whatever might be lurking in it.

Despite the nervous pounding of her heart, she had had enough of his bullying. *No*, she thought, *not really bullying. It's just that he takes no notice of me because he only cares about his stupid blood-debt.* Leaning back against a ruby outcrop, she was too hot and sticky to be bothered about his ridiculous Ship.

The Axe kept on worrying at the crystals, snapping over his

175

shoulder, 'Quick, Tohalla!'

She fanned red dust away from her face. 'No, Ain. Edrach can help you.' She added nastily, 'Where is he, anyway?'

'Guard keeping. Now on come, will you? The rain's coming!'

Tohalla quirked her face into a supercilious grin that was wasted on his back. Overhead the sky was that pure blue you only get in autumn, deep and clear. Yet somewhere over the heat-hazed marsh arrow-falls called, invisible, to show the year had turned.

'How d'you know what Edrach's doing?' Tohalla said angrily. 'Or even if he's still alive? You don't care anyway, do you? Not now he's too old to be useful to you.'

That stopped the Axe. But only for a moment. Still picking away with his spear-tip he said, 'That unfair is. This Ship just as much to Edrach means as it to me does. You the only one are who to the stars doesn't want to go. You the outsider are, not me. Not Edrach either.'

'But he's still an after-thought, isn't he? He's old and ill and you've just left him behind, your own flesh and blood, practically. He cared for you – '

'You him behind as well left, Tohalla!'

'Yes, but – ' she faltered, stung by guilt, ' – but I don't know my way in this Green-forsaken wilderness!'

'Well now you your conscience have sopped, you can stop worrying. I'd know if Edrach dead was. He wide is sweeping.' The Axe stopped just long enough to wipe the sweat off his forehed. Red smeared his temple. *Like blood?*

'Tohalla, you've got to help!' The Axe whacked the crystals in frustration, turned to glare at her, wild-eyed. 'This the first time is since I was promoted that the marsh low enough is. I five years have waited. And now the arrow-falls the rains are singing! Help me!'

But, abruptly, he abandoned her in disgust. Tohalla could hardly make out what he was saying as he banged at the mud-spattered Red: 'Hnh! Just like a Green! You for me not a hand would turn. Nor for the planet.'

And though she hadn't moved, a ripple of water tickled her toes.

Tohalla recoiled from it. *He's right! It* is *rising!*

'Ain – ' she said, scrambling to her feet in panic.

He glanced round, at the water-level, at her face. 'Didn't you the arrow-falls hear, Tohalla? The rains over the Northern Hills have broken. Now crystal shift! I must the doorway find.'

'But there isn't one! This isn't – '

Desperately the Axe locked his spear beneath another ruby plate.

He wrenched at the haft, muscles straining. A single red crystal creaked, spun loose, but there were the deposits of centuries still to break through. And the water was rising.

'Ask – Marchidas, Tohalla – of the Green,' he panted.

And there, in that other life she had been given, Tohalla found the knowledge; back when Leftant Vassily was dying on a harsh red planet that was not her home, before the messengers had been found, before the dying Book had faded into a sullen, growling glow. And tradition had fleshed the picture out in Marchidas's mind.

'There still a chance exists.' Vassily coughed. Under her withered breast the knife-hilt held back the blood its blade had pushed into her lungs. Kalinskaya wanted to pull the knife out, but Vassily wouldn't let her comrade do that. Death was close enough without choking on her own blood.

'Keep record in the Log everything that has happened, Tatya. They – ' she nodded feebly at the children waiting beyond the tattered awning Tatya Kalinskaya Kerchanova had rigged to shade her from the alien suns. 'They the truth must know. Teach them specifications – procedure – everything from the readouts. How Earth to find. Tell them what – what Ain Tsui did. No! No – I'll do it.'

Kalinskaya hated to hear that pettiness in Vassily's voice. Thirty years they'd known each other. In all that time Leftant Vassily had been so strong! Now she sounded like an old woman. She seemed to have forgotten how Loi-Tsu had taken the Mosckva's log. Kalinskaya put the First Officer's personal log in the groping hand.

Leftant Vassily thumbed the record-button lovingly. 'Civilization. Good thngs as well as bad. I wonder how Sergei is. Now I'll never see him.'

Vassily pushed back a strand of dull grey hair from her fever-slicked face. Then, with Kalinskaya helping her hold the book close to her trembling lips, she said, 'My children. All our children. Don't believe Jameson – or Loi-Tsu. They with Ain Tsui was working. Tsui wanted us to stay forever on this mudball, because he sick of war. This what happened.'

The closer to death she came, the more her memory grooves slipped their tracks. English was her third language; her accent grew thicker, the language took on the pattern of the deepest grooves: the speech of her childhood. And the sons of the crew would learn their lessons from her – and from the technical readouts of the Mosckva.

'So,' she said at the end of her tale, 'I can only believe that the same action which wrecked the Mosckva perverted all our instruments as well. Listen to specifications. Learn them. Because one day, in the southern marshes where the river spreads, you our ship will find to take you to the stars.'

And when the Crew had lived out enough generations to become the Sons of *the Wolf, Marchidas in her turn parrotted all the redows she had to learn before she could be promoted: 'Maintenance access in each tail-fin, one metre by one metre ... Crawlspace ... Throw wheel to enter hatch ... Command module bridge on B deck ...'*

Tohalla's lips were mumbling the ancient words. And through her mind cut the Axe's desolation. How could she not help him? And behind her, thrashing through the rising waters, Edrach was coming in answer to the raw need of the Axe's plea.

Heedless of the sharp-cornered growth Tohalla slipped into the ochre marsh. Wading out to meet Edrach, she hugged the old man briefly, appalled at his breathless exhaustion. 'It's all right,' she said quickly, 'you go on. I've got something in my pack.'

Edrach's bloodshot eye twitched a wink at her; he was too out of breath to say anything. But his belief in her heartened Tohalla. She splashed away to the bank, hauled herself to the pack she had left in the shade of the living rock.

Grabbing something from it, she plunged back into the muddy shallows, not thinking now of the creatures that lurked below the surface. Forcing her legs to move against the turgid waters as fast as she could go, Tohalla still had time to see the faintest smudge of darker blue on the heat-hazed horizon. Rainclouds! Then she was working forwards through the rank, resisting marsh, holding something high above her head.

She reached the red mound. Edrach and Ain were picking feverishly at the arching crystal spire. Ain snatched a moment to glance at her; he grunted as if surprised to see her there. But only a moment. His red-smeared arms were trembling but he made himself work on.

Tohalla slipped the string from the neck of the water-proof bag she'd got from her pack. Neither man noticed her. Pouring white powder into the palm of her hand, she sprinkled it with water and mashed the paste onto the winking red.

The crystals bubbled, dissolved.

Now the Axe took notice of her. Ignoring the sting of the paste on her cut fingers, Tohalla said, 'Salt! Remember Adiockle gave us some? Here.'

The ancient enemy of the Red. As the three aliens on this planet attacked the sparkling crimson, it subsided to a dull, acrid smear and Edrach wiped it off with the side of his hand.

'Look!' he shouted. A patch as broad as a man's chest had sunk between the clotted rubies. Edrach reached into it: a hollow gonging sounded as he tapped the dark surface at the bottom of the hole. 'Main –'

178

'–tenance access one metre by one metre,' the Axe and Tohalla echoed.

'See the edge of it?' the Axe yelled excitedly. Marsh-life clanged at his shout, whirring into the air in thick swarms.

Under the advance-guard of ragged cloud, warm water lapped about their knees. The access was chest-height. Tohalla and the Axe slapped salt on the crystal's wound, tracking the crack round the access under the centuries' glittering growth.

Edrach said over the hiss of the dying crystal, 'Before you in the bridge drown, I the Ship will raise.'

Tohalla slathered more salt-paste on; there wasn't much left. The Axe prised plates off with his dagger now he knew which way to go. And no-one followed Edrach, not even with their gaze.

Chill currents began to swirl around their ankles, a relief from the heat of their labours under the fiery suns – and a threat of what was to come. Warmer water stroked their thighs. The access wasn't half uncovered when the ship lurched.

Fright speared Tohalla.

'It only Edrach is,' the Axe said. 'More salt here.'

'There – there isn't any.' Tohalla rinsed the last salt from the bag, dripping it into the crystal above the Axe's knife. It wasn't enough.

The Axe jostled her aside. 'Then give me space, Toh.'

'But the Ship – it moved!'

He only grunted, though the Ship shifted dizzyingly beneath them. Taking sure hand-holds Tohalla climbed past him to see what the danger was.

At first she could see nothing beside the ominous banking clouds to the north, nothing else that might be a threat. If it were some huge and hideous monster, it was out of sight below the wind-rippled marsh. The light was turning livid now, and the choppy surface threw back the glare in dazzling patterns that filled her vision.

Making her way along the low, curving rock – *the roof of the Ship!* – with the crystals cutting into her feet, Tohalla could barely see. But surely the – the Ship was longer than she remembered it?

Then, squinting against in the fiery bewilderment of the light on the glittering marsh, she saw a dark blob. *The monster!*

Tohalla hefted her dagger, willing herself not to turn and run, not to miss. She raised her arm and as the shadows of it fleeted over her eyes, the blob resolved itself. Edrach.

Edrach and ...?

He was backing away, his hands uplifted against some solid black bulk. Tohalla dared not throw the dagger for fear of hitting him. In an agony of fear and indecision, she somehow found the courage to slide down into the water, fighting the urge to run away. She had to get close enough to attack the monster and rescue Edrach. A step nearer, and something moved beneath her heel. Tohalla gritted her teeth. Another step ...

But he didn't need rescuing. Edrach was spreadeagled against a living stone. And it was walking after him.

So amazed was she by this sight that she only just recovered in time to move out of his way; he had no awareness of her. Tohalla watched him sidling round the living stone, pressing it forward now with the heat of the suns at his back, urging it by some strange power of his will to nudge its way under the Ship.

Tohalla saw the whole Ship move a fraction. Just a fraction, but a girdle of dull watergrowth showed above the dazzling surface of the marsh. And the living rock, ochre from the suns' side, settled lower in the water, darkening where the water splashed.

Tohalla waded over to Edrach. Marsh-creatures writhed out of her way. She had to beat down her panic, speaking with her lips almost closed so nothing flew into her mouth. 'Can I help, Edrach?'

But the grey-haired Wolfman turned slowly to the shore. Tohalla saw clearly how effort had reddened his face. An ugly tracery of swollen blood-vessels marbled both eyes, even the blind white one. His massive shoulders were bowed, his heaving chest hollowed. Wrapped in his world of the Red, he didn't see her. He didn't hear her.

A wall of cloud bellied out across the suns and the light shut off suddenly. A cold current was plucking at Tohalla, wrapping her tunic around her legs. She had no idea what to do.

Edrach was coming back again, moving backwards with another living stone seemingly glued to his hands. The Axe was battling the layers of red; crimson crystal fragmented to his frantic attack.

And there was nothing Tohalla could do in all this alien Red to help.

The first outwatch of raindrops burst around her. She stood mid-stream, watching how the marsh dimpled and fountained, hearing the rain zinging on crystal in a thousand muted keys. The wind whiffled hostility; on the sad, moist air there was nothing that smelt of home. Tohalla felt utterly alone, isolated from the desperate need of her husband and Chosen Brother. The Sons of the Wolf.

And she was far, far from the homely Green.

Finally the water slapping at her chin made her decide. She couldn't stay here, not in the middle of the buffeting current. The Axe would never do it. He'd have to come back another year, a long time in the future; the scene leaped ready-dreamed into her thoughts. *We'll settle down quietly, maybe near enough the Green to visit, we'll have children, Edrach living with us –*

Tohalla made her decision, moved.

The Axe screamed and the wind drove his words to where Tohalla shivered on the bank, 'I've done it!'

'*No!*'

Even as her anguish echoed through the greyness of the rain, Tohalla felt the loving touch of Edrach in her mind. And it was like the warmth of an arm around her, though Edrach knelt on the lip of the access.

'Come with me, Toh!' the Axe shouted. 'Touch the stars! Find our path through the winds of the star-sea!'

But the Axe was standing on the Red, one hand flung high against the soaring spire of rain-washed crystal.

Gently Edrach used his mutant gift. He touched their minds together, Tohalla's with Ain Tsui of the Battle-Axe, of the line of First Captain. Fierce and bright was Ain Tsui's, vindicated, aflame with triumph and the lust for conquest of the gulfs between the worlds. *Erth, Tohalla, Erth!*

You'll fall! It'll never fly (dark pain of broken bones and metal piercing their bodies. The baby crushed –)

And Edrach strained to hold the contact with nothing in their awareness of himself but the friendly earth-smell.

We again will rise, Tohalla, like an arrow-fall in autumn! And the Crew my name forever with the Ship will sing: Ain Battle-Axe! Captain Ain Tsui's broken faith is mended!

Tohalla's shock: Broken faith? But Good Captain brought his children here for safe-keeping!

No, thundered the Axe, and Tohalla crumpled, her hands over her ears. *He no Good Captain was, but a madman who the Ship wrecked us here to trap! (Harsh confusion, wires burning and the slant-eyed Captain firing bursts of killing light; metal melted through the smoke of scorched bodies.) Don't you understand, Tohalla? That the blood-debt is! That's what he to my line left! We must fly, for Marchidas my mother's sake, and her father's, and all of them back to first Crew. Because Ain Tsui us here marooned, and he our way-finders broke so that we the Ship couldn't find.*

No! No, no no! she shrieked, and Edrach's face whitened with her pain but it didn't touch the Axe. Tohalla's thoughts spilled violent into their minds: *He was our saviour! He brought us from the smoking wreck of Erth's battles!*

Tohalla! The Axe hurled his thoughts like a command. *The water coming in is! It round my feet is! Come, Tohalla! If the Captain so good was, why did he the Ship crash? Why did he the building machines smash?*

He didn't! He didn't!

But the Axe wasn't listening to her. *He the speak-machine burnt, so no-one near us ever again would come. He said this planet all of us poisoned, and not to come looking.* He lied, *Tohalla! And he the Drone-Ship away sent, so your Greens all the sleeping-ones couldn't have: not the animals, not the people, not even the things that build.*

Tohalla peered through the slanting rain, astonished. The Axe answered her unspoken query, and under his answer rolled Edrach's unshakeable belief:

Sleeping children, and auchses, and medicine, Tohalla. He them killed! He the Drone-Ship undirected and she cried. (Puzzlement; the Wolfmen didn't understand, but they believed.) Vassily heard her. Ask Marchidas.

But Tohalla said, *Good Captain killed children? While they were asleep?* And the sick greyness of the rain-swept marsh was the colour of her soul.

Come, my Tohalla. Or does marriage for nothing in the Green count?

She remembered Edrach saying, 'Or loyalty not in the Green is?' And in words she yelled, 'You can't break my faith, Wolfman! I married you in the Green and you stole me from it, but I'll not risk my baby's life in the sickness of a broken Ship.'

Tohalla! (Despair and fear and loneliness arced from Ain's mind to hers, and Edrach was the messenger.) You've got now to come! The water the Ship's innards will kill. (She saw with Ain's eyes the scurf of drowned crystal surging round his feet into the access.)

No, Ain, not this time. We'll come again another year, I'll do anything –

We it can't leave, Tohalla, not when we so many lives have waited. Now is when the Mosckva *the sky must embrace. Now come, Tohalla, before the water you from me cuts. Before the sky between us falls.*

So confused! Loneliness, longing; you saved me, Ain, now you want to kill me. Pain. All the time, pain. But louder than anything her mind in lurid swirls yelled *fear!*

He played on it; she felt him play on her fear and loathed him for this second attempt at emotional bullying. His mind tried to hide his cunning even from himself, but Ain mind-spoke: *You alone in the Red will be. No-one you to help with the baby-birth.*

And Edrach, his life worn out in this search, turned away from it. *I dying am. I the world where Marchidas was can't leave.*

But – (The Axe was stunned.)

But – (Tohalla couldn't believe that shining sincerity.)

Edrach said, *The blood-debt pay, my Chosen Sister's son. But us here leave, so there someone will be your battle-poem to sing. And your love to Tohalla give, who so much for you has given. Now go! And mind the vacuum doesn't get in –*

The access slammed shut. Dashing rain from her eyes, Tohalla saw Edrach's head above the water, coming to her out of the grey desolation. She was terrified for Ain, sure he would drown in the marsh-bound Ship and at the same time sure it would fall from the dying skies. And from him she felt no mind-touch at all. The current rose frothing around the dull red of the Ship ...

Edrach waded to her, needing her help to haul himself out of the white-capped torrent. He lay gasping beside her, and Tohalla shielded his face from the stinging rain lest he choke.

And nothing happened, but the flood climbed slowly up the Ship, and the rain slackened, and the sea of clouds wept for Tohalla because she couldn't cry for herself. *I wish I was home. Even with Larnis. Even with Worut ...*

Then a roar like thunder came from the marsh, and Tohalla thought it was the Ship.

But it wasn't. Edrach dragged himself to his feet and pulled Tohalla up the sloping bank at a stumbling run. A towering breaker ripped down the channel from the north, a mountain of water that chewed the marsh with trees and corpses as its teeth. And when Tohalla looked back, the tail-fin of the *Mosckva* was only a scarlet needle.

The Axe was trapped beneath the bore.

'Edrach!' she screamed.

The old Wolfman knew what she meant. 'No, the Axe – not yet dead is.' Edrach stopped to gather breath. 'But what he – can do when the Captain the – bridge burnt, he doesn't know. The – redows and the reality – two different things are, like a landscape and a map.'

Tohalla asked no more questions; Edrach's great frame was shivering. She tried to warm him with the heat of her body but though lighter grey patches thinned the clouds, still it gusted rain. *What's it like for Ain, down in that darkness beneath the marsh?* she wondered, but she couldn't picture it. *Did the tiny point of ruby mark his grave?*

Fading to a drizzle, the rain waited with her, dwindling like her hope. *He must have drowned! They thought it had rusted through ...*

Edrach coughed, tried to suppress it, coughed again in a great tearing spasm. He was shuddering so hard that her body was vibrating too. 'My pack.' Tohalla could hardly hear his whisper, but she paddled down the streaming slope to get it – if it hadn't been washed away.

It was still there. Edrach had thrown his pack higher up the bank when he saw the rain-clouds. Tohalla hadn't; everything she had brought from her home was gone. *My husband's gone.*

When she laid the rolled-up Wolf-hide on his knees, he brought out a handful of vermilion branches. He turned over a few rocks and on their dry underside he made a little spire of the red stuff. And touched it.

Tohalla couldn't be bothered to ask. *Ain ...*

And the red stuff smoked into flame. From the corner of her eye she saw it through the mizzle but her gaze was locked on the crimson spar in the marsh.

Then the wind sang the flame into motion, and Tohalla saw it, incredulous. It went out –

No! A flash of suns' light dimmed it, but the fire was there.

From the marsh the backwash lashed noisily –

Not the backwash, but water cascading off the rising Ship.

The *Mosckva* lurched clumsily, like a chicken learning to fly. Hope leaped in Tohalla, plummeted as the huge thing fell back into the sucking swamp. A croak of horror wrenched her throat open.

But from the slimy, mud-caked ugliness staggered a part of the Ship, still rising. The command module.

And sparkling red it soared beyond the rainbow.

184

INTERLUDE

Backwash

Thick dusk hung in the corners of the Househall. It was too early yet for the candles to be lit. Not until Granamyr came in from milking the spineders would there be any other light than the fires at each end of the Hall; it would have been wasteful. In the friendly gloom Tohalla could think what she chose.

Nine years.

When the ruby that was the Ship vanished beyond sight, Edrach and Tohalla nursed each other south-east towards the winterground; the Green was too far for her baby's birth. Besides, Edrach had a mission there.

But the Autumn rains brought landslides and floods. Then early snow caught them on a hillside, and they built a dug-out with turves of mountain red, as Benhannon's people had. There, where the first crimson tendrils coiled above the snow, Tohalla journeyed through pain to bring her daughter into life.

Edrach trapped and hunted and coughed, and Tohalla called her daughter Vernal, a name for the Green. She nestled the baby in tideswool and wolf-hides, and whispered to her of her father the Axe, bound out along the star-trails, and teethed her on a bone that Edrach polished in the fire-lit dark.

Tohalla learnt to trap, and dig crystal-roots, and shared the cooking with the man who was more than brother. Without the Axe it was easier to weave a harmony, and Vernal copied their laughter.

When the lean times were gone with the frost and Spring had put new flesh on them, Edrach gathered his strength to lead them to the winterground before it was too late. He could hardly restrain his pace with his urgency to bring them the news that the blood-debt was paid at last.

But by the time they reached the winterground, there was almost no-one there to tell, only two old men too weak to last a summer's trek. Nevertheless Edrach chanted the song of the Axe Shipfinder in his old, cracked voice while Vernal crowed and played with Tohalla's hair. Though one old man slipped into the sleep of senility, the other cried his joy for the coming of the star-kin. With Marchidas's grand-child in his arms, Edrach knew his triumph was complete. There was only one more thing he had to do ...

How many scenes pushed into Tohalla's mind from their last journey together! Vernal's first steps from Edrach to her mother's arms; the little face beaming as she played peek-a-boo; Edrach's contentment as he sat warm by Tohalla's side with Vernal's fingers tight about his thumb. And his gift to her as he lay dying from his fatal fall: his life, and the Axe's, in the red hearts of messengers, with a blank crystal for her to record her own.

Edrach smiled at her even as his one eye grew dull. His numbing hand still held Tohalla's in his feeble grasp and the crystals spilled from their wrappers on his chest. 'Don't cry,' he said. 'I everything have had: Marchidas, and the Axe, and you, and Vernal. I the Ship saw on its homeward flight. Now I tired of coughing am, and you your own life must choose. Sail like the arrowfalls, Tohalla, not where the wind wills, or on others' tides, but where you will.'

But Tohalla had chosen the Green for the sake of Vernal, because she thought it would be safer there.

Nine years, and Tohalla was still in the Househall, not even on Housefather's platform now because of that taint of Red. Still playing with other people's children, still telling them stories in the growing dark where her words could hide from Housemother ...

There was noise aplenty, though, to cover up her tales. Bored children played and quarrelled under the trestle-tables; on his platform Housefather roared over a game of shove-bean with his cronies. Inwatchers whispered flirtation by the darkening, wind-beaten windows. Rain hissed over the sad, stubbled fields and down the chimneys onto the fires; from where Tohalla sat at the bottom end of the Hall, she could hear its sizzling death. And Housemother was safely bossing the women who clattered in the kitchen.

In the dreary wait until evening, until light and dinner and music, Tohalla laced an exotic picture of words and hung it shining in the gloom:

186

'And Edrach, trembling between hope and despair on the sodden bank of the marsh, suddenly shouted, "He's alive! I can feel him – he's alive!" '

Around Tohalla, on the chair-arms and in her lap, the children's faces split in grins of relief. What was the use of a tale without a happy ending? They moved restlessly, freed from the spell of adventure, but Daker bounced up on his knees – his movement pinched Tohalla's thighs against the chair-seat – and said, 'What happened next? Did he find the star-family?'

Peeping surreptitiously at the kitchen door, Tohalla lifted Daker and his splinted arm to a more comfortable position, which he promptly wriggled out of. But there was no sign of Housemother so she went on, 'Well, I don't know whether he found them or not. If space is big enough to hide a planet in so nobody knows where it is, the Axe might take ages to get to where they are. But I like to think he did find them. He was a good tracker. We'll know one day.'

'What's space like?' Roeisin wanted to know.

Tohalla puffed a rueful laugh. 'I don't know, Rosy, except that it's big, with light places and dark places, and stars as big as lanterns to guide you. And there's vacuums in it.'

Roeisin was four, so of course she said, 'What's vacuums?' Her round little face was enchanted, her eyes big and wondering. Briefly Tohalla wished her daughter was like that. But she wasn't. She never had been.

Tohalla half-sighed. 'I don't know. Some sort of monsters, a body would think. But the Axe can handle them. He can handle wolves, can't he? And one day, the Axe will come back with the star-family and we'll never be all on our own again.'

Roeisin and Misha were quiet then, dreaming star-families as they wanted them to be, like mothers and brothers who didn't boss them about. But Misha was always quiet.

Not Daker, though. He wanted more excitement. 'What did Edrach do then? And how did he magic the fire in the rain?'

Still no sign of Housemother. Most of the women in the Hall were gossiping; it was too dark to sew. If they paid Tohalla any heed at all, it was a quick glance to make sure she was still entertaining the children so they could, for a while, get on with their own lives. Those here were one with Tohalla's conspiracy. But she'd catch it if she took too long …

Tohalla smiled at Daker. His half-blond hair spun out as he shifted energetically. 'The Wolfmen have a special thing in their minds that

187

makes them very close to the Red,' she said. 'Not all of them, just some. And in Edrach it was specially strong. He thought at the wolf-fire branches, and made them burn just by touching them.' *How Vernal used to laugh when I made the sparks fly from the branches when I was learning! When she used to run and tell me everything, when she came to play with me on the Edge. Before she found out what being a Green meant ...* 'I used to be able to do it, a bit.'

Tohalla knew she shouldn't have said that. *What if he wants me to show him?* Hastily she went on, missing out the alarms and hard dangers of the long trail back. *If Housemother finds out ...*

'As for what we did then, well, a body was sure Edrach was sorry he hadn't gone on the great adventure, but he knew he wasn't well enough. He'd told me before ever we set off that he was dying, only I didn't really believe it then.'

I. Tohalla had learned that from the Wolfmen. Now, thinking about them, this sin against the Green came back. 'Besides, he was a very special person. He wanted to take care of Marchidas's grand-daughter –

'Edrach shared his Wolf-hide with me. He told me how to find fuel from the hearts of the purple brush where the rain hadn't got it. And he told me how to brew medicines for both of us that put new life into the empty spaces of the old.

'When he was stronger, we walked through the rain down the trail to the winterground, because once we were there we would be safe. And Vernal was born –'

'That's boring!' Daker said. 'You didn't make it an adventure.' The little lad's face showed how disgruntled he felt. 'I'm going to play.' He jumped up – and gasped. His sudden movement had jogged his broken arm. Last week in the first real frost of autumn he'd made a slide on the ice by the trough. Forbidden of course, and now he knew why.

Tohalla held him fast, hands around the five-year-old's tight little stomach.

'Let a body go, Tohalla! Let me go!'

People were peering at them through the shadows. Apprehensive, Tohalla shushed him. Even Roeisin was tugging at the hem of his shirt. 'A body can't, Daker. Sorry, but you're not allowed to play yet in case you hurt your arm some more.'

'Well tell me something interesting, then. Like about the other Ship. You know, the, um, Dream Ship.'

Tohalla fussed about, settling Roeisin and Daker one on each knee. Misha simply sat balanced on the chair-arm. He was five too, but his flabby limbs never seemed strong enough to help him move much. Housemother couldn't blame the child's parents for not wanting him in their way – but she did. Because he haunted Tohalla and Tohalla was, in some irritating way all of her own, Red-tainted.

With all her fidgetings, Tohalla had covered her search for people who might object. She couldn't see any of them in the Hall, though more people were sifting in from the raw night. Each time the door opened, smoke billowed from the fireplaces like suspicion.

'Go on, Toh. Tell us about the Dream Ship.'

'All right, Daker, hold your spineders.' She smiled at him. 'But it's not a Dream Ship. It's the Drone Ship. In the winterground, they say it landed in the south. Maybe crashed, the way ours did.' Tohalla hid the knowledge of how Good Captain had wrecked the Ship for his twisted dream. She dreaded what Housefather would do if he ever found out about her heresy.

Taking a deep breath, she went on, 'And it had machines in it, and babies of all sorts of people and animals. Some of them might have survived, the way our grandmothers lived through the wreck of the *Mosckva.*'

Daker sighed. 'Is that all? Hasn't any of them seen it? Why didn't you and Edrach go and look for it?'

'Because I wanted to go home –' *Not come home. They don't want me here – That was my decision and look what's become of it. They won't even let me talk half the time, and Vernal hates me …*

'So Edrach wanted to bring Vernal and me here before he died.' *Chosen Brother. My Chosen Brother, cradled in a sapphire tree in the arms of spring. You your Ship have found, to take you to the stars … Eight years ago.*

Roeisin managed to sneak a word in edgeways. 'But you said, before you said, there's a, a strange thing.'

Tohalla listened to her patiently, knowing it took time for a four-year old to stumble through words to her meaning. But it mattered. For the sake of the Axe, of Edrach and all the Crew who lived and died in the Red, Tohalla had to break down the prejudice. And maybe the lives of all in the Green depended on it, too. They were still dying of their ignorance of the Red.

'That's what they told me in the winterground, Rosy. There is something strange. There's a big desert whose edge is as straight as a furrow –'

'Oh, Mum!' None of them had seen Vernal crawl out from the game under the trestle-tables and come over to stand, suspicious, by her mother. 'Why do you keep talking about it? Housemother says you haven't got to. She says you've got to forget about your horrible time in the Red.'

Tohalla hissed, 'Keep your voice down, Vernal!'

Nine, and full of scorn for her mother, Vernal said, 'Well she does. She says you should be glad you're back in civilization. You don't have to eat disgusting dead things here.'

Tohalla looked at her daughter in exasperation. Vernal was dear to her for her own sake, and for the sake of the Axe whom she so much ressembled, but she was more than ordinarily trying. She could feel the girl's mind rejecting her. *Not a Green mind at all. She knows it. And it's my fault ...*

'Vernal, a body can't forget the Red. Not only is it most of the planet, it's also where your father's people came from and where you were born.'

Daker looked at Vernal with new respect, as if he had suddenly connected Tohalla's stories with the reality of the child who stood before him, suddenly invested her with the glamour of the exotic unknown.

'You're lucky, Vern!' he said. 'You're different.'

Anger flamed red patches on Vernal's cheeks and she struck out at the boy on Tohalla's lap. Her smack caught him on the side of the head. Daker rocked back, shrieked with the shock to his broken arm.

Vernal yelled, 'I don't want to be different! I want to be the same!'

Later, in the widows' room crowded with beds, Housemother said, 'If I've told you once, Tohalla, I've told you a hundred times. No good can come of the Red.' It was only the beginning of her scold.

But you didn't think that when you betrothed me to a new strand, thought Tohalla, across the current of angry words. *And I have to talk about it. We need to understand each other, us and the sons of the Red, because we need each other if we're going to survive and grow.*

'And that's why, Tohalla, I'm sending Vernal over to the New House. She wants to grow up as a good Green, and I won't have you standing in her way.'

Tohalla stood abruptly, blazing with fury. Housemother stepped back a pace, frightened of her own daughter. Tohalla would never have knowingly hurt her, but Housemother didn't know that. Housemother thought of all the time her daughter had spent in the savage Red ...

'You keep away from me!' shouted Housemother. 'And from now on, you can keep away from all the children, too. Look what you've done this evening, for a start.'

'You can't take my daughter away from me!'

'Can't I just! And you needn't think you can go sneaking off to that feeble-minded Adiockle of yours either, or Trinamine. You're not going anywhere near the Edge. You can just stay here and take care of the old folk. You can't corrupt Mevagrin, at any rate – '

'No, because she's deaf!'

Housemother's words rolled on, ignoring Tohalla.

'And your weaving – plain stuff only, none of your filthy patterns. I'm going to make you work so hard you won't have time for all these nightmare stories. I won't have you setting yourself up as something special, turning people's heads inside out with your nonsense.'

Later, long after Housemother had slammed out of the widows' room and the old ones had come up and gone to sleep, Tohalla sat by the window watching the Amethyst Moon wheel past the stars. In the passage outside the door, she could hear the inwatcher yawning. And there'd be other children upstairs in the girls' room where Vernal was probably asleep; if she wasn't, she'd be resenting her mother for getting her into trouble.

Only an occasional sob roughened Tohalla's breathing now. That was one of the benefits of being thirty-six. You learned to scab over your emotional wounds so the sting hid underneath. At least Agosta had been wryly sympathetic, and Caramon had crept in too and shared her mind with Tohalla. She'd turned out well, had Caramon. Sixteen, and smiling, and swelling with a child. Tohalla told her it was a boy.

Tohalla's eyes sought a ruby point between the wind-scoured stars, but it wasn't there. It never was. 'Oh, Ain!' she whispered. 'They're taking Vernal away, just like the Wild Men do, or mutinas. Help me!'

But echoing in her skull in place of dreams, Tohalla heard and saw her daughter cry, 'I don't want to be different! I want to be the same!'

On Longnight, Tohalla saw Vernal.

'The Red Woman's weeping,' said Larnis on the wagon through the wet and tilted fields. She said it with ill grace, giving in to the pestering of her son before Tohalla did. Neither motherhood nor being Housefather's favourite had made Larnis any less sulky.

The wagon-bed creaked and the still, damp air didn't blow the unpleasant scent of the spineders away. A lantern swung dizzy swirls of light on the road to New House. The great hoofs slurred on the stones that had sunk in the winters of rain and ice. Housefather had been delighted when Granamyr suggested gravelling the road, but as yet they had only hauled enough from the shore to reach past the lea.

Of the dozen that made up the party, there were Granamyr and Larnis, because Housefather thought they should take over New House when the present Housefathers there died. *If Ain had stayed, it would have been us*, thought Tohalla. *Maybe.*

There were Larnis's children, brats who usually had tats in their hair and holes in their clothes. There was Asdra, a strapping bully of fifteen going up to labour on a new plank-walled barn, and two lads of similar age. There was Agosta, skilled at birthing, who was prim and strait-laced when Housemother was looking, and great fun when she was not.

Lastly, amidst blushes and giggles, was a young couple. Tonight their Ripeness would be declared by the Housefather who would welcome them to the new rooms he'd had built after harvest. And on Longday they'd be wed in the new orchard of saplings that sprang from the Redwood's burnt earth. Everywhere the Green flourished, life wheeling through its seasons; Spring's birth, Autumn's fruition, then the slow melting back to feed a new generation.

Ain was gone. Worut – Tohalla no longer shuddered at the memory. She had gentled him with pity that had showed in her caring mind-touch. Worut had learned – something. In time ... but he didn't have time. His pallid flesh now nourished the earth of Rosaria. And for all his juice there'd been no seed. Tohalla's hair was long again. A badge of shame. 'A curse of the Red to mar the fair Green,' said Housefather. So everywhere suspicion fell on Tohalla's daughter.

Only Tohalla loved Vernal, so pretty, so quick, in whose being flowed an alien blood. But Housemother ignored the way everybody looked at Vernal askance. She was a new Strand, wasn't she? Half-a-dozen boys could pick her. If Housemother's plans overcame the opposition. What else did it count for, being Housemother, if she couldn't get the unfortunate girl a husband?

Her breath puffing white on the chilly air, Tohalla rode the wagon, trembling against hope that this time Vernal wouldn't turn her away. But Larnis had been busy with her tongue, and Coril, and Worut's kin, and ... And children learn quickly who's acceptable and who's not.

Tohalla thought, *What is there for me to do, if they won't let me love my own daughter?*

'Come in, come in!'

Light burst out of New House on a wave of sound, the lantern-beams freighted with dream-smoke, the laughter woven with the scent of joyberries. Tohalla swallowed. *Has she come out to meet me?*

Everyone tumbled out of the wagon in a crescendo of greetings. Yes, there she was! Vernal, pushing through the people in the doorway.

Tohalla's heart overflowed with joy and love and pride. Tohalla smiled wide. It was a smile that couldn't contain her exaltation, but it didn't match Vernal's.

Vernal's smile was close-mouthed.

Shy.

Vernal stopped, her wavy hair crowned by the lamp-light. Slim, beautiful in her soft new Longnight dress, beautiful anyway with her heart-shaped chin and rosy with the echoes of her summer freckles.

'Go on. *Go on*, Vernal! Kiss your mother.'

Because there was a hand at Vernal's back, propelling her. Yelena Housemother had to force her to come forward.

Tohalla stooped to hug her daughter. She devoured her with kisses, took her by the hand to lead her inside with the chattering throng. Vernal walked stiffly beside her mother.

Not just shy. Holding back, afraid of what they'll say.

'Come and see what a body's got for you,' said Tohalla. Sitting on one of the long benches down the side of the New Househall, she pulled out a packet from under her thick winter coat.

Larnis unwrapped the offcut of cloth. Inside was a roll of something soft, as green as the pine-boughs that hung on the walls to defy the winter-death the Red Woman brought. Tohalla put her arm around Vernal, stroking her back as her daughter unrolled the tideswool dress. Tohalla hated sewing, but it was as finely-made as she could: there was love in every stitch, in the yarn she had spun and in its weaving.

'But a body's already got a dress for this year!' said Vernal. 'Erm – uh, thank you, Mum.'

Tohalla's hand stopped its stroking, started again. 'It's all right, Vernal. It's just that this tideswool wove up so soft a body thought you'd like it. Never mind.'

'What's this?' Vernal's fingers were busy on the small thing wrapped in the skirt of the dress.

It was a doll, coiffed with real hair, Tohalla's own from her first Ripeness to Pierse, lighter then, almost the same colour as Ain's in the winter. Dressed in tideswool, a skipping-rope sewn in her hands, and with a tiny, heart-shaped face. When Vernal had been sent away at the beginning of Winter she'd held her favourite doll tight for comfort.

'Oh, Mum! A body's too big to play with dolls.'

'But you could at least use it as something pretty to hang by your

193

bed.' Even Tohalla was shocked at the acid in her own voice. Little girls had to grow up sometime.

'Well, all right.' Vernal tried to sound grateful. 'Thank you very much, Mum. It is pretty.'

It.

'Come away and play for us, won't you?' said Yelena cheerfully. 'You won't mind us borrowing your clever mother, will you, Vernal?'

'*Play?*' *Music? Doesn't she know Housefather won't let me? He said music's too powerful for someone steeped in the wickedness of the Red –*

'Mmm,' said Yelena Housemother. 'Naecre made us a zither. It's only wood instead of plastic, but we strung it with wire we got from the Iron Men and it doesn't sound too bad. We were all dancing until the Inwatch said you lot had come.'

So she doesn't know! And oh! How I've missed playing ...

And underneath was the knowledge of how Vernal shared her mother's love of music. *Perhaps* – though Tohalla wouldn't acknowledge the thought even to herself – *perhaps this will bring her back to me.*

How strange to be sitting on a Housefather's Platform, by a Housefather's fire of dreamsmoke on Longnight. Nine years –

'A body's a bit dusty,' Tohalla said doubtfully, settling the precious instrument on her lap. How weird and familiar the contours of a zither felt against her body, through her dress. *Once I belonged.*

'Well,' said Yelena, smiling, 'you can't be worse than any of us. And I remember you playing years ago.'

Flexing her fingers hesitantly, coaxing a tentative chord from the badly-tuned strings – she tightened a couple of keys – Tohalla began to play. The flutes and drums took their time from her. Any mistakes were covered by the clumsy tromp of the dancers' feet which all but hid the melody anyway. And Tohalla guarded the sweetness of her voice ...

Vernal crept nearer.

All the old favourites, one after another, mixed slow and fast so the dancers could catch their breath. The sharp green scents of the pine and bay festoons mingled with the dancers' sweat and the sparkling lilac haze of dreamsmoke.

Vernal drifted over to sit on the top step where the music wrapped her in its magic of mood-shifting. Her smile was dreamy, then bright and lively, then softened again to hope, to cheer.

And once Tohalla's fingers made friends with the cutting iron strings, her eyes kept straying to her daughter, bewitched.

It came. It happened. At last the hour-candle melted low on the sand in the niche behind Housefather Andret's platform.

'Play something gentle, to calm them down before I direct them for the next year,' said Housefather Andret, while the dancers clapped and the musicians rested after a long dance. Andret was smiling.

Tohalla smiled.

Not looking at Vernal, Tohalla rippled a rainbow of sound from the zither. Once or twice, when she'd first come back with Vernal snuggled in her cot and the old ones slumbering while Housefather shouted in the harvest, Tohalla had stolen a moment of magic in song.

The moment was now. Vernal's eyes were enormous, as limpid as Ain's on a sunny evening. Soft and softer, like diamante dew on the red Autumn brambles, Tohalla drew forth a song of the Crew. A song of love and hope, reaching across the velvet blackness to star-kin beneath the lanterns strung in Space. The words didn't sound like that; more like any song of yearning, but Tohalla knew. And she reached out to touch her daughter's mind. For a heartbeat Vernal came with her. Tohalla's voice arced like a red crystal soaring beyond a rainbow –

And Vernal knew.

She yelled, the single word, 'No!' But emotion bound Vernal's vocal chords and the yell strangled in her throat; hate and terror tied tight limits to her self.

And, like a word of the song that fitted in the chorus, Tohalla sang, 'Yes!'

Her mind admitted no doubt; she could not bend the truth that the rest of the world *was* there. Ain had found the Ship; had ridden it outwards to the stars, and there in Edrach's memories hung his sureness, inside her.

Just for a song's breath, Vernal had known.

And rejected her mother in spite of it.

But Tohalla's radiant triumph faded before Vernal had choked herself into self-control. Because rooted at the bottom of Vernal's soul was horror at the alienness of Tohalla's mind, of Tohalla's world. *And Vernal knows she's a part of it! Vernal loathes herself because of me!* For though Tohalla had tried to hide it, she was no longer of the cosy neat homeliness encompassed by the Green.

Tohalla tracked down her errant mind-reach, brought it firmly under her control. Forcing a smile to cover her shame as if at a false note, Tohalla struck a normal chord, strived for a normal tone. And no-one knew what had happened but the Wolfman's wife and his daughter.

Later, after she had played for the strand-naming as if it had been the old days when she was part of something so similar in the old House and its Hall, Tohalla was allowed to put her daughter to bed in the girls' room. Yelena thought she was doing her a favour.

Vernal turned away, but Tohalla kissed the back of her head and said, 'Wherever I am, however far apart we are, you are always in my thoughts. I always love you, Vernal. I'm sorry that being who I am, I've made things difficult for you. If I could have put it all from me, I would have. But thanks to your father I don't have the choice, and I owe Rosaria too much to hurt her with a lie. You'll be all right in this world, Vernal, if I'm not in it.'

In all the long speech, Tohalla left pauses for an answering whisper, but Vernal never spoke.

'I love you, Vernal. When you grow up, reach out to me with your mind and I'll be there. My thoughts will always be with you.'

I.

And Vernal pulled the covers over her head.

Early in the morning, her eyes red-rimmed, Tohalla asked Yelena's permission to slip out to her aunt and Trinamine at the Edge. Yelena knew she shouldn't, but she gave in before the bruised pain in Tohalla's eyes. But she made Tohalla promise to be back before Redsun was a finger's breadth above the headland. Tohalla set off in the luminous blue of the last of the night.

The new striding-post didn't – stride, that is. Instead of straddling the wicked honey spikes of the Edge, it was a mere tower built four-square on the once-burnt land of the Intake. This Housefather didn't have the plant-wisdom of that old one from times before.

And there was no-one there.

Tohalla turned on the moist, Red-spattered mud. Faintly it squeaked below her boot-heel; the earth sent up a rich odour that was not yet entirely of the Green. Above the headland, the sky was paling so that the land was more black than the charcoal of the sea. From here she couldn't see New House; there were no lights yet in the old, nor any sound from the night-beasts of the Red sleepily going home.

Desolate, Tohalla turned back to the splintered wood of the tower. A whisper of smoke from the chimney spoke of a banked-up fire but no-one answered her call.

She panicked, shouted and was aghast at her temerity in breaking that lonely silence. From beyond the Edge the Red shrilled back her alarm.

Have they all been killed? Fear was a prickle on her insteps, a pain that knifed her gut. *Have the Sons of the Red – Pull yourself together! Think!*

From across the field came a faint halloo.

Tohalla whirled. Muffled in a bulky coat, Trinamine waved frantically in the pre-dawn light.

Tohalla ran to her. Trinamine ran too, her short hair standing all awry. They met in the middle of the bare, rain-washed field. The first thing Trinamine said was, 'Ssh!'

'Where were you?' gasped Tohalla. 'I was out of my mind – '

'In the comfort of the striding-post, the old one. You don't still think the Wolfmen are just waiting to be penned up in here, do you? It's the Iron Men that worry me, and they won't stir 'til Winter's gone. Come on, come and have something hot. I thought you'd never get here.'

The old striding-post rose as it always had by the banks of the stream that fed the valley, yet there was no amber glitter between its legs any more. It still rang reassuringly as Tohalla followed her friend up the steps in its bark, though, and no outlander's hand flung a discus at her for a joke. Muted by distance, the faint chiming of the Red still hung a counterpoint on the soft air.

A warm fug reached out to embrace Tohalla as she stepped down onto the curving floor. Light laced in through the lattice but the rosy glow of the fire was stronger, shining off plates and chairs and knives. Adiockle said, 'Well come in and shut the door, then. I'm in a draught.'

It felt like coming home.

Tohalla kissed her aunt's wrinkled cheek, hugged her bony shoulders. Adiockle felt old but the firelight was kind. Sibulkrin was dead and composted five years ago; it was Trinamine who strolled around the curve of the lattice while Adiockle ladled out stew – it might well have some Red-meat in it but Tohalla carefully didn't ask – and raspberry-leaf tea.

Tohalla rested the plate on the hearth while she shifted her chair to the one place its odd legs balanced the seat level. It was automatic. With the cup cradled in her hands, she blew across the top of the scalding tea but made no move to pick up her plate. Even in her misery the whole atmosphere of the place was balm to her wounded mind.

'Tell us then, Toh!' said Adiockle briskly, yet not without sympathy. 'I haven't got time for long silences these days. Sibulkrin's always calling me on.'

'Tell you what?' Tohalla answered, pretending interest in her tea, but neither her friend nor her acerbic aunt spoke. Daylight crept, slowly stronger, through the lattice.

197

Trinamine poured herself a drink, at ease. It was Adiockle who said eventually, 'I'm not pandering to your whims by asking you why you've come out here at this time of day when you're not supposed to be here at all.'

Trinamine said, 'You just did, Adi.'

Adiockle ignored her. 'Now get on with it, Toh. You'll have to be back soon. Tell us why your eyes look like a nest of Red-mites.'

Tohalla laughed wryly in spite of her grief. 'You always did have a taste for flattery, Adi.' She sighed. 'It's Vernal. She – she doesn't want me.' Hopelessly, Tohalla began to cry, not ashamed here of her tears with the people who loved her.

'I knew it!' said Trinamine. 'You haven't got a man so it had to be a child. They let you come up to see her, did they? Big of 'em.'

Adiockle made flapping movements with her hands. 'Hush, Trin, let her get a word in edgeways. I suppose the child's too busy trying to fit in to want a mother who's seen some of the Red.'

Tohalla lifted her tear-starred eyes to her aunt's. 'How did you know?'

'Don't you think I haven't eaten the Red out here all these years? No, that's not right. You know what I mean. Here, you, Trin! Get that stuff out for Tohalla. Oh, get on with it! You know, the things I've got hid in the floor.'

Trinamine, with her usual economy of movement, peeled back the rug and prised up a whorl of wood. Her un-capped head bent low as she reached in for a bundle to lay on Tohalla's lap. Three parcels rolled out of the headless Wolf-hide.

Tohalla caught them before they fell. Her hands brushed the gut sacks: dead animal, yes, but more than that. Dried brown squirls marked the rolls one from another, but Tohalla made no move to open them. Daylight rolled in more broadly, casting perceptible patterns on the floor.

Tohalla gasped between her sobs, 'They won't let me do anything for her. If I could, if they'd let me, she wouldn't. It's not fair!'

'Oh!' She hit the heel of one hand on her head, a punishment, an appeasement of emotional pain. 'I sound like a child!'

Tohalla wanted them to deny it, but they didn't. In acceptance they waited. 'But it isn't fair. All the time, right from before she was born, I could do just about anything with children, but I never could with her. Not once she could talk. Not once Housemother and Coril and Larnis and everyone got at her. She can feel me in her head, I know she can, but she won't accept me.'

198

Her words became wails; not elegant, not heroic but true. 'I can't do anything for her!' she sobbed.

Feverishly her thumb stroked the heavy things in her lap. 'I suppose they've faded too!' Tohalla said bitterly.

'They haven't,' said Adiockle, 'not even Marchidas's out there still growing. And Trinamine's renewed them, up and down the edge of the Redwood. What you are still exists out there.'

Tohalla gave Trinamine her gratitude in a warm look before anger clouded her gaze again. Her voice thick, she said, 'All my life I've been what other people wanted, gone where they wanted me, done what I was told. Sometimes it was even what I wanted, too, or I found ways to enjoy it because it was all I had. And I've had wonderful friends or I couldn't have borne it: you, Trin,' Tohalla reached to squeeze her friend's hand, 'and you, Adi, once I'd found you, and Edrach and – sometimes – Ain. But Ain's gone, and Edrach's dead and it hurts. Then they keep me apart from you, and they've taken my daughter's mind away from me. If we'd stayed in the Red, they couldn't have, but I couldn't have kept her alive.'

Tohalla stopped. She felt the words wash out of her and there was nothing left. Nothing once the words had gone, taking with them the memories.

Red light stabbed across the room from side to side. The rim of the sun showed and, obedient, Tohalla stood, the bundles held awkwardly against her.

'This is the last time. This is the last time I keep their stupid rules. They can't stop Rosaria growing, even here.'

She turned to face her friend and her aunt, looked into their dear faces to imprint them on her memory. 'This is the Axe,' she said, and unwrapped the first packet, careful not to touch its contents yet. One day soon there'd be time. She'd make time.

'This is Chosen Brother, who chose me to be his sister too.'

Tohalla laid them side by side on Adiockle's knobbly knees. 'And when I've gone – you knew I had to go, didn't you, to find the Dream Ship? ...give these to Vernal when she needs us. Because one day she will need us, even me, only her mother ...' She cut herself off, snapping her teeth down over her bitterness. 'And this is me.'

She laughed, a wild outburst that struck sparks of sound from the ironwood room. 'This is the first thing I've ever done that's all my own decision. I'm – I'm learning to sail like the arrowfalls across the wind. I'll see you before I go.'

For just a moment Tohalla waited, wanting them to dissuade her or

199

bless her or – anything.

Slowly Adiockle said, 'Good luck, Toh.' Trinamine inspected her friend up and down. 'You'll do.'

Snatching up her coat, Tohalla ran to the door-hatch, stumbling on the curved floor and laughing at herself. Her footsteps gonged clumsily down the notched steps.

'Trin?' Adiockle said with a jerk of her head. It was unnecessary. Trinamine was already in the doorway, watching Tohalla run leaping into the swath of Redsun's light gleaming on the wet furrows. Before she sank below the breast of the hill, Tohalla turned and waved.

On Adiockle's lap, sparkling red in the light from the doorway, lay the hearts of three messengers.

PART THREE

Mindsail

CHAPTER ONE

To Run the Unshadowed Plain

Tohalla fell into the camp. Painfully.

She had been marvelling at the arrowfalls swooping north on the winds of Spring, not really concentrating on her journey because the memories of Marchidas and Edrach were watching through her eyes. They had known, so she knew, that the winterground camp was around here somewhere, but the poignant downcurve of the arrowfalls' flight had ensorcelled her with wonder. Marchidas and Edrach had brought her this far when the Iron Men could have killed her on the banks of the Big River, or the roving bands of comets, or a hundred poisonous crystals in all the shades of death. Some of the memories were worn and faded like her own; she did not know exactly where the camp would be this year, either.

Still, confidence was limping in her, weak but perceptibly growing. She had even crossed a crimson valley where a herd of razorbacks ran down a thieving geyrlizard. And the memory of Vernal ghosted after her.

But here in the winterground was safety; why should she fear? In this haven even the sons of the Red held their own kind sacred so that new bloodlines could shift between ...

The trackless hillside gave way beneath Tohalla's feet and she was falling. Something soft was winding about her, suffocating. Dirt spattered into her mouth when she jerked her head backwards to breathe. Her innards wrenched upward with the force of her fall.

She struck bottom. The jarring winded her. Then a searing agony lanced through her shoulder; choking, blinded by grit, she heaved herself aside from a banked-up fire. And stopped.

A spear, half-seen in the shadowy pit, pricked her throat. The man who held it recovered quickly from his surprise. His silhouette was aggressive but immobile. At least there might be hope ... Trapped as she was, coughing, she could do nothing; her smothered limbs wouldn't move. She was helpless, unable even to call for mercy.

The fumes of her own burning hair smeared her vision. When it cleared, the soil had washed out of her eyes with the tears. The dark outline above her watched her cough and writhe.

One side of the pit collapsed further. A shower of earth erupted outwards and its centre was a dagger in a woman's hand.

Redspeech stabbed at Tohalla's brain. Ice-cold, with a background of rage, it said, *You die if you here to attack are, winterground or no.*

I – Edrach – I can't move! In my wolf-hide ...

The man jerked his head but already someone else was pushing Tohalla over – she gasped as her wrist grated under her hip – to get at the wolf-hide on her back. Tohalla couldn't see whether the searcher was male or female but whoever it was they casually put a knee in the small of her back to hold her down. They tipped everything out of the rolled-up fur.

Tohalla heard the things falling and being shovelled aside behind her. The dust beneath her smelt of ashes ...

The searcher grunted, stopped. Tohalla knew what they had found. *But which one?* Which of the copied messengers?

Suppose this group thought they were mutinas, she and the Axe and Edrach?

Pinned motionless with her face pressed to the ground, Tohalla waited. For death or not-death that she couldn't see ...

After both suns had set for Tohalla and endless night had come, the searcher said incredulously, 'The Ship found is! And this one there was!'

'Let me see,' ordered the man, and snatched the chunk of messenger. Then, pressing its needle tip to Tohalla's exposed nape, he wrapped his palms round the ruby crystal.

It was Edrach. (Tohalla flushed with relief.) *Behind the casual lifetides of smaller things the darkness of Edrach's first awareness focused. Out through his long, bitter childhood of rejection because of his deformity came one good thing: his promotion to Chosen Brother, and once Marchidas had chosen him, things were never so dark in him again, not even when he thought her dead. At least someone had loved him for what he was ... The diamond-bright explosion of joy when Marchidas wasn't dead at all, and her child by Benhannon that should have been his ... Oh, the pain of that birth when Marchidas died! And the knowledge of the Ship, and the long furtive waiting for the Axe to mature while they skulked away from mutinas and Iron Men raiders.*

And that other sister who had chosen him: Tohalla. A muted daystar of deep pleasure, was Tohalla to Edrach, not the colourful ecstasy of youth but the softer, warmer happiness of maturity. It was enough for Edrach; more than enough for Tohalla herself. Even here in the threat of the winterground her mouth could not help smiling ...

Then Edrach scrambled over the Edge; it glittered behind him, behind the Axe and Tohalla as they escaped from the Green.

The Ship! The Mosckva! *It really did burst free of the flooding marshes, and rose with Marchidas's son to a red star in the heavens so help would come again to the sons of the Crew.*

Then Edrach struggled with his growing weakness to lead Tohalla back to the safety of her kind. Even after a season's rest in the winterground he was worn out.

Perspective shifted: he was lying with his head in her lap, a fan of rose in his hand.

Tohalla begged, 'Don't die! Please don't die! You'll be strong again, I know you will!' And a baby cried for a pool of refracted light that she couldn't grasp on the Redwood floor.

Edrach tightened his hold on the messenger; the crystal felt sharp in his palm. His gaze reached up into Tohalla's; his was open, caring. 'I don't mind, Tohalla. My body aches. But I in the messenger will live, and in you. Make a death-song for me, Toh.'

He rested then; even whispering strained his throat. (Now Tohalla could feel it.) *He heard her say through her attempt not to sadden him by weeping – he loved her for that – 'I will, Edrach. I'll put in Marchidas, and your promotion, and the battle with the mountain-lizards and –'*

Edrach moved his lips, but no sound came. She held a gut-length of water for him to sip. The water felt cool going down inside him. 'Don't forget the Ship, Toh.' Breaths came farther apart now. Not breathing was so restful and he was so tired. 'I my Ship – have found – to take me – to the stars.'

He had finished. There was nothing else he had to do. A golden glow through the curving branches of the Redwood showed the distant Edge. Tohalla was safe. He could rest ... rest ... res ...

The man took the messenger from the back of Tohalla's neck; the searcher lifted his knee. There were other figures now, summoned by the Redspeech. The man yanked the tight-twisted skins off Tohalla – *So that's what it was! No wonder they were hostile if she'd fallen through the roof of their shelter* – and dragged her, not ungently, to her feet. She never did find out who the searcher was.

'Regrets,' Tohalla said. 'I didn't know your camp was here or I'd never have put my foot through it.'

The man, nearly as tall as Edrach but well-formed and swarthy, said, 'You Green, what do you here want? All our world to burn?'

Uncomfortable, Tohalla nevertheless forced herself to meet his eyes. 'I the Green have left to find the – the Drone Ship.' She almost said 'Dream Ship'; ever since she had found that the Green no longer wanted her, she had been dreaming of it.

He thinned his lips in what passed for a smile. Squatting beside her – she heard his knees crack – he brushed fallen soil from the hairiest arms she had ever seen. 'So you think it still exists?'

Tohalla pushed a blackened strand of hair out of her eyes. 'I the *Mosckva* saw, and touched, and with salt its surface uncovered. I watched the Axe take it up above the skies. Why shouldn't the Drone Ship still exist?'

'You out of practice with our speech are, but you're trying.' The man nodded, his ranks of claw and bone rattling on the carpet of his chest. 'Chosen Sister, na? I Mauritz the Carver am. For a day or two, because Spring is, you here can stay if you us help. We a lot to do have. We a Green could use. Here.'

He handed her the messenger of Edrach's life, wrapped in its bladder. 'We about to eat were. Kari a nest of groundhoppers found.'

Whether or not they would treat her burnt shoulder or the hookweed ulcer or her other trail-wounds, Tohalla was grateful even for meat.

Three days of hard work followed but at least it was a respite from loneliness. This branch of the Crew had long since given up the quest for the Ship because they were so depleted in numbers but they still migrated; Mauritz, digging alongside her, said, 'Game scarce around the winterground grows with so many over its hills hunting.' Wordweaver's Crew, it seemed, were camped a day's walk to the west but Wordweaver herself was dead.

Mauritz seemed friendly, good-humoured even, and he never asked anyone to do anything he wouldn't do himself. He was curious about the planting in the Green and could have asked questions all day. His big, square teeth like a spineder's often flashed in a grin; Tohalla found herself more and more attracted to him despite his strange growth of hair, but it was still a guarded friendship on both sides. He had heard of the burnt black lands of the Intake.

206

In clearings they planted fragments of edible crystal or forage growths to lure the animals back. Tohalla found it strange how the presence of others in the lilac forest took away its beauty but made it seem more welcoming. Once, as Tohalla squatted at the planting with Crew either side of her, Mauritz speared a ripperclaw that was sidling up behind her. He laughed and rolled her over when she tried to thank him, and made a joke of it with his friends, but his wasn't a cruel humour. As the spring suns polished the new Red and they ate a cold nooning, Tohalla wanted to ask him why he hadn't got a woman when it was obvious several would have been willing, but she didn't dare. And whenever he sought her out, it put a smile inside her. When she glimpsed herself reflected in crystals it seemed the lines had faded from her forehead. Perhaps outside the Green to be thirty-six and single didn't mean you were useless?

After so long on her own, though, it was good to get away by herself from time to time; the Crew's insatiable curiosity about the Ship and its finders wore her down. She had become more accustomed to silence than to chatter.

Yet the thing that struck her most was the casual way they all seemed to do what they wanted yet their actions spun together with no more friction than there was back in the House. Mauritz even let his Crew talk about what each of them wanted to do. And every mortal thing they possessed, from long-knives down to their cooking-pans, was patterned in any way its owner had fancied and Mauritz could carve.

Housemother would never have believed it.

On the last night before Mauritz led his people seawards, he took her through the moonlit forest to cut dreamwood. Several times he seemed about to say something, then his face would clear beneath the bars of shadow.

When their knives slashed through the amethyst prisms he said, 'So you tomorrow to find your Dream-Ship go?' He put a hand by hers to free a splintered crystal. His skin was warm on her fingers; the hairs on his wrist tickled her.

'I have to,' she answered, seeking for comprehension in his bearded face. 'I don't know if I'm wrong, but it seems important to me. Maybe,' she laughed nervously, 'maybe it's the only thing that can unite Rosaria. Besides, it's the only thing I've ever decided all by myself. I daren't give it up – I'd be lost.'

'Then you right are. And brave. Not many even that do.' His eyes smiled within their net of lines. 'But feast first, is?' He slapped her lightly on the shoulder, stepping past with the weight of dreamwood in the crook of his arm. 'On come, Tohalla of the Dream-Ship. You all right will be.'

And all the way back through the moons-drifted forest his arm brushed hers.

In the winterground they feasted on an old stringy landstalker that had bogged itself down. Then, with the dreamwood burned down past blue flames to embers, its hazy smoke spread glittering through the shelter.

The talk languished. Two men began arguing about something and nothing, and their insults reminded Tohalla of a snippet she had overheard on her first night, 'She looks as boring as the rest of the Greens,' though the girl who said it had been reasonably friendly since then. In the dreamsmoke that was isolating each of them in her or his own thoughts, the pain of that casual contempt magnified against the two men's weaving argument. ·

'Enough!' Mauritz roared when one man's hilt strayed to his dagger, 'Tohalla, you Edrach's life-message brought. Can you now his death-song make?'

Nervously she looked around the circle of faces in the fire-light. With the zither she might have moulded their emotions, but with words?

She took a deep breath. 'I owe it to Edrach,' she said. 'I'll try.'

In a song that ranged from the Nameless Desert to mountain heights, Tohalla made a melody whose words drew courage sun-sparked on the blackness of fear and being different. Sharp was the song of Edrach's Wolf-slaying with the words bright points for his cutting blows.

Tohalla sang Marchidas: Winter-cold her loss on the snowfield and the soaring joy of her return.

She sang Edrach's gentle bravery and his humour, his striving always towards hope. It was a good life. And at the end of it came the sunburst of the *Mosckva* rising.

Silence spread, but for the tent-flap's movement. Dreamwood's flame had crumbled to ash while she sang, and the Red night's discord tinkled undisturbed.

Did I do it wrong? thought Tohalla in gathering dismay. Mauritz Captain stared at her, the fret of dreamsmoke seeming an extension of his hair, his beard, binding him to his people and to her. But his words cut her hard as a knife, 'I never a death-song with a tune before have heard,' Mauritz said suddenly.

Tohalla cursed herself for letting Edrach down. So many memories in her head – how was she to sort it all out? *I should have known a death-song was only a poem …*

But the tall man who made patterns on everything went on, 'In the Green some good is, if you death-songs like that make. Twice in our hearts Edrach lives. And you us from guilt have freed: we right are no more Summer-treks to make because Edrach and your Axe the Ship have found. And because of Edrach and Ain Battle-Axe and Marchidas and you, one day the star-kin to Rosaria will come.'

From under his beard he untied a thong with a single grey, chased claw. Crosss-legged, he reached awkwardly over and placed it at her feet; the dark hair of his arm brushed soft on her knee. The one who had said Tohalla looked boring pulled a clip with a dangle of wolf-scales free from her coiled hair and passed it around the circle.

One by one they sent tributes that gleamed in a small pile before her. And Tohalla the outcast felt tears roll down her cheeks.

Mauritz pointed from where he and Tohalla lay in cover on the hillside. He had brought her this far south but further he wouldn't go.

Close to her ear he said quietly, 'I to my Crew must return. But they say the Drone-Ship beyond the Unshadowed Plain lies – though I never have heard that anyone it seen has, not since the monster Ain Tsui the Ship split.'

Around them the last fringes of orange scrub were crackling in the midday heat but out on the high plain the music of the crystals was different. It was softer, less metallic, and its high and low notes flowed to a rhythm faster than dawn, noon and sunset. Nothing grew out there that would come higher than her ankles. Nothing vegetal, that is.

Gently laying one hard-skinned finger on the inside of her wrist, Mauritz whispered when she looked at him, 'Be careful.' He nodded at the undulating ground with its dull fur of purple-blue growth that hazed to grey on the distant horizon. 'Wild Men you from far away could see. Or Iron Men. Or a geyrlizard. If you seen are, for you death is.'

Pressed down and sweating from the heat of both suns in a cloudless Spring sky, Tohalla could smell herself but there was no water around except what she carried in the coil of gut. *I wonder what Vernal's doing?* She said, 'Why is it called the Unshadowed Plain? And why can't I cross it at night? It'd be cool then.'

'You'll see the Unshadows before nightfall. There a wind is getting up. And at night, when the grazers feed, the high-dogs come hunting.

You off the Plain before nightfall be. But don't in the Straight Desert sleep.'

Tohalla felt alarm slamming through her system: nervous sweat prickling in her armpits, a jolt in her belly that suddenly squashed her lungs out of their pattern.

'What do I do if I am seen?'

Mauritz squeezed her hand to give her comfort. His fingers were warm on hers in the heat of the day. 'Then you fight.' He reached over to touch the massive claw at her throat, brushed the wolf-scales back from her temple. 'Though maybe your ranks will them deter.

'But the Drone Ship nowhere else is, or we it would have found. I think. Beside, the Unshadowed Plain too big is for you to skirt, and anyway, the Spring the Iron Men out to the west will have brought. This safer is – if you with us don't want to stay?'

Tohalla turned her head. Her chin scraped on twigs of fallen crystal as she looked at Mauritz. His masculinity attracted her and she was lonely in anticipation. *Vernal! Why aren't you with me?* She could stay, have children with this one, weave a life for herself from the strands he offered ... maybe even fetch Vernal ...

But it was not enough. Vernal wouldn't come and something was missing – not just to know if the Drone Ship existed and why she wept. Something more.

Tohalla smiled – *If the Drone Ship cries, does she also smile? And why is it a* she *rather than an* it? – and the smile brought an answering gleam of creamy teeth in his tanned face. Not like a man of the Green, he respected her answer, 'I like you, Mauritz. I'd like to stay. But I can't. I've got to go on.'

Mauritz shrugged a cheerful acceptance. 'Well, maybe one day you back will come. We with the arrowfalls travel, north in Spring and back in Autumn when the land has been renewed. If you that know, you us in the winterground can find. Maybe when we the other Crews about the Ship tell, there peace will be, and a chance to grow.'

Mauritz knelt up and planted a kiss on her cheek. 'You us a gift have given. One day someone to you will give the gift you want.'

He stroked her arm; it drew the fire of sensation through her skin because once Ain had done that on the scorched earth of the Intake. Her breath hissed inwards and she kissed him compulsively, then pulled herself away to start her long run over the Plain of Unshadows. Mauritz waved, but she didn't see.

Walking or running over the blue-purple plain, Tohalla found the

210

footing awkward. Her body felt no older but when she stopped to catch her breath, lines and shadows round her eyes mocked from a thousand crystal reflections. *Half my life gone ...*

The double-pyramid crystals were hard, sharp-edged as Mauritz had warned her. At least running took away the aches of fear and gave a good reason for her heart to pound under her ribs. Her twin shadows broke and bounced sideways over the crystals, but there was something not quite right about it. Looking at it made her feel dizzy, so she kept her eyes on the horizon as much as she could and hoped she wouldn't fall.

A dusty wind breathed the soft scent of the crystals over her, cooling her skin. It was like nothing she had ever smelled before. Tohalla remembered when she had first realized she couldn't smell the sea any more, that first time in the Red with Edrach and the Axe. Funny how she always thought of Edrach first though he had not been her body-lover. But he had loved her mind and soul ...

She stumbled, cursing herself for not watching where she was going. A glance behind showed that the rim of orange scrub had disappeared under the folds of the plain. Leaning her hands on her knees, she stood panting but the fear of high-dogs, whatever they were, made her break into a trot again. The suns were half-way down the heat-paled sky and the horizon hadn't changed. *I'll never make it before nightfall ...*

Hours later, when her trembling legs could hardly walk, Tohalla took another pull at her water-gut. Not much left. Sweat had crawled between her breasts, evaporating to a white itchiness. She was close to exhaustion but fear drove her on through the solidity of the hot air.

Two threatening specks in the sky spiralled downwards. Tohalla almost fainted from fear but a group of comets far in the distance broke into a run ... She stared round wildly, cowering, but the geyrlizards hadn't seen her. The geyrlizards' stoop brought one of the comets down; its wail of alarm broke its back on Tohalla's ears.

From somewhere she found the courage to move while the monstrous lizards were gorging on their kill.

The wind was stronger now; hot but at least it was moving. Tohalla scanned the sky. Late-afternoon clouds were herding westwards. Doggedly putting one foot in front of the other, Tohalla watched them dully. Maybe they'd bring some relief from the blazing suns. There was a sore patch where her bouncing wolf-hide had ground the crusted sweat into her hip. The searing heat, unlike any she had known in her home in the north, was squeezing the life out of her with its implacable ferocity.

Then the first cloud hid Whitesun. The mauve crystals chimed high, piercing notes and – shifted, dizzying. Tohalla fell.

Hard sharpnesses cut into her in a dozen places. Her hand bled, stinging where she had tried to break her fall. When she tried to scan around her for menace, waves of giddiness swept through her; the ground looked as if it was moving.

But it wasn't. Where the cloud cover brought relief from Whitesun's burning, the crytals paled, though all around they kept the darker hues that protected them. And when another cloud sailed in front of Redsun, another colour-change drew lighter patches in a shifting counterpoint. Where the suns didn't touch in the cloud-shadows, the double-pyramids paled. The whole plain seemed to ripple disconcertingly.

Eventually Tohalla gathered her wits enough to start walking again. Redsun arrowed down crimson on Whitesun's centre, balancing in a wobbly egg-shape on the horizon. Crystals jangled in the diminishing heat, singing its departure. Thicker clouds stabilized the earth in purple.

What if the people in the winterground were wrong? What if the Dream-Ship isn't this way at all? If only I had the whole Book, not just fragments from other people's heads. But the Book is with the Axe – and if it was right, why hasn't he come back? Shivering now with more than sunburn, Tohalla heard an animal's hoot and began to run.

Eventually, Tohalla stumbled to a halt in the starless dark. Whimpering as something brushed her knee – *Animal! It must be a high-dog!* – Tohalla panicked. Then she realized she had run off the rim of the Unshadowed Plain, for the thing was unmoving, no animal but some growth she could not see. Almost sobbing with relief, she groped her way into a denser patch of darkness to pillow her burning head on the coolness of the ground. She just had strength enough to pull her wolf-hide over her.

In the rain-sodden dawn Tohalla creaked to her feet. Her tunic and the cuffs of her leggings were clammy, weighted down with water where the wolf's-hide had slipped off in the night. Once she had wrung out her clothes and wrapped the soft hide around her against the chill, she observed her surroundings.

Moisture beaded the Red with grey pearls, softening it. Here and there in a steep gully, clusters of chameleon burst yellow on her eyes; tufts of hookweed showed a dull, soggy brown between strands of lilac wood. And the air smelt so fresh it might have been made new that morning. The world hummed a tinkling melody especially for her and she smiled.

Best of all, though, was a freshet frothing white. Making her way down to it, Tohalla drank deeply and cooled her sunburnt face. The water stung her skin.

As she straightened, a gleam of translucent red caught the rising suns.

A messenger! Maybe I can find out what lies ahead.

With the thought came a hint of anxiety but she was so used to the feeling, travelling alone, that she shoved it into a corner. Neither Edrach nor Marchidas had ever travelled this way; they could have no warning for her.

Buds of icy pink formed incipient fans around the heart of the messenger, growing fast in the early Spring of this south-land. Tohalla knelt to cup the glowing ruby from which they sprang. She cleared her mind.

Like sun through closed eyelids patterns whirled shadowy through her. Small lives impinged on her; for a moment she *was* a comet with red-mites burrowing into her skin, scratching on this convenient growth. Then, with messenger fragments caught in its spines, it wandered on. Contact abruptly broke.

Disconcerted, Tohalla leant back on her heels. And saw the high-dog.

Its ridiculously-long legs had brought it all but silently within a stride of her. A spray of razor-thin teeth dripped saliva; backthrust claws unsheathed. Its black-hole eyes were level with hers. Like the wolves, it used the messengers as traps.

She fumbled for her spear without taking her eyes off the downswept fangs, couldn't grasp it as it rolled among last year's broken crystal. Still in the thrall of the messenger, Tohalla could feel the hungry cunning of the high-dog, had difficulty communicating with her own limbs.

Marchidas and Edrach swept through her. *Too much, too soon.* Tohalla felt that only the shaft of her gaze kept the beast from attacking. Her wet fingers still couldn't clutch the spear.

She felt her muscles contract with the high-dog's first movement. All the pain she had ever known burst black inside her, imagining the great fangs lancing into her body: childbirth, the fall into the winterground fire, the searing of her wrist in the battle with Wordweaver ...

And the high-dog whistled with her pain. *She felt her tail arch up in agony.*

The beast fled from the pain she had sent, its blue-grey body rippling away on its stilted legs. Only the sharp scent of it stayed.

Marchidas and Edrach had tried to warn her. Tohalla remembered the Axe standing wolf-guard in the clearing outside the Edge.

She vaulted the stream and ran.

Bursting through a stretch of semi-arid scrub, she stopped. Straight as a furrow the earth turned cinder black in a line from east to west.

CHAPTER TWO

The Broken Dream

Nothing grew. Half-crystals stopped, cut off, turned to ash. Nothing overflew. Tohalla felt her thoughts themselves amputated, unable to reach beyond the barren wastes of the Straight Desert. The very silence was a palpable thing that hissed menace in her ears. Like the desert itself, stretching out its ugliness as far as she could see, the silence seemed unending.

Something must have carved all life from that desolation, some implacable thing that hated the least living creature, animal or plant. Not so much as a red-mite crawled in the sullen gravel. Beneath the lowering clouds only dust-devils defied the stillness.

And I thought I could cross that?

Aghast, Tohalla crept away into the scrub. Better the high-dogs than that massive destruction. *But how can I go back and admit I've failed? Not only that – where could I go back to?*

She retreated, hunkering down beyond the brow of a gentle hill, her arms wrapped tight around her body. Unthinking, she squeezed the wolf-claw Mauritz had given her. Gradually the soft, habitual music of the Red calmed her. 'Before any decision, eat or drink – if there time is,' Edrach used to say.

A handful of wolf-fire taken from her pack was slow to ignite. Tohalla cursed her own ineptitude but she couldn't find the fire-box Benhannon had once given Marchidas. When it did burn, the dryest fuel she could find was still wet enough to pump out smoke at every breath of the damp wind.

While she boiled broth, Tohalla's sodden clothes clung to her, wringing from her sunburn a soreness that irritated. Yet as she changed into something drier, it began to rain again, a depressing drizzle that chilled her. Acids from her worried empty stomach flowed stinging into her gullet; when she tried to spoon up the broth that wasn't yet ready, she scalded her mouth. It did nothing to improve her temper.

All her anxiety spilled outwards from the black, bleak devastation.

Reluctantly, leaving the dried meat simmering to flavour the broth properly, Tohalla went back up the slope. She had to see the Straight Desert in reality to stop its ghost clouding her mind.

Wrapped in the changing hues of her wolf-hide, Tohalla climbed one of the low hills and lay beside a yellow chameleon cluster. Around her the rain drew a pattering tune from the Red; below her, on the sullen cinders, it sounded as sad as rain upon a shore. Otherwise nothing had changed. The charred earth stretched beyond the horizon, its edge –

From this height the edge seemed to curve a little. Suddenly excited, Tohalla laid her spear level with her eye. *Yes! It curves inwards off in the distance, such a slow curve it seems straight.*

Maybe there's a way round it!

It was the first hint of hope Tohalla had felt. Slightly cheered, she finished the broth and set off, keeping to the scrub because it felt less unfriendly than the eternal charcoal wasteland … Not once did she catch even a glimpse of the far side of it.

Three days' travel showed her there was no end to the devastation. Or not one she could reach before her food ran out. Even a stream she found turned aside at the edge of the Straight Desert. Here on this side were tree-crawlers and ground hoppers and the myriad facets of coloured crystals singing in the evening light.

Beyond, only a tired smell of ashes.

But there was a crack in the steppes of charcoal earth, a single flaw in its evenness that pointed the way she wanted to go. And the wind dropped one lonely crystal fragment on the dead black ground.

That sultry night Tohalla watched the Straight Desert pale beneath Gold Moon's sweep. There was a shadow of a shadow …

Patiently brushing off the crawlers – she had regained her immunity to the red-mites – Tohalla lay longer, waiting. The Amethyst Moon courted a humming sparkle from the crystals around her. Its swift gravitic pull lured summer-ripe buds spattering upon her in the dark.

Memories of Vernal brushed at Tohalla. *If only I'd taken her to the Dancing Forest!* She sighed, brightened. *Maybe Caramon will. Maybe when I bring new seeds from the Dream Ship she'll love me then* …

Lost in echoes of the Dancing Forest a deeper note was buried.

216

Tohalla caught her breath. The deeper note was there! Beneath the Amethyst Moon the blackened earth rose in a tortured dance. Beaten upwards by a surge of sound that centred on a straight line radiating from the other side. Inevitably the line shrank as it coincided with the focus of her vision.

Even here in the shelter of the scrub Tohalla could not defend herself from the sound. Hands jammed against her ears, she writhed as the wave of sound separated into a thousand different notes that each vibrated one part of her. Lungs and guts and brains jumbled jostling against her juddering bones. Heat boiled through her; the roaring in her ears cast dazzling rings of light across her vision. Life receded. She was trapped inside her –

Body. Tohalla turned her head, surprised it responded. The neap tide of sound had gone; dawn lay upon the land. And dew steamed upward from the scorched Straight Desert. Its one bright brave crystal might never have been.

Stiff, she lurched back to her camp of the evening before. Before. She would never be the same again. Neither food nor drink could still her shuddering. Her mind didn't seem to belong to her …

She looked around. Where had the morning gone? Rednoon shimmered on the crystals. Lilac spearwood breathed its sweetness over her; Summer was close. And, subdued, forgetful ground-hoppers belled in simple pleasure.

Laying almost her last messenger-bud on her joined palms, Tohalla imprinted the message she had learned in the night; each trembling fear that had touched her so that anyone who followed might be warned of the hot noise. And she recorded how, farther back, the Ship had been found and was gone for help, with her hope that somewhere ahead the Drone Ship might lie. If she didn't make it, perhaps some traveller in the future might …

If the Straight Desert didn't go on for ever.

Then, when she had planted the crystal as almost a prayer for the uniting of her world and the star-kin, Tohalla stepped onto the hot black earth.

Because if the thing came only once in four days, she might yet have time to cross the Straight Desert.

The noon stillness was less uncomfortable than the heat rising from the ground. Hours later when the dust of her walking lodged sharp in every crease of her skin, the evening breeze skirled cinders against Tohalla's flesh. Her scorched boots protected her feet less and less; the rags she bound them with wore quickly through.

217

But the desert did not stop. Now the scrub hills had crawled below the horizon behind her, there was only that crack in the earth to guide her.

Might get lost in the dark, Tohalla thought, wondering if it was her own thought and whether she was still Tohalla. Dwarfed by the unending black, identity somehow wandered away, her essence evaporating like sweat into the burnt air. Sometimes she wondered what she was doing here when she could have been home with her daughter. She could have ridden the *Mosckva* at the Axe's side – *But we'd have been outsiders there too ...*

She stood stock-still. It took time for her to realize that her feet were no longer drifting along beside the fault in the earth that guided her onward. *Outlander.*

They'll be glad of news that the Ship's gone to find the star-kin.

She was walking again, without volition.

The twilight showed a faint gleam beside her flapping boot when she climbed down into the deepening crack so she wouldn't lose her way in the dark. A lonely gleam: one poor pink crystal.

Through sooty lips her parched tongue said, 'I am Tohalla. I have found the Ship. I am Tohalla.'

A night without end: the nightmare of everyone who's been ill, or hurt, or watched over someone who has. *The ground's above me.* Tohalla probed at the puzzle. *I've fallen.* And, later, *I ought to – to get up?* After that, practice helped her solve the riddle so that she kept stumbling along within the ever-deeper fault. But it was still night and the flashing motes in Tohalla's eyes hid the stars.

Worse, Tohalla had miscalculated. The hot noise was coming back.

The bones of the earth shook, growling. The walls of the crack radiated heat, but something called Tohalla kept walking into its depths because it was all she could do. Above her head the walls of the crack crumbled.

Walk, and fall, and get up.

Hot cinders sparked in her hair. She batted at them, shouting, 'Go away!' They wouldn't listen. They danced in the darkness around her. They smelled horrible in the wolf-hide. They hurt.

Again that black incandescence dissolved her. Tumbling gravel rained down on her where she lay, but Tohalla was not inside her body to know it. She left in a shriek that said, 'Help! Ain!'

But it might have been 'Pain'.

It did help her, though. The machine responded to voice commands.

218

CHAPTER THREE

Disillusion

It wasn't meant to be like this. Lush greenery swathed mounds that might have been houses and some that weren't, but the trees had no purpose and the flowers bore no fruit. Hot air floated strange green odours into the broad space floored with dust. Rainbows walked in cascading scents. There was not a crystal to be seen. Mid-morning shadows arrowed from useless objects she couldn't even identify, but hardly anyone was about. Certainly no-one was doing a hand's turn.

But that wasn't what was wrong.

I was supposed to walk in and somebody stole my moment of triumph! Now nobody even notices me. I didn't even get here by myself –

How did I get here, anyway?

The thought rushed through her like a tide in her blood. Unnerving. Her breath shortened until she felt dizzy. Forcing herself to slow her heartbeat, her respiration, Tohalla stopped.

I was walking. Where from? Where to? What's going on?

Panic struck again, a force that existed physically. Tohalla sat quickly on the dried earth before she could fall beneath the pain that assailed her chest, her stomach. Other aches settled in as a background to her anxiety.

'My – my spear's gone!'

Unaware that she had even spoken, Tohalla searched around with her hands, suddenly afraid to turn her head in case *something* lurked behind her with unknown weapons. Fear grew.

But there was no shadow reaching past her. Only her own. She couldn't feel her wolf-hide and her pack had gone as well. Everything vanished. Everything she had brought from her former home in the Green – there were only her scorched clothes and the ranks that Mauritz had given her.

Tohalla huddled, her arms around her knees, waiting for inescapable doom to overtake her. The rending fangs, the piercing longknife.

Nothing happened. The suns brushed her with their heat and a breeze wandered through her hair, bringing with it the tang of the sea. Tohalla wondered at a level below perception.

Everything remained as it was.

Eventually her dread subsided and Tohalla looked around, vaguely disappointed. Distant figures crossed from mound to mound, paying her no heed; there was no-one in the sun-baked expanse close by.

If nobody's going to come and discover me, she realized, *I'd better go and discover them.* Then embarrassment numbed her aching legs until she felt as weak as a lost child, but she made it across the dazzling square.

At the door of a structure that looked more like a house than any of the other mounds, she hesitated. There were neither outwatchers nor inwatchers to tell them she was here (whoever 'they' were). What should she do?

Tohalla called, 'Hello? Is anybody there?' but nobody answered her quavering voice. She pushed the door. It didn't open.

Examining the door, she wasn't even sure that's what it was. It had no handle on its surface; she could find nothing on the bulging steel oval to indicate its function. Yet there seemed to be a path leading up to it, a track of beaten earth between haphazard flowers.

She banged at the metal; it was suns-hot beneath her hands.

No-one came.

Yet there seemed to be some sort of music inside. Not the comforting music of the Green, or the Red, that existed to weave links between the lonely. Uneasy, Tohalla listened, smote the slippery surface again. Lifted her hand to thump louder, head half-turned to see if anyone else was coming – and almost hit someone who suddenly appeared instead of the door.

'Scrag off!' he said fiercely. (Tohalla had an impression of a vast, pale man whose head – shone? – against the black of the interior.) 'Can't you read doors?'

Tohalla backed up. Before she could speak the metal curved shut with a snap. A bee bumbled into it, bounced off and droned away in a melody that had no need of her.

Rootless, shrivelled under the nooning suns, Tohalla wandered lost.

Soren's house was green, among other things. Green for the earth that fed him, sienna for the bones of rock whose flesh was his sweet curving hills. Silver windows threw back the suns' light shaped into crescents. The door was a waterfall.

Tohalla didn't know it was a house. She had been walking for what seemed like hours – were the suns here wrong that they wouldn't mark the passage of time? – not brave enough to approach another mound. Now and then she would catch a glimpse of someone in the distance but she never quite managed to catch up with anyone. Besides, what could she say? Out here in the burning heat of the afternoon, the mounds seemed fewer. They were all different, meaningless shapes.

Faint and thirsty, she saw only the liquid arabesque of plashing water. Bathing herself in its coolness, Tohalla gulped down handsful of water from its gleaming cascade.

Only then did she see the curving passage behind the waterfall, ripe with the scent of mushrooms. If she could rest a while out of the glare of the suns …

Just a few paces behind the falling spray Tohalla thought she heard music. Curiosity gave her strength enough to try and find its source.

The passage was taller than head-height, and not completely dark. Faint curls of light glowed in different colours and diminished, hanging in the air.

Tohalla started when she first saw them, her hand reaching for her missing knife, but they made no move down to her level. And the drop-like jewels faded in evanescent sapphire or emerald or topaz, seeming too soft to hurt.

Intrigued now at the way the gems grew larger the nearer she came to the atonal music, Tohalla walked on, beginning to perceive the connection.

'It's music in the air!' she gasped in wonder. The radiant colours winked out.

'Oh,' she exclaimed sadly. 'I've frightened it away!'

Dejection made her voice swoop down from its high-pitched excitement. Then jewels coalesced from the sounds of her words. Tentatively she reached out to touch an amber one in the half-dark.

It popped when she touched it, bursting like a bubble. Spots of some substance dropped on her fingers. Guiltily, Tohalla put her hand behind her back.

'Carm in!' called an unseen speaker. At least, it sounded like that but Tohalla could not reproduce the exact way of speech. Male, a rumbling from a deep chest. *Is he angry? Is it a trap?* Tohalla couldn't read the emotional freight of his lilting intonation. But she knew she had to find out. *Hiding out here isn't going to do me any good …*

Speech: *Is it someone talking, that weird jumble of sound? To me?*

After that, though she called softly so that the lovely gems of light might cheer her into courage, Tohalla saw only the dim passage, unadorned.

Hesitantly she stepped towards a hint of brightness that looked like daylight. Rounding a corner, she saw that it was.

Not bright enough to dazzle her, nor to hide the figure of an immense man lolling on a bed.

He smiled a little. 'Who're youah t'day?' *Is that what he said?*

'Tohalla of the Loom,' she said. 'We found the Ship and I've come to tell you.'

'S – th k agin.' He raised his eyebrows in surprise.

Tohalla could see no weapon in the room. *But would I recognize one in a place like this? Are those winking lights a threat or a song?*

Not understanding his words, she answered his expression, 'I said I've come to tell you that the Ship's found and the star-kin might be coming soon.'

'Well th's fi. Setun te me all 'bou it. N' a drink?'

He doesn't believe me! thought Tahalla, to hide from herself the fact that he didn't seem to care. *Perhaps he just doesn't understand?* But she perched gingerly on the edge of some sort of press almost opposite him, so that she could rest her sore feet. Angular metal boxes either side of the press formed some kind of barrier across the room, almost from side to side.

The man was already waving at an array of drinking-vessels that were clear as water. Liquids of different colours caught the light that filtered in from a thousand star-shaped holes in the walls. Tohalla could hardly tell exactly where outdoors ended and this place began, so many vines and plants rippled their leaves in the breeze. She found it strange to see green, too, so far from Housefather's vale.

'Chamomile,' said Tohalla belatedly. 'I could do with something to calm me down.'

Her attention was riveted on a sort of pear-tree that grew up an inside wall to spread its canopy under the ceiling. Both fruits and bell-like flowers glowed with the delicate sheen of pearls, phantoms of the rainbow. A strange flat sheet seemed to grow from the lower branches, rippling through she could feel no breeze. It stretched from branch-tip to trunk, a rich reddish brown of fibres laced with writhing tendrils. Yet the leaves of the tree were – well, green.

He'd been talking. 'I said, "I haven't any chamile, but if you want to calm down, try this." ' His accent was beginning to settle into a more

222

recognizable pattern, Tohalla found.

'Sorry. That'll be fine. Thank you.' *Or should I say 'gratude' like they do in the Red?*

He was leaning sideways now on a multitude of pillows, helping himself to a bottle and cup that were translucent. He didn't need to take a step; the shelf was well within reach of his long arms.

'Cheers,' he said, handing her a cup that she could see through containing a liquid that she could not.

Taking a drink – Tohalla found it reasonably agreeable though it seemed hot when it hit the pit of her stomach – she observed him. It was hard not to stare.

Taller than Edrach, even, the man was massive in proportion, running to fat. His hair seemed to grow out sideways in ledges but at least it was a normal colour: an undistinguished brown. He wore some sort of loose leggings in turquoise, with a tiny sleeveless jerkin of the same shade traced with looping silver and flowers that shone like coloured crystal fragments. Brown eyes and brown brows punctuated a face that was florid underneath its tan. Tohalla, remembering how they did things in the Red, was too shy to ask him his name. She supposed he had already told her while her thoughts were ranging round the room. She would not insult him by asking again.

'So leaven my life with all this,' the man said – she thought. It didn't seem to make much sense, though. His huge, spatulate fingers were stroking the embroidery on his turquoise jerkin. Only now and again did he glance up from his hands to her face.

'Again?' Tohalla asked, meaning him to repeat his words so that she might understand.

The brown eyebrows rose in surprise. 'You mean you've told me all about it before and I've forgotten?' He tutted in self-disgust. 'Typical. Well, tell me again for the pleasure of it.'

She did. Marchidas's death-poem, and Edrach's, with her life and the Axe's woven in between. Many times she hesitated, wondering if his closed eyes meant he was bored, or the flutter of fingers on his jewelled jerkin was a sign that he was no longer listening. But whenever Tohalla stopped, he would look up with a queer little smile to say, 'And then?' or 'What happened next to that?'

The flowers on his window-vines were curling into sleep when she'd finished between her hesitations and self-corrections. It seemed that the pears on the inside tree were brighter than the evening light.

'Fascinating, Loom.' Thick lips curved into a smile that almost showed his teeth. 'Have you had this story long?'

223

Tohalla met his gaze, trying not to be disconcerted by it. 'The parts I've lived took nine years, but the Sons of the Red have been trying to find the Ship almost since they lost it. The last bit, the search for the Dream Ship and the Plain of Unshadows and the Straight Desert, that's only been since my daughter would – would have none of me.'

He puffed the slightest gust of laughter down his broad nose. Tohalla jerked bolt-upright on her seat. *Does he think it's funny that my girl's a – a stranger?*

'Don't you laugh at me!' she shouted, taking the finger of his derision from her deepest wound. 'Generations of men and women have died trying to find the Ship, and all you can do is giggle like a stupid child.'

Still smiling, the man leant forward, laying a hand on her knee. 'I'm sorry, Loom –'

She shifted her legs sideways out of his reach. 'My name's Tohalla! Only the Axe and Chosen Brother gave me that as an earned name, Tohalla of the Loom, because I was the only one in the whole of the Green who'd dare put a pattern into my weaving, or listen to the song of the Red, or anything.'

Compressing his mouth – Tohalla could see he was trying not to laugh at her – the man said, 'Do accept my apologies. Far be it from me to take over their preserves.'

'If I had the messengers you'd soon find out!'

'Ah. But you haven't, have you, Tohalla? How unfortunate.' Sarcasm slithered around his words but they themselves were sympathetic.

Tohalla couldn't think of a suitable reply. She kept silent, offended.

The man sighed, pulling at his quivering lips, and said, 'I thought it must have been recent, or I'd have come across it in my mi –'

His eyes flickered to the tree.

Uncomprehending, Tohalla asked sharply, 'In your what?'

That only sent him into further paroxysms.

Only the thought that she needed something from this man kept Tohalla in the pear-lit cave of a room. It didn't make her like herself any better.

Tohalla hated herself for accepting but there was nothing else she could do. It was hard enough to be laughed at and called a liar, but when her empty stomach rumbled just as she was answering, 'No, thank you. I'd rather starve than eat here,' he merely grinned at her and said, 'And of course you wouldn't know to ask for food the minute you were past my hills, would you?'

'I don't need to ask for help,' she said. 'I can take care of myself.'

'In your Red, maybe. And that's not what I meant, is it? But you wouldn't last long against my watch-lions. Nothing gets past them. They'd eat your – wolves? – alive.'

'Ha! I got here all right, though, didn't I?'

'Ha yourself, Tohalla. You won't get out past 'em because it's dark now. So unless you tell me who you really are, you're stuck 'til morning, though I guess that's what you wanted. From the Vigilantes, are you?'

She jumped up, her hand reaching for the long-knife that should have been at her belt. She didn't know what Vigilantes were but if they were his enemies and he had her trapped …

The man didn't move from his indolent slouch. 'Yes, Tohalla, very convincing. I don't mind playing along.' His tone changed suddenly as he became the courteous host.

'Do, please, join me for dinner, Tohalla. Nothing extraordinary, but my friends will be delighted to make your acquaintance. It's always nice to know who's on which side.'

Feeling rather foolish, Tohalla let her empty hand fall. Eyeing him with dislike she said very clearly, 'Since I appear to have no choice, and since I need you to introduce me to other people who'll listen to me, I'll stay.'

Very dignified, she sat down. He said, 'I thought you might. Do you want to keep that ridiculous disguise on –' he made a gesture as though to push away the smell of her '– or would you rather have a wash?'

In amongst the strange odours of his cave-house, Tohalla was suddenly conscious of the sweat that had dried on her body and the acrid stench of her scorched hair. She could imagine how her splash in the waterfall had smeared the ash on her. *He's so neat and well-groomed …*

Tohalla swallowed. 'If you'll show me where the compost is – '

He laughed. 'Well, if that's what you wash in, of course, don't let me stop you.'

'Well what do you wash in?' Her anger seemed to amuse him.

'Water, of course. You'll find it a pleasant novelty.' He waved at the doorway behind her, the one she'd come through. 'Down there, first on the left.'

But the passage was dark and she only found the waterfall by following its sound. At least its moon-silvered chill kept her awake.

Nobody seemed in the least bit surprised about the Ship being found. They laughed in all the wrong places, and applauded her at the end like a child with a party-piece, and Tohalla couldn't understand the half of what they said, especially when they gabbled to each other. She'd wanted him to find someone who'd believe …

Apart from that, Tohalla remembered very little about the dinner except her exhaustion. The very strangeness of it all wearied her still more, and her burns and grazes stung. Besides, she was so self-conscious when they all belonged and she didn't, and the drink did something to her head: like dreamsmoke, but it seemed to put them all on one plane and her on another. And the news she had brought only set them laughing more. *How can I ever have thought they'd believe me? Me?* And the knowledge that had burned so long inside her, the surety that she was a failure, dragged Tohalla down.

At one point she awoke suddenly – *Have I been asleep?* – to hear her captor say, 'She didn't even have the presence of mind to ask me my name.'

A woman with bronze-green hair lolled against him, slack-mouthed. 'My dear Soren, who in all the settlement doesn't know your name? Especially someone from Council.'

'Exactly,' he explained patiently. 'That's why she didn't need to ask.'

'Oh,' slurred someone else. 'You mean she already knew?'

Tohalla said suddenly, 'I didn't!'

Soren laughed. 'A bit too late to be convincing, Tohalla.'

Later Tohalla seemed to hear Soren say, 'Ssh! Not now! I've got other plans for the Vigilantes.'

What can't they do now? Tohalla tried to make her stiff lips frame the words in darkness.

And, unaccountably, it was morning.

Her head ached; bile dried her throat. But the flowers on the vine trumpeted their blue, wide-awake against the lattice of star-windows. Someone in red was asleep on the couch in a dappled pool of suns' light but there were no other signs of the party. Her captor was nowhere to be seen.

Tohalla tiptoed past the russet thing that flapped at her approach, though there was no breeze stroking the emerald leaves. Heart in her mouth, she stole softly to the passageways.

'Oh!' she exclaimed as Soren rounded the corner.

'Going somewhere?' he asked.

Chin up, Tohalla spoke defiantly. 'Yes, if you'll let a body. You can't keep me here forever.'

He stepped back, sweeping her a mocking bow, but she didn't

226

recognize the gesture. 'I don't want to. Tell your masters they've failed. But do thank them for a very entertaining evening. I haven't been so amused in years.'

Words formed a cataract on her tongue, a dozen sentences to spill out her scorn on him. He waited with exaggerated politeness as she stammered.

In the end Tohalla said too loudly, 'Oh, what's the use? What's the use of anything I ever did?' Crimson flushed her face, hiding her freckles. She stared at Soren, hate for herself in her eyes, but all he saw was the hatred. 'Thank you for the food, if not the hospitality.'

Flattening himself against the wall as if she needed more room to pass him, Soren said, 'By the way, dear, I'd get those burns seen to now. They've served their purpose, wouldn't you say?'

CHAPTER FOUR

The Killing Machine

No large carnivores lay in wait beyond the waterfall but the suns' heat hit her like a hammer. After only a few paces her footprints were dry in the dust; a dozen more steps and the beads of moisture on her skin had dried. The redness of her sunburn set up a renewed protest.

Automatically she began to make her way downhill. The House in the Green lay nestled in its cove; perhaps the heart of this place did too. Maybe Soren, if that was his name, was only some kind of half-tame Wild Man. Maybe there'd be other people who did listen.

Maybe she'd find the Dream Ship.

Maybe Vernal would want her if she went back to the Green.

Here and there trees lined the broad walkways. Wherever possible Tohalla kept to their shade though some of the trees gave little enough of that, with only strange tufts of greenery bursting from the top of knobbly stems.

Even the exotic-scented air was languorous. Bees murmured between flowers of red and mauve and gold. Snatches of conversation drifted from vine-covered humps that must have been houses but Tohalla was weary now – or was it nervous? – and kept a lookout for something shaped like the Ship. Difficult when outrageous frothing greenery cloaked every structure ...

Turning corners left and right and left again, Tohalla came to a wide avenue that dipped downwards. The mounds were closer together now – *Can there be that many people?* – and tall figures sauntered around in colours, in black tunics and white robes, in spots and stripes and patterns like flame. No-one was spinning or weaving in the shadows. Eating, drinking, though it wasn't yet noon by either sun, and children ran around half-clad without anybody watching over them. Occasional fences didn't seem to keep anybody in or out.

None of them paid her any mind. Tentatively approaching one couple, a man and woman with hair flowing over naked skin, Tohalla said, 'We've found the *Mosckva*. The star-kin are coming.'

Amused, the woman said, 'Of course they are. They always are,' and strolled on, still chatting to the dark-haired man beside her.

Open-mouthed, Tohalla watched them go, wondering if they'd understood her, if she'd understood the woman. It was hard not to stare at their unclothed bodies. Her cheeks burned.

In another few steps down the hill, the sea exploded upon her vision. Excitement rushed through her; Tohalla didn't try to explain it to herself but the familiar white-capped surf on the aching blue sea reminded her of home.

Almost running, Tohalla passed the weird houses and other structures that were higher but were still not a ship. At the end of the avenue a white balustrade barring the blue stopped her.

Puzzled, she looked downwards. A cliff with not-quite-hens roosting on its ledges dropped jaggedly to the distant beach. Streams of flowers waved above the restless motion of the sapphire tide; bleached grass clung to the auburn rock.

Even the sand was not the colour it was at home.

A path zig-zagged downwards to her left. She followed a group of girls down it. They hadn't yet reached Ripeness by the seeming of it but boys were waiting at a turn of the path to fondle them suggestively. Tohalla blushed.

Waves rilled pleasantly cool on her skin when the first sting of salt had faded from her sores. There were no tidenets, no sea-stalkers, no tideswool. People here apparently thought it was all right to paddle; even adults were splashing up to their chins, yelling with laughter. The suns were burning her back. She hesitated, watching the others, decided.

Tohalla ducked her shoulders under, gasping. Her cropped hair had reached past the nape of her neck in her journey through the Red; now it floated like pale watercress and something nibbled at it.

She stood, shrieking, floundering towards the shore. No-one cared.

Tohalla stopped shrieking, embarrassed. With only her feet in the water, she observed. The sinuous silvery things at her heels did her no damage. Eventually Tohalla lay back to rest her head on the sand and let her body drift gently in the swell.

Twin shadows crossed her; she sat up suddenly. A man was wading up out of the sea with one of the silver things impaled on his spear.

'Sorry, did I splash you?' he said. His voice was light and rich as buttered toast, his words clear.

Tohalla shook her head and sent bright water spinning from her flying hair. 'No. What's that?'

'Wrasse. D'you like it?'

'I don't know. What do you do with it? Is it dangerous?'

He laughed, not unkindly. 'No, of course it's not. You eat it. Want to try some?'

'I don't know,' she said again, cautiously this time. *Is he Council? Vigilante? – Would I mind if he was?*

'Come and try some anyway. I've got plenty of fruit if you don't like it.' Her mouth watered at the thought of luscious fruit.

When she stood up he looked at her various wounds in puzzlement. His grin faded. 'Who're you today?'

'Tohalla of the Loom.' She borrowed what they appeared to use round here for a greeting. 'Who're you today?'

The muscles around his mouth tightened, deeper wrinkles formed around his eyes. He looked like he'd prefer to cancel his invitation. 'Tamdaintre. And I always am.'

He set off fast, not looking back. *It's as if he's trying to forget I'm here,* Tohalla decided. *But he's the only one who's talking to me at all. I'm not letting him get away.*

Yet.

He wore some sort of blue leggings cut off at the knee. They were old and faded, not like everyone else's garish clothing, Tohalla noticed. He was tanned a dull brown though a puckered scar drew a curve of silver-pink across the back of one calf. His hair was shorter even than a farmer's; white streaks showed in it despite its sea-slicked darkness.

Tohalla tried to step only on the sides of her feet because the sand burnt her lacerated soles. She fell further and further behind Tamdaintre *(Did I hear that right?)* but she wasn't going to run to catch up with him. Somehow that would have hurt her pride.

One behind the other they passed the base of the steps and the people crowded there *(Why do they stick so close together when there's all this great beach?)* Tamdaintre waved or called to some of them; not gladly, just in acknowledgement of their greetings. Tohalla felt foolish, spare, like a spineder behind a plough.

In the shadow of the cliffs the sand was blessedly cool on her feet. Tohalla made better time now it was possible to use the reaching stride of the Sons of the Wolf. Soon she could have touched the soft skin of the man's back. Though he was slim and well-muscled, there was the first faint tiredness of the flesh that age brings. Tohalla wanted to see him from the front again.

Where the cliff dipped, sloping backwards now, Tamdaintre scrambled up a steep bank of sand and waited, holding a hand out to her. Letting him pull her up, Tohalla joined him on the bottom of a rising path.

'D'you kow who I am?' he asked.

'No. Do you know where I come from?'

'The Vigilantes?'

Eyes level, Tohalla as tall as he was, they studied each other's faces. His showed laughter-lines, and patience-lines, but in his blue-grey eyes the colour of her nothern seas there was calm, a vast reservoir of balance to give him centre. It was a feeling that only Edrach before had given her a hint of, and she welcomed it with a nameless relief.

'No,' Tohalla said at last, 'look at my wolf's-claw, and these scales. These are ranks from the Red. Look at *me!* You know I don't come from here. How could I have anything to do with your Vigilantes?'

He chuckled derisively. 'You think because of who I am that I know everyone in the Two Hundred Thousand? Who else would think like that but Council?'

Tohalla's mouth hissed in a breath of surprise. She knew the numbers, two, a hundred, a thousand. But put them together? It was unthinkable! *There couldn't be that many on the whole of Rosaria!*

'Are you fine?' he asked, sounding concerned. His strong, slender hand came close to her arm. She saw the movement; he noticed the direction of her gaze and stopped it instantly.

Wondering what she had done to offend, Tohalla nodded.

'Think you can make it up the cliff? My home's a good way out from here.'

She said, 'I've walked mountains that make this a wrinkle, on my way to the Unshadowed Plain.' And it was his turn to look surprised.

Outside his home was a smooth white wall that wouldn't have stopped a toddler, it was so low, but it seemed discourteous not to use the gate. It was black, of panels of metal curved into flowers, and it was round. Not flat, but shaped like a ball. It rolled out of the way when Tamdaintre flicked it with a finger. He left it open.

There were lines of vegetables growing fiercely in the sun. Tohalla didn't recognize some of them but the whole thing seemed so reassuringly normal: a garden, a chicken-run, benches leaning against the wall. There was even a loom half-strung in a corner of his yard. More strange to Tohalla, he'd taken the trouble to plant flowers in tubs, their scents and colours all mingled together. She wondered why he'd caged the plants that way.

'What d'you think of it?'

Tohalla stopped staring. 'It's like a real garden! Only I keep seeing those flowers here and I don't know what they're for?'

'I don't get you. What d'you mean, for? They're not for anything, they're just pretty, that's all.'

'Do you mean,' she asked him carefully, 'that they don't have fruit? They're just patterns?'

'No, they're real enough. They –' He broke off, looking at her. 'That was a good one. I was almost caught.'

He turned towards the open hole in the smooth face of the cliff that served him as a door. She started to speak but he overrode her. 'Let's get a drink, shall we? What would you like?'

Tohalla touched his arm urgently, wondering if it was against some code but needing to turn him back to face her. 'Believe me, Tamdaintre, believe me, please. I'm not trying to catch you. I don't come from – what did you call it? The Two Hundred Thousand.' His scepticism was obvious but she poured her words out, avid to convince him: 'If only I could touch your mind I could make you believe! Let me try.'

'Not clever enough.' The suns shone in his eyes. He squinted against their fierceness, his face closed. 'Not subtle at all. Now I know you're Vigilante.'

Her hand fell from the warmth of his arm. Tohalla fought to keep the pain out of her expression. Her voice trembled but she ruled it with icy control. 'I came only to tell you all the Ship is found and the Axe is riding the seas between the stars to pay off his blood-debt. He's fighting the vacuums to fetch the star-kin. Surely you want that, the friendship of the people out there? To be part of Erth's family?'

He snorted derisively. 'We all want that. What else is the point of the Two Hundred Thousand? But we wait and they don't come, so we wait some more. They won't come now. It's been too long. Besides, everywhere else on this forsaken planet is dead black cinder. So don't give me all that garbage about crossing mountains. No human being'd last five minutes out there. Take your delusion and your trickery back to Jerad. I'm not giving him any excuse to have me sliced up.'

Tamdaintre turned away.

232

Tohalla took her hurt out of his garden, stepping over the low wall. As she walked away alone she looked back just once. Something bright sparkled on the russet warp of the loom. Tamdaintre was invisible in his house in the sheltering auburn cliff but a jaunty whistle showed he had forgotten her already.

Up and down hills, between the house-mounds of a hundred different shapes. Tohalla pounded angrily along the paths of dust or dull red stone, her feet throbbing. She almost welcomed the pain to feed her anger, her desperation. Whenever she met someone she babbled out her message of hope, to be met with mockery or a facile pretence at agreement. ('Not another one! Best humour her,' an old man said to his wife, and asked Tohalla who she was today.)

Some ignored her altogether. When she asked in despair, 'Well, can you tell me where the Drone Ship is then?' nobody seemed to know that either. A growing hopelessness enveloped her but she kept walking. Around her was a place she didn't belong.

In the dusk, lights pricked out inside the houses but there were always some mounds in each cluster that didn't hold the twinkling and chatter of a hearth. Tohalla identified with their sadness and limped on with the sores and burns of the Straight Desert repeating time and again that there was no welcome for her here.

The Two Hundred Thousand stretched endlessly with crowded rows of buildings rearing to the skies, or scattered low-strung house-mounds. Sounds of cooking wafted food-scents to tangle with the perfume of the night-flowers. The Amethyst Moon and Gold Moon wheeled above the leafy gloaming; she remembered their familiarity in the combe with Vernal asleep in her arms. Inside her Marchidas and Edrach spread their memories too as a blanket to protect her from the chill of loneliness.

She found a valley in whose tree-clad steepness were no house-lights to show she had no home here. Unconsciously, Tohalla rambled down into its depths, not knowing she was hiding because the pain of isolation went with her. Her bare feet slithered on fallen leaves, stirring up a rich odour of moist earth. Evening breezes scraped twig against branch; the foliage murmured a rustling. Some fowl swooped away, disturbed by her passage. When the clatter of wings burst away into the silent, empty skies her heart-beat calmed again. Then there was only a crimson flag of cloud in the star-hung purple that deepened to full night above the trees.

But the tangle of exuberant greenery was unlike the tidy orchards around the House where she was born. Whatever they said here, that was real too. *Wasn't it?*

'I remember.' Tohalla's lips moved just enough to reinforce the words that circled in her mind. 'I'm not crazy. It was real, the Red and the Green. It is real. I am Marchidas. I am Edrach – *No! I am Tohalla* – and I wish I'd never come here.'

And before her eyes was a huge black cave.

Its maw was a circular cavern, perfectly round, unnaturally so. Tohalla crept into it curiously, the hollowed sphere smooth beneath her toes, not even wind-blown leaves to crackle where she stepped. It seemed warmer inside the cave and Tohalla realized that her arms were rough with goose-bumps raised by the night chill. She felt her way round the walls but there was nothing to alarm her.

Gradually the warmth soothed her and she began to feel her tiredness steal along her limbs. Lassitude robbed her even of the sharpness of despair. Tohalla curled up in the bottom of the cave, watching the leaf-shadows on the threshold dance in the light of the Amethyst Moon. Sleep cuddled her in its peace.

A vast rumbling jerked her awake. Something big and menacing blocked out the moonlight. The cave shivered at its passage. Whatever it was, it was coming closer.

Tohalla sprang aside, scrambling for a toe-hold on the curving slope. Her blistered feet bled. The thing ground nearer. Fear bit into her.

She scrabbled higher, forcing her sleep-deadened fingers to cling to the slick surface. Now the thing was almost upon her. Panic swamped her. She hadn't so much as a knife …

There was a loud click. Dazzling light blinded her. The monster's sound was a roaring in her ears. She screwed up her eyes, forgot to breathe. Marchidas's death was in her. Tohalla cowered from it, sure she was going to die. The grinding howling thing was almost upon her –

Nothing happened. The glare, the mountain of sound were still there. But Tohalla realized she was untouched. *The thing hasn't seen me!*

Through slit eyes she peeped. The monster was melting into the wall at the back. No, the wall had opened somehow and the thing was rumbling along a brilliantly-lit passage. Tohalla crept along behind it.

Didn't the Moskcva *sound like that when it took Ain? Maybe this is a machine too. Maybe it'll take me to the Dream Ship.*

The thing took no notice of her. Walking more boldly now, she followed it. *The* Mosckva *didn't hurt me, did it? I won't be afraid. I won't be …*

The light didn't seem very bright at all once her eyes had got used to it. Then, braver still, she leaped up on some projection at the back and rode the machine for what seemed like hours. *But I haven't an hour-candle to tell …*

234

Eventually the light faded out altogether. Mouth so dry she couldn't even swallow, Tohalla perched alone on the black machine in the blackness. The sound of it battered echoing at her ears. Warm air rushed by her, faster and faster; the machine was going more swiftly than a razorback could run. She would have jumped off if she hadn't been so afraid. She wished she hadn't come. Who knew what was down here lying in wait? The wind sucked her breath from her. *What if the air runs out?*

But it didn't. Even terror dimmed with boredom. Endless night gripped her so that light and life seemed impossibly remote. She had always been driven headlong into darkness.

Then the howling whine changed pitch. Tohalla clutched her ears, trying to keep her balance because the thing's motion had changed suddenly. Her head catapulted against the unseen metal. She almost fell off. But the metal wasn't unseen any more. She could just make out its bulk against a paler blackness. The ordinary blackness of night.

The thing rocked on its legs – *(Did it have legs? Or wheels like a cart? I don't know)* but now she was clinging on. It slewed sideways along some sort of gully. Overhead, friendly stars winked at her though to the sides was only smooth, charcoal solidity.

Suddenly something clanked upwards, some sort of projection that rose twice head-height from the front of the machine. It swivelled, an extension reaching over the lip of the gully. Incomprehensible. Tohalla knelt up to peer ahead.

And fell.

The hot noise had come like a wall of sound collapsing in on her. Tohalla had found the evil that caused the Straight-Edged Desert. And it came from the Two Hundred Thousand.

Only the fact that the hot noise was focused on the Straight Desert saved her. Staggering against the whirling gale of sound Tohalla ran.

The sides of the gully were too smooth and high for her to scramble up them. She careered into the tunnel, hands outstretched to fend off whatever might be in the darkness. She ran until exhaustion forced her to a walk. But Tohalla dared not rest. The killing machine might come back.

Leaden-limbed, she urged herself to move as fast as she could. Her lungs were on fire. She felt that any moment her heart might tear in her chest. Yet she kept on, stumbling where the floor curved, her toes scraping until they bled.

Then from behind her came the echo of a roar and she knew that the killing machine was returning. Tohalla tried to outrun it but in her haste

235

she fell. Her shaking legs wouldn't carry her so she crawled. She could do no more – but it wasn't enough.

Perhaps I can crawl up the sides out of its way? Yet the tunnel itself was narrower than she remembered the cave. She felt the eternal dark tube closing in on her like a geyrlizard's gullet, and the killing machine came up behind her. Its rumbling shook the tunnel and ground through her very bones.

The roar shrieked up an octave, two. The walls of the tunnel began to glow. Tohalla dragged herself upright, made herself limp forward, casting anxious glances over her shoulder at the deadly black hulk which filled the space behind her. Ahead, the lighted tunnel stretched into infinity. There was no way out. Tohalla stopped struggling and turned to face her death.

The killing machine said, 'What can I do for you?'

'What?'

'What can I do for you?' the machine repeated.

Tohalla began to laugh. With machine patience the thing waited; Tohalla soon sobered up. 'You can take me out of here,' she said.

A metallic arm swooped out at her. She retreated but the machine said, 'Sit on my arm. I cannot get by you otherwise.'

Clinging to the scaly metal, Tohalla rode back down the white-walled, reverberating tunnel.

When the machine finally stopped its deafening progress in the spherical cave – the machine lit that for her too – Tohalla said, 'Thank you.'

Oddly it replied, 'You are welcome.' It made no move to release her but asked, 'May I further serve?'

Tohalla hesitated. She was hungry, homeless, sore in a hundred places, but all these things seemed too trivial to ask of such an object. And she was baffled by the Two Hundred Thousand. Perched on the metal-clad arm of the killing machine, Tohalla felt her confusion rise.

She said, 'Take me to Ain Tsui's Drone Ship.'

It carried her through a winding walk at the bottom of the valley. Its route twisted under the lightening sky. From a leafy ridge Tohalla watched Whitedawn slanting silver over the rippling sea and her heart soared with the beauty of it. From every tree songs rose: Tohalla supposed that the Green here sang like the Red, not knowing the sound came from birds the Drone Ship had seeded centuries before. Ain Tsui's decision had robbed her of this part of her heritage.

Other machines were abroad. One crawled along the beach below, combing rubbish from the soft white sand. Another culled grass that

236

grew rank between the scented rows of a flowering beanfield. Even when Redsun was a handspan above the horizon no people were out working. Tohalla realized people weren't necessary, and a frisson ran through her but the lush beauty of the sweeping bay thrilled her mind to forgetfulness. From beyond the horizon mist rose, rolling forward with the dawn wind in a shimmering, sun-pearled cloud.

Tohalla was glad she didn't meet anybody. She would have been embarrassed – an adult being carried like a child. But how her body ached! *I'm too old for all this running,* she thought wearily.

At last the machine set her down on a rocky promontory. 'My treads find the rocks uncomfortable,' the machine said incomprehensibly, but Tohalla understood at least that she would have to walk from here and said thankyou for the ride.

'It was no trouble. May I further serve?'

'No, thanks.' Tohalla looked around the heaping brown rocks. 'Erm, where's the Drone Ship?'

It pointed but Tohalla still couldn't see. She didn't like to ask it again. Stepping hesitantly over the red-brown stones, she began to climb. Only a few steps up the hill she came across what might have been a trail worn hollow by generations of footsteps.

The machine rumbled away. Uncertainly she waved to it but the killing machine didn't wave back.

Tohalla picked her way over the barren piles of boulders, still not sure what she was looking for. The point of the hill was still some distance above her but nothing stood out in any special way. The lonely beach was far below her with its fringe of trees; not much grew up here, though odd tufts of grass and tiny flowers clung in crevices. They cast long shadows in the early morning light. Bird droppings painted white streaks on the rusty tumble of rocks. But there was no trace of a Ship like the one that had taken the Axe.

Her footsteps clanged hollowly. *I'm standing on the Dream Ship! This hill is the Dream Ship!* And the realization burst in her body, a fountain of joyous hope.

Tohalla knelt, picking at the rust and sand that covered the metal. Not rust, but a form of corrosion, though Tohalla wouldn't have known the difference. After almost three hundred years it didn't matter anyway. The Dream Ship wasn't going anywhere.

Walking around the hill-top, Tohalla discovered why. A boulder the size of the House in the Green had fallen on one end of the Ship. Other, smaller rocks had fragmented part of it, probably in the crash, she realized.

Amazement that men could make anything that big numbed her

237

brain. Awe made her clumsy: her toes, clawing for a hold on the red rocks, would slip when she turned to stare at the sheer size of the Drone Ship. Ever and again as she clambered around the rock and metal slope, Tohalla stopped, wondering if the star-kin were – safe. She was no longer sure she wanted them to find Rosaria. The first Housefather had recorded in the Book how her people had fled an Erth riven by war.

But the Axe had gone to find the star-kin. And she had helped him.

At first she didn't realize that she was looking at the door. A crack in the metal might have been a fissure in the rock. 'It's too straight, though,' she whispered. Tohalla no longer knew whether she should open the door.

'It's made to a tolerrance of point oh-oh-oh-one, but it's not rreally strraight. The crrash warrped it.'

Tohalla's heart jumped. The voice was a women's, still talking, but there was no woman there. Unless, like the killing machine, the Dream Ship –

'Did – did you say something?' she quavered.

'Yes. I said nothing's what it appearrs. The doorr only seems strraight.' The unseen was chatty, confidential, the accent thick with some alien stress on the consonants, a lengthening or shortening of the vowels. But the words were very slow, as if the Drone Ship were tired.

'Are you the Dream – I mean, the Drone Ship?'

'Yes. What did you think I was, the Empire State Building?'

Even the Ship she had dreamed of for so long treated her with sarcasm. Tohalla swallowed. 'Can I come in?'

'Why not?'

The door slid aside, graunching sand and gravel along its runner. But its whole, huge vastness moved to let her in. When she stepped into the echoing, empty space, Tohalla felt as though she'd been eaten by some towering monster.

'Can I get out again?' she asked, and her words came back at her from hard and distant surfaces.

'Wheneverr you want.' The Ship was still quiet though its words came from all around Tohalla. 'What *do* you want? A new bathrroom? To get rrid of those frreckles of yourrs?'

Listening to the casual scorn, Tohalla didn't know any more. She felt very small.

The echoing silence lengthened. Slowly Tohalla walked across a deck, her footsteps raising dust that drifted red through the white space. It took her several minutes to reach a normal-sized door that groaned aside when she approached.

238

On the other side of it, still white, were shelves and shelves, all empty, rising from floor to ceiling of another room that dwarfed Tohalla. Sinuous cords were looped into place by clamps with dead-eyed lights. 'What was all this for?' she asked, drifting towards yet another door.

'Forr the ova – the eggs. Fifteen hundred human, a thousand cattle, two thousand mixed fowl, merrinos, saddlebacks, whites. Canarries, blackb'rrds – in therre was the seed,' the voice added as Tohalla walked through the next immense room.

'What was in that first big space?'

'That was forr the machines. You came in through my carrgo hatch.'

It went on and on. Half the things the Drone Ship told her, Tohalla didn't understand, any more than she understood merrinos or saddlebacks.

Sometimes she had to climb over twisted metal that the crash had tortured into cruel outcroppings. The spine of the Ship seemed to be broken. Easing herself over a rupture where the white walls were stained with smoke, Tohalla asked it, 'Is this why you weep?'

'Who says I weep?'

'The – the Crew.'

'There wasn't any crew. I was unpeopled.'

'I'm sorry,' said Tohalla, because the Drone Ship didn't sound very happy. But the Ship persisted, 'What Crrew?'

'I meant the Crew of the other Ship, the *Mosckva*.'

'They'rre dead, all of them. The Captain said so. I hearrd him say this planet killed them. Therre's nothing of Erth can live outside my defences. Not that they'rre mine any morre. They don't need me.'

Tohalla was overawed by the vastness of the Drone Ship's desolation. To comfort it she said, 'Some of them survived. Ain Tsui's child did. I was married to –'

'I wasn't. I was a human perrson – at least, the memorries of a human perrson they imprrinted on my circuits. I would have been with the Captain if I could but he told me to crrash. He told me to send worrd that this place kills as it killed him. He said they all died. That's why the sonic lances maintain a corrdon sanitairre. No-one goes out to death; and morre, nothing can get in.'

Tohalla didn't feel up to telling the Ship it was mutinas who killed the Captain because he was trying to kill them. Instead she asked, 'And did you send word?' but the Ship wasn't listening.

'He told me to crrash, and I did. My prrime duty was to obey the Captain, wasn't it? But my prrime duty was also to bearr all these young. So I cheated him. I crrashed and I sent the message, but I kept them all

239

alive. I've suffered from cognitive dissonance everr since then. Poorr Captain Tsui! I can rrremember weeping when my memorries had a body but I don't have the cirrcuits for it now. I'd weep if I could. I wish I could ...'

'Could you send another message?'

'What? No. He orrderred me to shut down communications. Besides, it's been almost thrree centurries.'

'I order you to open them up again.'

'You can't. You'rre not Captain. Captain's dead. Everrybody is dead frrom the Mistress Ship, and no-one but crrazies everr come to see me.'

Tohalla said, 'I'm not —' but she was suddenly aware of her tattered clothing, her barbarian ranks cut from dead animals, the wolf-scales in her scorched hair. She tried to swipe off the smears of cinder but the Drone Ship said to itself, 'I wish I could weep ...' and though Tohalla pleaded for hours it would not signal Erth.

Redsun was a scarlet globe on the crest of a hill when Tohalla came out again. Layers of cloud strung red nets across the sky. Tears blurred their edges in her eyes. A sharp evening breeze struck her aching head and flapped the remnants of her tunic. She shivered with more than the chill.

Nothing's any use. Whatever did I think I could do here? I should have accepted Housefather's will and stayed at home ...

Tohalla leant wearily on a boulder that still remembered the heat of the day. Utter lassitude pervaded her being. Her throat was dry and swollen from the long argument which she had lost and the Dream Ship might have won: it refused to signal Erth, or even to admit that it still might be able to. It had laughed when she raged at it, sneered when she pressed the ranks of pads in every conceivable, futile pattern.

And from the moment it said, 'The purrpose of the colony is to preparre for the incomerrs,' and she had answered to a deafening silence, 'But you sent the message! There won't be any incomers,' Tohalla knew she had lost. The Drone Ship had lost, and all the seeds it had borne.

Only Ain Tsui had won.

A dark finger of rain reached down from the clouds, striping the faded rose glory of the sunset, but not until the first raindrops burst upon the rusty rocks did Tohalla get up strength to find shelter.

Not for anything would she have gone back into the echoing loneliness of the Drone Ship. She would take her emptiness to one of the empty house-mounds they had built for the colonists who would never arrive.

240

As she walked the maze of tight-packed houses, Tohalla tilted her head to the slanting rain. Some found its way onto her tongue, but not much. The wind picked the rain up and flailed her with it until she felt wet to the bone. The warmth of her body retreated to its centre, where she could not find it. Her vitality was low. Hunger was an acid hollowing her out. One foot in front of another, Tohalla plodded heart-weary through the darkness and the mud.

So close to the Drone Ship, the lightless houses among the crowded mounds were fewer than where she had awakened. Laughter and arguments and a moan of love-making rang out in the darkness, leaving her alone.

Was it only this morning I had hope? But there's none now. I've found the Drone Ship and it did nothing. I brought the message to the people here and that accomplished nothing. There's no place for me here and I could weep a thousand years before Vernal would have room for me in her heart.

One foot in front of the other, and the mud squishing up clammy between her toes. *The Crew are slaughtering each other. There's nothing but blood in the Red. What was that the Drone Ship said about the sheer size of space? The airlessness? How stupid I was to think that vacuum was a simple monster! I let Ain go to his death alone.* Black slime splashed her from head to heels.

There's no point to my life. There's no point to anything.

Yet at last the habit of survival made her think to try saying to a blank mound, 'Open up.' And it did.

Then it bathed her with hot water, conjured fire from the air, and when she had eaten and drunk – *At least I can do that for myself* – she dragged a mattress and silver blankets in before the fire's scant company, and slept.

241

CHAPTER FIVE

The Vigilantes

It was the Red Woman's nails that awoke her, clawing aside the glass to get in at her. Fragments of crystal, the enemy's claws, screeked across the panes, shattered on the floor. The breath was torn from her body. In her brain, *inside it*, was a tingling so fierce that her pulse pounded. The Red Woman was suffocating her!

Tohalla screamed herself awake. The pain, the tingling breathlessness was real. Panting in fear, Tohalla clutched her chest to try to steady her galloping heartbeat. *I'm dying!*

When she turned to it in the darkness, the fire had gone out and a squat black thing was watching her. Only slowly did Tohalla resolve the unearthly tapping: hail had broken a window and was dancing on the splintered glass on the floor. The blackness was no monster; it was a machine. The Red Woman was a child of Green nightmares and this child of the Green was far in time and attitude from her home. *Vernal* ...

'Make a light come on,' Tohalla ordered. Cold and yellow, the ceiling started to glow.

'Light the fire.' A fire burned on logs that didn't, but at least the ruddy, shifting light was familiar, yet the worst of the nightmare was still within her. Though she tried to breathe slowly, her face was still hot and her head felt like it had pins and needles inside it. Tohalla was terrified.

'Make me feel better,' she croaked. The machine rolled towards her.

Twitching, Tohalla forced herself to allow the machine to touch her wrist, her jumping chest. A thin claw sprang out of one metal arm. Tohalla backed away on her knees, gasping. 'No!'

'Would you prefer a tablet?' said the machine, 'Or medicine?'

'Medicine. Are you sure it'll make me better?'

'Quite sure. Stress disorders are common in this colony. Drink this. And this. You will be fine by tomorrow. Perfectly well.'

Tohalla slugged back the medicine, letting its strange taste roll down her gullet, and sipped the hot herbal drink the machine gave her to follow.

And her burning skin grew cooler. The tingling left her head. When she laid the fingers of her left hand on her right wrist, there was no frightening haste in her blood and the heavy thudding of her chest faded.

After it had fixed the circular window, the machine suggested sleep. With the memory of the fear of death reverberating through her, Tohalla found it hard to let go. She wished Edrach was there. Or the Axe. Or even Pierse. *I wonder if Vernal sleeps sweet dreams?*

Then she woke, surprised it was morning and she was here to welcome it. Though life seemed grey, it was at least lighter and more familiar than the blackness she expected of death.

She chose a dress of green from the lavish collection of colour in a closet. The fabric was soft and clinging but the long skirt fell in whispering folds around her ankles, and though the material wasn't patterned, its colour changed from young wheat to deepest emerald depending on the light. It was the nicest dress she'd ever owned. *No. Not owned. This house wasn't waiting for me. I can't fit into its expectations.*

Still Tohalla spent some time twirling round in the stretchy, low-cut dress, delighting in its flow. After one look, though, she shunned the full-length mirror. It showed her skinny, her forehead lined and dark shadows circling her eyes whose colour was emphasized by the green of the dress. She hated seeing those eyes looking back at her, and there were grey streaks showing in her shoulder-length hair. Tohalla almost ran to a different room, and combed out the tangles by touch.

It was still raining. Not much light flickered through the vine-hung windows but the yellow glow was there at her command. For a while she turned it on and off but that got boring. Exploring the six-sided rooms was fun for a time, some empty, some filled like the main one with boxes in shades of cream and grey: other machines. She didn't know what they did and so she couldn't tell them to work. The one Tohalla thought of as 'The Machine' was helpful but Tohalla soon tired of feeling so ignorant. She was too exhausted to concentrate on its explanations for long.

The machine did everything for her so there was nothing to take her mind off her problems. She was lonely.

At noon she ate again for something to do, picking incuriously at the strange-smelling fruit but the machine told her it would wash up. Tohalla felt grey, pointless, depressed. It was a horrible feeling that seemed to stretch forward forever. She couldn't shake it off.

'All right,' she said at last. 'How do I meet some people?'

'Go to a public hall,' the boxy machine said, 'or the gymnasium, or the library. Can you read doors?'

'I don't think so.' Tohalla remembered the man whose head had seemed to shine behind the curved door.

'Then send me to find someone whose door is open.'

Tohalla said hastily, 'I don't feel like it. It's – it's raining.'

Apparently the machine thought that was a good enough excuse but it didn't stop Tohalla knowing she was a coward. Her experience in Soren's place, and with that brown-haired man Tamdaintre, made her feel too shy to meet someone else on their home ground.

She opened a window to watch the leaves drooping dismally under the weight of the rain. Sighing, she asked, 'What's a library?'

When it explained, Tohalla was staggered at the thought of half a million books. She summoned her courage to ask, 'How do I get there?'

'I will take you. And I will keep you dry.'

So now I'm doing what a machine tells me. Tohalla thought bitterly. *Well, why not? Everything I've decided for myself has turned out wrong. And I thought I could fly to freedom.*

Her legs curled under her on a platform on the machine, Tohalla sat with a portable roof spread over her. They rolled past house-mounds that blended in with the rain-dreary landscape. On the pink wall of one that didn't, someone had daubed. *No Infringement.* Many of the houses had a circle of blue and white and green enamel, or a copy of it grown in flowers. It obviously meant something, but not to her.

There was so much she couldn't understand that Tohalla didn't even bother to ask the machine. Her tiredness had come back; she was in two minds about retreating to the house again. Then she decided not to be so scared. *Pull yourself together!* she ordered, but she couldn't. Anyway, she would have been embarrassed asking the machine to take her back before she'd done what she set out to do.

Two or three times, on bare patches between the smothering greenery, they passed other *No Infringement* signs written in jagged, angry capitals, and on the library door below the disc of shining blue-white-green was gouged *Outlaw Mindsails*. Idle curiosity wasn't strong enough to make her ask what it was about. Tohalla was trapped inside the confines of her own being.

The library was a ziggurat, each floor smaller than the one below. From each of the balconies a garden trailed flowers or leaves, looking bedraggled in the downpour. Hardly anybody was inside the building. The few who were seemed too busy even to look up from their cylinders or the crackling paper books; Tohalla didn't dare interrupt them.

No matter how vast the floors of the library, there was no echo, because soft blue matting was underfoot and in the cabinets of cylinders. The circular pattern of blue-white-green swirls was repeated on each wall. Someday she'd get round to asking what it meant – if she ever met anyone she could talk to.

The first book she tried didn't work at all, just droned in a slurring bass, like Housefather's Book. Then, plucking another cylinder at random, one that spoke clearly this time, Tohalla thrilled, listening to a voice talking to her from ancient Erth. She touched and fondled the cylinder, remembering the time in the Red when Edrach and the Axe showed her the Book of the Crew. But the ear-plugs the machine told her to wear on the talking books *(How strange! Once I thought there was only one anywhere)* hurt her ears, and the sight-books looked like a snow-storm.

The machine let her take a written book, whose every page looked just the same. 'Look at that handwriting!' Tohalla exclaimed. 'As straight as a furrow.'

'That is because machines wrote it.'

'Oh.' Tohalla's depression returned.

In a glass-walled garden on the top floor, the machine told her she would find some company. Tohalla hoped someone would take pity on her but the sparse crowd between the trailing plants ignored her.

'What am I doing wrong?' she whispered to the machine.

'Because you are on your own, they think you want to be. They do not want to infringe. Go and ask those three there if they want a drink.'

Tohalla could not forget how her human conversations had gone here. Nervously she said, 'But what should I talk about?'

'Talk about mindsailing.'

'I don't know anything about it.'

'Then now is your chance to ask.'

Drifting hesitantly towards a table where two men and a jolly woman were talking, Tohalla stopped, half-hiding behind a rope of fronded creeper. Presently they looked up and the pale blond youth broke off in irritation as soon as he realized Tohalla might be listening.

It was too late now to back off. Tohalla muttered, 'I – um – Would you like a drink?'

'Got one, thanks,' said the woman. 'Why don't you sit down, though?' She was a little older than Tohalla, pale-skinned with dark red hair curving to a sudden stop below her ears. Tohalla thought she looked like a mushroom. But she smiled and looked friendly. So did one of the men, younger than the red-head but so like her he must be her son.

The other youth, the angry blond one, took a swallow of his drink and said, 'It's an outrage, I tell you. They have no right – '

'And they have no right to sail so close to other people's bubbles. What else can you expect?' the maroon-haired boy answered just as passionately. He turned to Tohalla for support. 'What d'you think?'

Tohalla said, 'I'm sorry. I'm at a loss. I don't know what you're talking about.' She introduced herself, feeling awkward.

The blond boy paled still further. Staring accusingly at the red-haired woman he said, 'I thought she was a friend of yours.'

The red-head smiled with some secret satisfaction. 'I've never seen her before in my life.' Grinning up at Tohalla, she patted the bench beside her and the wanderer sat down on the furry padding. 'Forgive our manners. I'm Valtisane. This is my son, Erin, and his friend, Anstrew. Pleased to meet you, Tohalla.' The boys, who sat facing them, murmured courtesies.

In a louder voice Valtisane ordered drinks, seeing as Tohalla hadn't. 'And what'll you have?'

Tohalla said shyly, 'The same as you.' A blue machine glided over with a pitcher and beakers in a recess in its top. Valtisane poured.

The beaker's made of glass! realized Tohalla, amazed at such extravagance. *Unless they can make glass here? Or,* she thought gloomily, *a machine can.* 'I'm sorry?'

Valtisane repeated, 'I was just wondering where you've sprung from. I thought everybody in the Two Hundred Thousand knew about it. Or aren't there any Vigilantes in your neck of the woods?'

Too wise now to admit she came from beyond the Straight Desert, Tohalla said cautiously, 'Not really. We've heard of them, of course, but we don't really know the details.' *So the Two Hundred Thousand is different places! That's why they didn't know where the Drone Ship was.*

'They're next best thing to murderers!' burst out Anstrew, the blond

246

boy. He was about seventeen, the age to be angry at things you can't put right. 'They – the Vigis, that is – they caught some friends of mine sailing. Now one of them's next best thing to a cabbage. He just lies there, screaming his head off. The Vigis have got no right – They must have been sailing themselves, or they'd never have caught Yuri. He was to fly –'

'Oh, come on! I've seen –' The boys resumed their argument, intense, turning to answer each other's point with a hostile reply. Tohalla could hardly make sense of what they said.

Valtisane leaned so close to her that her hair almost brushed Tohalla's forehead. Taking pity on Tohalla's obvious bewilderment, she talked quietly, her clear voice carrying under the angry tones of her son and his friend. 'It's this mindsailing, you see.' Valtisane went on hastily, 'Don't think we're mixed up in this, because we're not. But so long as there's no infringement, I don't see any harm in it, do you?'

'I'm – I'm not sure.' Tohalla rescued a glass that Erin nearly upset with his extravagant gestures and put it safely in the middle of the table.

Valtisane shared a mother's smile with Tohalla, then continued, 'Well, I can quite see that some children need excitement. It's hard on them, isn't it, when all we can do is wait? But to go round frightening the life out of folks who aren't expecting it – Well, can you wonder at it if an old wart-nose like Jerad takes it upon himself to form a committee?' Sounding as if she'd like to throttle the man, Valtisane added, 'He's the sort that'd form a committee to pick his nose. Your councillors the same, are they?'

Tohalla nodded dumbly.

'So this Jerad digs up some old mindsail that Tamdaintre made years ago and he and his old buddy-boys go up a few times to put the wind up the lads. Next thing you know, they're infringing *him*, giving him nightmares, making him remember things he hasn't done, popping up every time he goes to the toilet. Can you wonder at it?'

Tohalla said, 'You can't, can you?' and wondered if it was the same Tamdaintre. *It's not surprising he was so touchy if he's involved in all this tangle of yarn.*

Fiddling with her glass mug of red liquid to hide her awkwardness at this strange conversation, Tohalla didn't notice the muscular woman coming up behind her.

'All of you come with me,' the strange woman barked.

Tohalla jerked around on the bench. Half-hidden by a festoon of ivy the woman jabbed some unidentifiable weapon at them. Tohalla recognized the threat if not the object.

In anger or in fear the woman's voice rose half an octave, 'Get a move on, sailors. Jerad's impatient.'

Tohalla glanced at Vatisane and the boys. White-faced, they were obeying. Tohalla stood too, reaching suddenly for the black muzzle of the thing in the woman's muscular hand.

Someone unseen clubbed her down. In a haze Tohalla cursed herself, with the anger of Marchidas and Edrach weighing hard on her through the tumbling mist. Falling, she heard Valtisane shout 'No!' but light exploded in her eyes and everything went black.

Anger returned. No, it was voices, other people's anger, no concern of hers. Then hurt arrived in her head and Tohalla was herself again and wishing that she wasn't. Half-slumped in a corner where she'd been dropped, she allowed her breathing to remain stertorous though she eased her chin up a little so that air came in more easily to her lungs. It took all of her strength even to do that much; with the full force of her will, Tohalla could scarcely move her fingers let alone retaliate. The smell of too many bodies was thick in the dank, airless space. She almost gagged.

To get away I need a plan. And, in time, *if I understood what was going on, I could work out what to do.*

Slowly meaning came into the words she could hear. 'But I heard you say you were a friend of that slime who crashed his mind into me!' A male voice, high with rage. *Jerad?*

Peeping through her lashes, Tohalla saw a grey-walled, windowless room and at the focus of a table in its centre a wrinkled man was yelling. At his shoulder was the squat, muscular woman who'd threatened her with a weapon in the library. Other men and women shifted so that the room seemed crowded but this man was obviously in command. He was a little man who'd been big. Fear had wasted him so that the skin hung on his frame like an empty bladder. Long, thin hair trailed across his white and lumpen skull.

Valtisane said, 'But –'

'You speak when you're spoken to!' shouted Jerad. 'I'll have the truth if I have to beat it out of your whining son.' He eyed the maroon-haired boy malevolently. The broad woman shook Erin with a viciousness Tohalla felt.

'Not me, Persis!' babbled Erin desperately. 'Well of course I knew

248

him, everybody did, but I never went with him. Nor did –'

Jerad pointed a clawed hand. 'You then. Anstrew, isn't it? You were the one that was with him.'

'No. No. I wouldn't. Honestly, I –'

Anstrew, like Tohalla, like Valtisane and her son, was too hurt to stand. The brawny woman – Persis, was it? – jerked her chin at the scraggy man holding Anstrew. At her sign he kicked Anstrew's ribs. The boy gasped.

'Well how come you got a sail then?' Persis asked him.

Anstrew twitched to another kick. Mastering himself, he pushed the blond hair out of his eyes and said, 'Lots of people got sails. I've had it for years.' He twisted his bruised head to stare at Persis, at Jerad. 'You've got a sail, haven't you? And you, Jerad?'

Jerad shot a look of reptilian hatred at the boy. Just so had the wounded comet's eyes glared hatred at Tohalla. She shuddered.

Jerad hissed, 'I never needed one of the abominations until your filthy kind started infringing the privacy of people's minds. Now, yes, I have one. I loathe it. I despise it. But I'll keep on using it at whatever cost to myself until our skies are swept clear and people can be safe in their homes once more.'

'But no-one's *in* danger,' said Valtisane. She shook off the hand that tried to cover her bleeding lips. 'Not from these boys. From you, maybe. That poor lad Garys is in the hospital and you put him there. Not us. You.'

Outside a frantic knocking had begun. Jerad's cronies cast desperate glances at their leader. Of a sudden they seemed to notice the damage they had inflicted on their captives.

'We'd better get out, Jerad,' Persis said, combing her fingers through her short, spiky hair. Another, the scrawny man, let go his hold on Anstrew, who collapsed to the floor. The thug said, 'What d'you think they'll do to us?'

Jerad seemed as worried as the rest of them but he held himself together by will-power. Tohalla could feel the strength of him as a twisted presence. He spoke low, violently. 'Nothing! Not to me they won't, or to anyone who stands with me for the protection of the innocent. I'm Council.'

The hammering was louder now. Outside, wood splintered. Jerad said hastily, 'But they might not understand.'

He jerked his head at Persis, who pressed a slim shaft against the far wall. A slot opened, melted wider. Jerad's followers – Tohalla counted six of them – slipped through it into its pearly depths. Somewhere at the bottom of that iridescence, Tohalla could see the green of rain-wet leaves.

Part-way through the molten doorway, Jerad paused to look cruelly on his prisoners. Somewhere behind Tohalla, out of sight, planks juddered to a thunderous blow.

But Jerad didn't care. Distorted by the strange doorway, he said, 'You'll make a mistake. Sometime, up in the skies, you'll make a mistake. Your kind always does. And then I'll have you.'

His fist clenched, savagely crushing something imagined. Tohalla felt it was her. Even as the wall healed to its matte greyness, Jerad vanished.

At the same moment, around an angle behind Tohalla, something smashed. Shards of wood flew past her into the room and from a recessed door Tamdaintre stepped in with an axe.

'Valtisane! Are you fine?'

Tamdaintre's concern broke out as he saw Jerad vanish. Kneeling swiftly by the woman, he touched the bloody cut oozing down her forehead, reassuring himself that it wasn't deep. The thought flashed through Tohalla, *I wish I had someone to care that much about me.*

'I'll live.' Valtisane strove for a lighter note. 'But my hairdo's ruined. I don't think any of us is badly damaged – boys?' They nodded wanly. 'And unless I miss my guess, Tohalla here's not as unconscious as she makes out.'

Tamdaintre hadn't seen Tohalla in her shadowy corner. Now he noticed her, the dried brown blood beneath her ear and the ugly graze along her cheekbone. She grinned feebly at him. 'Nice place you've got here.' Nodding at the small axe he had forgotten in his hand, she added, 'Mind, my husband's battle-axe would make that one look like a toothpick. Still, you cause enough trouble without. Thanks for rescuing us.'

Tamdaintre helped Valtisane tenderly to her feet. 'You don't want to believe what she says, Val. She's one of Jerad's lot.'

'Oh garbage, Tam. She doesn't even know what mindsailing is. She went for Persis – that's why they clobbered her. She's no more one of them –'

Tamdaintre interrupted. 'How can anyone in the Two Hundred Thousand not know what mindsailing is? It's a pretence – an obvious slip.'

The boys were on their feet now, holding each other up. Tam led them towards the recessed door he'd come in by, wanting nothing more to do with Tohalla.

250

'She doesn't know, Tam, really,' Valtisane said, pulling free of him. 'I'm not leaving her here.'

'Well if she doesn't, she's psychotic, but have it your own way. We can always turn her over to the spital with the rest of the Ship-has-come brigade.' Tamdaintre bundled Valtisane through the door ahead of him.

Making herself walk upright with all the pride of the True Crew as her example, Tohalla followed him. Outside, drizzle haloed lights strung from trees in the garden opposite and the night chill struck her. With no defences left, Tohalla shivered. On the point of saying she would make her own way, she stopped. There was no sign of the machine and without it there was no means for her to find the house-mound she was using.

Valtisane put her hand on Tohalla's arm. 'Come round to ours, Tohalla. Unless anybody'll be worried about you?'

'No, Valtisane, there's nobody left to worry about me. And without that machine I couldn't even find my way back to the place I've been staying. Thanks for the invitation.'

Valtisane's house was the usual single-storey building, half underground with a sunken garden behind it. But there the similarity with the place Tohalla had spent the night before ceased.

Stepping through the door was like entering another world. Outside in the sleeping walkways of the Two Hundred Thousand, their voices had all been compressed to whispers. Once the door clicked shut behind them, the boys began to talk with animation. Valtisane sighed with relief. Tamdaintre threw himself wearily onto a curving padded couch that fronted two sides of the fireplace. And in the friendly atmosphere Tohalla felt like she had come home.

Valtisane got her machine to ignite a blazing fire, light dozens of candles in coloured glass bowls, and fetch hot punch. Tohalla didn't know what it was but it smelt wonderful, and when she swallowed it she could feel its rosy warmth spreading outwards from her stomach. She settled back with a thankful sigh.

Then she sat up suddenly, guiltily. 'I'm sorry, Valtisane, I should have said before. Would you like me to fix your head?'

Valtisane's brown eyes regarded her curiously. 'How would you do that?'

Tohalla shrugged. 'Well, with a tisane of marigold to wash the wound.' She slid to her knees to examine Valtisane who was sitting around the angle of the couch. Tohalla reached up an arm to snag a candle from a niche above the fire. (*Just like in the House!*) and peered at the cut on Valtisane's hairline. 'Don't think it needs stitches, but all the same I think you should drink some comfrey, just to be on the safe side. Unless you've got any cobal crystals? Edrach used to swear by them.'

Valtisane ignored Tamdaintre's winking at her. Smiling at Tohalla, she said, 'No thanks. I'll stick to the usual, if you don't mind.' But instead of getting up and going into the kitchen Valtisane just beckoned the machine – hers was painted a cheerful scarlet with yellow trim – and told it to take care of them. And though Tohalla winced in anticipation the machine was delicate and thorough, even with her half-healed cinder-burns.

They don't need me here, thought Tohalla. *They don't need anybody at all. They've probably got machines for making love. They certainly have for everything else.*

For the sake of good manners she tried to throw off her feeling of bleak superfluity but much of the conversation was above her head. Yet when Tohalla suggested it was time to leave, Valtisane said, 'Oh, don't go! Stay the night so we can get to know one another better in the morning.'

Valtisane brought Tohalla a hot drink when Redsun was high in the sky, racing past ponderous Whitesun. Looking at her exhausted state, Tohalla wondered briefly if she had slept with Tamdaintre.

Tohalla had not long woken up in the room she'd been given last night and was wondering whether she should get up or if that would be an intrusion. She accepted the mug gratefully though her broken nails clicked on its unaccustomed hardness.

Valtisane groaned dramatically and sat on the edge of the bed. 'Oh, my head! I feel like I've got a hangover only I didn't have the fun of getting drunk.'

Tohalla smiled because Valtisane seemed to expect it but she didn't know what 'drunk' or 'hangover' meant. *Perhaps it's like having too much dreamsmoke?*

Tohalla sipped from the mug. The drink was pale brown, both bitter and sweet. She wasn't sure she liked it.

'Tam says you claim you're not from the Two Hundred Thousand.' Valtisane smiled. 'There's quite a lot of folks say that. Or that the Ship's landed and hang out the flags. You don't seem gaga though.'

Gaga? Not sure how much to say, Tohalla took another mouthful.

Valtisane went on cheerfully, 'Where d'you live now?'

'Nowhere really.' Tohalla sighed, looking at Valtisane over the rim

252

of the mug. Her eyes were dark-ringed still with accumulated fatigue
and Valtisane was motherly. Tohalla wished she could confess the truth,
but *gaga* didn't seem a good thing to be. 'I sheltered for the night in a
disused mound but I didn't like it much.'

'A mound?'

'You know, one of these glorified dug-outs. If I'm going to stay here
I'd rather have a real house but I don't think I could build one on my
own.'

Valtisane looked at her curiously. 'What d'you mean, a real house?'

Tohalla thought about that. 'Well, a house that looks like a house.'
Her enthusiasm lit her eyes, bringing out a sparkle in their emerald
depths and lending a touch of colour to her pale cheeks. 'One with a
roof-store, and the bedroom upstairs, and a kitchen that you can sit in
that's warm against the winter snows, and a hall that's cool and shady in
summer. And with a garden where you can pick your own dinner as easy
as finding the Red.'

'I don't know what snow is but we don't have it here. Anyway, what
d'you want to store?'

It was Tohalla's turn to look surprised. 'Food, of course. No.' the
animation died from her face and she looked more tired than ever. 'I
expect the machines store the food like they do every other Red-cursed
thing around here.' She put the mug down with a bang on the
night-table. 'Though I suppose I'm the last person who should say
"Red-cursed".'

'Why?'

'Because there are some good people out there. I'm not saying a lot of
them don't want to kill you as soon as look at you, but they're loyal and
kind. And they *do* things.'

'Mmm.' Valtisane watched her. 'Are you sure you don't want to go to
the hospital?'

'What is it?'

'It's a place where they look after people who're sick.'

'Or gaga, don't tell me.' Tohalla's eyes flashed with anger. 'Well I'm
not sick. There's nothing wrong with me that a little peace and quiet
won't cure.'

'All right, fine, you don't have to shout.'

'Sorry, Valtisane. I'd best be on my way.'

'No, I'm sorry, I shouldn't have infringed. You can be who you like.
Why don't you get a machine to build you your "house that looks like a
house"? But stay and have some breakfast first.'

'Let me come with you, Tohalla,' Valtisane had pleaded. 'It'll be interesting to see what your house turns out like. I'll lend you my machine.'

So now the two of them had walked out a long way from the coast, talking as they went. Valtisane was good fun, and a good listener too, and Tohalla was envious of her affectionate mockery when she talked of her son.

They reached a place where the last house-mounds blended into the rolling hills. Whitesun's fierce light was scarfed by mist though Redsun was bringing a blush to the fields of standing corn. On green slopes opposite birds were skimming above terraced vineyards. Nearer, on this more gentle knoll, orange-groves cast a net of delicious scent that snared Tohalla; when she found the tiny brook singing clear in its pebbled bed, she knew she had found the place where she wanted to live. *If I want to live.*

Firmly suppressing the thought, Tohalla said, 'Well, what d'you think?'

'I think it's fine. I wouldn't want to live so far from the centre of things, but if that's what you fancy, who'm I to say different? Only won't your house be visible from where the neighbours live?'

'Let it! I'm not going to bother them. Anyway, won't they like to see it?'

Valtisane puffed out a breath, considering. 'Well, I don't know. That's why we build so low, so our houses don't infringe anyone else. We want them to kind of merge in with the scenery.'

'Oh.' Tohalla put her head on one side and thought for a while. 'Still, if I plant on orchard in front of it, will that be all right? I mean, I'm not going to go round sticking myself in anyone's face or anything. I've had more than enough of people for a while.'

Valtisane said, 'Oh, I should think that'll be fine,' but to Tohalla she didn't sound convinced.

'I just thought it would be sort of friendly,' mused Tohalla, more to herself than to Valtisane, 'seeing other people's house-lights. I always thought that was so nice when I was up at the striding-post with Adi and Trin and Sibulkrin, looking down into the combe and seeing the lights of the House in the twilight and knowing that Housefather and Housemother were too far away to get at me.'

'Fine, then. Just tell the machine what you want.'

'Are you sure you can spare it, Val?'

The woman with the dyed red hair looked at Tohalla strangely. 'Of course I can! I'll just whistle up another one when I need it. But come on, will you? I'm dying to see what you think a house looks like.'

254

CHAPTER SIX

First Touch of Infinity

It was beautiful, at least that's what Tohalla thought the day her house was finished. When the machine and some of its companions had finished the walls, they were a pale peach because the machines had done something to the local stone when they ate it up and spat it out in a thick stream that soon became solid. They'd used some dark wood for the windows and doors that were proper rectangles, like in the Green. The chimney poked up through the roof of the storage-dome so she'd be able to smoke meat like the Crew did, and there was space enough for a winter's fruit. There was a porch at the back for tools and a thick winter coat, though Valtisane said she wouldn't need one. And Valtisane had brought some knick-knacks 'to give it a homey air', she said.

'I like your little orchard, too,' Valtisane added. 'Aren't you going to have any plants just for flowers, though? Otherwise it seems kind of mean.'

'Well, maybe.' The thought seemed revolutionary to Tohalla and she wasn't sure she liked it.

'Anyway, when's the party?'

'What party? What *is* a party?'

Valtisane explained. 'Whenever we get fed up of one house and go to another we have a party. Do, won't you? Or how else are you going to get to know the neighbours? And if you still want to know about mindsailing, make sure you invite Tamdaintre.'

'Is he – He's not your husband, is he?'

'Grief, no! He's far too intense and purposeful for me! Always has to be doing things, making things – why doesn't he just get a machine to do it, like everybody else? Anyway, you invite him. Do him good to see something different for a change.'

Without joyberry juice, or dreamwood, or even the flute, drum and zither for the dance-music, Tohalla was privately sure the celebrations would be useless, but she had promised Valtisane. *I wonder when Longday is? I should have been counting. At least Vernal's Ripeness isn't for years ...*

But the party was a great success. Valtisane helped with everything, or at least got her machine to see to it, but one thing she was good at was creating a happy atmosphere. It made her feel she was doing something useful. 'Anyway,' Val said, 'I like parties.'

Even Tohalla enjoyed the housewarming once her nervousness had gone, and revelled in all the gifts her new neighbours and Valtisane's friends brought her. But she found it strange dancing to machine music whose rhythm was inaccessible, until she remembered the wild melody of the Dancing Forest. Then it was a release.

Afterwards, when only a few people were left in a circle by the firelight, Valtisane disappeared. 'Weird, needing stairs inside a house! What do old people do?' she called from upstairs. When she came back into what Tohalla called the househall, she was carrying something over her arm.

Valtisane shook it out. It was a cloth, swirled with shades of red. Tiny beads in it caught and held the light of Gold Moon shining in through the open, night-scented window.

'What is it?' Tohalla asked, wondering if she already knew.

She did.

'It's a mindsail,' Valtisane announced.

'Well go on, take it,' said Valtisane, holding out the octagonal cloth on its cedarwood hanger. Her waxen skin flushed with pride. 'It's one of the best Tam's ever made.'

'Shut up, Mum,' said Erin from where he was lounging with his back to the corner of the hearth.

'Why? There's only us here. Who's going to button this down to Jerad?'

Tohalla looked around. Besides herself and Valtisane, there were only Tamdaintre and Erin.

'Please, Tam?' begged Valtisane, mock-winsome.

Tohalla watched Tamdaintre's thoughts play over his face. Candle-light shone on the tanned skin over his high cheekbones. He half-closed his eyes as he pondered, making them seem darker and more mysterious. Then, gazing up at Tohalla in her rocking-chair that all of them had played on that night, Tamdaintre weighed her in some private scale of his own.

256

Anxiety, and a measure of irritation, writhed in Tohalla's stomach. She hadn't seen him since that night he'd cut them free from the Vigilantes' secret house with his axe. This evening he'd been mildly courteous but beyond a few words of welcome to her new home, and a hand-thrown earthenware pot, he'd shown her no more interest. He'd danced, oddly graceful, with a handful of women and joined in some sort of circle dance that Tohalla couldn't follow.

And he'd laughed. A lot. Sharing jokes with other people. Once he'd laughed into a sudden silence left by a pause in the music and Tohalla's eyes had been drawn to him. As if he felt the weight of her gaze Tamdaintre had returned the look and Tohalla flushed, turning back in embarrassment to her partner who seemed annoyed.

Now, though, in the circle of four by the fire, Tamdaintre gave her his full attention. She stared back at him, thinking him rude, but knowing that he wasn't. She'd felt the force of Jerad's Vigilantes and knew he was evaluating the danger.

'All right,' he said at last. 'I have to admit I'm curious. But you two keep watch.'

Reluctantly Valtisane and her son moved from the enchantment of the firelit hearth. From his post by the door to the orchard Erin kept looking back.

'I mean it,' Tamdaintre said, and it was clear from his tone that he did. Chastened, Erin looked out into the moon-dappled night.

'Hang the sail up there, Tohalla. – No, it's all right, I'll do it.'

As though I can't do anything right. Tohalla's earlier overlay of good humour dissipated and she was floundering in the grey miasma of self-doubt once more. She almost snapped, 'Don't do me any favours,' but she knew how Valtisane had schemed for this. The least she could do was not disappoint her friend.

Dragging the table across to a place near the window, Tamdaintre unhooked one of the hanging baskets that Valtisane had filled with coloured ivies. Tohalla took it meekly. From her place by the back window Valtisane was careful to keep her eyes on the moon-threaded vineyards opposite.

When the sail was hung, he pulled it slightly this way, leant back, and fiddled it a little further across. Tohalla couldn't see what he was hoping to achieve with all his adjustments but gave in, as she had done for so long, to others' expectations. She began to get bored. Swallowing a yawn, she feigned interest but wished she were upstairs in her own hay-filled box-bed. *I'll set up a loom this winter and make myself some sheets ... I suppose tideswool is too much to hope for.*

At last Tamdaintre stepped down. Vaguely acknowledging to herself that she found him moderately handsome, Tohalla sat beside him on the couch when he told her to. The fact that he was attractive made her somewhat uncomfortable when he was so close.

'Look at it,' Tamdaintre said. 'That's right, just look at it. That's all you have to do. And hold my hand.'

Tohalla swallowed. His hand was warm upon hers, and his skin was cracked and dry from hard work, not like the soft, moist fingers of the man she'd been dancing with. But Tamdaintre's clasp was undemanding. From the corner of her eye she saw how Gold Moon wove gilding into the fine ends of his hair. Beside her, he too looked at the sail.

'See its eight corners?' he said. 'Look at how the pattern swirls in from them, all the different reds. See the pattern of the gold beads, like moonbeams on a spider's web? Look closer. See how the strands of reliesin weave in and out of the swirls? Concentrate. Concentrate …'

Tohalla moved restlessly and he tightened his fingers for a second. She could feel the power in his hands. *What's he doing? What am I supposed to feel? I don't feel anything. Oh!*

For the mindsail had rippled.

It's just the wind.

But it wasn't. 'That's right. See how the sail moves? See if you can move it. Fill it with your mind.' His voice was like a warm caress. Tohalla had a sudden urge to do what he wanted of her.

Staring at the red-gold sail, Tohalla tried to imagine it full. Billowing like her mattress cover on the line when she and the Axe – The house had been like a peak overlooking the meadow, the suns' bright sea – it had filled with wind as the sail was filling.

The mindsail curved, hollowed. It was beautiful. 'It can take us anywhere,' whispered Tamdaintre. 'Think of where you'd like to be. Anywhere.'

She was falling into the gold-spiced depths, the red a warmth around her.

How good it feels! she thought on a level below consciousness. It was a softness that gathered her in, comforted her. Tohalla sank into its rosy embrace, amber sparks like stars reaching down to her.

Of a sudden direction changed: she was falling *upwards*. Far below, breath faltered but Tamdaintre was there, holding her mind in the sureness of his. Wordless he told her *Don't be afraid. I have you safe. Let me show you* –

They swooped to ethereal night, bodiless, weightless, pure thought.

Hovering in the midnight-blue infinity above the crinkling sea, they smelt the pastel crash of breakers upon the sweep of sands. Around the bay on the charcoal curving land sparks flickered, lamp-lit houses. And sailing above them, serene, Gold Moon spilled its light through the radiant essence of Tohalla and Tamdaintre.

You see? said Tamdaintre. There was a smile within his thoughts.

Gold Moon's leaning crescent beckoned from above the hills. Tohalla pulled towards it. Tamdaintre hesitated just long enough to be sure she was safe leading, then they vaulted to her will over the waves of smiling earth. Outwards she drew him, past flickering violet lights that she could not comprehend, skimming tall stands of trees that were dark on the fair rippling fields. Away from all he knew.

Further and further inland where houses were lonely, until at last Tamdaintre paused their headlong flight. Looking back with his whole being, she too saw that the moonpath on the sea was only a far, faint golden thread. She could feel his wish to return.

For before them was the dead black waste of the Straight Desert. Yet the sum of Tohalla's essence lured her onward with hope and Tamdaintre could taste that hope even above the ugly tang of soot on his mind's tongue. For the time he let her sway him.

More and more as their thoughts fled over the charred earth Tamdaintre's reluctance dragged her down. But inside her was her own strength and Marchidas's and Edrach's. She knew the Unshadowed Plain stretched its purple crystals to the moonbeams and suddenly, there, ahead on the horizon was a fugitive glitter that swept Tamdaintre's doubts to tattered cobwebs with its wonder. And the wonder bore them upwards into the Red.

Over the amethyst ranges with their subtle, rich alien scents, Tohalla darted aside. The tiny dots of highdogs grew into a belling pack and the squat bulk of a comet keened its baby-scream and threatened them with its arm. From this height, with its bush of tail-spines lashing behind, it looked like the comets that roamed between the stars. But Tohalla snapped the skein of its screams and veered eastwards to parallel the coast. Beyond Red-crested dunes tidenets span their glassy strands for the wind to harp and the song of it pierced Tohalla's heart.

She turned aside, her thoughts blood-tinged with the distillation of a sob for the Axe and for her lost home. But Tamdaintre was there bound in the spell of marvels. With his support Tohalla used his eagerness to sail onwards into yondering.

For it came to her: *I could go home! Back to the Green that bore me. Vernal's waiting in the kiss of sleep.*

259

Now a new determination urged her. Tamdaintre ran before the wind of Tohalla's longing. In him surged the exaltation of this voyage and all its enchantments. Circling the flicker of a campfire of the Crew, Tamdaintre gasped at the savage grace of a warrior woman standing wolf-guard in her iridescent mauve-green cloak and the sharp-tusked mask of her Wolf-hide on her head.

Past the chequered fields of planting in the winterground – Tohalla smiled her triumph that her message had helped somewhere. Past gleaming snakes of water in the delta of the Big River with the soft sour smell of marshland. Tohalla beat upstream in aerial motion to investigate a smudged red glow; it came from a pit in wounded hills – *Benhannon's people, the Iron Men who like to inflict pain …*

Both of them were glad when Tohalla led Tamdaintre flashing to safe beauty among the Dancing Forest. He saw it both dry with lumpen stolid cones and in Tohalla's vision with the wild dance of lightning: rain-lashed, the glowing hearts of the trees rejoiced in a savage mazurka while the sapphire branches chorded music from the gale. Tamdaintre would have lingered there, washing his soul in the harmony and light, but Tohalla pitched him onward until the cold topaz glitter of the Edge brought her plunging to a stop.

Riding her mental turmoil, yawing with indecision, Tohalla could not make herself take the last tidal leap over the fear-spiked Edge.

I was nothing there! All they wanted was a brood-spineder and I wasn't one. I failed them.

There's the old striding-post. How softly shines the lattice with firelight and good cheer. I wonder if Adi's still alive? Or if Trinamine is? And did they give Vernal –

I didn't belong. I wasn't what they wanted so they gave me to a man they feared so much they kept him in chains. And when I did what he wanted like a goodwife should they wouldn't let me back, not really. What poor Vernal suffered because of me –

But how easy it would be! Just to sail along the tumbling stream, down to the House. See the inwatchers as silhouettes, glide past them, up to the Girls' Room where I was so happy when I was loved. Before my poor little babies – But Vernal! The one thing I made right! To see her in sleep. –No! I can't! I ache for –

What if she's over there instead, across the hill in New House? Where would she be? Would she want me to glide into her dreams? Would she smile? Or would it be like the last time? I love her so much – but I'm not what she wants! She hates me. She hates me!

Palpitating with her doubt, Tohalla's mind pitched like a dying geyrlizard and Tamdaintre was too close inside her to help.

Trin couldn't have given Vernal my heart in a messenger. No. She's not old enough. No – it's not that. Vernal doesn't love me enough to risk the taint of the Red. I'm not fit –

I CAN'T DO IT! TAKE ME BACK, TAMDAINTRE, TAKE ME BACK!

Tohalla's anguish scorched whatever it was, the mental power that bore them along in the aura of the sail. She saw everything dim, darken. Almost nothing left but black. No sense of self to hang before the wind of passage. Fluttering, wounded, she dragged them down in a plummeting spiral.

Tamdaintre's mind tossed rudderless with the shock of it. Yet in his heart there was a fire of inner certainty. He knew who he was and his purpose. He spread a canopy of himself for them both and, limping, reeled their self-cores home to his roots in the Two Hundred Thousand.

They fell, tumbling into their bodies. Like a fall in a nightmare it twitched them awake. Gravity leapt and their flesh was pinned to earth.

CHAPTER SEVEN

A Self to Hold

'I can't! I can't!'

Tamdaintre's arms were around her, their smooth flat muscles holding her tight to still her shudders. It had been so long since anyone held her like that. The Axe rose in Tohalla's memory and a fresh burst of grief renewed her sobs. Around her voices babbled, 'What? What's wrong with her? Where did you take her?'

Tohalla felt Tamdaintre's chin move against her hair and knew he was looking at Valtisane and Erin with some message in his eyes that made their pestering cease. She was grateful to him.

In time the warmth of his body got through to Tohalla. When she grew calm enough to stop hiding her head and to start feeling embarrassed, she saw that someone had folded away the mindsail and re-hung the pot of ivy.

Tamdaintre – she tried not to think that he had seen her failures from *inside* – leant forward and lifted up a mug of something hot whose steam got through the thickness in her nose. With the messenger plant at least it was only other people's memories that they pushed into your head.

But this! This was a live being, free to poke around in the crevices of your head, weighing and judging your thoughts in the alienness of their scales, examining your failures as though you were some sort of –

I'm no good! Not as a mother, not even as a wife. Not a Green. Not a proper woman. I'm old and ugly and unlovable –

Tamdaintre touched the skin of her cheek and she sniffed and mopped her face then drank that same bitter-sweet liquid Valtisane had offered her before.

'Gratude,' she said. 'I mean, thank you.'

Valtisane gave an odd little laugh. 'I should think so too! I had a fine old time of it rattling around in that peculiar kitchen of yours with never a machine about to make it for me.'

'Sorry.'

'Oh, don't apologise. I like new experiences.'

Erin put some more wood on the fire, keeping his gaze so pointedly averted that Tohalla knew the body was trying not to stare at her.

What did he see in my face? Was it as naked as when I saw Ain at the messenger?

Tamdaintre took a swallow of his drink, one arm still resting lightly on Tohalla's shoulders. 'She was right, you know. We're not alone on this planet. There's a great sweep of glitter out there, plants like crystals of red and purple and blue with people living off the land.'

Valtisane said, 'There can't be! – Sorry. Go on, Tam.'

Tamdaintre's lips quirked in a lop-sided smile. 'There's even a couple or three tiny settlements where they're trying to grow green crops like the machines do here. And we're cut off from it by a great black belt of cinder.'

Tohalla hiccuped on a sob. 'You saw it all, didn't you?'

He answered her urgency with a tightening of his arm that felt very good. 'Yes, I saw it all. I saw what you saw.'

And what he saw was my failure …

Erin was saying, 'That's impossible! Everyone knows life's impossible out there. The Ship –' His mother kicked his ankle and he stopped.

Tohalla felt Tamdaintre looking into her eyes and she couldn't bear the weight of his gaze. *Why did I think I could fly like the arrowfalls? How stupid to believe I could just walk south and find the Drone-Ship and it would all suddenly be all right, even Vernal? To think I could just walk back into the Green and they'd be glad of me … Why didn't I just die?*

She stared at her fingers tracing the circle of her mug's rim. She didn't see the tiny crease of puzzlement which came and went on his face. He was trying to work out whether she wanted him to have understood what occurred at the House in the combe. Or not.

'Did you –' she began huskily. 'Do you know what happened at the Edge?'

Tamdaintre took his time working out an answer. 'They rejected you,' he said carefully, quietly, his words a whisper in her hair. 'Because you were different. And they alienated your daughter from you. I didn't understand it all, but I understood that much. If you'd like to, sometime when you feel you can talk about it, you can tell me. If you want.'

Tohalla made no sign that she'd heard him, just kept staring down at

263

her fingers. She couldn't imagine that there'd ever be a 'sometime'. There didn't seem to be any reason for her to keep on living. She didn't seem to belong in life.

I. If I want. It's because of me that everything's gone wrong in my life. Why couldn't I want what they told me I did? Poor Vernal.

'Well,' said Valtisane, standing up when the silence had become too uncomfortable to bear. 'I – um, I think I'd better get this young man home to bed.' She drifted around, picking things up and putting them down again, a mug, a candle-stick. 'That is, unless you'd rather we stayed? We'd be quite happy to, wouldn't we, Erin?'

'What? Oh, yes,' her son said sleepily.

Tohalla worked up a smile that seemed cut out of someone else's face and dropped at random on hers. 'It's all right, Val. Thanks all the same. And thank you both for coming. I'm sorry …'

'Oh, we've enjoyed outselves.' Valtisane even managed to say it as though she weren't embarrassed too.

Erin followed his mother across the bare, echoing boards. 'It was a great party.' His voice was flat. 'Thanks.'

It was quiet after their voices had drifted away through the orchard and over the wall that was a wall. Finally Tohalla said, 'You don't have to stay, you know.'

Tamdaintre traced a delicate spiral on the bare skin of her shoulder. 'I think it'd be better if you weren't left on your own tonight.'

Tohalla made a tiny movement of her head that might have been a nod. She was wondering if he had felt the grey desolation that had torn a ragged hole across her being. But she said nothing, not wanting to admit she was afraid to be alone with her thoughts.

And the sky pearled to the azure of morning. Little by little, not knowing when, they slept.

In the daylight existence stretched out, dreary and infinite, before her. *Unless –?*

There were jobs to be done. Even though she didn't feel like it, Tohalla forced herself to make a herb tea for herself and Tamdaintre. For a long time she couldn't even bring herself to do that. He didn't say anything, just smiled if their looks happened to cross, and finally Tohalla roused herself sufficiently from the bleak futility of it to go out into the kitchen, put wood in the stove and boil the kettle.

Long after they had finished their tea, Tohalla sat slumped with her elbows on the kitchen table, and Tamdaintre stayed opposite her. At last he said, 'I'll get last night's drinking bowls if you'll wash 'em up.'

It was too much trouble to argue with him though she wished he would go away and leave her in peace. Sulkily Tohalla washed the crockery, wishing it was proper wood like they used back in the Green. But it wasn't; a pot broke when she dropped it. Tamdaintre stood watching her, leaning hipshot in the doorway. That annoyed her too.

It was Whitenoon before they'd cleared all the debris from the party. *Everything takes so long. And what's the point?*

In her turn Tohalla leant back against the stone sink eyeing her tormentor balefully.

'I've got some leek seedlings that are ready for transplanting,' he said. 'Come and get 'em.'

She shook her head. 'No, thanks.'

Tamdaintre answered, 'Well, I haven't got room for 'em all. You'd better come and get 'em. You wouldn't want 'em to die on account of you, would you?'

Tohalla clicked her tongue in disgust and sighed. 'All right. You win. Just this once, mind you.'

Dragging her feet through the dust, she followed him. At first he waited until she caught up but every time she fell behind again. People looked at them strangely as they walked one in front of the other but finally Tamdaintre linked arms and moved her along at a faster pace. Tohalla found it annoying but at the same time his touch was a comfort on the inside of her arm.

It took a long time to get there but at last there was the low white wall around his garden and the house that was cut into the heights of the brown cliff. Across the wide curve of the path in front of it lay the sea, sparkling blue beneath the paler mirror of the sky. It was a long way down to the rocks. Tohalla's head was aching with tiredness.

'Come in and have a drink, Tohalla.'

'No, thanks. I'll just have those plants and be on my way.'

'Well I'm having a drink first. I'm thirsty even if you're not.'

Tohalla turned to face him, a bitter light in her green eyes. She was so pale that her freckles stood out dark across her cheeks. 'You don't fool me, Tamdaintre. I know what you're trying to do. You're watching me to make sure I don't do anything stupid, like jump off the edge of that cliff !'

'Yes, that's what I'm doing. You're too valuable to do something like that. Besides, it slopes out here. You'd probably just break your legs and then some machine would come and haul you off to the spital. But they're your legs. It's the only law in the Two Hundred Thousand: don't infringe anybody else's life. So go ahead. Be my guest.' His face carefully neutral, he swept a wide gesture at the broken edge of the pathway. *Even with him watching, I'd like to jump and be done with it!* But he went on, 'Anyway, I'm having a nice cool glass of pineapple juice. Want some?'

Something nice and cool ... It sounded good. To end broken on the savage rocks – the pain, the fear that maybe she wouldn't die after all –

Her green gaze buried in the earth at her feet, Tohalla nodded. And with the knowledge of her cowardice stalking her, she turned away from death.

Life went on, somehow. Everyday tasks seemed monstrous, impossible. Tohalla put off the simplest things for days, unable to face them. Grease darkened her unwashed floors and the dishes in her sink were rank and smelly. She would look at the mess and know she should do something about it but somehow the long days fled and there was no time. Tohalla would look around and evening was upon her.

Outside, in the hard heat of the southern Summer, the garden grew overgrown. Tohalla planted and watered and weeded sometimes but her heart wasn't in it. *I should have stayed in the Green. Or died in the Red when Vernal was born. Better to have gone with Ain to meet death in the awful void between worlds than know such pain.* But she carried on hoeing, somehow sure that if her garden died there would be nothing left of her at all.

In the first days when she felt able to work among the growing ears of corn she felt a faint shadow of pleasure, knowing that she was giving life to seeds that would otherwise lie fallow. Then she realized in disillusion that the machines would have nurtured them if she had not. Even colours seemed dim in the barren perspective that engulfed her, but at least she could count the new shoots in her garden and see that they were growing bigger every day. Spring, and Summer, and the habit of Autumn harvest.

Tohalla thought sometimes of Edrach though his memories stored inside her seemed very distant. *How could he live, knowing his was sterile? How could he go on, club-foot and gotch eye, even after Marchidas died? He was so cheerful, my Chosen Brother and hers. I wish I was as brave as him!* And gradually the certainty came to her that it takes courage to live as well.

Lucah, her neighbour, came to lean on her wall, watching her curiously in the afternoons. One day he spoke, laughing at her determination to do without machines. 'A waste of effort, girl! How can you even think you can take care of your carrots and maize as well as a machine can?' And he laughed his old, dry cackle, while his plump wife Jade elbowed him in the ribs.

But despite his jibes and Jade's endless, useless advice, on the days when they didn't come Tohalla began to miss them.

Valtisane came often to see her, and Erin and Anstrew and their friends. Tohalla couldn't think why. She had nothing to say. Some of the youngsters never looked the same two days running; their hair would change from long blue to short silver or they'd laugh weirdly, compelled now to some oddness by drugs or a strange, sacrificial asceticism. Tohalla thought *Some of them are as lost as I am.* She came to understand why the greeting was so often, 'Who are you today?'

Sometimes the boys or their girlfriends would beg, 'Take us to the world beyond the Straight Desert.'

Tohalla always said, 'No. Not today. I don't feel like it.' But it was just an excuse. She wouldn't mindsail whatever they said or did. She wouldn't expose her painful inadequacy to anyone else.

Sometimes, though, when elongated shadows brought coolness to the pink and gold of evening, she gave in to their badgering questions. Sitting under wide eaves of her house that *was* a house, sipping some new potion that Valtisane had brought for her to try, Tohalla told them, and Tamdaintre when he dropped in, 'There are wolves that hunt by the power of their minds because they're deaf.'

'How?' Tamdaintre asked, and Tohalla didn't realize that she had brought curiosity to the Two Hundred Thousand. In a world where everything is done for you, curiosity had never been needed.

'If the prey is nearby, they feel its thoughts.'

'And if it isn't?'

'Then they find a messenger – that's a fan of rose crystal that stores the memories of anything that passes. And they know if the prey was hungry, or thirsty, or ready to fight.' Without knowing it, Tohalla sighed for the heart of the messenger that was her. *If only I still had it, perhaps it could teach me to be me again. I wonder if Vernal's learnt to spin –*

'What about those comet-things we saw, with their rattling tails of spines?' Tamdaintre asked in the silence that stretched empty as evening.

So Tohalla went on with her stories, still doing what other people wanted, not reliving her life because it was as if all that had happened to someone else long ago, but talking of the other beings that used the red messengers, and of the hatred between the Red and the Green, and the Iron Men in their stinking, fiery pit and the Wild Men who

267

were the outcasts of all.

And they said, the people who came to visit her, or invited her to meet their cousins or sons, that the only ones who had ever talked to the Drone Ship – because it was no longer a Ship she could dream of – the only ones in the Two Hundred Thousand who ever sought the Drone Ship out were gaga.

Not one of them had. (Tohalla dared not call them friends. She didn't deserve friends.) Not one of them had ever been curious about Rosaria beyond the burnt black land that the killing machines made. They half-doubted that the machines made it anyway. They didn't really believe any of Rosaria would support life. Not even Tamdaintre – before he sailed with the impulse of Tohalla's mind.

'So please will you tell me about the Red?' was just a prompt for her to entertain them with something different. And because they'd never known anything but the freedom of idleness they made her feel a freak when they asked, 'What was it like when Housefather bossed everyone about? Why did they do what he told them?'

Or they'd ask the one question whose answer eluded her: 'How did you get into the Two Hundred Thousand?'

Yes, life went on, with the grey spectre always inside her. Waiting for – something.

Leaves crackled under her feet one night in the Autumn that she could not sleep. There were many nights like that when Tohalla roamed what she had been taught to call streets, or shouted her anger into the storm-tossed howl of the waves.

Tonight, though, with the blustery wind rattling dead leaves against the fences, hardly anybody was about. Tohalla was sick of the eternal questions people she hardly knew kept asking her. She was glad that the stinging, wind-borne dust penned them in their half-hidden houses that were ashamed to be seen.

Clouds like the ribs of a basket contained the light of the crescent moons. She was driven like the cloud-shadows far from the house that was a house to an area she didn't know.

A tall man passed her, head-down, cowled against the cutting edge of wind. Then stopped.

'Tohalla?'

She walked on but he turned and ran a few steps to catch up with her. 'Tohalla?'

Irritated, she halted. She had no choice because the burly man was

268

blocking her path, which did nothing to improve her savage temper. 'Well?'

He threw back his cowl and a gleam of moonlight that had escaped its prison shone briefly on his fleshy face. 'It's me, Tohalla. Soren.'

She side-stepped and he fell in alongside her. 'So?' she asked rudely. A spatter of cold rain lashed them for a moment, then was gone.

'So I want to apologise.'

No answer.

Matching her stride he said, 'And tell you something you want to know.'

'Like what?'

'Like how you got here.'

Tohalla stopped motionless in mid-stride, her thin face turned to peer into his. He said nothing. 'Go on then,' she prompted.

Soren shook his head. 'Not here. It's too blasted cold. Come to my place – it's only round the corner.' But he wouldn't say more until they were inside.

CHAPTER EIGHT

The Forbidden

Now that she knew what it was, Tohalla found the mindsail dominated Soren's room.

Banked-up machines hummed or blinked lights or made Soren's words hang in gleaming colours on the air. The rampant vines etched their green mass against his star-lattice windows and lolling on his scarlet-quilted couch, Soren kept saying, 'No! Not yet! Try this combination first.'

His fingers fiddled with a keypad that rested on his stomach and a different medley of scents swept her patience thin. The presence of the room seemed to press solidly in on her. Tohalla said again, 'But you promised to tell me how I got here!'

He told her, 'Ssh! In a minute. I'm concentrating. I want just the right mix –' Soren's preoccupied drawl broke off and Tohalla strove to encompass her impatience and master it. For she had seen the watch-lions rampant through the lattice.

Tohalla swallowed another mouthful of fruit-perfumed wine and the pearly lights of glow-fruit swirled upside down in the ruby depths of her glass. Even so what her eyes returned to again and again was the mindsail which hung quiescent from one outswept branch.

It wasn't how she remembered it. In fact, she realized, it was a different mindsail altogether. Tiny beads, specks of stained glass or gnarled seed-pods, were interwoven with the russet threads of the reliesin. They formed a pattern that she couldn't quite work out. It meant something. From her seat that was soft as a mountain of turquoise cloud Tohalla studied the meaning that was hidden somewhere in the design.

Still staring, she absently tossed back the rest of the wine.

Fragments of some melody spun a background of dreams to her absorption. Unnoticed, Soren watched.

And the mindsail slowly filled. Tohalla scarcely noticed how she was drawn into it. She was borne aloft, falling upwards into the welcome of the mindsail's red embrace. And Soren was beside her.

Before she knew it he showed her the sleeping hillside that was his home. They were high above it, seeing its stars of gentle light shine forth through the green tangle of vines. Stately, gold-furred and feline in their grace, the watch-lions arched, then curved their necks to drink at his silver-swift stream. They were like jewels with the beauty of Soren's land as their setting.

It's wonderful! breathed Tohalla's soul.

Soren's mind smiled at her, a strength in him that she could feel. *If I keep you safe*, he thought, *will you sail with me? I'll show you treasures you have never seen ...*

Rapt, her spirit acquiesced with a kind of mental nod. In her was the same joy and wonder that she had felt once before, with Tamdaintre. She scarcely noticed that Soren's feelings were not her own. He kept them shielded as he drew her gently down into the crystal depths of the sea, where fish spun moonbeams through arcs of inky coral. For Soren had heard of her refusal to take minds out to the heart of the Red, and he was careful not to peer into her privacy.

Soren showed her marvels that bored him with their familiarity, because he had a plan.

And the flickers of violet luminescence were thick around them.

Tamdaintre was waiting on her porch at noon the next day when Tohalla came back. In fact he'd been waiting since shortly after Whitedawn. He noticed straight away that she seemed more relaxed than she had in months, her face less strained.

'Hello!' she said cheerily, setting down the bulky wrapped bundle that Soren had given her. 'Are you feeling fine?'

In point of fact he was chilled with the thin, sea-tanged rain that slanted through the air. So was she but it didn't seem to matter.

Hardly hearing what he replied, Tohalla continued, 'Come on in and have a glass of wine. What brings you here at this time of day? I thought you'd be fishing, or weaving, or something busy-busy. Hasn't the virtuous Tamdaintre got anything to do?' She was sorry as soon as she'd spoken that her teasing had come out sharper than she'd meant it to.

His bootheels hammered over the boards of her househall, louder than hers and slower. 'I've got plenty to keep me occupied. Look here, Tohalla, is it true?'

Kettle in hand, Tohalla came back from the kitchen. Some of the brightness had faded from her face but she still looked happier than she had since the night of her housewarming. 'Is what true?'

Tamdaintre ignored the hardness of her voice. 'That you've been sailing with Soren.'

'What if I have? Why shouldn't I? Anyway, what business is it of yours?'

'I make the best mindsails, Tohalla. You know that. But I wouldn't given Soren one of mine. And it was one of mine, I'd swear it was. He took it.'

She shook her hair, its ends still pale with streaks from last summer's suns. 'He wouldn't do a thing like that. Besides, what makes you think it was one of yours? So what if I did sail with him? I enjoyed it!' she added defiantly.

Tamdaintre looked into her eyes that were on the same level with his. There was still that self-containment in his gaze that attracted her but her anger had her on its leash. 'How did you find out, anyway? Have you been spying on me?'

'Not spying, no. But I was out last night and I saw you. Did you think I wouldn't recognize – one of my own sails?'

She ignored the second part of his question with its little pause that made her think he'd been going to say something else. 'We didn't see anyone!' she said loudly. Inwardly she wasn't so sure. There was so much about mindsailing that she didn't know yet ...

Tamdaintre took a step closer. He was so near now that she could smell the pleasantness of his rain-washed skin. Taking the kettle from her fingers, he passed her and went to fill it from her water-jar. 'Didn't you see those purple glows all about you, Tohalla? That's what you look like when you're mindsailing. Well one of them was me.'

Furious, she snatched the kettle back, holding it to her chest. Water sloshed over both of them. 'Then you *were* spying on me!'

Equally angry, Tamdaintre stared at her. 'Can't I get it through to you that I wasn't spying? I happened to be nearby –'

'Oh yes!' she yelled sarcastically.

'And I felt your mind. One of the other lights was Jerad and his Vigilantes. I headed 'em off for you or you might –'

'Might what? Anything you can do, Soren can do.'

Tamdaintre stalked out of the kitchen so fast she had to step out of his way. At the door to her bare-leafed orchard he put one hand on the

272

jamb and looked over his shoulder. 'He's using you, Tohalla. He's got something in mind and I don't know what it is. I don't like the idea of you being mixed up with him. You take care of yourself, you hear? And don't let him take you out after dawn.'

'Why not?'

'Because the suns' light disrupts your energy.'

'Ha!' she replied scornfully. 'You're just trying to scare me. Well it doesn't work, all right?'

But he was gone down the muddy path that twisted between the apple-trees and the bird-pecked cherries rotting on the branches. Tohalla felt unaccountably sad when Tamdaintre disappeared out of her gate.

She set up her loom in the roof-dome where some heat came through from the chimney at her back. Val's machine had made the loom for her, the way she remembered from her home in the Green. Treadle, stone warp-weights, and the bench before it, it was all so familiar.

And yet different. The tight-woven wattle overhead was protected by some clear plastic so that it wouldn't need chinking with clay come the snows. And there weren't going to be any snows anyway, Valtisane had said.

Yet the ripe smell of dried fruit and Autumn apples were comforting. A gable window the machines had built into the dome added clearer light to the stripes from the wattle. A cloth-covered jar of ginger-beer on the windowsill added its fizzing amber scent to the atmosphere of her dome and bunches of herbs rustled in the still air when she moved.

Then Tohalla took the light, bulky bundle that Soren had given her. Trying not to think of Tamdaintre and the sense of foreboding that he had left inside her, she rolled aside the crackling plastic and took the reliesin out of its wrapper.

Who Soren had got to spin it for him, she didn't know. From what she'd heard of his strange acquaintances, Tohalla didn't think any of them had done it. They were not the type to do hand-labouring but the stuff was too uneven for it to have been spun by machine. Besides, Soren had said, 'The best mindsails are all worked by hand.'

Tohalla ran her fingers over the rough strands. Reliesin was taken from the inner bark of some tree she'd never heard of. It was supposed to have come from Erth but Tohalla doubted it. The prickly russet fibres and their odd powers seemed more like some spawning of the Red.

273

Untwisting a hank, she tied strands of it to the warp-weights and set up her loom. Since she was unused to working with such coarse stuff, Tohalla knew she should make a practice square but the magic of the reliesin lured her. She made her first throw with the shuttle.

Though the prickles stuck in her fingers, she was soon caught up again in the soothing rhythm of the weaving and all the sweet memories linked with it. Now the memories seemed real and vivid. *How strange that only yesterday my life seemed as faded as the growling of the Book! Was it really ten years ago – no, more like eleven! – that Asdra was chasing Caramon round my loom in the sunny yard and the Axe came to talk to me?*

The swift passage of the twin suns abruptly cast Tohalla into shadow. Surprised, she looked up. Crossing to the window, her back unexpectedly stiff, she saw Whitesun trembling on the rim of the hills. But today her time had not been lost like in those sad days before. Looking behind her, a square of mindsail glowed ruddy in the drying light and her garret seemed more companionable for the work she had done in it.

Smiling in the twilight, Tohalla made her way downstairs. A ghost of sadness still shadowed her but for a while her activity had pushed it back. She thought, *Perhaps if I ignore it, it'll go away*, and smiled again at the childish associations.

She wasn't due to see Soren until tomorrow night but loneliness didn't weigh on her. In the morning she'd go down to the beach and collect some shells to decorate her next mindsail. Or maybe to the woods to get some of those beautiful pods to make beads for it. The idea gave her a pleasant sense of purpose.

She soaked her fingers that the rough reliesin had scraped raw. Sitting with her hands in the bowl on the kitchen table, Tohalla gazed idly round the candle-lit room and was struck by how squalid it looked. She wrinkled her nose. *Smells sour too!* She began to put it to rights.

Later, when the Amethyst Moon was the merest sliver of a haloed crescent that presaged rain, and a chill breeze was blowing in off the distant bay, Tohalla was startled by the squawking of birds in her orchard. *Someone's coming!*

She jumped up uneasily and went to the door just as footsteps rang on the boards of the porch. Someone knocked.

'Who is it?' she called, nervous now that her life had begun to take on some meaning. Before it wouldn't have mattered if someone had –

'It's me, Val! Why, who were you expecting?'

Tohalla opened the plain plank door to see her friend's creamy skin and red-dyed hair. Best of all though was the smile of one friend to another. Tohalla grinned cheerfully back. 'No-one. Come in! It's good to see you.'

'And you.' Val peered around the househall and as much of the kitchen as she could see through its open door. She sniffed the fresh smells of soap and brine and a bowl of crisp red apples on the table by the window. 'You're feeling fine, aren't you? I can tell. Just look at this place! Don't tell me you and Tamdaintre – '

'No!' Taking hold of herself Tohalla said more calmly, 'I don't know what it was actually. Unless Soren – '

Tohalla wasn't allowed to finish her sentence either. Valtisane exclaimed, 'What, you and Soren? I thought you had better taste.'

A flush flooded Tohalla's pale cheeks. 'It's nothing like that! We just went mindsailing, that was all, only it was wonderful! We swam right down in the sea and into a cave where a shaft of moonlight's trapped on the water and, and – '

Valtisane crouched by the fire, rubbing her cold hands in the heat of the blaze. Black trousers as broad at the ankle as a skirt would have been shimmered in the flames' dancing light. Her blouse was exactly the same red as her cap of hair. 'If Soren's giving you the guided tour,' she said drily, 'you can bet he's got something else lined up for dessert! Moonlight and caves? Not his sort of thing at all.'

Tohalla began to take umbrage but, sensing this, Valtisane quickly changed the subject and the rest of the evening passed pleasantly. Only when she was saying goodbye under the broad sweep of the eaves did Val bring up the subject again.

'Maybe Soren's just lulling the Vigis, but all the same, Toh, I'd watch it if I were you. Jerad's got his eye on him.'

'Curse Jerad! Why doesn't someone stop him and his bully-boys?'

'Perhaps,' Valtisane said slowly, 'it's because most folks in the Two Hundred Thousand agree with him, his ideas if not his methods. A girl got killed out mindsailing last week.'

As excited as she had been the first time Pierse asked her to walk outside with him, Tohalla stopped outside Soren's gate. Really it was not so much a gate as a break in the scattered line of stones that marked his borders. Fumbling round the bundle she carried under her rain-proof cloak she pulled out the mind-key he had given her. It was too dark for her to see it but she knew it by the touch: a slim rod the length of her hand, tapering to a hollow point at both ends.

Tohalla stepped across the gateway. Involuntarily she screamed as two leaping animals sprang out at her but she pressed the mind-key to her lips and said the code. At the same time she jumped back into the muddy street but there was no need. The moment she said the code-syllable the watch-lions heard her frantic thought, *Stop!*

They froze in mid-stride, the one in the air falling to land stiff-legged with a clang. Cautiously Tohalla crept forward, ready to run back to safety, but they made no move.

She touched one. Under its coating of golden hide it was metallic, its massive shoulder reaching her chin. Its fluid, animal power was imprisoned in heavy iron. One steel-tipped paw was lifted, ready to strike; its jaws agape showed gleaming fangs. Inside its eyes was a glow of machine intelligence. Only its solidified skin held it back from grim slaughter.

Chills stalked her. Tohalla could not help it: she ran.

With the mind-key she commanded the waterfall to open. An arched lintel rolled out of the rocks between the grassy banks and the water parted. To either side the quicksilver liquid draped the opening but with a stride across the hollow place Tohalla was on the wet floor of the tunnel's entrance. Looking back she saw the waterfall sliding into its channel; there was a tawny gleam as the watch-lions slowly began to move again but she was safe.

She wondered why Soren needed such fierce defenders. Was it as Tamdaintre said, that Soren was trouble?

Calling out his name, Tohalla watched her two tones solidify in glorious bubbles of shining ruby and sapphire. And Soren answered her call.

Pastel light framed him when he came out to meet her. He was even broader than the first time she'd seen him, muscles running to fat, but his brown face made a smile and welcomed her.

'You brought your mindsail? Good! Come in and let's give it a try.' Only as an afterthought did he say, 'Are you fine?'

When, sitting beside him on his scarlet couch with drink in hand, she said, 'You were going to tell me how I got here?' Soren answered, 'That's not important. Just look at your sail and let's give it a try.'

Tohalla struggled to get up from the depths of the soft, clinging couch. Soren grasped her wrist hard. Trying to contain his impatience behind a gentle tone, he said, 'Don't fail me, Tohalla of the Loom! You're special! With all those Red powers behind you we can –'

'Not until you tell me how I got here! Let me go!'

'Sit down then, Tohalla, and I'll tell you.'

276

Sinking down reluctantly on the scarlet billows, Tohalla stared at him. His dark, hooded eyes held some secret that made her nervous but Soren said off-handedly, 'It's obvious. You say you called out in the Straight Desert? Well then, the machines are programmed not to hurt anybody human. The machine heard your voice and brought you in to safety, semi-conscious. You certainly didn't ask it for any other help. You probably struggled and said 'Put me down!' when you came round, and it did.'

Tohalla felt cheated. *If it was true –*

Soren snapped, 'Now let's get on with it.'

'But – but why didn't I remember?'

Soren clicked his tongue in irritation. 'You were so frightened that you blanked the whole thing out in your sub-conscious. Now will you stop interrupting? You've got a lot to learn before –'

He broke off but it made Tohalla even more nervous. 'What were you going to say?'

Soren's fleshy features rearranged themselves in a smile. 'Before you're mistress of this new craft. Remember how good it felt last time? Well then, just relax and trust me.'

The mindsail she'd spent so much effort on! Would it work? Curiosity got the better of her.

Tohalla leant back, facing the russet sail she had made. Her first one. She'd make better ones when she understood the nature of reliesin, but already she felt some binding roots growing between her and the fibre that seemed somehow aware.

Beside her, through her white silken sleeve, she felt the heat of Soren's arm.

Abruptly she sat up. 'I'm not going out there again – not to the Red. Or the Green!'

Soren gripped her hand moistly. 'It's all right. You won't have to. I won't make you do anything you don't want. Trust me.'

In that strange Winter without snow, when the things Val called roses still bloomed on what should have been Longnight, Tohalla found herself telling Tamdaintre about Winter in the Green.

They were sitting over the remains of a meal at Lucah's house. Uphill, through the thick twilight, Tohalla could see the first trees of her orchard and through Lucah's open window they could smell the faint sweetness of his garden. Murmuring fans swept warm air through the room and his machine hovered behind the table, eager to serve at the slightest word.

277

Lucah's hair was a chequerboard of amber and coral. Gilt limned its ornate wedges and peaks. Tohalla couldn't take her eyes off it.

He laughed. 'Like it, do you? My Jade here always does my hair special if we're having a party.'

Naïve, Tohalla asked, 'Does this count as a party, then?'

Lucah laughed again and the others joined in, friendly not mocking. Lucah was always laughing – at Tohalla and Tamdaintre for trying to live without machines, the way she was still depressed sometimes, at anything.

Jade said, 'Of course! We don't like them big noisy affairs you go now with Soren where people spill cake-crumbs behind the cushions and puke drugs all over the mats.' She swept imaginary crumbs off her comfortable stomach and winked.

Lucah snapped his fingers and their machine, blue and silver that had painted itself like stars, poured more wine. Tohalla still hadn't learnt to like it much.

'Oh, yes.' Lucah's thin old voice was positive. 'We used to go to those big things down to the Civic Halls in Mistyvale but we like it better now with less noise. Hated that organized jollity. Enough to put anybody off.'

His wrinkled features beamed round the S-shaped table at Tohalla and Tamdaintre, Valtisane and her latest partner Lian. 'Me and the wife, now, we like it better –'

He broke off, turning to Tohalla. 'Are you expecting anybody?'

The focus of all eyes, Tohalla said, 'No.'

'Well a light's just come on in your dome window.'

Tohalla leapt to her feet, her thighs catching painfully on the edge of the table. Tipping her chair backwards in her haste she ran for the door. In two strides Tamdaintre caught up with her.

'You can't go alone, you fool!' he said, pulling her backwards. 'What if it's Vigis?'

'Let go! I can't stay here and do nothing.'

'But if they are Vigis, you know how they operate. Never send one or two. And if you do manage to fight them off, they're Jerad's so he'll just call Council and say it's you that infringed and you deserve it. Listen!'

Faint on the moist gloaming came the sound of breaking wood. Whoever it was, they didn't even try to hide their gloating laughter.

'My loom! My lovely loom! Look at it!'

Tohalla stood half-way through the trap-door, staring at the devastation in her roof-dome. Wrecked, splintered, its pieces hurled

278

any old how among her sacks and barrels, the loom was unrecognizable. On the step behind her Tamdaintre put a comforting arm about her shoulder. Even the half-finished bolt of woven reliesin had been pulled free. Only odd wisps clung to the fragmented wood. Even her warp-weights had gone, one thrown through her window so that the damp night blew in. Flour-sacks had been axed open; dirty white tracks mixed with a jumble of herbs where the hanging bunches had been torn from their hooks.

'That's all I was,' she whispered. Tamdaintre thought she added, 'All I had to show for my imprisonment here.' She backed down the stairs.

'We'll build you another one, Toh.' Tamdaintre stood aside to let her past, his dry fingers stroking her arm. Of all the things he might have said: how he'd warned her not to sail so often, not to go out night after night with Soren, that Soren was trouble – out of all these possibilities Tamdaintre chose, 'You and I, Toh, we'll build you a better loom.'

'Did you hear, Soren? I had night-visitors,' Tohalla said too brightly the following night. It was late; she'd had to wait until his dinner-guests had taken themselves off. Listening to their voices from the next room where she hid, she wondered idly which were his bed-guests too.

'No? What sort of visitor? Tell me.' Soren heard the fierce gaiety in her voice and was glad, but he cloaked his gladness with spurious sympathy. It was what he'd been waiting for, after all. The Vigis and he were old enemies. He'd let himself be seen around with Tohalla, flaunted their friendship – and not three nights before he'd swooped Tohalla's latest mindsail so close to one of theirs that he'd frightened the wind out of their sail. He told Tohalla it was an accident. It had only been a matter of time before the Vigis paid her a visit.

After Tohalla had spat her acid phrases, while Soren hid a grin, he dwelt on the meanness of the minds that had conceived such an outrage and she was ready for his lesson of hate. He said, 'Let's pay 'em back, Toh. Let's teach 'em a lesson.'

'How?' she said simply.

'Like this.'

It was one of Tohalla's own, her fourth mindsail, better than the ones before as she learnt bit by bit to know the secrets of the reliesin. Interspersed were shining, wrinkled seeds and polished stones she had picked up in her rambles on the shore. And it was keyed in to its maker's mind in some fashion that Tohalla didn't understand but felt on an instinctive level.

It was a brilliant mindsail she had made. It flew her – and Soren – with very little effort. Only, because she trusted him for all the joy his teaching had given her, she relinquished the 'lines' that steered them. With deft mental flicks Soren led her not past but *to* the violet glows that danced beyond the first russet warmth where the mindsail spread its canopy.

Travelling through the air, minds flying while their bodies were safe inside Soren's green-hill house, they barely grazed one purple shimmer. Tohalla's mind shied in panic.

For inside the violet brightness were souls unbound by the limits of flesh. Those souls recoiled aghast at the invasion of their nakedness by Soren and Tohalla. And Tohalla felt she had been stripped.

Someone had pried apart the crevices of her mind where she hid her fears and shames, trampling through her to leave slimy tracks in her thoughts.

Just for a second. Then Soren pulled her free of that livid abasement. Beyond it was a mental abyss whose winds shrieked upwards as Tohalla fell. It seemed that the crash would kill her.

But Soren spread his power and the mindsail almost cracked with the strain. Yet it held. A scant body-length from tearing destruction the sail boomed open and Tohalla drifted safe in Soren's mental embrace.

Wafting through a gentle orange-grove, its perfume massaging the stress from her being, Tohalla listened.

You have to shield yourself. Here, like this: and Soren showed her how to grow protection. It never occurred to her that Soren hid his thoughts from her. Or that his aura was dark and nebulous and not a clean bright light.

Let's try it again, Tohalla. If you do it right, it won't hurt us or them.

It's not right! she thought. Soren felt her revulsion, fed her anger.

Didn't you feel the same when Jerad's mob invaded your house? Smashed the things you loved? Didn't you feel dirty?

Her anger carried agreement. Inside himself Soren smiled. It had been a close-run thing; her mind was so powerful, nurtured by Red-speech, by Marchidas's and Edrach's inborn, cultured skills, that he had almost failed to stop that death-bound plummet. But with Tohalla's power – yes. The thing was almost in his grasp.

They're strong, Tohalla. We have to be strong to stop their evil. To stop the Vigilantes invading anyone else.

Still Tohalla hesitated, rent by fear and indecision. A wave of fury ripped through Soren, so sudden that he couldn't shield it in time. Tohalla's mind jumped like a startled razorback.

Hastily turning his anger to advantage Soren told her slyly, *I was just remembering Hsü, a friend of mine, what she was like when the Vigis got hold of her. She's – gone now.*

I'll do it! shouted Tohalla's mind, and on a wave of exultation realized that Soren had given her a new purpose in life, ready-made.

So began her learning of infringement.

CHAPTER NINE

Target Vigilante

By day Tohalla helped Tamdaintre craft a loom. From his store of timber she chose the frame by touch, knowing when the wood felt right for her purpose. As Winter gave way to the riotous explosion of Spring in the Two Hundred Thousand Tohalla grew stronger, healthier. The wounded look she had worn for so long was lost in peace and the drawn hollows of her face filled out. She grew confident enough to wear the clothes she'd made on her first loom: a cream shirt, russet leggings.

With Redsun rising at the centre of Whitesun's broader disc, Tohalla learned to plane. The broad morning light on Tamdaintre's terrace gilded her nose with freckles; his tenor rose with hers in harmonies that sped her loving polish along the rich grain of the wood, and her hair, pale bronze now with the southern suns, streamed free as a warrior's streams, proudly.

She helped him with his garden and he shared Lucah's mockery in hers. Cheerfully they splashed for clay in a stream-bed, to mould new warp-weights. While the suns were bright in the blue of the sky above the smiling bay, you could say 'Tohalla' and Tamdaintre would be there.

But the nights were her own – and Soren's.

One evening with the winds of equinox drifting pollen from flower-starred bushes, Tohalla smiled and sighed. She was sitting on a bench on the sunset-side of Tamdaintre's cliff-house. From the kitchen window he asked, 'What's up?' A delicious smell of Spring's first salad came out with his voice.

'Oh, nothing. It's just so beautiful here! Look at that: Redsun's touching Whitesun's rimtop down there, see? Summer'll soon be here. With those palms outlined against it, it's as lovely as – the Green.'

'D'you miss your home still?' Tamdaintre could picture it now, from that one mindsailing visit and from a thousand fireside tales. But he never mentioned it unless Tohalla did.

'Sometimes,' and the yearning was a counterpoint to her voice. He knew she was thinking of Vernal, wondering what she was doing, hoping she was happy, torturing herself lest Vernal had forgotten her mother.

Tamdaintre came outside with two frosted glasses of lemonade. He handed one to Tohalla. Fruit swirled under its pale surface.

'Thanks, Tam. Oh, that's good after a hard day with a hoe!' She liked looking at him, finding peace in his frank, open face. His high cheek-bones, perfect lips and strong, square teeth, and the friendship in his eyes had all grown dear to her. Returning to her earlier subject with determined cheerfulness, Tohalla added, 'But the Two Hundred Thousand is beautiful too. Is the number of people always the same?'

'No.' He swallowed a mouthful of his drink, settled beside her on the wooden bench with the warm, smooth rock at his back. 'It's growing, not as fast as it once did, though. One day it'll be the Three Hundred Thousand, I suppose. It was the Ten Thousand when it started. But there's lots of unoccupied land yet.'

Tohalla sighed less happily this time. 'And I suppose then the machines will burn another range of hills. Edrach was right. One day the Green will kill the Red.'

Tamdaintre looked at her, comfort in his level grey eyes. 'Don't look at it like that. You've changed the way some of us think about the rest of Rosaria. You strengthened Mauritz's belief in a more settled way of life. Maybe the Red and the Green can learn to mix. Who knows? Maybe even, one day your Axe will fetch the star-kin home.'

'I don't think so, Tam. The spaces between the stars are too big. I suppose he's dead by now and we'll always be alone here. And that Erth-disc you see everywhere with its blue seas and streams of clouds won't ever help the incomers feel at home. It'll always be just a symbol. Every time I go to the library I find another lot of books that you can't see for white blurs, or books you can't hear because the power in them's gone. D'you ever wonder if they'd look on us the same way we used to think of the Wolfmen? They must know so much we don't ... But think what it must have taken them to send us here to a place where we can grow. To be part of the star-family again ...'

Tamdaintre must have known the picture of the Axe was in her mind. 'D'you want him to come back?' he asked curiously.

'I don't know. He'd be sad to see how fast the Green has taken over down here.'

That wasn't what Tamdaintre meant but he let it pass. In companionable silence he and Tohalla watched while combers crashed far away on the soft, golden sands of the beach, and sea-birds whirled overhead in a sudden gusty wind.

'Oh!' Tohalla exclaimed, when the hills had quenched even Whitesun's fire. 'I should have gone sooner!'

Coldly Tamdaintre said, 'Soren again?'

She nodded.

'How are your watch-lions, by the way?'

Tohalla now had watch-lions of her own prowling in her garden by night. That was another bone of contention between them, even though Tohalla had given all her friends a mind-key. She had many friends now, but she wouldn't sail with any of them any more. Only Soren. Because she knew all the others would be horrified if they discovered the revenge she planned. *Will Soren say we can do it tonight?* She stood up.

'You're thinking about him already, aren't you, Tohalla?'

Tohalla flushed with the anger so many similar conversations called up. 'What right have you to tell me what I can or can't do?' she shouted. 'I thought that was all part of the Two Hundred Thousand – that there's freedom here. What right have you?'

'None. And if you notice, I didn't tell you anything.'

A hard expression was on his face. Tohalla was not to know it hid his hurt. Nevertheless she felt a sense of guilt at provoking it.

'I'm sorry, Tam. But it'll be all right, truly it will. Only I can't explain now. Will I see you tomorrow?'

'Mmm. We were going to the reliesin-wood, if you remember.'

She was half-way down the path already. Ankle-high shoots burgeoned green beside her feet. 'Goodbye, then, Tam. See you tomorrow.'

But he was wondering what she had to hide behind watch-lions.

Tohalla saw someone again, standing in the garden opposite Soren's house, watching her. Her steps quickened nervously. She didn't know him but when she had described him, Tamdaintre said he was a Vigi called Kester.

Don't be ridiculous! she told herself. *How can anybody get past Soren's watch-lions? We'll be all right.*

But she was glad to get in and see her fourth mindsail again. It hung in all its simplicity beneath the unnatural tree in Soren's unnatural, machine-cluttered room.

It was such a contrast, that room with its ranks of coloured, winking lights, to Tamdaintre's homely cave. Tamdaintre's place was plain, with polished wooden furniture and woven hangings brightening the sienna walls, but Tamdaintre's welcome was stamped on even the natural scents of the air. It was fresh, the few things made with love ...

Yet her mindsail glowed under the living pear-light in Soren's shadowy, overcrowded room. And the mindsail gave her a more natural welcome than Soren's toothy grin. Something rang not quite true in the way Soren received her, but she couldn't pin it down. His little, pink mouth stretched, crowding his brown, fleshy cheeks. And underneath his commonplace greetings was a fierce and watchful – something.

'Are you – ' he began, and at the same time she asked, 'Can we do it – '

Soren grinned again *(like a hunting wolf,* she thought) and he finished their sentence: 'Now.'

He pulled her roughly onto the jagged scarlet of his divan, breathing fast. Tohalla smelt sharp-tanged sweat spring out from his armpit as he grabbed and held her tight. Nothing gentle, nothing loving. He was on fire to begin his personal plan ...

Swiftly now she could adopt the mental posture that gave the breath of her mind to fill the sail. Soren thought at her *So strong tonight!* but his confidence wasn't shaken. Whatever her strength, her skill did not yet match his.

Their double being was borne aloft as the reliesin sail swelled to their presence. First the disorientation of the upward fall into its soft copper colour, then elation as their spirits soared and the Two Hundred Thousand lay stretched beneath them like a physical map. But more than that: now she was attuned, the violet bubbles of other people's thoughts shone bright for mindsailers, very faint but perceptible for those whose thoughts were safe at home.

Only tonight they weren't safe.

You remember? asked Soren.

Everything you've told me.

But he hadn't told her everything.

They swooped down the wild warm winds like a geyrlizard stoops on its prey. Above them the stars flickered as though the gale would blow them out, so low and trembling were they in the midnight sky. Below, the faint mauve of strollers grew thicker in the winding streets as they neared the Council House, and the green-strung roofs of homes swept dizzying beneath Tohalla.

It's glorious! she cried, thrilling to the flight.

But Soren answered, *Concentrate!* and Tohalla's joy was shadowed. They flew on, past silly gangs of youths who tried to net them with infringement. Each glistening mass of thought tasted different but that was part of the game. When you want for nothing sensation is everything.

A couple – does gender have a soul? – rose crazy in their path. Rapt in each other's minds they were oblivious in their act of love. Tohalla was too full of wonder *(Why didn't Soren tell me you can make love with your whole being in the mindsail?)* to make a move.

But Soren reacted just as their rocketing mindsail skimmed the surface of his and Tohalla's. Giant sparks cascaded from the interface, violet lightning that burned – but Soren shielded Tohalla as well as himself.

The other couple plummetted. Horror shook Tohalla so that she almost fell too, but the couple saved themselves almost at ground-height and limped home, their souls wounded.

Concentrate, blast you! roared Soren through Tohalla's mind. *The Vigis are faster than that!*

Inside himself he sneered as Tohalla was stung by his criticism. But without her knowing he was feeding more anger into her mind to fuel her flight. Savage joy sped her, and his arrogance. Ahead was the glassy tower of the Council House aglimmer in the starlight: their target.

Dagger-quick down the racing wind rode Tohalla. Adrenalin drove her in exultation towards the black-windowed tower. Beside her, inside her, was –

Soren roared, *Shield!* as a livid bubble burst upwards towards them. He dragged her down slanting. The enemy mindsail whooshed past, turned, corrected. It was so close that Tohalla was aware of a massed crew, four or five of them.

We're outpowered! she yelled and her mindsail sagged. The ground began to leap up at her.

Get a grip on yourself, you fool! There's too many of them for fast manoeuvres. They'll be forming committees – Look out!

Faster than he'd hoped the enemy recovered. They were matching Tohalla's accidental drop. Soren took advantage of it, sidestepped their mindsail using Tohalla's fear to boost speed. The outer rims of the thought-bubbles scraped past, flaring on contact.

But Soren was dragging Tohalla sideways and up. The enemy

thought-sphere was dashing itself downwards, five wills trying to flee in different directions. The sail's aura was rudderless. Fear of falling is the most primitve fear of all. And the enemy mindsail crashed on the reefs of terror. Far below, hormones flooded into the Vigis' bloodstreams, spearing hot needles into panic-filled brains, crashing rough-shod through the hearts' normal rhythms. The Vigis' terror was physical pain. Tohalla looked down in her sail's upward surge. She felt an impulse to pity but Soren used one of the tricks he'd kept secret: yes, Tohalla looked down. But her sight was filled with the infernal light of conquest. The joy of triumph dazzled her – as he'd meant. And her power was his to command.

Quick! urged jubilant Soren. *Before they come back!* But he knew that they wouldn't come back tonight. He'd tasted insanity before.

Sweeping her along on the wings of exultation, Soren's mind licked the air for a trace of Jerad's taste. And found it.

This is the bastard who invaded you! he said, and in echoes of emotion poured hate into her mind, down in the subconscious where she wouldn't know its source. But she felt her hatred grow until it was a consuming incandescence.

This way! He pulled her and the mindsail swept through glass and curtains, past the prickly barriers Jerad trusted, that were no more than dead talismans.

Soren gave her no time to hesitate though she tried to slow his headlong flight. Adept at using her own power against her, Soren wasn't even checked. Like a discus from the Red he hurled the mindsail into Jerad's purple essence.

Time stopped. For Tohalla, feeling *was*, and was with great intensity. And the feeling was Jerad's as, not touching him yet, they observed, and Tohalla watched and felt in growing horror.

Jerad lay frozen between sleep and waking, vulnerable, his mind open to every passing thought.

Jerad lay fretting because he wasn't asleep. He tried to lie still and an itch began on his instep. When he wriggled sideways to scratch it, breakfast crumbs lay under his ribs. Even his machine-made silver sheets were seamed with wrinkles from all his tossing.

He tried to still his thoughts: *think of black velvet. It's smooth, it's soft, black as night, gemstones are its stars. Why doesn't Glaedwin wear the necklace I gave her? Is she having an affair?*

Oh, blast it! I'm supposed to be going to sleep, not thinking of her. I've got to get up in he asked his pillow the time yet again and it whispered, 'One-seventy-six.' – *In five hours.*

Beside him but too far away to touch, Glaedwin turned slightly. A faint, irregular snore drifted across to Jerad.

He clenched his teeth until his jaw ached but there wasn't another snore. In time he managed to make his breathing less angry. Jerad was on the edge of sleep –

Glaedwin snored.

His eyes flicked open, hot and dry in his head.

Vaguely scratching his wrinkled belly, Jerad calmed his angry mind, thinking of Persis. Her strength. Her ingenuity between the sheets. And as always when he thought of Persis's hard body on his, the things she did to him, a spur of guilt made him swallow. *Nobody knows. It's all right.*

Unless some bastard mindsailer's been watching, feeling how good the pain is ... Some infringing bastard.

I wonder if she's caught anybody tonight, her and my Vigilantes? Some infringing bastard ... I hate them! What if it's someone they know? Would they tell me? They haven't brought many up before me recently ...

Are they on the level? Have they sold out to that bastard Soren?

Not Persis. But she only brought me two last week and there wasn't any proof. The thought was a worry that nagged him: Persis and Soren? *Remember at that dinner four years ago?*

No – Soren's got that gaga woman in tow now. She should be in the spital. If I catch her I'll put her there, unsettling everybody with her blasted lies. Even that eyesore house of hers is an infringement! But I'll fix her! Anyway, how can Soren stand sailing with the stupid bitch? Maybe Kester's lying. Or Persis? Are they trying to hide something ...?

Glaedwin sighed in her sleep, her thick lips drubbing together. Jerad bounced noisily in the bed but she was drunk again. She didn't wake. Jerad loathed what she'd become.

I'll show you, too, you old faggot! I'll get rid of you. I'd like to strip the skin off your fat gut. (The pictures were bright in his mind.) *Burn your nipples. Watch you bleed, you ugly bastard!*

Soren swooped. Seized upon the thought and turned it inside out in Jerad's mind so its hatefulness was paraded. Blazed it dark and triumphant, letting him feel Tohalla's disgust pass with violence into Jerad's secret ways.

Every meanness from earliest childhood, every snatched toy and deceit – Soren dragged it out into the open like some hideous banner. Soren emblazoned Jerad's sick, secret joys, the twisted pleasure when he punished some infringer and blood spilled red, the way he loved destroying some mindsailer's intimate possessions, his glee at their

288

nauseated discovery of his violations. And Tohalla saw him masturbate over the wreck of her loom.

Then Soren spewed out what he had stoked up in Tohalla: the force of her rage burst in on Jerad like a tidal wave, seeking out the lines of weakness to score Jerad with loathing.

And the acid of self-hate gnawed at Jerad's heart, for Soren showed Jerad to Jerad in a fire-warped mirror he'd moulded from Tohalla's power.

Soren loved it.

CHAPTER TEN

The Uses of Remorse

Tohalla fell for eons back into her body. When her mind dropped into her, her limbs thrashed on Soren's smothering covers, settled, trembling with the shock of her fall. Agony possessed her. No awakening could be worse.

Beside her, Soren shook off his own marginal horrors. And laughed.

'What have you done to him? What have I done?' she shouted, all but incoherent. 'You – you used me. You tricked me! You lied to me! You used me!'

Still laughing, his derision echoing in Tohalla's skull, Soren gasped, 'You said that. Now, if you're nice to me, I just might let you go.'

Tohalla tried to roll away from him over the patterned silk but the yielding couch smothered her. Soren, effortless, pressed her down with his weight. Just the touch of his flesh, the stink of his sweat, nauseated her. Half under him, she heaved upwards but she couldn't shift his bulk.

'Keep that up,' he said, hot, moist lips by her ear. 'I'm enjoying it.'

She turned her head and bit him. 'Enjoy that then, you –'

But she had managed to free one hand from the divan's slithery embrace. Catching a corner of her polluted mindsail, she yanked. The stiff russet cloth broke free of its cords, the batten at its top falling on Soren's head.

As he struggled to uncover his face Tohalla seized her opportunity and slipped heavily onto the floor. One arm strained still beneath Soren's shoulder but she punched him awkwardly in the throat and rescued her arm from the obscenity of his touch.

He flailed the batten as if to fling the mindsail aside. Tohalla grabbed it, rode with the direction of his movement and tore it from his bloated fingers. Reversing it, she brought the batten down hard on his solar plexus.

He groaned as the air rushed out of him but breath did not return. Tohalla dropped the tainted mindsail in the empty fireplace as though it were some pus-laden rag. *Oh for some wolf-fire!* but this was the mechanical Two Hundred Thousand. A machine did her bidding.

The diseased mindsail burned in roiling sulphur clouds.

Tohalla fled down the tunnel, slid to an unsteady stop behind the waterfall, which showed four reflections of gold in all its falling silver. The watch-lions' eyes!

Down the tunnel behind her Tohalla heard the first stirrings of Soren – something falling to the floor, a moan of intaken breath. The sound of his inarticulate gasp hung in the air before her like a jaundiced tear.

Tohalla scrabbled in her pocket for the mind-key. A groan wrenched from her; the mind-key was in her cloak and her cloak was in Soren's room.

Echoes of Jerad's torture reverberated inside Tohalla with her own fear: Soren had put ideas inside her mind. She no longer knew which were her thoughts or his implanted sickness. She would rather face the watch-lions than Soren. *What else might he do to my mind?*

She could see the watch-lions' watered-silk hides pacing beyond the falling beads of the cascade. Sharp claws curled into the grass.

Small heart – wasn't that what Marchidas said? Memories from the Red were clear and clean. Behind she heard Soren stumble nearer, bulky, menacing, hurling things out of his path.

Small heart.

Kneeling at the lip of the waterfall, Tohalla fought to forget herself and the horrors in her mind. To think no thoughts of Soren, coming to get her. To be one with the rippling water. To be transparent yet star-silvered.

Will-less, what was Tohalla's essence shrank to no more substance than the sheen on the streamlet's flow. *Small heart ...*

And the metal beasts who were keyed to alien thoughts could not feel Tohalla's mind.

Her body slipped limp into the limpid waters, bumped along the stream-bed watched by the puzzled watch-lions. There was not enough in her to remember to breathe. Ebony and argent, the stream flowed over her eyes, her mouth.

But the quicksilver thread of her consciousness knew when the water had borne her past the flowered stones of Soren's border. Oh, but what effort it was to grow enough strength to breathe, to want to *be* again when being was so hard. So many choices, this living outside the Green. So many wrong decisions without Housefather to tell her what to be. How much easier to lie in this silken stream, cool water flowing into her, stroking away the pains of life in her lungs.

Silver and black. And then just black.

Involuntary spasms shook her diaphragm. She choked. Sat up coughing, water-blinded, cold. And was Tohalla again.

'Whassa – What's the matter? Who is it?'

Tohalla called again, softly, not sure of her welcome in the hour before dawn.

Tamdaintre saw her silhouette in the rugged hole he called a window. 'Toh?'

'Y-yes. Can I c-come in?'

She saw him sit up, throw the covers off then snatch one up again. With it clutched around his waist he shuffled to the door.

'You're soaking! Your hair's wringing wet! Whatever is it?'

He took her inside and threw towels and some of his clothes on the bed. 'Here, Toh, you get these on. I'll get the fire going.'

'But Tam! You don't know –'

Her voice shook with cold misery. Tamdaintre drew one finger up her arm. At even such a light contact Tohalla quivered.

'Tell me later. Let's get you warm first.'

'But Tam! They'll be coming to get me.'

Tamdaintre bent to the fireplace set in one wall. 'They can do it just as well if you're dry. Come on now.'

And when she was dressed in his trousers and warm shirt that almost fit her, Tamdaintre sat beside her on the oak settle by the flames and said, 'So tell me.'

Dark-eyed with fear and horror, she did. Outside the first streaks of daybreak frosted whiteness on the sky.

'What will I do, Tam? I – I don't want to go back to the Red but the Vigis'll kill me. And Vernal –' Her whisper trailed away to silence.

Tamdaintre was quiet for so long that she thought he hadn't heard. Or that he was framing a rebuke so horrific she would never recover. Tohalla put down her empty cup and stood to creep away, but at a gesture from him she sat again, mute.

'We'll have to mend him,' he said at last.

Tohalla jumped to her feet, drained of all colour. 'I can't! I can't sail again, not after –'

292

'You can.' His calm grey eyes printed faith onto hers. 'You have a power that no-one's matched before. Didn't we sail further than anyone's ever been on your first attempt? Even in daylight you can do it. Share your power with me and we can do it. I'll help you.'

'Why should you?' Tohalla asked, unbelieving, untrusting. 'After all you told me about Soren ...'

'Two reasons,' Tamdaintre said, drawing her over to where a coloured weaving hung beside a window. 'First to help you right a wrong. And second because when the rest of the Council decide to act, there'll be slaughter in the Two Hundred Thousand if we don't. Anyway,' he added, dragging the settle over to her by the window, 'it's half my fault. My partner and I made the first mindsail. And after she left me I carried on.'

Hurrying to help him Tohalla said, 'I thought there had always been mindsails here.'

'No. I guess we've known about reliesin for a century or so – something to get us high without drugging us, to ease the isolation between our minds. Here, sit down before you fall down.' He sat close beside her, feeling her shivering still. 'But Risande made the first sail. She said it would only cause trouble but I kept on at her. Maybe I shouldn't have.'

'What happened?' Tohalla asked.

'She got fed up with the way I live. Got into drugs, orgies – any of the things people do to keep the loneliness out. Anyway, give me your hand. That's right. And feel my mind in the sail.'

Strange to sail in the white world of first light. Rising through the redness of the mindsail into ghostly sky, Tamdaintre led her back to the Council House. Thought-bubbles were misted, atremble with the coming dawn, cowering in houses. Suns' light disturbed the reliesin; already there was a slick of colour in the east.

Quick now. Tamdaintre said. *There's the tower.*

Tohalla felt no soaring pleasure this time in the sailing but Tamdaintre's mind was a friendly warmth that mingled with hers. She could feel his determination. And he was open to her in a way that Soren had never been, in a way Tohalla had never imagined possible ...

And from high above the flat-roofed tower they dived straight down. The web of streets with their prisoned houses rose up at them, dizzying, frightening then terrifying.

No, Tam! We'll crash!

How can we? You sailed beneath the ocean, didn't you? We've no bodies to

293

crash. Our minds can sail through vacuum or to the burning core of the world.

The tower speared up at her. Tohalla almost blacked out with fright but Tamdaintre gave her the trick of it: *It's fear that kills. Would I hurt you?*

The thin wild gale whistled upwards. Like a javelin Tamdaintre hurled themselves down. Terror sang through her, wind on a tide-net, and Tamdaintre hung the trick before her, the click that turns off fear.

Their spirits plunged in through the roof and swooped at the speed of thought to Jerad's muddied aura.

Violet bubbles clustered round the raving man on the bed, hands stroked back his hair that spiked upwards from his sweating scalp. Sparks shrieked lilac at Tohalla – Tamdaintre's thought-sphere ground against the edges of others.

Not hiding, Tamdaintre stoked himself on power from Tohalla's mind. Quick as a single vibration of the highest note of a zither, he played jets of self-worth into Jerad's wounded mind. They laved along the acid paths of shame leaving healing where they washed away the pain.

So fast was it that only now did the figures round the bed react. Slow shock checked action. Before Tohalla had time to taste the poison of their hate and fear Tam flavoured it with kindness. And dragged Tohalla sideways past the useless spiral barrier.

Outside in the east a flat crescent of white fire burned upwards into dawn. Gilt clouds outraced the free-flowing winds. Somewhere a cock crowed. No other sail drew a violet cargo of thought-light into danger.

The sun pulled strength from them but Tohalla and Tamdaintre shot onwards beneath the essence of his mindsail. Weary as they paced the sun, they searched the damaged Vigis out and healed each wounded sailor. And Whitesun was half up with small Redsun a drop of blood rising at its top.

Each second drained more energy into the killing suns. Tamdaintre was faint now, a pale shadow beside her. Too weak to shield, he knew he was too far gone to limp back to his body, and Tohalla heard him.

The reliesin vibrated as Redsun pulsed into view. Her despair mirrored his. When the slow bulk of Whitesun rose in its entirety, Tohalla's essence and Tamdaintre's would shimmer into nothing.

In her mind she could see it: in Tamdaintre's homely cave-house their bodies would decay untenanted. Tohalla knew a feeble urge to dissipate in the dawn, her spirit a part of Rosaria floating forever. *What use have I ever been?*

And no answer came from Tamdaintre beside her.

Fear sparked into fire: *Tam! Where are you? Don't die!*

Above the first green of gardens in the new day she searched weakly for him, called his spirit-rags to shelter in her mind. She gathered him into her very core and strove onwards for his sake.

The vibration was strong now, plaiting her senses into a tangle of discord. Dislocated, she didn't know where she was, where her body was. Or Tam's.

I am Tohalla. I am Marchidas, but the thought was flimsy. *There was Edrach, shrivelling on the pyre of sapphire wood I lit when Vernal was a baby. And the Axe, that I never saw hold an axe in the Red. There he goes. Look at him soaring in the dazzling Ship above the rainbow.*

She was drifting, wafting apart, flailed into death by the particles of suns' light.

The Ship! I am Tohalla – Marchidas – and I have found the Ship to take us all to the stars. And she saw through Marchidas's eyes the ruby spire of the tail-fin jutting from the marsh. *The flood of welcome in Edrach's eyes!*

Fulfilment.

Belief.

And below her soul that cradled Tamdaintre was the white wall of his garden on the brown headland. Falling, senses tumbling, she saw the salt wind in the flowers, smelt the sparkling blue of the horizon.

Beside her Tamdaintre's body on the settle twitched as she poured him into it. *Loyalty in the Green is!* she thought drowsily.

And, smiling, Tohalla drifted into the new day on the wings of sleep.

CHAPTER ELEVEN

Mindsail

Afternoon stung Tohalla's eyes when Valtisane slapped her awake.

'At last!' Val exclaimed. 'I've been so frightened! I've been trying to wake you up for hours.'

Tohalla struggled upright, pulling her numbed arm softly from behind Tamdaintre's shoulder. She shaded her eyes with one hand, a tender smile shaping her mouth. A faint pucker was between his thin eyebrows but the rest of his face was smooth in sleep.

He stirred slightly as her hand eased his head to a more comfortable position. Tohalla stroked his cheek lightly with one finger. The corners of his lips tugged briefly upwards and he slid into a more natural slumber.

Tohalla yawned and stretched but she didn't move from Tamdaintre's side. 'What's the matter?' she whispered sleepily.

'Council have outlawed mindsails. And you two are up before Jerad as soon as he's back on his feet.'

Another yawn threatened to crick Tohalla's jaws. 'Why? We put him right again.'

'Oh, wake up, Toh!' Valtisane clicked her tongue in annoyance. 'I suppose I'll get no sense from you 'til you've had a drink.'

'Mmm.'

Valtisane moved away to the dead fire, making no effort to be quiet. 'Blast it! Why can't the idiot have one machine at least?' She bent her red head to blow on the fire and clouds of ash swirled into her face. Still, she had seen Tohalla tend a fire before. Taking wood from the box, Valtisane soon had the kettle sitting on a respectable blaze. It didn't stop her complaining.

'Here,' she said, coming back with a hot tisane. Tohalla took a mouthful. It was horrible – her friend must have used some cooking-herb rather than a tea. Her eyes watered.

'Better?' asked Valtisane hopefully.

Tohalla snuffed with laughter. 'Much,' she said, but she was too bone-weary to get up and make a proper drink. 'Anyway, what's all this upset? If this Council of yours isn't meeting for days, there's plenty of time to do something about it.' Her arms stretched lazily.

Valtisane looked at her in exasperation. Tohalla noticed that her eyelashes were dyed deep red today to match the maroon of her hair. It put red highlights in her hazel eyes.

'Stop grinning like a gaga, Toh!'

'Oh, I can't be solemn today. Tamdaintre's alive!'

'Not for much longer.' Val sounded serious. She laid a dimpled hand on Tohalla's arm. Her grip was surprisingly strong.

Tohalla raised her brows, her mouth muffled by another yawn. She was too happy to be worried.

'Vigis, Toh. There's too many people been stirred up this time. Between you and Jerad's mob, you've got half the Two Hundred Thousand up in arms. What did you really do last night?'

Tohalla heard the tension wring her friend's voice higher. 'Tell you in a moment, Val. Do you think they'll do anything, really?'

Valtisane squeezed so hard her rings pinched Tohalla's skin. 'They will – and soon. As soon as they've talked themselves into it.'

'What will they do? You told me the only punishment is shunning and Tam and I don't care if we never see another machine in our lives.'

'You will, Toh. If only that was all! Council might shun you but that's just the start. No more food, no more tools, or clothes, or medicine – no more anything! No more house –'

'So what? In the Green we made everything for ourselves. As long as we've got friends …'

'You won't have. You think Lucah and Jade will give up everything they've got for the dubious privilege of hearing your outlandishness? D'you think I'd let Erin give up his future here for you? No friends, no girlfriends. Everyone! Everyone we're friends with will shun us, or they'll be shunned, out and out, from one generation to the next! D'you want that for my son, Tohalla? Because I don't!'

Valtisane was panting, too angry now to stop her tirade. 'But that's only Council!'

Tohalla snatched a gap to say, 'Not now, they won't. Not Jerad. We mended him, and Persis, and everyone Soren damaged.'

'You can't, Tohalla! You can't do that to people, go round meddling with their minds. It's the only law we've got here: no infringement! You're not even supposed to live in a house that interrupts everyone's view like yours does, remember? The Two Hundred Thousand means everyone can live like they want, but only so long as they don't interfere with anyone unwilling.'

Tohalla tried to hush her friend so that Tam might stay asleep. 'What was I supposed to do?' she whispered fiercely. 'Leave him sick in his mind like that? But he's fine now.' She shrugged. 'Don't worry, Val. Jerad may have outlawed mindsails but he won't do anything else. He's scared we've got too much on him. There'll be no threat to you.'

'But the Vigis, Toh! Don't you understand? There'll be thousands of them, burning, smashing – if they work themselves up enough they could easily kill! It's only happened once before but there's no saying if what you did won't tip 'em over the edge again. We could all be slaughtered!'

Serene in her exhaustion, Tohalla shook her head. 'It's simple, Val. We'll burn our mindsails for them. Tell Erin – tell everyone! We'll burn them on the beach at sunset by the wreck of the Dream Ship.'

The red-hazed air was heavy with anger. In the dying of the day the mound of reliesin glowed a poignant russet. Here and there facets of metal winked like falling tears; a tangle of smashed timber glittered with broken beads. Above the surge of angry people the sea-birds mourned, disturbed. Their pale underwings flashed back the sullen light like the flames that were to come.

Thousands had come to watch the mindsails burn. They blackened the sprawling beach in a smear that spread its tentacles up onto the broken hill where the Drone Ship lay trapped. Some were even standing knee-deep in the waves that frothed at the edge of the darkling sea.

And hundreds, fearing retribution, had come to cast their mindsails on the heap that rose tree-high beyond the rocks. In the front of the crowd Tamdaintre stood next to Tohalla. Grim-faced they waited for the destruction of something meant to bring joy.

Tohalla stared at the pyre, trying to pick out her mindsails and the wreck of her new loom. *Is it always going to be like this? You make something and they spoil it like they did with my Vernal? I remember her bringing me star-flowers in the Red* ...

From the edge of the town a machine rolled, parting the stream of latecomers. Tohalla watched a way clear before it, thinking bitter thoughts about the supremacy of machines. And as it rolled over the sand, the sound of many voices talking drifted away on the wind.

298

Jerad, paler and more shrunken, sat on the black machine's platform. The machine stopped. Even so Jerad's hair flicked upwards at the ends, the grey strands crawling across his fleshless skull. On a robe white as purity the Erth-disc symbol glowed to show he held the power of the Council. In the weight of silence made more ponderous by the smash of the surf, he addressed the shadowy throng.

'This is an abomination,' he said. He didn't even bother to stand up but commanded the machine to ignite the kindling jammed into the logs of the platform.

Electricity carved jagged blue through the air. And the wood roared into fire and the fire roared through the mindsails. Choking sulphur streamed off into tattered clouds red-lit from below.

The crowd fell back. Tohalla coughed, held up one long, green sleeve to shelter her face. *Green for birth and death ...*

Sparks flew from the crackling blaze. The heat was appalling.

Driven by the fierceness of the conflagration the thousands reformed man-lengths back into the dark. Waves sucked at Tohalla's ankles but she could not have fallen, so tight-pressed were the people. Nevertheless she stumbled and Tamdaintre held her up.

A cry went up from somewhere, echoed and repeated. 'The reliesin-wood's on fire!'

Tohalla turned with the rest. None of them had expected this. Jerad had ordered his machines to fire the wood. It burned, a vast and lonely beacon of blood-red and acrid yellow on the dark horizon.

There was no shunning. What need? Wherever a mindsail was found it was destroyed.

But on Longday – ask a machine when that is – in the heart of that long, hot southern Summer, Tohalla gave a party that started in the sunshine of her leafy orchard. Gone were her watch-lions. Tohalla had nothing to hide in the house that was a house or in the garden with its Summer's crops.

She had made her decisions. No longer would she look at her life in the light of other people's dreams for her, nor allow herself to be swept along like some piece of self-less flotsam. Tohalla had discovered an amazing truth: *This is my life, to steer and to enjoy – as much as anyone can without hurting others.* And she was learning, one way and another, not to hate herself for what she was.

Tohalla wore a crown of plaited corn. Her long dress gleamed apple-green, and it was embroidered. Wondering, Valtisane watched the joy on Tohalla's face as double shadows shrank to one beneath a single chestnut. Tam wore green too, and there was pride in his face reflected from his bride's as she sang her strand-naming right back to the cramped hold of the *Mosckva*. Not one there could match it. They were born from nameless eggs. And no-one even thought of cutting Tohalla's suns' bright hair.

Then everyone came forward to kiss the bride and groom. Valtisane still laughed at the idea of marriage but she whispered, 'You've chosen well,' to Tohalla, and hugged her. And she said the same to the slim bronzed man whose hand Tohalla held.

It was a good party in Tohalla's Summer garden; she'd even used machines to make something like joyberry-juice, something like dreamsmoke. Tamdaintre had made her a zither. Its tone was softer than the one of plastic but Val was not the first to say, with a softness on her motherly features, that she liked Tohalla's songs.

Afterwards amid the laughter in the leaves, while sound-machines played songs not heard on Erth in three hundred years, Tohalla and Tamdaintre danced with their friends, but there was a special look on their faces when they were in each other's arms. And the wind mingled her gold hair with his silver-streaked brown. Grey eyes locked in green, they shared their trust in the future.

Past moonrise when the last guests had called their cheery goodnights, she and Tamdaintre sat – one last time? – on her porch. The spreading eaves caught the wreathing dreamsmoke that drifted from her windows. Faint firelight danced on the little hard apples growing on the nearest tree. Tohalla stroked a song softly into the warmth of the night. Sharing its spell, Tamdaintre leant his head against her legs. The song was of Longnight in the Green. Its chords drifted away past Lucah's lights that twinkled through the trees.

'Are you ready, Tohalla?'

'Tamdaintre, I am.'

They grinned in cheerful humour and stole away. They'd prepared the hiding-place beforehand: everything was as ready as it could be.

In a wild wood beneath the Amethyst Moon they lay on a mattress perfumed with hay. On its leaf-dappled pattern they shared a caress that lengthened from tenderness to passion.

Above, in the branches of the tree that might have been oak, the mindsail rippled. The last mindsail? Tohalla had hidden it with Tamdaintre's blessing out here in the backwoods near the Straight-Edged Desert.

His tongue flicked pleasure from her skin; he matched her shivers of delight when her gentle skill heightened his joy. They came together,

300

skin to skin, mind to mind, and neither could tell where one finished and the other began. The physical became mystic ...

Overhead the mindsail filled. They rose through its design that both of them had made: a blue-green disc ice-capped and woven with the love of home. A hand reached towards it from the red berry that was Rosaria.

Falling upwards into the mindsail's welcome, they let the russet warmth enfold them. In sea-washed glass of emerald and turquoise the design lured them on.

Perspective shifted: a moon-path kissed the bay that held the Two Hundred Thousand. Now Tohalla learnt what she had seen only from the outside: the glory of minds intermingled with love which accepted the good and the bad.

Ecstasy exploded them so that they felt they could encompass all Rosaria with their love. The warm breeze kissed them. Tohalla's spirit laughed for joy and Tamdaintre understood.

Swinging over her firelit house with its echoes of peace yet to come, she said, *I choose another brother and you are more than that.*

His mind smiled in hers as his body did in the moon-shadowed forest. *More than sister, I love you. Down there is our child as a gift to Rosaria.*

His laughter changed. *Look, Tohalla! There's more than us mindsailing tonight!*

She laughed too as she perceived the flicker of a thought-sphere the colour of the Amethyst Moon. *Let's outrun them!*

They swooped in exultation beneath Rosaria's skies. Here and there above the sleeping streets other mind-bubbles irised in violet but their pursuer came on. Yet with Tohalla's Red-born strength and Tamdaintre's mastery of the art they began to outdistance that flickering follower.

And, unknown to them, other parts of the pattern began to ripple outward in the Two Hundred Thousand ...

Out beyond the hot-noise's run they fled in merriment which lifted them over the charcoal desert. They skimmed the shifting moonglow of the Unshadowed Plain, delved into the bowl of night where the Big River uncoiled its shining streams, and still the pursuer chased them.

It's Soren! she thought so low that she hoped he wouldn't hear them.

Can't catch us! Tamdaintre challenged and Tohalla laughed.

This time she leaped the cold amber spikes of the Edge. She swirled invisible, Tamdaintre inside her, through the bright lattice of the striding-post where old Adi snored faintly from her sleeping-wools and Trin fletched an arrow and watched the Edge. Trinamine's thoughts tasted good like the scent of a fresh-turned furrow.

And one ruby heart of a messenger was gone!

Enchanted, Tohalla flew to where the combe cupped midsummer's warmth between its headlands. Wasn't this Longday? Wouldn't Vernal be in the girls' room in the dreaming House? Surely Housemother –

It felt so right it had to be true. And it was.

Her curly hair sun-gilded, Vernal lay sleeping where once Tohalla slept in hope. Tohalla's mind kissed her daughter's and the little girl exhaled a happier peace. Vernal smiled at her mother, held the heart of the messenger to her in her dream.

In exaltation Tohalla winged upward. The same moon-path on a different sea flew her over the tidenets' glassy strands and she shared their chords with her lover.

Minds bright with laughter they looked back to where Soren still gamely pursued.

In the Two Hundred Thousand torches flared through the streets. Angry men shouted, holding up this river of fire. For the Vigilantes had kept back some mindsails too.

Half the torches split off, heading for a house that was a green hill. But the other half, led by a pack of watch-lions on chains, marched raging towards the distant woods. The watch-lions snuffed for a taste of the minds they hunted.

And under a monarch of oak two smiling bodies slumbered, untenanted – small heart – but very well hidden, breast to breast and thigh to thigh beneath the Amethyst Moon.

Soaring on the wings of exaltation Tohalla speared upwards, with Tamdaintre to strengthen her nerve. High above the heartland of the Green, he pointed back down to where the inwatchers' lanterns glimmered through the windows of the House.

Are you sure, Tohalla?

She flowed her thoughts to hold him in a stronger embrace. *Tamdaintre, I love you. And I'm sure. You?*

Yes. His thought was full of faith in her – and in the others inside her. For in their memories was stored the knowledge of the Log-book of the *Mosckva*.

Her laughter rang clear as the bell of some creature of the Red. Tamdaintre shared it.

In the face of this ultimate challenge, Tamdaintre aimed the

302

mindsail whose coat of arms was Erth. With him, twin-souled, Tohalla sailed past the beacon constellations to defeat those monsters of the seas of light whose shores are those same stars. Like a comet Soren fell behind them. Who knows if he reached the Two Hundred Thousand as an incandescent arc across the dawning sky?

But reaching out to embrace their long-lost kin, the stars sang in silvery welcome.